THE NUDE DETECTI

G000164455

I

THE NUDE DETECTIVE

Dedication

Thanks to my kick-ass, wonderful partner, who supports my crazy projects and who helped me make this one better.

THE NUDE DETECTIVE

Contents

Intentionally left blank

Prologue

[Ethan] - Of course, you'll want to know why an almost thirty-two-year-old multi-billionaire like me is hiding inside Gwen's pantry, as naked as the day I was born.

No clothes within reach, the door is stuck an inch and a half open, admitting a revealing searchlight-like stripe across my chest and thigh and illuminating my deep red blushes. Through the gap I can hear Gwen, who cheekily trapped me here, chatting freely to Marion, who is completely oblivious to the awful shock awaiting her if she casually reaches in for some pasta. I'm backed up hard against boxes of mac and cheese, holding my breath, with the sound of my blood banging so loudly in my ears, I'm sure it can be heard in the corridor.

It's obvious to me that Gwen covertly invited Marion over and planned her arrival for the most opportune moment—a moment I would be at my most vulnerable. Dr. Gwen Walsh is my fun, gay neighbour. I've been great friends with her for a year now, and she has a power over me, which I will explain later. How do I describe Gwen? Imagine Charlize Theron with her blonde hair cut pixie short. She's a raging 29-year-old trapped in a 55-year-old body and determined to wear it out. Her curvy 185 pounds are topped off with grey-blue eyes that don't just smile, they giggle, yet somehow always hold wisdom. Around Gwen is an air that you are always in her movie. And maybe we are.

As instructed, I came to Gwen's apartment prepared for an ordeal. She had me go into the bathroom, strip naked, and come out wearing nothing but a towel and an awkward smile. She had me stand in the centre of her apartment with my hands on my head, with me hoping the towel wouldn't slip off my waist. Having a washboard belly does have its disadvantages, so I tried to keep my butt flexed to give the towel something to purchase on, and I kept my breathing even and shallow. Even though the blinds were all drawn, and Gwen had seen me naked before, the unpredictable doctor had my adrenaline coursing through my body, and likely for good reason. Gwen picked up my neatly folded clothes and dropped them into a tough-looking leather case that had a hefty-looking combination padlock. In the pocket of my pants was my apartment key. I live in the unit across the hall from Gwen.

Gwen circled me a couple of times, then playfully tugged at the towel. Not hard enough to dislodge it but enough to make me imagine a breeze. Then she sauntered slowly, window by window, and opened each blind.

The good doctor leases her apartment from me and decorates it as she chooses. She has done such a fantastic job I'm sure it draws many looky-loos, who, if they looked today, would see her latest decoration: Me!

The apartment was bright, airy and cheerful. The sun, flowing in the wide full-length windows, lit up the creamy mushroom-white walls and plush deep sofas. Below the arched ceiling hung grey wooden beams, contrasting with twelve-inch planks of polished maple below. Sky-blue and mustard-yellow throws and pillows brought out the red and brown tones in the floor, walls and window frames, which were a subtle backdrop to the one strong colour in the room. A striking picture hung boldly over an ivory baby grand piano. The expensive print in the silver frame was of a tall, languid, sexual woman stalking across a ballroom floor in a scarlet, off-the-shoulder dress, with an unknown purpose. Her gaze was on something in the distance, but in this setting, she appeared to look out onto the luxuriously appointed, four hundred square foot deck I was hoping I would not be visiting in my current state.

"Hey, it's broad daylight, Gwen!" I reminded her, somewhat defensively. In the middle of Yaletown's condo land, there was a real possibility of being spotted, which of course was the point. Gwen said nothing but continued to open the blinds until there was bright daylight and possibly curious, laughing eyes streaming in at me from all angles. Gwen walked around the elegant glass case housing the *Sonos* sound system to the leather bag and, picking it up in her left hand, walked over and stood behind me, deliberately in my blind spot. I did as instructed: hands on head, eyes looking directly in front of me. *She wouldn't, would she?* As I was looking around trying to see things without moving my head, I noticed Gwen had moved all of the throws and blankets that normally festooned her apartment to the far side of the suite, and the one piece of cover within reach was wrapped around my waist, slipping lower with each nervous breath I took.

Gwen strolled slowly around me again and stopped dead in line with my nervous face, grinning at me with mock menace. She glanced at her watch, and the grin widened to Cheshire cat proportions. Suddenly she reached down and snatched away my towel, dropping it into the case. Holding eye contact, she growled, "Don't you move a muscle, sir!" With a flourish, she stepped to my side, put her arm around my shoulder so the case dangled in front of me, then *flash*, an old-fashioned instamatic camera materialized in her other hand and took a selfie of the two of us. She was saluting, and I was almost doing the same. I was about to complain but there was a knock on the door. I gulped. *Who could that be?* Our little game was a secret and would stay so under the terms of our agreement, but to get to the penthouse apartments you needed a key or to be buzzed up, so you had to be on the guest list.

"Coming, sweetie!" Gwen yelled, as she snapped the leather case's combo lock shut, then threw the bag through the open door onto the patio. To my credit, despite my sheer panic, I held the appointed position. I could feel Yaletown's gazing community staring, and I wasn't about to follow the case out into their full view; but Gwen was about to let a stranger — or worse, someone I knew — into the suite.

"Quick, into the pantry," said Gwen, pushing me towards the stained mahogany walk-in unit and slapping my butt hard to get me going. I bolted into the sanctuary and pulled the door behind me.

Marion had arrived innocently at the door with flowers, a bottle of wine, and some sort of dessert that I heard Gwen "ooh," "ah," and "you didn't need to" about. I was still trying to close the door fully, but it had jammed against a lone screw mysteriously driven into the door frame. *Hmm!*

I heard the girls pop the wine, laughing and flirting – as nervous 'newly-mets' do – as they settled in for a night of pasta and deepening of their relationship. Gwen had told me about Marion, the latest potential love of her life, whom she had met last Saturday at *The Crazy Bean*, the coffee shop Gwen owns and runs by the water taxi stand in Yaletown. I had closed a case, and so, under the terms of the *arrangement* I had with Gwen, I was there for what she called sarcastically my *treatment*. As I stood there embarrassed, shivering and red as a beet, I realized Gwen had upped the stakes yet again.

"I'll just fetch us something to nibble," cooed Gwen, as she pulled the pantry door wide open. I was totally exposed, my hands desperately trying to cover my pride, pressing backwards even farther, and up on my toes, trying to somehow sink back into the back wall out of sight. Gwen stood at the threshold looking over her shoulder at Marion, who was thankfully just out of view to the left, presumably sitting on the couch. I'm sure the placement was all carefully thought through and choreographed by my Machiavellian neighbour. I'd felt seconds away from discovery, which was the point, but I doubted Gwen wanted to see Marion run screaming from the apartment and have to explain to her why there was a naked guy hiding in the pantry.

Gwen had stepped in, pressed the Polaroid into my hand, leant close and whispered, "Run when the coast is clear." She giggled, pressing her spare key to my unit into my other hand. With another rough slap on my butt, she turned and picked a tray of chips and dip she had prepared earlier from the shelf, then left the pantry, kicking the door closed with a snick against the screw.

"The weather is awesome, Marion. Let's move on to the patio." I heard Gwen's voice fade away and cautiously pushed the door open a couple of inches, glancing into the empty room. I let myself out into the hall after a quick check that the coast was clear, stepped across to my unit, and let myself in with the key provided, relieved it matched the lock. The way Gwen was behaving that night, it occurred to me that she might have given me a fake key, leaving me trapped nude in the hallway.

I slouched with a gasp of relief against the now firmly closed door and tossed the cheeky selfie of us onto the hall stand. My heart rate was far from normal, but was at least heading the right way. I guess I should explain how I got myself into such a predicament with Gwen.

1: A PI Is Born

My name's Ethan John Booker, and I am embarrassingly rich. I say embarrassingly because I don't really like to talk about it, and I detest those who have it and flaunt it. I'm old fashioned that way, and to be anything but humble about it seems crass, ungrateful, and invites bad karma. That said, bad karma could also come from not enjoying my enviable position, so I'm not afraid to spend my fortune, and I admit to owning enough gadgets to make James Bond jealous. I just don't brag or rub it in peoples' faces. OK, I flaunt it a little, but not over people. It is a humble sort of flaunt.

Like most spoiled rich kids, I need something to do. Da likes to farm, Ma likes to run companies, but having tried both the mud and the boardroom, I know those worlds are not for me. Neither parent tries to guilt me into following in their footsteps. They really only expect me to follow a few rules: Rule one – you must have fun and live a life you love. With the resources we have it is inexcusable to not shape your life to be what you want it to be. What a waste otherwise. Rule two – you must do good deeds from time to time with what God and a massive inheritance provided.

Warren Buffett apparently once said, "A very rich person should leave his kids enough to do anything but not enough to do nothing." I admire that, but my folks didn't limit me in that regard. I could definitely do absolutely nothing and stay in the lap of luxury for a hundred years. But Ma and Da instilled in me the desire to experience and live life and to help those who need it. Now, by help, I don't mean charity work, although the family runs several charities and donates such a fortune each year we could make a small country blush. Nor do I mean just handing out money in the street to people I come across, or friends with debts who could use a hand. I do help my friends of course, sometimes openly and sometimes discretely, but that doesn't qualify as good deeds. The way I have chosen to "do good" is to solve problems for people that no one, especially the law, can help.

As a kid, I was a detective story nut. Everyone from *Bogart* and *Bacall*, to *Bruce* and *Cybil* in *Moonlighting*; *Ironside* to *Sherlock Homes*, *Ellery Queen* and *PD James*. I read everything I could find and watched everything on the TV or the big screen. But most of all, I loved the stories where the detectives used gadgets: The aforementioned *Bond*; *Artemus Gordon* in *Wild, Wild West*. *Inspector Gadget* even. The idea that cunning technical trickery and disguise can win the day is wired somewhere deep inside me.

I graduated in 2006, which – if you do the math — is a year later than I should have. I spent a few years travelling and working for Ma and Da in various positions in their companies, to learn about business and get an idea of what I wanted to do with my life. One day in December 2009, in a jazz club called *The Cellar* in Kitsilano, I met a guy called Aki Naru, and that night changed the course of my life. Aki, 74, was a Canadian Armed Forces lifer. He had made sergeant when he stood down from active service. He lived in Sechelt on BC's

Sunshine Coast and had driven down and caught the ferry to stay in town for the week. Despite his military training, and with everything to do with his age, he had been mugged and lost his wallet. He had dutifully told the police, and of course they were sympathetic, but with their lack of resources and overabundance of cases, they really couldn't help. I heard about his sad tale from Detective Sergeant Marcy Helen Stone, nee Bremmer.

Marcy and I seem to have intertwined fates. We had dated briefly at the end of my last high-school year. It was a culmination for me of the crush I'd had from my youth. We were childhood friends and flirted often, but until that particular summer of love, we hadn't crossed the romantic or physical threshold, and I could never fathom what held us back. Marcy was just finishing a diploma in criminology at Camosun College, and we both spent time at our respective families' cabins, which were adjacent to each other on Gambier Island, and we'd had time on our hands. She revealed she was dealing with an abusive mother who, with the help of alcohol and drugs, was dealing with an abusive husband. She shared some of her experiences, which had been horrific, and had gone some way to explain the polarity of the siblings: Marcy, her older brother Billy and little brother Max.

It is my experience that kids come out of broken homes either broken or incredibly resilient. Marcy proved to be the latter. She was in no way interested in a long-term relationship, but that glorious summer, she helped us both discover more about sex than I thought possible: when to rush and be frantic, and when to slow down and take a long, lovely time; what a woman really wants, and not...Hefner and friends; what to say, where to touch... how to handle those inevitably embarrassing moments. Dignity. We went our separate ways as close friends, and my heart almost broke.

Marcy worked hard — with purpose and passion — to join the Vancouver Police Department, the VPD. A period as a volunteer special constable, more schooling, and her proudest day, graduating and getting her badge. She left me behind after that summer and pursued her life and career, but we kept in touch. She grew into a beautiful woman second — and detective sergeant first. Seeing her as an adult, you are instantly struck by her sense of readiness. She stands upright and square, feet apart, about to sprint somewhere or jump like an athlete. She has a great figure, exuding fitness and hardness, but her face softens the effect. She has shoulder-length black hair, rarely out of a ponytail, surrounding a face with high cheekbones, which could be Hispanic maybe but for her very white complexion, and red lips. Sandra Bullock meets Krysten Ritter. With green eyes. I still carried a big torch for Marcy.

Marcy called me one day and asked me to meet up with Aki. I think she knew that in those days I was quite adrift, partly because I was still processing the death of my best friend Max, her brother. She held that talking things out was good therapy, and while it was a shame that Aki had lost his wallet and credit cards, talking to Aki about his military experiences, and what it must have meant to Max to serve, enabled me to get to a better place and deal with some misplaced anger and guilt.

While reminiscing with Aki, he told me his biggest sadness about the theft was that he had lost a photo he kept in his wallet, which was all he had left of his daughter. This poor guy had lost his wife and daughter to a house fire when he was fighting in Afghanistan and had come home to a black cindered house, instead of a wife at the door and a little girl running up the path and flinging herself into his arms. All of their possessions, memories and vitality — gone in a few hours of thick, black smoke. Part of what he had put his own life on the line for—gone forever. No foul play suspected, just a simple faulty electrical connection. His life torn apart by weak wire and plastic. His picture, and his dignity, stolen by punks or addicts he had spent his life providing with the liberty to fuck themselves up.

This all happened long before we published our lives and photos to the cloud, and so all he'd had was this one picture, wrinkled and faded, but now gone, along with $67 cash and some plastic cards.

Without Sargent Naru's knowledge or consent, I went to work on his behalf and, a week later, and some $46,000 invested mostly in bribes and private investigator fees, I had tracked down the mugger and persuaded him to show me where he had dumped the wallet, which still floated among some waste by the train lines in East Vancouver. Luckily the picture was salvageable, if a little damp. It cost another $2,400 to refurbish it, and I had a few copies and enlargements made before I caught the short *Harbour Air* float-plane commute up to meet Aki, ten days after our first meeting. We met for lunch at the Lighthouse pub, which had been the China Gate restaurant when Vancouver hosted the World Expo in 1986 but had been relocated in 1988 to nestle in the crook of the Sechelt Inlet.

I handed Aki back his daughter's picture and, ok, by this time, I was so pumped I admit to getting a little dramatic. I convinced the staff to play Amos Lee's version of a song called *Sweat Pea*, which was Aki's nickname for his daughter. What else could happen? The guy broke down and hugged me on the spot; we were both more than slightly misty eyed, and we are still friends to this day. As far as he knows, I saw a mugger by coincidence that matched the description and tackled the guy and retrieved the photo. We still meet once a year in a jazz bar or go fishing somewhere up the coast, and he buys me expensive brandy all night and won't hear a word about splitting the tab. And I let him.

This experience taught me that not only did I have some talent for detective work—I truly loved it. This passion, backed up with having an almost inexhaustible supply of money, made my chances of success higher than the average bear. Kind of like Batman, but without Robin, the fighting, and definitely no Lycra.

Soon afterwards, The *Ethan Booker Private Detective Agency* came to be, complete with an honestly obtained PI licence—a silly piece of paper I am insanely proud of. I can get quite excited about a new Aston, or Huey, but doing things with my own mind and hands, like cooking a great meal or playing the piano well, is ridiculously rewarding for a stupidly rich guy.

The agency doesn't have offices and I don't advertise, and the 'detective agency' façade is more of a cover for something a little bigger and more effective. Over the years I've met some other PIs and some honest cops and helped a lot of folks with problems big and small, so I get most of my clients through word of mouth.

I have a couple of simple rules: I have to like you; I have to be drawn to your problem; and you have to pay something you can afford. I never tell clients I have the resources I have; I try to appear to be just another guy making a living. I'll always research my clients ahead of accepting their case, and I always come up with a price that is within their means. Yes, hypocritical I know. They don't get something for nothing, even though I have almost everything for nothing. But them's my rules. None of which explain how I got to be buck naked in Gwen's pantry, but I'm getting there, which leads us back many years, to the Bremmer case.

2: The Bremmer Case

It was May 24, 1995; I was 12 years old and far from being a full-fledged detective. But I remember being as angry as a 12-year-old can get. It wasn't the anger of being pushed or from losing something; it was the red-faced screaming anger you get from being humiliated unjustly by a bully in front of the girl you have a crush on. A bully who is too big to take on without taking a hiding, and he knows it, although you are tempted anyway. William H Bremmer — or Billy Bremmer as we knew him — was 16, fit, and an arrogant jerk. Billy was the older brother of Max, my closest friend, and whose sister Marcy was 14, very hot, and the object of said crush.

We had hung out with the Bremmer's for many summers when we came over to Gambier island. It was a case of the haves and have-nots. We were rich, although we played it down; you couldn't get more down to earth and modest than Ma and Da. There was not much difference between our cabins, but people find out things at school and there were inevitably reactions, good and bad. I had tried to get Max to hang around his older sister Marcy and their friends as much as possible. Montel's *This Is How We Do It* and Seal's *Kiss From a Rose* were summer anthems, and Bryan Adams' Have *You Ever Really Loved a Woman?* —a portent for hopefully good things to come—was racing up the charts to the number one spot.

Ma and Da were planning a quiet night in, as Da was grumpy. Mr. and Mrs. Bremmer would join them and there would be BBQ and beer — wine for the ladies — and Da would come around. Da was gloomy because Elizabeth Montgomery, the actress from *Bewitched,* had passed from cancer the previous week, — she had been someone Ma had graciously poked at him about being his 'hottie' — and George Forman had just been stripped of his boxing title for refusing to refight Schultz. Both combined to put him in bad humour, and our family system dictated that Ma would cook him his favourite dessert, and he would burn some cow on the grill and he would have a grown-up beer with the Bremmer parents.

Us boys were keen for the excuse to make ourselves scarce, and there was talk of a boat trip over to Woolridge Island, a tiny rock a quarter mile across the bay. There was nothing really there but a few trees, rocks, and, most importantly, no adults. We teens would escape there on occasion in our boats, take our ghetto-blasters, light a fire, and hang out where adults would not smell pot or notice we had snuck some brewskies out of the beer fridge. Likely our parents were smoking pot when we were not there and hoping we wouldn't smell it on them. Well, Ma might have been. I couldn't imagine Da doing anything mildly drug related.

With school just finished for summer break, this was the first couple of days at the cabin and the first escape to Woolridge of the season. We would be back a few times over the break. I had raided our cabin's supplies, including two beers from Dad's fridge, some food, and a Sade CD — in case slow dancing was called for — and had walked over to the Bremmers' to join the party. We all talked in their kitchen as things got organized and parents fussed, but soon we were set to go. The group was Max and me, Marcy and her friends Katy and Beth, and Billy and his pal Odd Wayne. I often tried to find out where he got the name 'Odd,' but people just laughed outrageously, winked, and changed the subject.

Marcy and her friends had arrived the night before. I hadn't seen Marcy since Easter, and the three months had seen a growth spurt in several key zones. I'd had a bit of a crush before, but now I wondered if I could be in love. Marcy was a bit of a tomboy, with black hair cut short, a slender figure, perky pointy features, and deep blue, almost violet eyes. The smoky look was heating up thanks to some new makeup, new hips and somewhat fuller breasts. I remember hearing the term 'fuller breasts' before, but the word 'fuller' had just re-formed in my pre-teen brain. I thought fuller meant larger, and they had grown some, yes, but that wasn't it. They had a new roundness and said "hi" when I glanced shyly their way. That is what fuller now meant to a 12-year-old boy.

Katy I knew, as she had been around before, a brunette but with round eyes and a rounder figure, short and cute and curvy, but not special the way Marcy was. Beth, a redhead beanpole, had sprouted north-south, but not yet east-west. Max and I had spent the morning switching from cool and aloof to puppy dog to sporty to annoying and back again, trying to tune in to the girl group and trying to get traction. Katy and Beth wanted little to do with Marcy's younger brother and his annoying buddy, but Marcy was friendly to me, and we eagerly caught up on our news.

The seven of us were making our way to the dock to board our outboard-driven whaler boats when Billy's dad intercepted us in something of a mood. Teens have a radar for angry parents, and all of our radars tripped as one as he came down the path towards us.

"Billy, come here, boy!" yelled Mr. Bremmer. Billy roughly pushed past me and walked over to his dad, shoulders squared back, playing his young buck role to the full. His buddy Wayne followed him over for back up but looked less sure of himself. Mr. Bremmer had a predatory aspect when sober and calm, but a few beers in with a burr up his butt, he was unpredictable, so the rest of us hung back. But when Da wandered over to see what the ruckus was about, we ambled nearer to see what was up.

"Give it up, Billy," ordered Mr. Bremmer.

"Give what up, Dad? I ain't got nothing," said Billy.

"Don't make me search for it, son," said Mr. Bremmer in a quiet and dangerous tone, which drew us all forward to hear. Somehow the quiet voice was more sinister and captivating than if he had shouted. Billy held his tongue and just looked back insolently.

"There were two mickeys of tequila on the counter when you kids were getting ready to leave, and now there is just one. Now I don't mind you liftin' a couple of beers – hell, I'd be disappointed if you didn't – but there is no way four boys and three girls are hanging out in the dark with no adults, with hardtack liquor flowing!"

I could tell Da agreed with him because the slightly amused look dropped from his face and he looked stern, as he began to understand what Mr. Bremmer was on to. I don't think Da was even OK with the beer, and he would have had a heart attack if he knew the older kids had pot stashed in their bags. Billy just shrugged and held out his bag for his dad to inspect. Mr. Bremmer hesitated then had a look inside, reaching in to move things around.

"OK, nothing there. Wayne, sorry, I got to check your bag too pal," said Mr. Bremmer, with a little less confidence. After a check of the girls, also revealing nothing, Mr. Bremmer looked at Dad and then at me.

"You sure, Jake?" Da asked Mr. Bremmer and received an embarrassed but firm nod in return. "OK, Ethan, sooner we do this the sooner you can be away"

I had known Max was clean as we had been together the whole time, and neither of us went near the counter where the Bremmer's kept their booze. Loyal wingman that I can be, I opened my bag for Da's pro forma inspection. I wasn't paying Da much attention, as I was watching the girls to see if any of them looked like they thought maybe I was bad enough to be a 'bad boy.'

"What's this, Ethan?" asked Da in a quiet voice, and I turned to see what he had found, suddenly recalling the two beers I had snuck out. I hoped he wouldn't make an issue of it as the others no doubt had some.

I looked at what he had in his hands and time stood awfully still. So still in fact that even *time* was awkward and embarrassed. In Da's hands was not only the missing tequila, which was bad enough, but a clear bag of BC bud, papers, and a box of matches, none of which I had ever seen before. Nothing made sense. I checked the bag and it was mine and had not been mixed up. I looked from Da to Mr. Bremmer. Dads have a special skill at making you feel ashamed, but Da truly looked disappointed, which began to add some anger to the embarrassment and puzzled cocktail brewing rapidly inside me.

I looked at Max, who looked amazed and perhaps a little proud of me, and I might have imagined it, but I think his head bobbed back and forth a fraction signalling masculine respect, and I thought *not helping Max*. I looked at Beth and Katy, who looked accusingly and angrily back at me as if possession of tequila was akin to attempted rape. Finally, I looked at Marcy. Despite the war going on inside me — of hormones, confusion, defensiveness, and affronted righteousness — I fell in love with Marcy right there. Out of all of them, I could see faith in me in her look. A faith my own Da apparently didn't share. She was puzzled, yes; angry at someone, yes; but it wasn't me. She was there for me in that moment and our eyes met. "Come on Mr. Booker, Ethan wouldn't do this..." she said, looking at Da. How brave. Up to that point I had just stood there with my mouth hanging open, but her faith and bravery spurred me to action.

"Da I...you know me. I don't steal, Da. I can't explain this stuff, but I don't steal," I pleaded.

I could see it have some impact on the emotional cocktail he was barely containing, but he said, "Well, I wouldn't have thought so Ethan, but there are two beers here from my fridge. I know Jake doesn't drink the dark beers—he's a lager man."

"That's right," said Mr. Bremmer, again not helping. I could see where Max got it from. Marcy clearly took after her mother.

"Ok yes, I took the beer but…" Da had stopped listening. Looking back, I'm not sure if he knew what to believe, but he is a simple guy and I was guilty of something, and consequences had to be borne.

I think he wanted to take me back to the cabin, cool off, and sort out the situation in the cold light of day, but Mr. Bremmer chimed in with, "A hiding might be in order Booker."

Dad stopped and looked at Bremmer, but I missed that. He looked at me and subconsciously placed a protective hand on my shoulder and pushed me forward, but I missed that. Marcy shoved her friends towards the dock, chastising them for something they said, but I missed that too. All of those things I recalled later, replaying the events for the tenth time from memory, my subconscious filling in pieces I'd missed in real time. I missed all of these things because I made eye contact with Billy. There wasn't really a smug grin, or a twinkle in the eye, but something passed between us. As I held his gaze, I remembered him pushing past me just minutes ago, and I knew he had slipped his contraband into my pack as he went past. And then I saw his face change, and that he guessed I had just worked it out, and his look of innocence, put on for the adults, now contained a hint of *not too quick on the uptake are you Booker?* I was flushed with rage and the sudden knowledge I was his patsy and there was nothing I could do about it. Hot tears welled up and I turned my head and followed Da, so important was it to me that Billy didn't see them. One thing being slow and a dupe, but another him pointing out me blubbing, in front of Marcy.

Dad led me back to the cabin. A couple of times I started to talk, to explain, to blame Billy, but each time the look of anger, embarrassment, and disappointment on Da's face stopped me. Part of my rage now transferred to him. *He should know me better. Trust me more. He brought me up and I've done all I can to live up to his high standards. How can he believe I would steal? Well, aside from the two beers of course. Shit! Shit! Shit!*

I wondered if he worked it out, or at least had some doubt, but the man that is my Da would not embarrass Mr. Bremmer in front of his kids, with no way to prove it. He was sorry Bremmer didn't see the rotten egg he had in Billy, and the special souls he had in Max and Marcy.

In 2004, Max didn't make it home from a tour in Afghanistan. An IED took him completely, and also took half of a fellow soldier. At the spit and shine military service for Max, Da went up to Mr. Bremmer, who was still clutching the Canadian flag in his hands, and with a hoarse voice and wet eyes, he separately told both Mrs. and then Mr. Bremmer that he thought the world of

Max. But as Da passed Billy, he didn't meet his eyes. Just walked right by him and left him hanging. Thinking back to that day of shame, I suspect, with hindsight, Da knew something of what was going on between the Bremmers and had concluded that Billy getting a beating from his Da wouldn't have helped. Wisdom of age.

But the souls of the righteous didn't matter to me that night, just the soul of the mean and twisted. I was sent to my room to cool off and imagined Billy telling the others what a bad lot I was, poisoning Marcy against me while they danced and partied. All of the things I could have and should have said played in a constant loop in my head, fighting with the actions I should have taken, warring with the feeling of cowardliness for doing nothing. Anything but think of the awkwardness and confrontation that was to come in the morning when we all met up again.

But then something happened. Something so far-reaching in my life, it would eventually lead to me being naked in Gwen's pantry. I had an idea.

The idea started with reaching that point when rage gives way to acceptance and you begin to rationalize. My subconscious knew I couldn't be mad at Da. He was too good a man who loved me wholeheartedly and unreservedly and was trying to deal with a tough situation many dads have dealt with over thousands of years. Some trick of the subconscious moved me from anger at Da, to wondering what Da would do if faced with the same situation? How would the man I probably admired most in life without being conscious of it, and depended on more than I realized back then, have handled things in my place? Da was farming stock and a big guy, and as direct as they come. Never a detour, always a direct line, from point to point. Even with the age difference, I would bet Da at 12 would have punched Billy at 16 were Da in my shoes that night. I can still recall the moment when I realized I didn't have Da's strength, but I did have his blood. Da would get even—not angry. And so would I.

3: Mission Impossible

Trips to Woolridge Island were special but somewhat formulaic: head over about seven; hang out until after dark, which was about 9.30 pm on those summer nights; light a fire; wish we had brought more food and beer, which we never remembered to do; and come home a little cold and hungry at about 11 pm. Much later than 11 pm, and there might be trouble.

The parents wouldn't go to bed until we returned.

It had taken me a couple of hours to calm down and come up with a plan and so time was now pressing. It was a long-shot plan, and much could go wrong, and in fact did; but when young and driven by a great wrong, you are not always smart.

The Woolridge routine came with a long-established safety plan. My folks are big on safety planning and so we had always agreed that should there be an issue on the island, someone would fire off a flare for help. This really had to be a last resort, as a flare might bring the coast guard or other help, which was great if needed but would be awful for something frivolous. In the event of a flare going up, assuming the parents saw it, one of them would take the other boat, which was the same size as the first, and motor over to investigate. This was in the days before many of us had a cell phone, and back then, there wasn't even a cell signal within ten miles. Now the big problem with the safety plan was that Da may have had too much to drink by then, and given his mood around Lana Turner and Foreman, compounded by his troubled teen, Da would have had several beers, as would Mr. Bremmer. In a real emergency, they wouldn't hesitate no matter how drunk, but if they had another option, they might take it. I knew Da would be cautious about going out in the dark on a small boat, half cut. There was a fair chance I would get to redeem myself somewhat by piloting him over.

It was dusk already, and the tide was slack, which meant I could swim across to the island and put my plan to work. I looked around for my Bermuda shorts, then recalled they were with all of our wet gear, drying on the porch where the adults were drinking, and therefore out of reach.

I snuck out the back in a T-shirt and shorts and, taking a wide birth around our cabin, made my way to the dock. I checked the wind, which was low but was blowing back towards the cabin. Starting the second boat would make noise, and there was a good chance I would be spotted in the failing light. I'd swum across to the island before and was a confident and accomplished swimmer. It was only a few hundred yards, but I had never done it alone, and never in the dark. Beside the dock was a small lockbox in which we kept spare gas, ropes, and other items. I rummaged inside until I found an empty gas container and a short, thin rope. Then I thought of a snag.

I was going to do something that could cause a great fuss, and if it came to light that I was behind it, then I truly would be in trouble. If Ma found wet clothing in my room, she would ask questions. So, with it being near dark, I stripped off and hid my clothes in the box, tied the rope to the gas can and my wrist, and lowered myself naked as a jaybird into the Howe Sound and started stroking confidently for Woolridge Island.

I wasn't too many yards out when the cold water and darkness combined to give me second thoughts. But again, my Da came to mind: How mad he would be if I got hurt and how mad he would be if I chickened out now. Actually, the adult in me today knows that the latter was not true, but the youth I was then was not as smart. So I struck out again and, after what seemed like a very long time, came up to the small beach on Woolridge where their boat was drawn up and a fire was lit.

There was music playing, Jamiroquai's *Return of the Space Cowboy*. The group was sitting in a semicircle around the fire, facing towards the water: Katy and Beth to the left side, nearest to the boat; Max and Marcy in the middle, behind the first; then a little gap, and Wayne and Billy on the right-hand side. My temper started up again seeing them, but then I realized it wasn't much of a shindig and the mood was subdued. Beth and Katy seemed to be having a lively two-girl party, but the others were somewhat quiet. Now I became worried the night would end early, before I had a chance to work my mischief.

Their boat was at the waterline, about 40 yards from the group. I watched from the water, which thankfully was in the shadows of an arbutus tree to which the boat was moored on a long line. The moon was out, and I was a little worried someone would notice me emerge from the water and move to the boat, but after studying the scene for a few seconds, I was sure that the glow of the fire would spoil their vision this far away. I skittered as far over to the left as I could without having to climb out over the razor-sharp barnacle-infested rocks.

I crept up to the boat, keeping as low in the water as I could, disconnected the outboard motor's gas bottle, and swapped it for the empty one I had brought. The bottle with gas in it was three-quarters empty, so it contained enough air inside to float when I towed it back to Gambia island. I stood slightly to scan the boat, found the backup container, and took that out too. I was on a roll because that also had enough air in it to float, otherwise I would have had to hide it in the trees.

As I tied it onto my tow rope, I reflected—not for the first time—how weird it felt to be so far from my clothing, carrying out such a dastardly plan. It felt weird but electrically thrilling, and I felt powerful and in the driving seat. I would be back in my room when the party broke up and they would realize they were stranded and out of gas. They could just wait until morning, but they'd know they'd be missed. They could fire the flare or wait, but one way or another someone would have to come and rescue them. One thing that had been drilled into us time after time was good boat work. Our parents only trusted us out on the water after we could prove how responsible we were. Billy was in charge due to his age, the fact it was his family's boat and he was the oldest, and his arrogant take-charge nature. I knew he would have checked the gas before leaving and would not be able to explain how he had endangered the group. His dad would come down hard on him. He was supposed to look out for his sister, and perhaps worse, in Mr. Bremmer's world, not embarrass Mr. Bremmer. Perfect.

The smile that was forming on my face vanished when I heard voices approaching. I took a step towards the water and saw nothing but a brightly lit, slightly sloping beach and gently lapping waves reflecting the moonlight. I would be seen if I tried to escape to sea, so I pivoted, crouched low and scampered up towards the tree line, where I got a nasty surprise.

The shadows hid a large rock formation that blocked an escape along the beach, and I would have to heave my naked ass over in the bright moonlight to reach the tree line. There was sea on one side, highly illuminated rocks on another two sides, and the only remaining path was towards the fire and the approaching people. I was naked, wet, and clearly up to no good. If discovered, being laughed at by the girls and beaten by the boys would be followed by a meeting with Da I really didn't want to experience. I was in trouble.

They say necessity is the mother of invention, and I've believed that firmly every night since that night. I could see the outline of two shapes heading my way, and it had to be Beth and Katy, given the others seemed to still be silhouettes in the places I had seen them earlier. I quickly slipped the rope off my wrist, dropped the gas cans into the boat, then I rolled in the sand. My wet naked body caked quickly in itchy sand and I backed myself up to the rock face and into the deepest shadows I could see, and lay as flat as I could, shrugging myself as deep into the sand as I could in the scant seconds available. I took the deepest breath of my life and held it and prayed to God — whom I realized guiltily I hadn't talked to in a while — offered a deal or two, and waited to be spotted, humiliated, and have the rest of my life dissolve into tragedy. I caught a small break, as passing cloud dimmed the moonlight. It seemed even the moon grimaced and shut one eye at my embarrassing predicament. The effect was dappled splodges of soft light and shadow, creating a slight camouflaging effect.

Beth was yelling back to the group that she and Katy had some more beer in their bag in the boat and would bring it over. They were both wearing cut-off jean shorts and bikini tops, and both stepped up to the boat and out of sight of the others. I was pressed flat into the sand about 10 feet from them, partially obscured in sand and shadows. But I don't think they would have seen me if I had been in neon orange flashing coveralls, waving the Canadian flag. All they could see was each other.

Now up until that point, I had seen several people kiss in real life. There were some older kids at school of course. There was Jared the Cowboy's party too. Jared was a Persian guy who had a huge thing for pointy cowboy boots and country music, hence the nickname. There was a lot of necking there. But I had never seen two girls kiss before. Of course, I was a man of 12 and imagined it often and had seen it on the TV once or twice, but never in real life. As Katy reached up to Beth, moved Beth's hair to the side, and stepped in and kissed her, it was the most erotic thing I had witnessed up until that day of my life. In part because they were both girls, but mostly because they were so intimate. They had no idea I was there, and I felt a twinge of guilt. Their world had just reduced to them in that moment, and the kiss was so tender and sincere. I had never, ever witnessed such a pure and raw act and was immediately overcome with two sensations. The first was the most mature feeling I may have ever had to that point. I wanted to have that. What they had. That moment where I was with another human being, hopefully Marcy, in an embrace where nothing but the two of us counted, and that it would lead to a lifetime of love and happiness. And the second sensation was the pain of a massive erection pressing into the sharp gritty sand. What? I was 12 and full of raging hormones. This was Max's dad's *Playboy* come to life. Judge me not.

I think I was still holding that same breath when the girls broke apart, grabbed the bag, and went back towards the fire. I let the breath out slowly, my eyes pinched shut trying to stop that image from decaying even one tiny bit.

I recovered after a while, grabbed the gas cans and took my woody off into the cold waves, which took care of things quite quickly. I swam back and climbed onto the dock, out of breath for more than one reason. I stashed the gas in the box and retrieved my clothes, then circled back to the house. I was pretty dry by the time I was close to the back door, so I pulled my clothes on and slipped inside. Nothing had changed and I could hear the adults still chatting and drinking.

It seemed to take an age for the flare to go up, but it was probably no more than 30 minutes. I heard the adults react to the white light that appeared out over the dark water with some cussing and worry noises. I came outside with what I hoped was an innocent but concerned look. Smug expectations buried deeply.

"Must be the kids in some bother," said Mr. Bremmer, somewhat redundantly. Dad said nothing but turned and looked at me with a penetrating glare like he was puzzling something out. I was just about to confess all, when he said, "Ethan, come drive the boat," and the three of us walked to the jetty, followed by a quiet Ma and a clucking Mrs. Bremmer. My breath caught when I noticed the dock was still wet where I had climbed out of the water, but no one else seemed to notice.

"It was only one flare so it can't be too serious," said Da.

We climbed aboard and I primed the outboard and Da pulled the starter cord. The engine caught straight away, Mr. Bremmer cast off the line, and we were across the bay in no time. When we pulled up alongside Billy's boat, I could tell immediately he was scared. The other kids were cold and quiet, but he was panicked and upset.

"Dad, I checked it before we left. In fact, there were two cans half full. I don't know how that happened," cried Billy. Marcy met my eyes and didn't look at all happy, but I didn't think it was directed at me; if anything, there was a warmth I had never seen before.

"Dad, it's nobody's fault," she said with resignation heavy in her voice.

"No Billy, you fucked up!" shouted Mr. Bremmer, making us all cringe. "You fucked up checking the boat over, and you put lives at risk. And now you're making excuses. If you fuck up, you have to man up!"

He was silent a beat, then said, "Ok kids, get in this boat. Not you Billy, there is not room for everyone. We are one too many. You are going to stay here on the island overnight and think about taking care of your responsibilities!"

"But Dad..." Billy started, but there was no arguing. Mr. Bremmer pulled off his jacket and threw it at Billy, who barely caught it before it fell into the water. The others climbed into the boat, and Mr. Bremmer pushed us back from the shore and stepped aboard. As I reversed us away into the shadows, I'm pretty sure Billy saw my expression. Hidden in a face that looked otherwise innocent, was enough of the truth so he knew. He didn't know how I'd done it, but he knew I was somehow behind his embarrassment. I saw realization dawning on his face and I bit down on my lips to stop the smug expression forming there. He had the rest of the night on his own desert island to try and figure it out.

I felt so smart that night fooling the adults. Years later Da and I talked about that night over a beer, and he explained he had never dreamt I was guilty. He had pretty quickly worked out someone had planted things on me and had caught the same look on Billy's face. But for reasons he wouldn't say at the time — Mr. Bremmer's abuse of his family — he had acted the way he had. But he had worried about it all night and had come into my room to talk it through, having given me time to wind down from my moral outrage party—and found my room was empty. He had thought I was off sulking somewhere, but then the flare had gone up. He had spotted the wet patch on the dock and worked out most of what was going on. He'd figured men had to grow up and fight their battles, and I had. He said it was one of his proudest memories of me. I guess he missed the naked, voyeur, hard-on part.

So, what does this tell us about why I came to be in Gwen's pantry, wearing only my birthday suit? There is a fair amount of research that early sexual experiences can lead us to eroticize situations, urges, and desires that stay with us for the rest of our lives. Some say, for example, that enjoying a mild spanking goes back to being punished at an early age. So, what did mother nature wire into me that warm summer night? Was it watching lesbians in their tender, exploratory youth? Was it voyeurism? Did it make me a stalker, or someone who likes under-aged girls? Was it to limit my ability to get excited to only moments of unique intimacy? Thankfully none of the above. That warm summer night, Mother Nature — love her dearly — took my hormone soup, heated it in the fire of fear of discovery, crystallized it with the pain of a woody on sand, into being highly turned on by the fear of being caught naked. Since that night, I've had erotic dreams of being stuck naked in church (no idea how I get there) or discovered skinny dipping by strangers wandering by or losing at strip poker in front of a room full of women. A fetish that has caused me trouble on more than one occasion.

Mother Nature is an entertaining but twisted bitch!

4: Rooftop Exposure; An Agreement Reached

So, twenty years later, how's this fetish worked for me? Pretty frustrating, actually! It's not something one can experiment with easily and safely. There is a thin line between the thrill of being scared of discovery and being a creepy flasher. A line I've stayed well clear of. I've dated often, but never intimately enough to admit to this odd kink. I'm a very happy and sometimes active sexual male, and I indulge my more straightforward and *normal* urges whenever I can. I've been nude on a nudist beach, and to be honest it was a total let down. The planning and build-up were arousing, but as soon as I stepped onto the beach, I knew it was a bust. There was no fear of surprise and discovery. Mostly just naked old people wondering what I was doing there.

But with a creative mind and limitless funds, there are ways. A year before what we shall henceforth refer to as *The Night of Gwen's Pantry*, I was standing naked on the roof of my building. The Booker Building is in the heart of Yaletown, and it is my building. A little ostentatious by my standards, but there you are. I splurged. There are 26 floors housing 80 units, crowned by two split-level penthouses that share a large roof garden. The roof garden is really mine, but if my neighbour Gwen wants to use it, she can ask, and I have always said yes. Access is from the corridor that separates our units. The elevator that serves our floor via a private-penthouse-only code is at one end, in the middle facing each other are our respective front doors, and steps lead up to the roof at the other end. Each penthouse unit has a fantastic deck, so the rooftop has been left largely unfurnished. It has an area with wood planking in case we want to set up a party, a small observation area in case we want to watch fireworks, or something not easily seen from the deck, and a small utility area for hobbies, star gazing or whatever I need.

One of the problems with limitless wealth is that it can make you greedy. I know that sounds silly, but not really. I could indulge myself in almost anything legal every day of the year and soon lose interest in it, so I have learned to ration. One of my rules is that I can only indulge my shameful fetish once in the week after solving a big case. The smaller cases don't count, so I really only have two to three chances a year to embarrass myself terribly.

I had just solved a case of financial embezzlement, which though satisfying— as the criminal was a jerk — is a case too boring to relay. But it did mean I was able to play, and I had a plan. The plan was an evolution of the last time I had risked my modesty. The last time I had gone up to my roof garden at night, left the door to the roof unlocked, making discovery a possible but rare chance event. I had screwed a time-operated safe onto the utility table. The safe can only be unscrewed when the safe door is open, as the bolts are inside. Into the safe, I put the key to my unit, all of my clothes, and my cell phone, and then locked the safe for an hour. I was stuck on the roof naked, and possibly discoverable. Gwen or the building commissionaire, Sandy, coming up to the roof was unlikely, and although my roof was overlooked, someone would need night vision goggles to see me in the shadows. Don't get me wrong, it was thrilling nonetheless.

I'd asked that our building manager employ Sandy as one of two commissionaires after solving a problem for Sandy. His real name was Mathew Brown, but being a light-skinned man of colour, he had grown up with the nickname Sandy Brown. Sandy worked security at a warehouse on the North Shore and had been framed by his employer for drug smuggling. Sandy was referred to me by another PI who was overworked and who I owed a favour. I had quickly proven by breaking in and planting hidden cameras that the employer was the smuggler and taken the evidence to the police. Given how I had obtained the footage, it was inadmissible, but it gave the police a start in on the drug ring. Sandy was released, but now unemployed with no references. Sandy had a wonderful wife and triplets, girls, aged four. I really liked him and his family, so I rented him a two-bedroom unit on the second floor, at a reduced rate, on the basis he ran building security and his wife ran a daycare out of space next to their apartment for themselves and people in nearby buildings. Even with the salaries I pay them, and after rent deductions, I'm more than breaking even in daycare income. Sandy had been doing a great job for 18 months.

The evolution I had come up with for my adventure that night was a serious increase in risk. I really needed to up the likelihood of being discovered. So, I asked Sandy to ensure the roof was checked once per night at midnight. He wasn't fazed by the request. Rich millionaires are eccentric, and I'm sure this was one of the more reasonable requests he'd gotten from our tenants. I then adjusted the lock of the roof so that you can open it from the inside but need a key from the outside. That key, and a key to my unit, I put in a box and attached that to one of my remote-controlled aerial drones. I use drones often as part of my PI work. I've hired some of the best and brightest engineers and operators and have all sorts of drones that do tricks that most of the emerging drone market has yet to come up with, but when they do, they will see there are several patents on the technology already owned by Ethan Booker and Associates. The drone I was using tonight had two features key to the mission. The first was that it could self-navigate to a predetermined spot. By placing the drone at the target spot and sending it a code, it could find its way back to that exact spot both vertically and horizontally. The second feature was, like all of my drones, it contained a map of all buildings and sensors to help avoid crashing. So, on this occasion, there was a drone sitting on the roof of another of my buildings waiting for a timer to send it on a journey, which would end with it landing on the roof where I live. It would arrive at 11 pm and deliver the keys needed to let myself off the roof and into my unit, well ahead of the scheduled inspection.

Now, I like the risk, but I'm not completely crazy. So, for the two nights before my adventure, I had the drone practise delivery three times each night and it made it flawlessly each time. At 9 pm I checked the drone remotely and confirmed it was active and counting down. I shed my clothes and went to the door of my unit. Checking the coast was clear, I let myself out, closing the door behind me. Now I was committed. I pushed firmly to test the door, which I had paid a great deal of money to strengthen with steel and high-security devices. No easy way back unless you have the key. I didn't think Gwen a 'peeker,' but didn't linger at the door in case she checked her security peephole. I skittered up to the roof and closed the roof door, so now felt doubly committed. Gwen could decide to come up without warning. Sandy could come early. If the drone failed to show up, I would have to choose between waiting for Sandy, banging on Gwen's door, or trying to break into the building. With that thought I crouched and ran across to the side of the deck above my unit and looked down onto the balcony that hangs off my kitchen. It was about a 15-foot drop. I could lower myself over the edge, hang, then let go, making it a seven or eight-foot drop and an interesting view for anyone in the city who happened to look this way, as it was well lit from my patio. I had left the kitchen door ajar. This development gave me mixed feelings. A relatively non-embarrassing but slightly dangerous escape route.

I walked back to the centre of the roof and sat in the canvas deck chair I had put out for this adventure. I spent the next one hundred minutes remembering previous outings, thinking of ways to improve this adventure for the future, but mostly imagining what would happen if someone came up onto the patio. I decided Sandy wouldn't bat an eyelid. He'd just believe I had decided to take a nude stroll. Lots of people are nudists. Although I get a kick out of these adventures, as time went on, I had to admit they weren't as close to the edge as they needed to be to scratch my itch. There was no easy way to make them less predictable.

I had deliberately not taken a watch but sensed the time for delivery was closing in. I wandered over to Gwen's side of the building, which was where the drone would appear. As I moved quietly to the edge, I heard music and saw soft lights flickering. I peeked over the top and Gwen was sitting on her deck taking in the evening. I was suddenly very aware of intruding on her privacy—and of being very naked and vulnerable. Throw in some sand and another woman and I could have been back on the beach 19 years earlier. Gwen had pushed her patio table to the right and was sitting on the left on a chair facing out into the night. She was staring intently out into the darkness, taking in the city scene. She didn't look relaxed. Her body posture was alert, as if she were waiting for someone, and I wondered if she had a guest. I eased back, not wanting to be a voyeur, and waited for the drone. I have drones that are almost silent, which I use for special occasions, but on this occasion, I had employed a standard model. Nervous and thrilled as I was, my adrenaline-fuelled hearing intercepted the soft whine of the six electric motors whisking the small craft through the night. Then I heard a chair scrape loudly as Gwen stood suddenly, as if she'd heard it too.

It happened seemingly all in one fluid motion. I saw the drone coming out of the darkness, and Gwen moved across the deck and grab a pole that was leaning against the wall.

She raised it up and out towards the drone. "Come here you pervy, sneaky bastard!" She wrestled to manoeuvre the pole rapidly into the path of the incoming aircraft. I saw Gwen reach up with a stupidly sized fishing net and snag the drone out of the air. Both impressive and devastating all in one fraction of a second.

"Yes! Frigging drones. Score one for team privacy!" yelled Gwen, at no one in particular, dragging her catch onto the balcony and laughing proudly.

The drones are programmed to go dead if they hit anything to avoid further damage to themselves or whatever they hit. A live operator can override at any time, but tonight the drone was on autopilot. It lay in her net and she kicked at it a few times. I saw her search for and find the camera unit, look into it, and give it the finger a couple of times before throwing a blanket over it.

Below on Gwen's deck was my drone, and my only easy way back. I did a quick mental inventory and couldn't think of anything on the drone that would easily identify it with me.

"Thank God," I heard myself say, then my hand clamped over my own mouth.

"Who's up there?" yelled an angry and maybe a little worried Gwen. *Shit.* I considered my options. I could run and hop onto my balcony, but the building security systems would show Gwen and I were the only occupants of the floor tonight. Still I could deny everything.

"Ethan, is that you? Is this contraption yours?"

Oh, she sounds mad.

"OK whoever you are, I'm calling the police, right now."

Shit, crap, bugger.

"Err, yes it's me Gwen, no need for the police," I croaked, not sure what else to do, before I realized running would have been the smart move.

"Where are you? What the fuck are you playing at spying on me. I knew you were a little different, but a pervert? A creep?"

"Err, not quite. Well, not that sort of pervert," I said quietly under my breath. Then more loudly I forced out, "It's kind of hard to explain to be honest Gwen."

"Hang on, I'm bloody well coming up there and we'll sort this out!" Gwen yelled, starting towards the door. Clearly pissed.

"Actually no, err... I would prefer you don't, actually," I said smoothly. Two 'actuallys' in one sentence. God damn it *man, take control. You're supposed to be cool in a crisis.*

"It's not what you think. That drone is part of a scientific and classified experiment and there is more secret equipment up on the roof," I offered in a somewhat sterner tone. "Sorry if I disturbed you but this relates to the business I run." "Well come down here and explain yourself or I will call the police and you can explain it to them instead," she shot back.

There was a long silence, then I peeked over.

"Well that would be kind of hard Gwen. You see the door is locked and the key is attached to the drone. Silly mistake. Locked myself up here and had a buddy send the drone over with a replacement. Didn't want to disturb you. And now I have. Sorry." That slowed her down a bit.

She chewed on it for a bit and then in a somewhat calmer voice she said, "So the key to the roof is in this box then? And what, you locked yourself out both of the past two nights, too, Ethan? Three times? What's going on? This is bullshit." Her tone was a lot less angry; it now was more curious. Ok, still a little angry. I then recalled my other danger: Sandy. *Crap! What time is it?* I came up with an explanation that sounded good in my head but less clever when I said it out loud.

"Crap, Gwen. This is really embarrassing. I lost a bet and have to pay off a dare. I'm afraid to say I'm standing up here buck naked, and my buddy had the key. I'm stuck up here until either he comes and lets me out or I get the key. The last couple of nights were practise runs. So, I know this is really, very weird, but I would really appreciate it if you would throw the box up and forget this whole thing. Dinner on me anywhere in the city if we are still talking after this. What do you say?" What? Yeah, I know. Pretty lame. But oddly she bought it. After a long think.

"Ok Ethan. Surprisingly, I might buy that a lot more than your 'secret science experiments' bullshit or you being a total pervert. But here's the problem: I throw like a girl. The chances are the box will end up down in the street."

"Good point," I said, somewhat relieved and keen to build some positive momentum here. "How about this. Why don't you come up to the roof door and open it, and throw the box through it, then go back to your apartment? I'll go get dressed, then we can have a good laugh about this over a glass of wine? I have some great wine and I'm at your mercy? Think about it?" She thought about it for a very long minute before coming up with a conclusion I hadn't intended.

"OK. Wait right there, I'll be just a minute," she said. She waited for my nod and vanished inside. She was gone a few minutes and I was beginning to think she had really called the police, but she reappeared. Gwen looked different, like she was through the shock and beginning to have fun at my expense. "OK, Ethan. I have a one-time offer for you. I'm nearly convinced. To check out your story I popped over to your apartment." She pulled a bottle out from behind her back and put it on the table next to herself.

"I chose us a 2005 William Fèvre Chablis!"

"You went into my unit?" I asked incredulously, which her look told me was a little cheeky under the circumstances.

"Yes, I wanted to check some facts before buying into your cockamamie story. I found a pile of clothes by the door. Nice briefs by the way. And I went and locked your kitchen balcony. Now there is only one way down from up there. My way. And here it is Ethan. I'm still a little worried you are a freak show. If I open that roof door, how do I know you won't attack me?"

I had no answer to that but to say I wouldn't.

"So here is what we are going to do. You've scared the hell out of me, and you need to pay, pay, pay. You can't go creeping naked on our roof and buzzing people with drones, Ethan. I'm going to pass you something up in this fishing net. Hang on." After some fiddling on her part, the net arrived about a foot below me, and I reached over and pulled out the contents. A pair of handcuffs and a blindfold. OK now who is being weird? I was already blushing red all over, but it cranked a shade or two. Fifty shades of red seemed fitting.

"So, I want to see you put the blindfold on, then turn around and put the cuffs on behind your back where I can see them. I want to hear them click tight. Only then will I feel safe and come and let you out. I'll bring you down here and we can talk this out over a glass of wine. If I'm happy with the explanation, I will let you go. If you are not happy with my terms, you can sort this out with the VPD. What do you say?"

What could I say? I had one 'Hail Mary' idea. "Gwen, I'm naked here. I don't think you really want to see me like this. You don't have to come up. Put the key in the net and pass it up. I'll be out of your hair without further embarrassment for either of us. Who wants to see a naked guy?"

"Oh Ethan, you play for the wrong team for me, and I have six brothers, so I don't embarrass easily. In fact, why don't I call them and see what they think of how you treat their sister? Last chance, Ethan!" Now she was beginning to enjoy herself way too much.

What could I do? Really. I put the blindfold on, turned around and put on the cuffs. A short while later I heard Gwen approach across the roof, and I swear I could hear her laughing, although afterwards she said not. I was cringing, sweating, and dying of embarrassment, yet little Ethan was clearly enjoying himself. Traitorous bugger. *You got us into this!* I thought. She guided me carefully down the stairs and into her apartment and out on to her deck. I heard some scraping of furniture then she pushed me down onto a chair. As I sat there trying to orientate, I heard another noise, like handcuffs being attached. The blindfold was removed, and I sat there blinking. I looked over my shoulder and the cuffs I wore were now attached to the metal railing by a longer pair of cuffs. And she thinks *I'm* kinky? As I was just getting my eyes adjusted there were a couple of quick flashes and I looked up and saw Gwen grinning over the top of a camera. She vanished inside and came back a few minutes later with two glasses and a blanket. Truth be told I was shivering, but I wasn't sure if it was cold, relief, or fear about what would come next.

After a few glasses of wine, I explained my shameful secret. She was very sweet and non-judgy. As with anyone moving into my building, I had researched Gwen thoroughly and knew she had been a professor of sexual psychology at the local university, and it seemed she liked to bring homework home. Gwen confessed she did like to play a little around the edges and liked to be in charge with her girlfriends and was quite expert in such matters.

21

We made a deal that night.

She'd decided to make me her new fun toy, as revenge for my scaring her into thinking her nice neighbour was a creep. She said it was the perfect arrangement. She was in it for the fun, not for sex, and promised to be very creative at putting me in awkward predicaments. She was very worried I would get into real trouble with my little games, and to be honest she was right. I nearly had.

The essence of the deal she offered was that I was to let her know when I solved a case, and she would arrange a game that would test me. We would do this for the next ten cases, and I would have to promise to follow her instructions on each occasion without question. If I agreed to the rules, she would trust me to keep the bargain but could release the pictures to the media if I reneged. If I said no, then she might release the pictures anyway, and I would get to meet her brothers. Or the police. By this time, I was pretty sure we were past that, as I had sat for an hour handcuffed naked, with a blanket covering my treacherous friend. It turned out to be the beginning of a lifelong friendship with Gwen.

Gwen explained that she considered this a form of BDSM, and that BDSM is consensual by definition, and I could always back out if she pushed me too far. We had safe words, yellow for slow down or pause, and red for stop, and we spent a while discussing what I think I like and what I would not do.

I found out later as we got to know each other that she had no brothers. She found out I could hack anything and next time she looked at her cloud storage, the pictures had Mel Gibson's head on them.

I had agreed to the deal; Da would be shocked if I reneged. We have played our game four times now, each time Gwen getting more creative and nearer the line. Each time more thrilling than the last.

And that fourth time, a year after it all began, I solved the Onion case, which led to me being naked in Gwen's pantry.

5: Marcy Owns a Piece of Me

The Booker Building, my home, is on Marinaside Crescent and has 26 floors above ground. On the west and south corners, False Creek Inlet sloshes by, separated from us by a road and a sidewalk festooned with cyclists, joggers, and step-counting strollers. It is zoned for mixed-use commercial and residential and has plenty of both. In the subfloors there is visitor and resident parking and a large private garage for my many vehicles. At ground level there are two restaurants, a nail place, some offices that turn over frequently, and Gwen's coffee shop, *The Crazy Bean*, often shortened to just '*The Bean*.' On the second floor is a general use gym and common area, the latter which is used for Sandy's daycare and other functions, and the remainder of the floor and all of those to the 20th contain apartments of various sizes, which would be considered upmarket even for Yaletown. The 21st to 24th are for my personal use, and from where I run several of my businesses. Gwen and I each have one of the two penthouses that occupy the 25th and 26th floors. She leases her penthouse from me, along with the space for *The Bean*.

The 24th floor is my private fitness centre. It has a well-equipped gym, sauna, steam room, a dojo where I practise my martial arts and defence training most days, and a 25-foot by 65-foot pool with a swim-current generator. To the side of the pool is a south-facing covered balcony that is a solarium.

The 23rd floor is a technology lab, where Darcy Fullerton is queen. I met Darcy and her sister Kelsie while working for Ma at Booker Sciences, a technology think tank Ma operated to create technology she sold to industry or kept and fed to some of our other companies. The company owns over 5000 high-tech patents, and a considerable number of those could be attributed to Darcy. Both MIT graduates, Darcy and Kelsie are the daughters of a Japanese industrialist father and a Norwegian mother who was a Nobel Peace Prize runner-up. Kelsie Kobe was younger, unmarried, and sported the family name, but Darcy had married Jimmy Fullerton, who owned a company specializing in military computer component fabrication for various top-secret weapons systems. Darcy loved to invent and was the force behind most of the toys I employ as a PI. If she didn't invent them, she probably modified and improved them. I get to use them, and we sell some of them to various military and defence contractors, security companies, and governments.

Kelsie was developing security systems and counter systems when I met her at Booker Sciences but had more of an operations bent than inventor leanings. When I started my detective agency business, I convinced them both to come and work for me in Vancouver. Darcy is to me what Q is to James Bond, and Kelsie is my head of operations. The 22nd floor is the operations floor, and I have a small team dedicated to security-related work focused mostly in Vancouver but able to turn their attention further afield if I need them to do so. There is a larger team, in a separate part of the floor, who look after my global business operations and oversee most of my other interests, which are not as much fun and which I generally try to avoid. Being responsible is often a burden. The 21st floor is my administration and legal team, which focusses mostly on my businesses, but I have a couple of criminal specialists on hand who can help with any of my PI needs. There are 55 staff who work on the four floors. Not a huge number given what they do, which is fast-paced and 24x7. They may be few, but they are the best in their fields.

Part of Kelsie's team's role is to monitor local, national and international events and flag items of interest to me or parts of my business. As I stood naked and breathless in my penthouse, having escaped the pantry encounter, a call came through from Kelsie. Mavis, my computerized and somewhat experimental house system, chimed and announced the call.

"Sir, there is an incoming call from operations. Should I activate the video conference system?" inquired Mavis. "Negative Mavis. Audio only, please" I replied, stepping out of view of the many cameras just in case Mavis got it wrong, as often happens. There was a click and then Kelsie herself came onto the line rather than one of her team. A sign something serious was happening.

"Ethan, sorry to break into your evening but we are monitoring a shooting and police response just east of Gastown, and there are several injuries and officers hit and as far as we can tell from the police radio traffic, at least one fatality. And sir, Marcy Stone was heard on the radio coordinating the response but has been silent for the last 90 seconds."

It felt like a huge vice had grabbed onto my chest and slammed the air out. I felt sick, but unlike the befuddlement I feel when embarrassing myself with my fetish, I become very cool, and very, very focused with faced with danger.

"I'm on my way down, Kelsie, and I want eyes on by the time I get there. And wake up a couple of our security details and have them on the ground pronto!" I commanded.

"We already have drones coming online and they should be over the site in under two minutes. Teams Charlie and Delta have been alerted and are rolling, Ethan," she replied.

My instincts had taken over and I was already through the living room and heading down the spiral stairs to my bedroom. From the closet I pulled on underwear, jeans, a sweatshirt, a quick-draw shoulder holster, and pulled a hoodie over the top to cover it. All of it grey or black. As I was slipping into a pair of sneakers, I pressed a discrete catch on a wall mirror to reveal a small black keypad. I entered a code that caused a hidden floor safe to tilt open, revealing a small collection of handguns and combat knives. I chose a Glock 19, which I quickly checked and holstered, shut the safe, and grabbed my wallet from the dresser.

I was dressed and armed and on my way within 60 seconds. I have a door from the suite that leads into a service riser which has a private stairwell connecting my suite with the four business floors, and as I descended to the 22nd floor, I marvelled at how Kelsie operated. She was always at least one step ahead of me and a savant at organizing rapid, precise contingencies and actions. As she was putting the call in to me, she would have instructed her ready team on what she needed. We keep four security teams in Vancouver; each team has four specialists. The teams typically rotate so one is on duty at all times, but all four can be called in if needed. Charlie and Delta were our two most experienced teams and would already be approaching a holding position near the shooting and waiting for instructions. Images from the drones would be relayed in real time to their vehicles to aid situational awareness.

As I burst into the operations area, I could hear talking from four different police radios, all going at once. Police radios are encoded these days and you need more than a simple scanner, but given we supply the technology, this was not an impediment to our eavesdropping.

Three of the six large screens in the operations centre had images from the three drones Kelsie has dispatched. Two operators were controlling the drones. One operator was flying the lead drone, and the other two drones were slaved to follow six feet either side of the lead. The second operator was working the cameras and other sensors. The pilot had selected a holding point on a detailed area map, and the drones were just completing the half-mile dash at maximum speed to the allocated spot on autopilot. As they arrived, they slipped into a hover, and then the operator gave each of the drones separate coordinates to move to, and assigned each slightly different altitudes. The drones took up positions on three sides of the shooting site, and the operator fine-tuned the cameras on each drone to maximize coverage of the scene.

"Drop two down about a hundred fifty feet," commanded the camera operator to get a better angle inside a building.

I stood in front of the screens and searched for Marcy, but all I could see were officers and EMTs moving rapidly around a small industrial-looking building surrounded by flashing blue lights. My mind was racing through actions I could take and just as quickly striking each of them. *No, I couldn't call her cell. She couldn't answer anyway. No, I can't go down there,* and so on. And then from the cacophony of radio traffic I heard her voice strong and clear.

"All stations we have BlueMan. I repeat, all stations, we have BlueMan. All hostiles are in custody, all hostiles are in custody. Harden up the perimeter and bring in the EMTs and crime scene teams. We have at least seven injured and one Red Team fatality." Over the next 20 minutes, I watched and listened to Marcy expertly commanding the conclusion of the operational portion of a takedown operation. With Kelsie proficiently and very secretly probing through the VPD computer system, we discovered Marcy was the local action commander for a raid on a suspected human-trafficking ring, which was part of an internationally coordinated task force combining the Canadian, US, and Brazilian serious crimes units. BlueMan was code name for the local kingpin, and he was now in custody. Go Marcy. In 30 minutes, I had gone from terrified of being discovered nude to terrified of losing a woman I'd loved from afar for over 20 years, to being incredibly proud and impressed by that same woman.

I thanked the team and left them to secure our resources, then went back to my apartment and took a shower. I knew she wouldn't answer, but I called and left Marcy a message anyway, being careful not to reveal I had illegally watched the end of her operation.

"Er, yeah. Hi Marcy. It's Ethan. It's been a while since we connected, and I wondered if you were free for dinner this week. Tomorrow would work best for me, if you are at a loose end. How about Blue Water?" I hung up. Blue Water Café was her favourite restaurant in town. She is a seafood girl.

Marcy knew about my money and she knew I had several business interests and owned the building I lived in. She knew I had a PI agency, and even referred people to me, but I always kept from her the extent of the resources I employed. As it sometimes bends the laws, just a tad, it would be a terrible conflict of interest for her. I knew she suspected I had some interesting assets, but she was smart enough not to ask.

After our brief summer romantic relationship back in 2004, I went on to university and Marcy to police work. We kept in touch but didn't spend a great deal of time together until Max's sudden and unexpected death thrust us back together in 2008.

I was a bit of a mess before then. I was at McGill University in Montreal and had fallen into the trap of being a rich brat. First year was great. I knuckled down and got good grades. Second year was OK, but third year, not so much. I was going on 22 and the world was my oyster and travelling and the joy of life fuelled by money was cutting into my study time. I wasn't even sure I would finish. What was the point? I never needed to work. Give the spot to someone who needed it. When Max died, I flew home and wasn't sure I would return. In fact, if I could think of a way of not telling Ma and Da I was flunking, I was certain I would not go back.

The Bremmer's had downsized when Marcy and Max had moved out, so Ma offered Marcy a room in our house while she was in town, which she accepted gratefully. While Max's remains were being repatriated, we had a week to console each other. In that week I was close with Marcy. I confided in her that I was thinking of dropping out and gave her my lame-assed rationale. We were sitting on the patio at my parents' house; they were out at dinner, still romancing at their age. I still hadn't worked out how to at mine. It was a sunny evening, and "Dock of the Bay" was playing quietly in the background.

After hearing my confession, Marcy sat a while without speaking, and then she seemed to make up her mind. She stood and asked me to stand, which I did. She looked me in the eye, and then slapped me hard across the face. Not once. Not twice. But *three* times. And then she started pounding me in the chest and yelling at me that I was a selfish and privileged brat. She broke down in tears and collapsed into me, as my tears mingled with hers while we held each other.

After some time, she told me that she and Max had always been blown away by how down to earth I was about being so rich. Max idolized me and cherished our friendship, in part because I was such a swell and normal guy despite my fortune. He was really upset at putting our friendship on hold while he went to serve in Afghanistan but had joined up to escape his parents at just 19 years of age, just as Marcy had fled home to the police force intending to solve all domestic violence cases single-handedly, or so she had naively thought. Together they had marvelled that even with the riches I had, I was humble, focused and diligent. They had envied the family and my parents, especially compared to the failure of their own, and the values I had inherited from my folks. Almost everything they didn't have, I had, and they couldn't wish it on a nicer guy. They had talked often about how they both loved me, which was interesting to hear, and how they were so proud of me. And now Max was dead, from serving his country, and I was turning into the stereotype Max had been so proud I was not. And she was 100 percent right. A kick in the nuts was probably more deserved than the slaps.

That week she told me the stories of her parents, which I won't repeat here, but they were disturbing, wretched, and painful. As we grew closer and grieved Max together, I think I was her family that week. She stood with us at the service and asked me to take her back to the ferry when she left to go back to work. We hugged and kissed quite platonically. Then I got my ass back on a plane to Montreal, extended my studies by a year, and finished top of my class in Computer Sciences. I have a small box of things from my time with Max, and I keep my graduation certificate and cap in there, along with other memories of him.

It was during our trip back for Max's funeral that I found out that she was romantically engaged to Terry Stone, who she went on to marry in 2010 and then tragically lose in early 2013. Terry ran the detachment of CBSA border guards at the Peace Arch crossing to the US. Between 2008 and 2013 I saw Marcy only five times, and two of those occasions were funerals to bury a brother and a husband. Terry had pulled a double shift watching for a particular individual crossing into Canada, who had been a no-show. He had a long drive from work to their home in North Vancouver, and his car left the road at 4:24 am and hit a telephone pole at 60 mph, killing him instantly. The police report suggested he had fallen asleep at the wheel, and they were probably right. I never discussed the accident's cause with Marcy, but it broke my heart to watch her go through the pain of losing someone she so clearly loved. During the next year her career stalled, and Marcy became a little withdrawn; I was quite worried she was slipping into depression.

After Terry's death, when I became worried about Marcy, I remembered how she had tuned me up years before. I gave her a call and we had dinner. Over dinner, I shared my concerns, and as I could hardly slap her face three times, asked her what I could do to help. At first, she denied being depressed but eventually broke down and admitted she was having trouble finding herself. She needed to somehow reboot and find her mojo again. I asked her if she could take a week's vacation and said we should take a trip, clear her head. She hesitated and I stammered, "I... I meant as friends, nothing more. No strings, just to get away." She surprised me and accepted, and I told her to be ready to be picked up the next day, and to bring a toothbrush and passport.

I picked her up in an SUV, with two shiny new racing bikes strapped on the back. She went along with me but didn't seem to relish the idea of cycling through BC's woods for a week. I drove her to Vancouver Airport and we wheeled the bikes onto a private jet, which took us to southern Italy, where we were kitted out with everything we would need. A crew moved our luggage from hotel to spa to hotel, and we cycled only much as we wanted, but in fact each day pushed ourselves harder and harder, exorcising our demons. It was a week of low commitment to everything but memories and hard work. Ok, we may have been committed to a lot of good Italian wine and pasta, too.

At the end of the week, we flew home fit and adjusted, and she left Terry behind as a loved and cherished memory, and not a millstone. Marcy attacked her work again with renewed vigour and got herself back on the rails with a vengeance.

A couple of months later it was my birthday, and I got a card from Marcy. It read:

Dearest Ethan,

That was one of the most romantic gestures, and most romantic trips of my life. Your timing really does suck doesn't it? Your high-school year, and now this summer. I've still got some work to do, but please don't give up on me, Ethan. Third time could be the charm.

Happy birthday.

Love Marcy

That was five years ago. Marcy still owns a huge piece of me.

6: A Mother Lost

Not unexpectedly, I didn't hear from Marcy that night. I dialled in to Ramsey Lewis on my *Sonos* sound system and tried to catch up on some reading. Darcy had flagged some technical white papers on emerging technology and some ideas on how we could exploit it, but my concentration wasn't up to the task. I would suddenly realize I had been staring at a page for a long time, skimming my eyes over it but not absorbing much. That is a dangerous game with Darcy, as she will quiz me and hold me accountable to give her intelligent feedback. Marcy, and how to kindle another attempt at a relationship, kept intruding. In the end I put the reading aside, stepped into some running clothes, and took off around the seawall.

Vancouver is built on the delta of the Fraser River and has a couple of significant inlets flowing to other bodies of water. The downtown core abuts the Burrard Inlet to the north and meets False Creek to the south. The two inlets, combined with English Bay to the west, essentially make downtown a small peninsula, which is tipped by Stanley Park. It is a beautiful second-growth protected forested area that is approximately six miles in circumference surrounded by water, float plane traffic, seals, seagulls, and a mountainous panorama across the bay to the north. The local mountains are about 3800 ft high, and that night, the tops were lost in a layer of broken cloud, turned a dusty rose in the dusk light. I picked a route that took me from Yaletown in the east, along the seawall paralleling downtown, around the park, back along the north side of town, and back to my apartment, which was about 10 miles in total. Sure enough, when I checked my watch GPS it was 10.7 miles, which I had taken at a leisurely pace and completed in three and a half hours. This awful time was partly due to the inclusion of a pause to take in the sunset, and two pints of Fat Tug IPA and some blues at Carderos, which is a character seafood and steak place nestled among Coal Harbour's many marinas. Some of my training runs are a lot faster, but I knew I had an appointment with Gia in the morning and being stiff and tired for that appointment would mean a great deal of pain.

After a shower and a solid and surprisingly undisturbed sleep, I awoke at 7 am, pulled on some trunks, and slipped down to the pool. After a dozen lengths to loosen up, I hit the sauna for twenty minutes and digested the financial times. The sauna is one place I can hang out naked and not look too crazy. The smell of dry wood, hot (electric) coals and eucalyptus scent combined with newspaper and sweat is unique. One of the benefits of being an eccentric billionaire is setting your own rules and your own pace, so I pulled on a vest, shorts and flip-flops and sauntered down to the main business office and checked the status on a few business items before wandering back up to the dojo for my appointment with Gia.

Gia Yui Mai Braekhus is my personal trainer and torturer. No, this is not another kink, although sometimes I wonder about that. Gia, a product of a German painter father and Japanese businesswoman, puts me through my paces thrice weekly in the gym for strength, shape and flexibility, and twice a week for martial arts skills. Today was the latter, which almost certainly meant a bruised body but not ego.

Gia was born in England but moved to Alicante, Spain, when just a few months old. Later in life she returned to live in England and competed in Taekwondo at the Olympic level. She became fluent in about a dozen other disciplines and weapons capabilities as a result of a short stint with British Intelligence.

She has striking rather than pretty features, which individually might almost qualify as ugly, but together and on her create an earthy beauty. She inherited her mother's colouring and stands a stocky five foot five inches. Gia's body is hard as nails, athlete muscular rather than bodybuilder bulky, but with her colouring gives the impression it is more sharply defined. Her abs have abs; her arms are elegant like Michelle Obama's, until she bends her elbow and muscles form. She keeps me incredibly toned and ripped, but I'm almost blurry or fuzzy standing beside her.

As I entered the dojo and slipped on a white training keikogi, or Gi – the standard martial arts uniform – I watched Gia completing a complex kata I didn't recognize, but that looked impressive and scary. I'm pretty sure she could do that in any biker bar in town and the place would empty before she finished.

I'd met Gia when I was interviewing people for the role. Kelsie had organized a shortlist of people to be flown in after a rigorous background check, and all four had met me here at the dojo at the same time. There was Gia, an ex-marine who was nearly 60 years old but looked like he could break concrete with his smile, an ex-Gurkha, and a scary-looking thin guy from the Bosnian armed forces. We stood in the centre of the mat and I planned to have them duke it out as part of the interview process. I knew they were all exceptional, so any would do technically, but I wanted to observe their character under pressure.

I explained I would ask each of them why they thought they would be best for the role, then watch them spar. I remember saying "ladies first" and turning to Gia, then I remember lying flat on the floor, small birds circling my head, after she sucker punched me.

"Mr. Booker. As a PI you might be forced one day to hit a woman in self-defence, and I suspect you might hesitate. I can cure you of that, but I will absolutely kick your ass if you ever strike a woman for any other reason." She said it with such a genuine and professional smile, I just stood up and thanked the others for coming and told them to enjoy two weeks accommodation and business-class flights home on me for their trouble. They all smiled, shrugged and left without a word.

Over the last few years Gia has worked me to a level of fitness and fighting ability I had never imagined I could achieve. I keep close to triathlete conditioning, can impress most gym bunnies on weights and machines, and should never lose a fight unless it is someone approaching Gia's amazing ability. But Gia always insists we try for better, and today was no exception.

Our-hour long sparring session included kicking my ass with karate, knocking my head around with kendo training swords, and culminated in a five-minute no-holds-barred street fight. Having your head in a leg scissor applied by your own pocket Amazonian until you tap out does have some upside, but Gia doesn't always release on command, and I'm pretty sure I was unconscious for a second or two.

I think I came back to the world of the living to a comment something to the effect of, "Learn how to toughen up when the going gets rough. One day, you may have to save that wimpy ass of yours with your last breath. You've got to build up your tolerance!"

*

After a stretch and a long, warm shower, and dressing in my Yaletown summer uniform of ridiculously expensive t-shirt, shorts and deck shoes (or sandals), costing more as they have to look really casual and not expensive, I crumbled and checked my messages to see if Marcy had replied to the voicemail I had left the night before. Nada. Then I went to *The Bean* ostensibly to check how Gwen's date went, but really because I needed company from someone who was not trying to kill me.

The Bean is a high-end, one-off coffee shop. High end because it has designer everything throughout, and one off because of Gwen. You could create the spaces as franchises, but they would lack the personality that is uniquely Gwen. Gwen's is to Vancouver coffee shops what *Cheers* is to Boston, only real, and Gwen is Ted Danson, Woody Harrelson, Rhea Perlman, and George Wendt, all rolled into one. Does that make me Cliff Clavin or one of the girls?

Gwen opened *The Bean* in 2009, when she quit teaching, and it thrived from the day the doors opened. In the heart of the tourist district, in a primo location, it is only ever patronized by locals, as there is rarely space for tourists. There is something Harry Potter about it, in the sense Muggles need not apply. The décor is cocktail-loungesque, leather furniture, velvet and, black tie, the food is healthy snacks and heart attack desserts, and the coffee? Heaven with hell's kick. Part of the magic that is *The Bean* is that there is never, ever, a lineup. If you are a local, you come in and are seated and served. If you arrive and there are no seats you are turned away. Many tourists are turned away, but I've never seen a local go without a seat. It's spooky. There was one close occasion, but Gwen kicked a young couple out of their seats — putting cushions on the bar for them — in order to seat Frank the Cap — whose cap is older than he is — and he must be soon to get his milestone telegram from her majesty for reaching his hundredth year. Frank the Cap is a quality guy, and part of history here, but not the main attraction as he is gravely quiet these days. The main attraction is Elvis, Cap's just-out-of-puppyhood, gangly legged, slobbery, grey mutt. He loves everyone, and they love him back. There will be playing, antics, stolen sausages if you are careless, pleading sad eyes if he can't steal your food—oh, and a lot of sleeping. If one sad day Frank doesn't roll in for his daily brunch, I'm going looking for Elvis.

Gwen typically takes the morning shift, leaves the middle shift to Derek, her manager, and comes by in the evening if she doesn't have a date or a neighbour to torture. It was nearing eleven when I pushed through the door and she wasn't there, which was unusual. Close friends of Gwen's typically bypass the greeter and go grab their own drinks from the pot. If you need something frothy, it's a good excuse to go catch up with Mike or Bennett, the baristas. Bennett was on today, so I strolled over and gave him my request: coffee art in a Grande cup.

"No Gwen today?" I asked.

"She was around earlier, then got a call from her date," he confided with a cheeky wink. "Something was up, and she took off and asked me to call Derek to come in early."

"Booty call?"

"Na, she looked troubled, ya know!" I took my coffee, grabbed a copy of *The Globe*, and sank into a leather seat by the window overlooking the marina, but I couldn't settle. I pulled out my phone and confirmed Marcy hadn't been hound-dogging me, which she had apparently managed to avoid entirely, and after a moment's hesitation I sent Gwen an "Everything OK?" text and got "No" for a reply. A "Can I help?" retort got an "Abbot and Hastings" response. We could hardly be accused of wasting words, but rather than chew up more bandwidth, I picked up my coffee and walked out. The taxi gods smiled, and I hailed a Black Top cab and was at the address she gave me in four minutes. Gwen was on the corner consoling a distraught Marion, unimpressed with my speedy arrival, as I paid and walked over.

"It's Marion's mom, Ethan. Gone missing again."

"Again?" I asked. Likely not the right question, but it popped out.

"Dementia's getting really bad," sniffed Marion between sobs. "But damn sneaky. Her home helper turned her back for a second, taking the garbage to the chute, and she was off. We've been showing her photo around the area for two hours and no one has seen a 73-year-old in a green housecoat in red slippers. I swear she is part ninja. She's done it before a few times too. She wanders East Hastings looking for my dad, only he passed in 1979."

Marion pulled away as a black and white patrol car pulled over outside a nearby 7-11 and she stepped across to talk to them to solicit their help.

"Sorry Gwen, I didn't realize you knew Marion this well for her to call you out on this."

"Neither did I," said Gwen. "She was never a serious date to start with. Do you think I would risk bringing someone I was serious about to risk bumping into your naked ass?" She is never one to miss a chance to make me blush. She continued, "She's nice enough but new in town. Recently arrived from Montreal to be near her mom. I guess she doesn't know many people. Do you have any private eye mojo to bring to bear or are you just cute moral support? Marion says her Mom will be within a few blocks, but with all the alleys and weirdos in the area, she could get hurt. The police will look, but it can't be their only priority."

"I can give it a go," I said. "Do you have any photos?"

"Marion has a bunch on her phone," replied Gwen, just as Marion returned, disappointed that Vancouver's finest couldn't work miracles. Well, maybe I could.

I gave Marion an email address for the operations centre and had her send through half a dozen pictures of her mother, taken from different angles. After a quick word with Kelsie, a hastily drawn-together plan kicked into gear. I sponsor a local school for aspiring actors who are a feeder for the movie industry. Vancouver is one of the biggest centres for movie work and is often referred to as Hollywood North. The arts school is a stepping stone for actors, makeup technicians, the talented people that create scenery, and some of the best special effects in the world. Why would Ethan Booker, PI and altruist, be involved in such a venture? I have a readymade workforce of trained actors and some of the best creators of disguises at my beck and call to deploy in my business. I once filled one of my restaurants with fake customers and met with a con artist we were trying to convince to introduce to his pipeline. I was disguised as an East Indian financier and was able to control the whole environment à la...Mission Impossible. A great plan thwarted by my mark being hit by a cyclist crossing Granville street outside the rendezvous. Twenty-eight actors watched as he was carted off in an ambulance.

Kelsie quickly arranged for ten students to come and help us, and they arrived in a van within 30 minutes, along with some of our surveillance equipment. The team dispersed in pairs into the East Hasting area. East Hastings is as bad an area as we have in Vancouver. Drugs, prostitution, and assorted people dealing with some pretty severe disabilities mingle with homeless in tent cities and criminals of all levels. For Vancouver it is grungy, but by the standards in many big cities it's fairly safe, which is why I didn't send troops to watch their backs.

They were armed with several types of rapid-fix cases, which can quickly be attached to poles, posts, anything metal or quick-glued onto any flattish surface. The cases were fabricated in different ways to blend in and look like part of the scenery. Mostly they deployed what we refer to as 'circlets.' A circlet is a little bigger than a man's dress belt and wraps around a power pole and fastens like a cable tie. The circlet contains eight very wide-angle cameras, which feed a small processor. The processor can send real-time video over Wi-Fi or cell, or operate in autonomous monitor mode, which was the plan today. Within an hour every street or ally corner in a ten-block circle of Marion's mother's house was being watched. The photos of Marion's mother had already been downloaded into the units, and the processor was performing real-time facial recognition on anyone visible within 30 feet of the unit's lenses. Overhead four drones hovered. At night the drones can fly low, just above the street lights, and get an angle to spot faces, but during the day they have to stay high enough to be invisible and blend into the ambient noise of the busy town.

Marion, Gwen, and I, supported by our team of helpers, walked the streets, checked parks, alleys, and doorways, but the chances of us spotting Marion's Mom were incredibly remote. It's amazing how an old woman in a housecoat and slippers can evade capture. Jason Bourne generally gets picked up pretty quickly even with all his training, but not lost old people.

Just after 3 pm, a unit on Cordova and Richards got a match. Marion's mother had stopped for a rest under a tree on a bench at the back of a small plaza. When she awoke and stood up, a magnetic camera on a parking signpost saw her, and within a second had compared her likeness to the five pictures stored in its memory, computed a 97% likelihood of a match, and begun tracking the owner of the face it had just recognized.

Tracking works in three ways: While in range of that unit, the camera brackets the target. The unit also communicates to other units in the vicinity all data it captures about location, colour, and so on, and those units attempt to pick up the target. Lastly, the unit communicates to the drones overhead, who lock in on the target. A signal is also sent to HQ, and in this case relayed to my smartphone, and within 10 seconds I could see the road sign camera live stream view, and an overhead view from a drone at 350 feet above the scene on a split screen. As Marion's Mom walked south on Richards, the drone overhead automatically adjusted its position to keep its target in sight, and the ground units relayed the image at intervals. Not wanting to reveal this technology, I arranged with Kelsie to direct two of my security team to intercept our wanderer.

"Marion, I've just had a call from one of my searchers and your mom is safe, and just a block away," I explained as I hung up my call. Half an hour and several tears and "thank yous" from Marion, she and mother were safely installed at their home and I was back in *The Bean* with Gwen. I gave Marion a tiny tracking chip to insert into one of her mom's pendants, and a hand-held tracking unit to shorten future searches during the next Great Escape.

Gwen was both impressed and grateful and insisted on giving me a free coffee, a chicken pasta salad, and any choice of dessert. We had a good catch up on her date, including a few double-entendres about my pantry adventure. While we were talking, Bennett came over and asked if he could take off early for his kid's birthday. Gwen had a sudden twinkle in her eye.

"Ethan, are you around for the next hour?" she asked. Not seeing the connection, and with little else to do, I said I was thinking of watching the Whitecaps game, but if she was going to put it on *The Bean*'s TV system I would likely hang around. "Good" she said. "You take off Bennett. I'll get Derek to run the barista and Ethan can run the till while I go run some errands. I've got an apron, Ethan, so you won't mess up your fancy clothes." I had helped out occasionally so was familiar with the till, but it was a pretty slow day and I was sure Dereck was capable of doing both and said so.

"Oh Ethan, I think you are forgetting our agreement," she said, with a wink only I saw. "I think our bet said I could ask for favours whenever I wanted to and you would go along. You've been so helpful today already that I hate to impose. But I will!" Bennett looked a bit confused but got while the going was good. There was no way I was getting naked in *The Crazy Bean*, but I followed Gwen out back to the storage room. Gwen handed me an apron.

"Keep your shirt and sneakers on but shorts and pants off buddy. Put the apron over the top and tie it at the back. A skinny fella like you, it should cover all of the way around." Pulse racing, I reluctantly did as I was told. To be fair, as long as I didn't move too much, no one would suspect I wasn't wearing shorts. I tried walking up and down and standing in a couple of relaxed positions, and nothing scary popped out.

I took a big breath, swallowed my fear, and wandered out and relieved Derek at the till. Gwen stood there smirking and leaning back, pretending to try to take a peek, but I was confident there wasn't much to see. After a while she got bored.

"Don't you have some errands to run?" I said pointedly, and with a sly grin she shrugged and wandered out of the door. I served a few customers over twenty minutes or so and chatted to Derek and Maureen, the greeter. At first, I was too scared to move and was sure someone would cotton on at any moment. The first few times the door opened I flinched in case a gust of wind might lift a flap on the apron. But after a while I relaxed a bit. I must admit, Gwen has a bit of a flair for this stuff. At the 30-minute mark I was almost disappointed to see Gwen come back through the door. She was carrying some small boxes, which she brought over and put on the counter.

"Oh, thanks Ethan, that really helped out. I had to run to Costco and get some supplies," she said as she passed me a box. "Be a dear would you and tuck that away. Till rolls. They go in the drawer at floor level under the till." We stood there looking at each other. Both deadpan. She knew she could outwait me. I took the box and stood back, imagining how best to bend and angle myself to avoid any exposure. I turned so my back was angled away from everyone and crouched. I think everything stayed put but did feel a little draft. I stood and surreptitiously smoothed down the back of the apron.

"These two go in the cupboard behind you. Spare filters. It's a little high for me. Would you mind reaching up and throwing them in the top cupboard? So handy to have such a tall man around!" It was so hammy that I was worried Derek and Maureen would think something was up, but they appeared oblivious. Actually, this one wasn't so hard, as there was a small partition between the cupboard and Derek. It was a long shot someone walking past the side window might get a glimpse. I waited until all of the customers were otherwise occupied and quickly stretched up and tried not to slam the cupboard closed after depositing the filters in my haste. OK, that time there was definite gaping. Still, got it done.

I was walking back to the till, but Gwen had one more surprise for me. "Oh thanks for that. One more thing. Would you mind coming around and turning the TV channels to the Whitecaps game? I know you wanted to see it, and other customers will too. We might make the playoffs with this game I'm told." I glanced to the counter where she keeps the remote controls. No remotes. I'm sure they were there just a few seconds ago and realized she had pocketed them while I was worried about my ass and the cupboard. This was going to be impossible. Two of the three TVs were fairly easy, as they were in a quiet part of the café. I walked over and stretched up. Oh. I stopped halfway up. Bum gape was not the only issue. I had to reach up so far the front of the apron rode up and I was pretty certain little Ethan would show his head below my hemline. If I turned around I was sure to show my ass off. I glanced at Gwen who was enjoying my discomfort way too much. Looking around I realized I had a moment with no one looking my way and I quickly turned my back and flicked the channel to 58. *Good. No one noticed.* Now TV two. I figured I could do the same thing and sauntered over. The angles were a little more awkward, but I could go for it. This time it would have looked odd if I turned my back, so I had to risk the front flash. Just as I was pushing the button, Gwen called my name in a loud voice on some pretense. I panicked and dropped down, looking as guilty as sin, but luckily her loud voice had drawn all of the attention in the room to Gwen. She looked miffed and said, "Oh, nothing, Ethan, I thought you were about to slip. Carry on."

The third TV was going to be impossible. There was a young couple right there. They were pretty engrossed in each other, but I would have to stand so close to them they would be sure to look at me. *Crap. Crap. Need a distraction.* I had an idea. I went over to the TV and fished my phone out of the pocket in the apron. I called *The Crazy Bean* and waited for Maureen to answer. In a God-awful Irish accent, I said I had a very urgent message for Donald Murphy, who had told me he would be there at this time. There were three customers who might possibly be a Donald. I saw Maureen looking around the room trying to decide what to do. Good — she was going to call out to the room. Timing was going to be everything. I hung up and quickly stepped to the couple and apologized for the intrusion, and the guy shuffled his chair to give me access. I stepped around so that as Maureen called, their heads turned from me, and towards her. In a big loud voice, Maureen paged the room for Donald. All heads turned away from me. *Excellent. Home free.*

But before I could move, the door opened, and in walked Marcy. I froze, and she saw me immediately. God is a woman and has a sick sense of humour. I was stuck. Marcy started to walk over. There was no way I was going to flash anyone, but Gwen wasn't going to let me go so easily. I glanced towards her, and she was grinning from ear to ear. She nodded towards the TV with a "get the job done boy" look on her face. I glanced back at Marcy, and then at the TV, knowing a quick lunge would never work, but assessing my chances desperately anyway. As I looked at the TV, a miracle happened: The Report on Business show suddenly flicked over to the Whitecaps game. I looked incredulously from the TV to Marcy to Gwen. The latter looked totally innocent and waved the remote control my way.

"Found it. You must have knocked it behind the till Ethan. Don't just stand there. Isn't this your friend? Marcy, isn't it? Ethan's mentioned you often, and I recognize you from pictures he showed me of you all as teens." Gwen had stepped over and had her hand on Marcy's arm, guiding her to a free table.

"Cup of coffee, honey?" said Gwen, in full-on flirt mode. "On the house of course. Ethan, I can take over unless you want to work the rest of the shift while I take care of your lovely friend here? Take your apron off and sit down. I'll put it away and get you both a drink." It was the epitome of innocence blended with sweet tigress. Her hand reacquired Marcy's shoulder as she stood behind her seat.

"Don't worry, I have to wash up anyway. I'll get the coffees," I said, leaning in between them to give Marcy a peck on the cheek 'hello' and breaking Gwen's grip in one movement. With my body wedged between her and Marcy, Gwen gave my butt a quick goose.

"Great," she said, stepping past me and taking Marcy's other arm as she dropped into a seat by the fireplace at Marcy's side. "I'll have a chai latte please," she yelled over her shoulder before turning to Marcy and saying, "He's been so sweet all day. Oh, love those shoes Marcy...."

7: **Faster Than Sound**

I came back fully dressed, the apron ditched, with a tray of drinks. I handed Marcy a triple shot macchiato and Gwen her chai latte, and pulled over a chair, reversed it, sat astride the leather base, and rested my elbows on the top of its back. Marcy was sporting her typical detective power-dresser suit. Grey, sharp lines, hard crease, subtly tailored to hide her gun bulge, yet also enhance her chest bulges which were doing well in her white cotton tank. Marcy is wonderfully configured. Perhaps I have always had a thing about women with prominent ribcages because Marcy has a great ribcage. I don't mean she is so skinny you can make out the individual ribs—quite the opposite. She is trim but has meat on her bones. I mean the bases of the two sides of her ribcage lift smartly out separately from her flat tummy like they were sculpted, and lean together to form a robust, broad and curvy chassis, which are topped off with wide, square shoulders. An educated observer might call it a structured physique, and I wouldn't argue. Combined with great posture and worked-out legs, it's quite the package. The only thing I kid her about are her police shoes. It's tough to chase down bad guys in heels, so she wears classy but tough-looking flatties.

After some small talk, Gwen eventually took the hint, made her excuses and went off to torment Derek. I popped my chair back under the table I had borrowed it from and plonked myself down next to Marcy. We made some more small talk, and I told her the public version of helping out with Marion's mom. Marcy knows I sometimes draw on the school for resources, but not about my army of gadgets. I've often thought about telling her about that part of my life, and always put it off until she crosses the line to be in that part of my life on a full-time basis. Which hopefully might be soon.

"So, I've been quite the little do-gooder today," I summarized.

"Fantastic. Boy Scout Booker to the rescue." She smiled and I swear the sun came out. "Hey, I dropped by to talk to you about your dinner invitation. I didn't want to just call and have you think that I was just blowing you off. Figured I would find you here. I'm sorry but I have to go out of town for a few days. Rain check?" I was quite disappointed about being put off, but pleased it was a rain check and that she bothered to go to the trouble of seeing me face to face. As she was telling me I noticed quite a bit of tension in her face.

"Everything OK? Family alright?" I asked.

"Yes, the family is fine. Work related." I know people well enough to know when I'm not getting 100% truth, and double so with Marcy.

"Mounties always get their man? Hunting someone across the globe?" I said lightheartedly, not wanting to pry into her business, but dying to pry into her business.

"Something like that," she said looking away.

"Well, I'd love to hold you to that rain check," I persisted. "Do you know when you'll be back?"

Before Marcy could answer, my cell rang. I have two ringtones. One for regular calls, and another for urgent matters. It was the latter that was sounding. I glanced at the screen and the number showing was the operations centre hotline. I smiled apologetically and mouthed 'sorry', while pressing the answer button and stepping away.

"Go ahead," I said as I answered. Almost before I had spoken, Kelsie's voice came through crisp, urgent and commanding.

"Ethan, no time to explain or answer questions. You are in grave danger. Move away from the windows and away from Marinaside Crescent. Leave the building via the ally exit and head north." I wondered for a heartbeat how the Ops centre even knew where I was, then recalled they track my cell as a matter of course. I didn't argue, but wasn't going to leave anyone, least of all Marcy, in the path of whatever had Kelsie so spooked. I stepped back towards Marcy and noticed she was answering her own cell phone. I grabbed her arm and pulled her up from her seat, explaining there was an emergency at the same time.

She was beginning to react when the large window to her left and the mirror on her right shattered, sending glass everywhere. We both dropped to the floor as two holes the size of golf balls appeared in the chair Marcy had just vacated. We were both processing the scene and concluding we were under fire when the noise of three shots — one then a pair — rolled in through the window. I looked at Marcy and there on her neck was a red laser designator light spot. Before I could react, the light jumped a foot to the left, and the floor at that spot exploded into a splintery mess, the thin laminate gone and concrete exposed and chipped. I grabbed Marcy and rolled over her so I was between her and the shooter and pushed her towards the back of the store. I crawled behind her as fast as I could.

I looked for Gwen, Derek, and Maureen, and they were all hunkered down at the far end of the store. One man was on his back with blood on him, but as far as I could tell in the quick head-bob glance I took it was from the mirror glass, and the blood was coming from a small gash on his knee. Judging by the size of the holes in the wall, and the delay between the bullet being fired and the sound following on, we were being shot at from a distance with a big, long rifle.

Marcy had her gun out and was on one knee peering around the till, seeking the shooter, but I tackled her as I went by and pushed her towards the storeroom

"Sniper. Long gun," I yelled, the volume a little excessive, as the shooting had stopped and it was actually silent. "Out of range for your pistol."

Marcy was a pretty cool machine in a pinch and began instructing everyone to move quickly into the storeroom and to bolt the back door, but to be ready to open it and run if the gunman entered through the front.

We were hunkered down for less than a minute, taking stock, catching breath, and covering the entrance, when my phone rang again and I picked up.

"Back door. Alpha team in a black Navigator. Twenty seconds. Tracking the police response. ETA one minute. The sniper is down temporarily but there may be others. Recommending evacuation."

"Acknowledged," I answered automatically, then turned to Marcy. "Those bullets were for you. Don't know what is going on, but my bodyguards are approaching the rear and we should get you out of here.

"I'm not leaving these people unprotected," she replied, not taking her eyes or gun from the doorway. I thought about it for a second.

"You are the target Marcy, and you are endangering them by staying. I'll leave my bodyguards here until the police arrive. You can hear their sirens already." Her instincts were to stay and fight. Partly to protect the others, but mostly she was exchanging 'scared' for 'mad' and wanted to shoot someone. But her training won out and she followed me to the rear door. I heard the car screech to a halt. I pulled back the security bolt, snapped open the door and was relieved to see three of the Alpha team deploying out of the car and adopting defensive positions, while the driver gunned the engine. I told two of them to go in and guard the store, and after some resistance -as their duty was to protect me not others — the two nearest us hurried off.

We piled into the back of the Navigator, the lead Alpha guy bundled back into the front and we took off. Dave Marwick was the Alpha team leader, and I asked him what the hell was going on. He seemed to know less than we did. They had been parked a block and a half away when they were urgently ordered to the rescue.

I called the Ops centre as we tore down Seymour towards Hastings. Kelsie answered and didn't wait to be invited to explain.

"Chopper One is just skids up from Pitt Meadows airport, ETA at the Vancouver helipad in seven minutes. Alpha team are being instructed to take a circular route to arrive there as Chopper One touches down to minimize exposure, and we will transfer you and fly you to a safe distance until we know what is going on."

"What is going on Kelsie?" I asked with an unfair amount of impatience, given she had just saved our butts and was acting with such efficiency.

"We were collecting the circlet surveillance devices used this morning and one of them registered a target. We thought Marion's mom had slipped away at first but it was a dark-skinned man carrying a case. I called Darcy and she explained the units had just come back from being loaned to the FBI for a trial. As you know, we are trying to sell them some. With your sudden call to deploy them, we hadn't wiped their memories. We just added a new target. The old faces were still in the system and one of them triggered a unit on Richards and Dunsmuir. The target was getting into a cab. We had one drone still airborne and we tasked it to track the cab. We called the FBI and advised them we were tracking a target they had added to the system. They have not been very cooperative and we are hearing nothing back from them."

I didn't comment that the FBI quartermasters she dealt with probably didn't have the operational knowledge or authority to cooperate and that few are as efficient as she was.

She continued. "We tracked the cab and the target was dropped off two blocks from *The Bean*. He crossed the seawall and walked in the opposite direction for 250 yards, then climbed onto the roof of a maintenance shed housing an air conditioning plant for a tower block. When we saw him assembling a rifle we alerted the police immediately. It was only when he took position and we were able to triangulate he was shooting in your direction that we connected the threat to you. I got through to you as he opened fire."

"Where is he now? Are you still tracking him?" I asked, stunned. Marcy was listening in as I had the call on speaker—amazed at the story, and equally amazed that someone was feeding me, a mere billionaire PI, this tale.

"Well, we um, err sort of lost the target," Kelsie said, uncharacteristically awkward. "When we realized what was happening, we um, counter-attacked."

"What do you mean counter-attacked?" I asked. There were no real offensive weapons on our drones.

"We... um... flew the drone directly into the target. We dive bombed him."
Wow. Creative.

"Well that explains how he missed Marcy," I said, recalling the laser designator jerking away. The drone must have crashed as he went for the kill shot.

Marcy added, "When the shot came in, I had just had a call to warn me. The FBI had a tip there was an assassin on the streets and alerted the VPD. We were on alert as we had heard a revenge contract had been taken out on me in connection with a takedown of a group I was investigating. The arrest occurred last night, which is why I was leaving town until it could be sorted out. That was a pretty fast reaction. This group has operated relatively freely, as it was very overt in its threat that it does not tolerate interference from local law enforcement. Arrests in Paris and Houston were followed by the leaders of the arresting team being killed within a week. One car bomb in Paris as the detective drove past, and the Texas killing was a close-range shot to the head while the detective slept next to his wife. She woke up a couple of hours later and found her husband dead next to her, a bullet through the eye. They think the killer flooded the bedroom with knock-out gas as there was no silencer judging by the scene and autopsy." Marcy stopped because I was staring aghast at her. "Don't look at me like that, Ethan, until you have at least explained all of this James bloody Bond shit." Fair point. I still had a lot of questions forming, but they would wait.

"Are you sending up another drone, Kelsie?" I asked.

"We have two already on station. There is drone wreckage, but the target has vanished. We are scanning and have sent the VPD a photo of the assassin. We are also loading and redeploying the circlets at as many likely locations as we can imagine.

"Good work and quick thinking, Kelsie. You and the team rock."

"ETA Chopper One is two minutes. Make your way to the rendezvous spot."

"Will do. Where is the Sea Star?"

"Stand by. Ah, the Sea Star is about twenty-five miles south heading for Seattle. Good idea. I'll have them reverse course and meet you north of the US border." The Sea Star is my local yacht. It has a helipad and can safely stay at sea and be defended. It would make a pretty good hidey-hole until we could get a plan together.

"OK, that is the plan. We'll take this half of the Alpha team for protection. Chopper One carries four, and we can fit in if I fly. The pilot will have to stay on the ground. Have another two security teams pick up some better protection equipment and grab Chopper Three and meet us this evening!"

We transferred to Chopper 1. This Hughes MD 500 variant has four seats. The normal configuration is five or seven, but I had this ride pimped up with more comfy seating and a small bar. I was current to fly and enjoyed the challenge. I'd only landed on the Sea Star once before, but the sea was calm and I managed to put us down safely after a couple of close attempts. It probably helped that I had consumed all of my adrenaline dodging bullets and training with Gia, so I was relatively calm executing one of the more difficult flight manoeuvres in a helicopter. Once we had been lashed onto the pad and I had shut the aircraft down, we retired to the saloon for a much-needed beer.

We collapsed into luxurious leather high-top club chairs, and I called into the Ops centre and stood the phone on the bar, speaker enabled. I told Kelsie that Marcy was listening, knowing she would modify her reports to not create a conflict of interest for our favourite cop. But there was not really anything new, so we summarized what we already had established. Marcy had previously told us the gang's assassin was known only as The Kingman, a feared enforcer and assassin for an international trafficking gang, but that he had gone to ground. Kelsie would use her contacts to learn more, but these things take time. She sent through photos from the circlet units and the aerial video stream, including some beautiful footage of the drone screaming at its maximum speed of 50 mph from 800 ft, smashing down next to The Kingman. The operator did a fantastic job aiming but missed. Drones are never flown deliberately into the ground and have several safety features designed to stop exactly this from happening, which he mostly managed to override or mitigate and got near enough, fast enough, to spoil the shot.

"Screw that he broke about half a dozen laws," exclaimed Marcy, appreciating the skill and risks involved, "I'm buying that guy dinner and getting him drunk when this is over!" We hung up and watched the Gulf Island scenery parade past our window for a few minutes while we caught our breath, formulated questions, and considered what we were prepared to divulge. Right there, in that moment, I made a potentially life-changing decision. Go all in. Well, maybe not revealing that a couple of hours earlier I was almost caught with my pants down, literally, but I didn't want any secrets getting between me and trying to kindle a relationship with Marcy. And I said as much.

"Look. I've got some secrets to tell you." *Gulp!* "You know, I really am a PI, but I may have gotten a little carried away funding my hobby, as billionaires are prone to sometimes. I promise I only use it for good, but I can't pretend I always stay totally within the conventional rule of law.

"The dinner invitation was thirty percent because I was worried about you. We may have listened in and perhaps peeked a little into your operation last night. But was a hundred and ten percent because I think about you so much and really want you in my life in a much bigger way. I don't like not having shared what I do, but God, Marcy, you are a cop and that would be awkward. But I'm done waiting and wondered where you were at emotionally. I planned to turn dinner into a date."

Marcy was grinning at me. It felt good. No one spoke for a while. "I said I needed a little time to get over Terry, and the third time might be the charm Ethan. It's been five bloody years! How long do you think a girl needs, you idiot? I had nearly given up on you." She took my hand and stood up.

"I'd kiss you but you are smelly and bloodied." This was true. "I take it this gin palace has a shower and a bed? The least a girl can do is scrub you down to say thanks for saving my life. Then I think we have some catching up to do."

I had so much emotion running through me in that moment it could have powered the Sea Star to Alaska. I just stared at her, and I think my mouth was embarrassingly wide open.

"What?" she whispered. "Can I help it if gun battles, brave rescues, and helicopter abductions to luxury yachts make me horny?"

I may have had a lot of different emotions running through me, but that statement made one particular emotion rise to the top. We retired to the stateroom and hung the 'do not disturb' sign on the door.

8: The Sting

By the time we emerged, the Sea Star had sprinted 90 miles north, it was late into the evening, and we were in Desolation Sound, a remote and beautiful area accessible by water and air only. Ironically, in 1792, Captain Vancouver had named it Desolation Sound as he said, "There was not a single prospect that was pleasing to the eye," which may have kept it so pristine that the BC Government turned it into a protected marine park in 1973. As I stared at Marcy as she pulled her hair back into a ponytail, I saw plenty of prospect, and five-foot six of eye-pleasing.

Desolation Sound is one of the most beautiful parts of the world, frequented by orca, grey whales, and huge salmon runs. Stunning lime-green outfalls from rivers mix with the dark blue of inland waterways nestled behind Vancouver Island, all watched over by towering 8000 ft peaks. Desolation implies lonely or deserted, but not in this case. Its natural beauty has caused people to travel for thousands of miles to enjoy it. You couldn't call it crowded, but it's certainly not empty. There are normally a few hundred hikers or sailors in the vicinity, and in the summer, you can count on one mega cruise ship a day passing through the deeper straights with a few thousand passengers enjoying the run between Alaska and Seattle or Vancouver. The Sea Star was in the area, but well off the beaten path and lost among the dozens of islands that frequent the Sound.

Kelsie had been hard at work. We had three of the four security teams on board, and Chopper 3 had arrived and lowered Chopper 1's pilot onto the foredeck. Chopper 1 had returned to Pitt Meadows, and Chopper 3 was now perched on the back of the Sea Star. Chopper 3 had an increased load capacity, able to lift off with 3500 lbs of cargo, and far better all-weather capability. It arrived with people and supplies to defend the ship from all but military hardware. I can afford the military, and could get it in certain markets, but I draw my line at mildly bending the laws, not flagrantly disregarding them. The Sea Star is a large yacht, and despite having about 40 people on it, still didn't feel crowded.

We emerged well protected and ravenously hungry. The yacht has large, grand saloons with luxurious cream sofas, sitting on polished pine boat plank boards, with swirly cloud lighting ceilings, but we both were drawn to the utility tables and bar near the galley. We hopped up onto high-top chairs and devoured a large breakfast despite the fact it was night time, almost as passionately as we had devoured each other for the last few hours. We hadn't talked much about anything. We were just close, intimate, and thankful to be alive.

As we settled into our meal, it was time to discuss things. I didn't touch the fact that Marcy had knowingly put her life in danger risking the wrath of the trafficking ring and The Kingman. I was living with a huge cold fear deep in my gut for her safety; but that is just how she is wired. Not stupid about it, but never backing down from bullies. I was very proud of her courage and told her. I think she blushed and definitely preferred that to being mothered.

"I've checked my cell and there is coverage here, which surprises me," she said. "I should check in with the office. Despite Kelsie telling them I am safe, they will be going nuts not hearing from me in person."

"The signal is local to the boat and relays via the ship's satellite link. But before you call in, we should think this through."

"What do you mean?"

"Well, who knew you were at *The Crazy Bean*? Even I wasn't expecting you. It's possible that someone was following you, which I think you would notice — being you and all — unless they are tracking you electronically. The drone footage didn't show The Kingman with a device or phone in his hand to track you, although he could have been talking to someone via an earpiece. But he looked to me like he was acting independently. It looked to me like someone knew where you would be and was seeking a favourable sniping nest. Before we call anyone, we should solve that riddle."

"Crap... I hadn't thought of that," she said. "And now that I think of it, why the long gun? I didn't know I was going to *The Bean* until about an hour before. I'd worked the case and paperwork until about five thirty in the morning and then slept. I had been up a couple of hours and picked up your message, then thought about calling you back, but then decided to take a chance and drop by *The Bean* on the off chance you would be there.

"I'd decided to drive out to Abbotsford and take a flight out from there to Calgary, then from there on to Grand Cayman for a vacation. I hadn't told anyone but my boss where I would lay up for a few weeks, but I did have one thing to do before I took off. Last night I was supposed to speak at a conference in the convention centre. We talked about the risk and agreed I would be OK as The Kingman would take at least 24 hours to arrive and try to find me."

"Did you tell anyone you were going to *The Bean*?"

"No one specifically, but I did tell our office management when I called in, and they post it on the squad room board for emergency contact reasons. You think someone in the squad set me up?"

"I can't think of any other explanation, short of you being tracked in real time. The long gun and the convention centre make sense. If they knew you would be on a stage at a set time. A pretty strong statement killing you within 24 hours of your operation. But even so, very quick to put that together. But if someone in your squad is leaking information to The Kingman, why didn't they tip the trafficking ring off and avoid the raid all together?"

"The raid was set up with the RCMP, as it is a federal crime. I was only the VPD liaison, but when it became apparent local knowledge was going to help in this case, I was promoted to task force leader on scene for the takedown, as it's my patch and I know the layout. The raid was to go down tonight, not last night, but an RCMP informant in the gang told us their meeting had moved up. I'd guess our mole was out of the loop for the date change at least."

"Did your boss know?"

"Yes, he was the one who told me. So it doesn't make sense that he is the mole. OK, I'll call him and get him to keep this mole idea to himself for now. I can't believe someone in my team would be working for these monsters!" she exclaimed.

"How about you invite him to the Sea Star to discuss it? We don't know who will be monitoring him in the office or his cell phone."

Marcy called Dennis Preece and had a difficult conversation. He wanted her back, and she refused. She said she had information that once he heard her out would explain, but that she wanted to meet him privately and not talk about it over the phone. When she explained he would be collected by helicopter he was very wary. One of his detectives was nearly assassinated then she mysteriously wanted to whisk him away out of contact with his safety net in strange circumstances. It was a testament to their relationship and his courage that he agreed. With it already being late we agreed to a pick up at 5.30 am to give us all a chance to sleep.

At 7 am, we were up and watched as Chopper 1 returned and dropped Dennis onto a pontoon dock the Sea Star crew had deployed. Chopper 1 took off immediately and banked back off to the east, into the recently risen sun. As the rotor noise faded, the crew pulled the pontoon alongside the yacht and we greeted Dennis and brought him up to the saloon, where breakfast was set for three.

"My God, Marcy, I hope you are not planning to expense all this," quipped Dennis as he took his seat.

"Sorry Dennis, the big boat was busy so we are slumming it," she shot back, not giving him anything yet.

As we ate, we filled Dennis in on our theory. He was shocked to say the least. The idea that one of his team was involved was hard for him. Most he had worked with for years and trusted with his life on more than one occasion. The newer members had come with solid references from people he had known forever, and he trusted their vouchsafe. But he couldn't deny the logic. Something was definitely very rotten.

*

We worked through what we knew over the next couple of hours, documenting who in the team was privy to what, and even considered people higher up the chain of command to Dennis — including some people in the RCMP detachment. It looked pretty likely that it was someone reporting in to Dennis, given how the last 48 hours had played out.

I was all for taking Marcy via private plane to a remote and undisclosed location for a month or two until the threat had been neutralized, but I was outvoted by them both. Now that it was apparent there was a mole, it had to be rooted out and Marcy wasn't backing away from helping Dennis with this ugly task. My arguments to let me be involved and leverage my resources were turned down by Dennis. Marcy agreed with him — and perhaps could have been persuaded — but his view was that this was a police issue, and civilians, no matter how resourceful, had no part to play. Everything from liability, forensic integrity and ethics, right through to chain of command issues, seemed to be a barrier to my helping. When I pushed, I even got a bit of a warning about being charged if I interfered. Of course, just for my own protection.

Dennis had just gotten off the phone discussing a plan to draw out The Kingman with his boss and an RCMP squad from out of province, which could not have a compromised connection to the local team. He had put forward my offer to use a cabin I had up at Stave Lake as a defendable place to lure attackers into the open, but this had already been discarded by the higher-ups who wanted to reduce the amount of involvement generally, and from external parties specifically.

"OK, looks like we have a plan Marcy. Sorry Ethan, I can't share it with you. If you could give us a moment, I will tell Marcy what I have been authorized to share."

"Bullshit!" said Marcy, before I could say the same. I was going to object to being cut out, and thought she was about to do the same, but she had a different angle.

"Look, Dennis. This is my ass on the line. Some people choked at standing up to the threats from this group, but I didn't. And you are going to keep information from me? If you want my cooperation — and dangle me out as bait — I want to be all in. No holding back on either side."

He considered this. I could tell from his expression he agreed, but that he had been given orders to the contrary. If he went back to them to say he couldn't control his subordinate, he would appear weak. Then a most bizarre thing happened: Dennis's phone chimed and he stepped away to answer it. His face went dark with anger, and his end of the conversation was all one word, either 'yes' or 'no.' There was the beginning of a longer objection that started with a "but," but that was cut off before it went far. When he hung up, his cheeks were flushed, and his eyes were shooting daggers in my direction.

"Mr. Booker. I don't know how you did this, but I am so pissed at you right now, and that is a bad situation for you. I really don't appreciate your buying your way into matters that are out of your league, just because your rich-boy pride is hurt and you are not getting your own spoiled way!" His glare was something dreadful.

"Back up here Dennis. You've lost me. What have I done?" I asked as we squared off physically across from each other.

Marcy stepped between us, more subconsciously than in an effort to stop a fight.

"That was the chief on the phone. Apparently, Ethan called someone who called someone else, who called someone who called the chief. As of now, we are going with Mr. Booker's plan. The RCMP task force has been vectored to focus on tracing the trafficking group's activities, preventing it from re-establishing and trying to roll up their operations back towards its leaders overseas. I've been told to leave The Kingman to the two of you, but to offer cooperation in any way I can."

I was stunned. I assured them I had called no one. It hadn't even occurred to me. I must have looked pretty sincere, as Preece stood down a fraction.

"Well how else can you account for it?" he barked. "It's pretty frickin' coincidental. Don't you think?"

"Den', he doesn't roll that way. If Ethan has a problem, he's very direct about it," interjected Marcy.

We were all silent for a few minutes. I poured us all a fresh coffee while we mulled it over. It was Marcy who made the leap first.

"I think I have a bigger problem, Dennis. We know this group is pretty connected. Don't take offence, Ethan, but those who don't know you would assume you are amateur hour, yes?" I reluctantly nodded at the logic. "As far as the outside world is concerned, I've just been jettisoned from the protection of a national squad of experts, to being alone with a PI from Vancouver to face a proven, motivated, and well-funded killer. This isn't Ethan interfering: it's something much more sinister. This is the trafficking group's work. They've isolated me from help and are setting me up!" This was shocking insight — which none of us wanted to accept — but it did appear to be the only explanation if you accepted that I had not interfered.

"Well," I said, breaking the silence, "I guess we have to show them they are messing with the wrong bloody amateur!"

The agreement we struck with Dennis before he boarded Chopper 3 and headed back to the office was that we would endeavour to set up a trap for The Kingman using my cabin in the remote lake area northeast of Vancouver. Marcy would be the only person representing the law on site. Her jurisdiction was questionable outside of Vancouver proper, so Dennis arranged for two RCMP officers from out of town to assist us, taking direction from Marcy.

I gave Dennis a secure phone that used Darcy's latest encryption technology, so we could stay in touch without relying on possibly compromised technology. We agreed that when we were set up and ready, we would have Dennis let it be known that Marcy was working remotely and she would call in to squad meetings. Our thinking was that The Kingman — or his mole — would be able to find a way to track communications back to the cabin, then move in for the kill. We would be waiting and take him down. If after a few days there were no bites, we would assume the subtle approach of letting The Kingman trace us had been too much for his resources and let some hint slip. We could think about what that could be nearer the time. Other than that, we agreed not to share any more details of the plan with Dennis, to ensure operational secrecy.

Marcy and I conferred several times with Kelsie on the plan, which we left her to put into action. We returned to our stateroom for a little more catching up.

It took 24 hours to set our trap, but it was a good one. We boarded Chopper 3 well-fed, dressed for the countryside, kitted out with the latest Kevlar protection, and armed for bear. We both had a good knife, two handguns, and a shotgun.

Chopper 3 flew low level into Vancouver, where we stopped for less than a minute and picked up two very tough-looking RCMP officers, Meeka and Justin. Neither wore the traditional Red Serge uniform of course. Both were in full-fledged camouflage, helmets with built-in communications, night vision capability, and three large bags of equipment between them.

We introduced ourselves as we lifted off to the north and banked east over the docks. The helicopter dipped its nose to pick up speed. Meeka was clearly First Nations heritage: short, wide, and very still. Stoic eyes. It seemed stereotypical, but he appeared to be connected to the earth, lakes, and mountains. Almost timeless. Justin was Caucasian, with jet-black hair, a matching beard, and sky-blue eyes. Probably against regulations, he had a very small tattoo on the left side of his face between his eyebrow and temple. It was like a backwards letter 'c' with a horizontal line through it. In counterbalance to Meeka's stillness, Justin was restless. Not fidgety, but his head was swivelling, eyes darting. Alert, and seemingly moving to tackle some problem, even though he was actually just sitting on the bench seat. They told us they were part of hostage rescue, and out of Ottawa, but nothing else about themselves. They exuded competence and professionalism, were understandably dubious about taking direction from a mere detective, and were clearly annoyed about my being involved at all.

We stayed low until we were away from the city and in the valley west of Mount Seymour, then climbed up and followed the peaks and valleys, staying off radar, out over Pitt Lake, and hopped another ridge over to Stave Lake. I didn't believe the trafficking group had military or even civilian quality radar capability, but these days they didn't need to. There are several public websites that show aircraft radar tracks drawn from civilian public radar feeds for commercial purposes. The images are delayed by a few minutes, to prevent them being useful to terrorists, but it would enable anyone to see where we went. We thought this tactical departure through the hills and treetops might be overkill, but better safe than sorry.

As we descended towards the clearing in front of my cabin, we looked down the lake and saw two tugs departing from the dock, pulling a barge of construction equipment and workers that had just finished some impromptu renovations to the cabin and the local area.

Stave Lake was created in the first quarter of the twentieth century as demand for hydroelectricity drove the construction of the three dams that backed up the Stave River and flooded the valley. Hudson Bay Company workers in Fort

Langley named it Stave River, as the trees lining the bank were ideal for manufacturing barrel staves, used in the export of fish. The native name for the river is long forgotten, but the modern-day Slo:lo and Kwantlen tribes refer to it as *Skayuks,* which ominously means 'everybody died.' I hoped we were not running into a fate similar to what my ancestors had inflicted on the indigenous people when they flooded the valley a hundred years ago. Meeka seemed to sit a little straighter as the helicopter turned into the valley, settling towards our landing clearing, and I imagined some spiritual sensation had touched him.

The 'cottage' was a four-room, polished-pine log cabin with an A-frame roof. Two sixteen-foot picture windows made the eyes above a mouth formed by a wide, deep deck that had a six-foot BBQ station at one end, making it look like a cheeky face. The whole structure was nestled in a discrete, gnarly cove on the northernmost part of the lake, on a small peninsula formed by the river outfall into the valley thousands of years before the dam made this space an idyllic lakeside retreat. It was now sporting bullet-deflecting, transparent Perspex over the windows.

We had modified the cabin to be a trap. Meeka and Justin would spring it from behind two barricades, strategically placed to provide cover and unobstructed fields of fire within the open-plan living space which formed the entire ground-floor. A panic switch at each station would drop metal blinds over the windows and doors. The plan was to lure The Kingman inside, then trip the shutters and take him down. If, in the unlikely event he got the better of Meeka and Justin, he would not be able to leave the premises and we could call in reinforcements, as the blinds could only be released from outside. The communications equipment was set up in the upstairs space, and the upstairs entrances had all been sealed with metal shutters.

As an extra precaution, a hide had been built in the trees, 30 feet in the air and across the clearing from the cabin. The hide was well camouflaged among the foliage, but also heavily insulated so that the occupants would not appear on thermal or night-vision scopes. Marcy and I headed to the hide, taking with us munitions and supplies for a couple of nights; Meeka and Justin withdrew into the cabin. The hide was already decked out with sleeping bags and a small portable toilet (fun times). One half of the hide had been painted with a backdrop so that, to the camera linked to the cabin's communications hub, it looked identical to the cabin's interior. As Marcy Skyped through to the squad room, it would look like she was sitting in the cabin's kitchen. The site had a very secure communications satellite link for our clandestine needs, and a separate low-grade commercial service, that we hoped The Kingman would have little trouble tracing.

For the final touch, Kelsie had flown in four ATVs, which were parked and covered in the woods to the north and had rigged a remote drone base half a mile from us on a small boat moored on the east shoreline. There were six drones based on the boat, which recharged and were maintained from there but controlled from the main operations centre. At any time, three drones were patrolling overhead using a mixture of audio, visual, movement and heat sensors. Kelsie had confirmed that the sensors in the drones couldn't see us but could make out Meeka and Justin at their posts in the cabin. She had the drones fly low and high and at most angles The Kingman might approach from, to confirm we were secure.

Nothing had been heard of from The Kingman, but we had to assume he was still in Vancouver as his reputation was that he was as relentless as he was ruthless. Preece had confirmed that he had communicated to the squad that Marcy had taken refuge in a cabin and would brief the team on the events of the attempted assassination at noon. Marcy made several Skype calls, including that one, over the course of the afternoon. We sat back to wait to see if our bait would be taken.

Excitement turned to boredom pretty quickly, and soon to fear of using the toilet in the hide in front of each other.

Risking a trip out into the woods was foolish. We might be spotted by The Kingman, but we would definitely be spotted by the drone operators. I really didn't want to pee in front of Marcy, but definitely wouldn't in front of my whole operations team. We agreed to a system where one of us would put on the comms headphones, crank up some music and face away, while the other took care of business.

We had arranged to do a communication check each hour and had recently completed our fifteenth check when Kelsie came on to the secure channel.

"Attention all stations. Drone Two, our high overhead view, has picked up a thermal image of someone walking through the trees approximately two and a half miles east of your location. To get there, one has to ride the long way around the lake as there are no roads nearby. We scanned back behind them, and there is an ATV parked off the track, visible by its heat signature. It's cooled somewhat so must have come in a while ago. Hard to tell, but the target appears to be carrying a gun case."

We heard Meeka and Justin acknowledge and concur they could see the same on the relayed video feed inside the cabin. We watched too, and for over an hour, the target picked their way carefully through the woods to a small outcrop approximately 900 yards to our east and about 120 feet higher than we were. As they emerged from the trees, the video feed switched from thermal to night vision and then to a combined multi-vision, a technology Darcy was working on. The target was quite visible in this mode and we could see him in a shooter's prone stance, covered in military clothing and equipment, watching our camp via a large scope, his rifle still bagged up beside him.

After nearly 25 minutes of nothing much, the target set the scope down and unpacked and set up his rifle. The rifle had its own scope, which he looked through and was obviously dialling in for range and wind. Meeka and Justin changed their positions inside the cabin to be behind the thick, main pine beams that supported the upper floor and roof. With a good night scope, they would be blurry but visible inside the cabin. The rifle was large, and would possibly even be a 50 calibre, which could punch through the door and perhaps even the thinner logs. Our hide was sturdy and safe from handguns, but a serious rifle would be able to reach us. We suddenly felt very exposed. We figured if no target showed itself, The Kingman would eventually have to wander down into the trap.

"Helicopter coming in!" Kelsie's voice made us jump. The channel had been silent as we watched the target approach. "We were watching all traffic on radar, and this helicopter had a flight plan past the end of the lake, but it just deviated north up the side of the lake and is descending towards you."

"Understood," said Meeka, who was the ranking officer. "We could have a problem if there are multiple combatants on that helicopter. Can you call for reinforcements? If it lands and we are seriously outnumbered, we will trigger the metal blinds and hunker down in here until the cavalry arrive. But it looks like a small bird, perhaps carrying four including the pilot. The sniper is the tactical advantage. We are fairly safe in here, but if Ethan and Marcy engage, it will reveal their position and the sniper will take them."

"If it comes to that," I said, "we will not leave you to fight for yourselves. We have a way of disabling the sniper, at least for a few minutes." Darcy had come up with a simple solution; I wouldn't let Darcy put offensive weapons capability onto the drones, but she had talked me into adding a flash-bang grenade to each drone. The drone can drop the grenade quite accurately and trigger it to go off on contact, or at any set altitude. Flash-bangs are used by military or paramilitary when attacking a site and they need to be able to surprise and overcome people, without doing a lot of damage. The grenade lets off blinding light and a debilitating bang, but is otherwise fairly harmless. Hostage rescue teams use them as a matter of course, throwing them into a doorway, letting them go off, and then stepping inside to tackle the occupants — who if not expecting it — are incapacitated for a few seconds. Even people trained to resist the effect struggle. Dropping a flash-bang on the sniper would have less effect, as it was not an enclosed space, but it would certainly ruin any night-vision capability for several minutes. He might even break position and run once he knew he was exposed, as he did in False Creek when he attacked *The Bean*.

We could hear the helicopter approaching and soon it appeared on the other drone's video feed, through which we could see it skimming low up the middle of the lake. The image was so crisp we could make out the pilot, but the passenger seat appeared to be empty. I looked back at the sniper, and he had switched back from the rifle to the funny scope he had started with. A horrible thought occurred.

"Kelsie, give me a shot from the high drone, infrared only!" I commanded, and a second later my fears were confirmed. The scene showed the cabin, lit up by various heat sources. The lake was a deeper black than the land, because it was colder, but both were mostly black. The sniper was visible as a blob from this height. The drone was up at 2000 feet to take in the whole area. But the worrying thing was a line that stretched out ominously from the sniper and across to the cabin, lighting it up like a Christmas tree.

"That's a laser-designating scope!" yelled Justin. I looked back at the image of the helicopter bearing down towards the cabin, and mounted on each side was a small pod. Either a machine gun of some type, or possibly a missile. We watched in horror as a bright light obscured the helicopter as it launched its payload and began rapidly tracking towards the cabin, eating up the distance as fast as we could compute what was happening.

"Get out!" "Cover!" "Run!" were several of the shouts that came over the link all at once, mixed in with at least two swear words. But before anyone could otherwise react, the cabin exploded and lit up the night's sky. Our hide rocked and we felt more than heard debris striking the outside. Our video feed was down, but we still had audio, and we could hear Kelsie asking more calmly than I could have done for a roll call. We checked in, but there was no word from Meeka and Justin. I explained we had lost visual.

"The helicopter is slowing to a hover over the cabin site. The cabin was levelled. The sniper has switched back to his rifle and is scanning the area. I don't imagine there is much for him to hit. Hang on! Drone Four has a view of your hide, and you are leaking light. Turn off your screens and lights immediately!" We complied, but she could still see us as a black area emitting heat from several small holes. We were holding our breath.

"The helicopter might have seen you Ethan, it is transitioning sideways across the clearing to get a better view, and it is turning away from the cabin to point your way. Prepare to evacuate. We are taking out the sniper, and suggest you run up into the treeline northwest. ETA of reinforcements is six minutes."

"That's going to be five and a half minutes too late!" said Marcy, to no one in particular.

"Flash-bang in four...three...two...one.... Now!"

As she got to 'two', we were already opening the back of the hide and dropping the rope ladders down to the ground. At 'Now!' we were halfway to the ground. We heard the grenade go off, and somewhere off to the east we could see a short glow, which faded quickly.

The helicopter had closed the distance and as we raced for the cover, we could see a second missile on the left-hand side, and what looked like a 50-calibre machine gun on the front. It didn't really matter which were fired: at this range we were toast. The pilot was jockeying his bird into position, being careful not to run afoul of any trees or posts. It would be only a few more seconds. Marcy and I both reacted the same way at the same time. We drew our handguns and opened up, pumping as many bullets towards the helicopter as we could. But either the range was too great, or the helicopter was armoured because the small sparks of the bullets hitting did little to put off the pilot. Suddenly, there was a new flash high off to the south, and a small bolt of light shot across the lake and struck the helicopter. There was a tiny but noticeable pause, and then the whole aircraft erupted into flames with an ear-splitting explosion, then dropped, spinning to the ground. Marcy and I looked at each other. We reloaded as we stepped down towards the cabin. If the sniper was now our only enemy, we wanted something big and solid between him and us. My cell phone suddenly chimed. It was Kelsie.

"Was that a ground-to-air missile?" I asked. "Did you do that?"

"Unconfirmed, but we think it was a missile. But we can't see anything at the source. We are moving a drone closer, but nothing is on the high overhead-sensors. The sniper is bugging out though. He has packed his rifle already and is heading back towards the ATV. We have two drones tasked on him and should be able to keep pace once he gets there."

"OK, we are going to check Meeka and Justin, but I don't think they could have made it given the blast intensity. If either is alive, we will split up, and one of us stay with them while the other goes after The Kingman. If they didn't survive, we both go after him. I know these logging roads fairly well." We scrambled down to the flaming devastation that used to be a cabin but could not get close due to the heat. We looked at each other and said nothing, but Marcy had tears welling up in her eyes, and I was fighting back the same. I couldn't tell if they were tears of sadness or anger.

"We'll take an ATV and head up the logging road in The Kingman's direction," I said hoarsely into the phone, trusting that they would pick up on the inference and I wouldn't have to say the two officers were dead. "At some point I will need to be guided to intercept. I can't drive and talk on the phone, so I'll pass you over to Marcy."

"The hell you will!" said Marcy, "I can drive these things pretty well. You get on the back and guide me."

Why do I surround myself with type triple-A women? I asked myself silently as I got onto the back of the scarlet-coloured ATV. Marcy started the engine, turned us and we jerked a couple of times as she got used to the thumb-operated throttle's bite, then we took off up the trail at an alarming rate. I ditched the manly 'hold onto the saddle with one hand' stance, slung an arm tight around Marcy's waist, and hung on for my life.

Kelsie told us we were paralleling the sniper, who had just reached his ATV, started it, had turned, and was headed back along the trail. I deduced that if we caught him in the bushes we would have an advantage, as one of us could drive and the other could shoot. But if he got to open ground, then he could keep us at bay with his long gun. Still, if we kept him pinned down that way, the cavalry would eventually arrive and win the day.

We raced through the woods on a path that would turn and then intersect his path. Our path was a good road and we were doing 30 mph or more, which was high risk in the dark with no headlights. His path was much trickier, and Kelsie informed us he had to slow down to navigate difficult terrain from time to time, so we were gaining rapidly. We reached the intersect point just as he blew through it, and we saw his headlights clearly through the trees. He was about 250 yards ahead of us and perhaps making a little on us. Now that we were on his more difficult trail, our additional weight was slowing us more than helping us. He somehow became aware of us, Kelsie relayed, and he put on a burst of speed. He broke out into a clearing and surged across it. We broke out twenty seconds later and the gap had visibly widened. We were accelerating hard after him when he jammed to a stop, grabbed his rifle, and dove behind his ATV for cover. We were stranded in no man's land. We could not make it back to cover before he got a bead on us, and we might not make it all the way to him to get in range of my pistol. I was about to tell Marcy to head back to safety, but she leaned forward and gunned the engine to its' max.

OK, decision made then. We were covering the distance at a terrific rate, but I could see him bringing the gun up onto the saddle to steady his aim. He looked incredibly calm and deadly, as if following some predetermined and well-practised script that would snuff us out.

I reached over Marcy's back and carefully took aim, which was impossible as we bounced around. I let a few shots go, hopefully it might force him to keep his head down, but he just ignored me. One bullet hit the tire of his ATV and it settled and spoilt his aim, but he just ignored it and realigned the shot.

We were suddenly only 50 feet away, and then 40 then 30. I was trying to anticipate which way Marcy was going to swerve so I could be ready to open fire with the rest of my clip, but at the same time I could see The Kingman was going to get at least one shot off. At that range, that rifle ammo would pass through Marcy and me and not stop for some time. Then I grasped Marcy's strategy: It was not a swerve and fire plan, it was a steam straight into the guy ramming plan. *Holy crap.*

As that realization formed in my mind, we had reached ten feet and were still accelerating. I leapt off to the left but Marcy just rode it all the way in to impact, making damn sure of the collision. There was a bang as the rifle went off, then a huge crash as the ATVs came together; then everything blurred out as I hit the floor, rolling over and over, land and heaven spinning wildly.

As soon as I could get a breath inside of my lungs, I levered myself up, in quite a bit of pain, and shuffled towards the carnage Marcy had caused. The Kingman was sprawled under both ATVs and was clearly dead. If not dead, he would have one hell of a neck pain, as it was at a horrible angle with what looked suspiciously like bones and a foot pedal sticking out of the side.

Marcy was on the far side, and I shuffled around the debris of bike and trees to her. She was lying on her back and I quickly ran my hands over her looking for bullet wounds. She was looking back at me, clearly winded, but she seemed OK. She was smiling. She started to laugh, but when it broke into coughing, I worried again about internal damage. I told her to lie still. She looked up at me.

"I nailed that sneaky fucker's ass to the wall. The VPD always gets its man." I flopped down next to her, cradled her head, and wiped away the worst of the mud. I examined myself and found part of a tree coming out of my side, but little blood; I counted a couple of broken ribs and my right ankle had begun to swell. This was going to hurt in the morning; I might have to cancel my session with Gia. It started to rain very lightly, and we were still lying like that when the cavalry showed up.

9: An Education

[Marcy] - The Kingman was confirmed dead at the scene. The last thing to pass through his mind was an ATV grill that contained the last bullet he had fired. Ethan and I were both field stretchered to a small clearing and airlifted directly to the pad at Vancouver General Hospital. We had police protection and Ethan's personal bodyguards. So we were safe—but I felt just awful. Firstly, for getting Ethan involved in a police matter at all; then for letting him risk his cute civilian ass with me at the lake; and finally, he had the worst of it from my crazy ramming manoeuvre. Being in the driving seat, I had jumped and rolled at the last second, sending the ATV on its way, whereas Ethan, not knowing what I was planning, had launched himself blindly into a bush that turned out to be tougher than it looked.

Within an hour of arrival at the hospital, I was cleaned up and discharged, but Ethan would be staying overnight at least, then bed rest was recommended once released. Slim chance, knowing wonder boy! Ethan lay back on the bed, mostly cleaned up and totally naked — with just a towel for privacy — while a nurse applied bandages to his side, ankle, and thigh. He was manly and stoic as she patched him up, but there was a shadow in his eyes about recent events. And something more, which my cop sense flagged as guilt, that I couldn't quite get a bead on.

"Pass me what's left of my pants," he growled. He reached into his pocket and took out his house key. "My place is like Fort Knox. I know you are Vancouver's finest," I rolled my eyes at this, "but who knows what else these creeps might have in store, or what they might have done to your house by way of booby traps." He reached over and took my hand and continued, "When I get out of here, let's take a break and find some sunshine to recover in." I bit back a prideful outburst and accepted the key. After all, I was going to be on gardening leave while Dennis sorted out the huge mess caused by the tragic and brutal RCMP casualties, so I had time to kill. I hadn't been lying when I'd told Ethan that five years was a long time, and I really wanted to give us a chance. The reconnection was overdue and the heat we had between us on his yacht was intense. Just the thought brought an electrical tingle to my neck, breasts, and belly. I blushed. Hanging out at his place would be a start at getting to know him again, and I wondered if he had a wardrobe of rugby shirts I could steal to relax in.

But there was something I was missing. He was focused entirely on me when we had sex, except there was a troubled shadow of...something. In those passionate moments I hadn't been aware of it, but reliving the moments later, which I'd done often, there was a ghost of something. I would have to puzzle that out.

After the nurse had finished and Ethan and I had kissed and cuddled. He mocked my ATV manoeuvre, and I had 'accidentally' made him wince by hugging him too hard. Then I got serious and pressed Ethan about the mystery missile. Dennis was almost split in half and spitting mad. Again. He was grateful someone had taken out those responsible for killing two of our own, and almost getting me too, but mad as hell someone had military-grade toys that he didn't have. I knew exactly how he felt, and I honestly couldn't think of any other explanation than Ethan's deep pockets and secret toy collection. Ethan seemed truly perplexed about it, too, and cryptically mentioned it was not the only puzzle he planned to unravel but would not be drawn to share more.

We lightened the mood by talking about where we might take off to and what we would do there but unspoken between us was a determination that we would not walk away from this until the threat was shut down. I left him as the drugs took hold and he began to drift, then caught a ride back in yet another black SUV with some of Ethan's private army. A crew was working hard on *The Bean* as we passed, and the Booker building gates were already open and guarded as we rolled straight into the private parking area. We didn't exit the hardened SUV until the steel doors were safely closed behind us.

We were met by a fit-looking woman who introduced herself as Gia, his personal trainer (something else to discuss when Ethan got home), who showed me into a private elevator and explained the codes to get up and down and gave me numbers to call if there was anything I needed. She rode with me to Ethan's floor and we wore polite smiles, but we were bristling at each other all the way up. No hissing or fangs, but lines being drawn. My line was between her and Ethan, but I relaxed a degree or two when I sensed that her line was between Ethan and danger and she was trying to decide if that included me. She escorted me to Ethan's door, where she left me. I sensed she was also relaxing as she seemed to have concluded I was no threat; and that rankled me over again. Plugging into Ethan's life was more complex than expected. But I felt motivated.

Ethan had told me Gwen lived across the hall, and I tapped on the door to let Gwen know Ethan was OK. The door opened quickly, and Gwen tried to drag me in to make a fuss of me, which felt welcoming. I agreed to pop back after I had a long, hot-hot bath.

I let myself into Ethan's apartment with his key and closed the door. *Yikes, a key to his place!* The lights came up slowly on their own. I waited a bit for Barry White to play, but not a sound. Feeling a little like a schoolgirl venturing nervously somewhere I shouldn't, I took a deep breath and enjoyed the scents of a well-groomed man and his macho apartment. The aroma brought a whirlwind of emotions and turbulent thoughts. But not as many, or as turbulent, as those that erupted in me when my eyes fell on the selfie picture on the hall stand of my naked Ethan standing next to a smiling Gwen.

*

I hadn't commanded my body to move, but in an instant Gwen was opening her door to my angry, urgent police knock, and I was in her apartment holding the photo a few inches from her face. I was trying to decide if I would throw the photo in her face and leave, punch her in the face and storm out, or pull my gun and shoot her. Or go shoot Ethan. I couldn't think straight, and my thoughts swirled. Getting back with Ethan was too good to be true. The last 48 hours had been crazy. And now this...what? The silence stretched out, and then further out, before Gwen eventually broke it.

"Well, honey," she started slowly, "I admit that's pretty awkward. I'm guessing you two are an item. At last!"

Silence again. I felt a stronger urge to shoot someone.

"I would bet my little gay tush that right now, you are thinking about running or fighting, and either way I couldn't blame you. If I were in your shoes, I couldn't possibly imagine that there could be an easy explanation that would make sense. Stupid bet? Not Ethan, no. Affair? No. I'm gay and too old anyway. Yep, it's a puzzler to be sure!" She paused again and considered me. She was wrestling with decision, and then she seemed to decide. "And you would be right, in that there is no easy explanation. There are glib, unsatisfactory, evading, condescending, and insulting explanations to be sure, but not easy. Nor helpful." Another pause.

Is she trying to drag out her last moments, or help me process what she's telling me? Hmm, the latter. Smart. I started to focus.

"I'll tell you something for free, though. I've seen the women Ethan has around him at work; some he has very casually dated, and most of them are smart and gorgeous, like you. But the thing is, he barely sees them as women. He goes and wrestles with that glorious martial arts trainer and, bruises aside, forgets her as he walks out of the dojo. But when I saw him at *The Bean*, stumbling and fumbling over his feet for you, I knew you must be Marcy. He's mentioned you over the last year. Often. Your on-and-off history. Your violet, life-filled eyes. So, as you work out this conundrum, start out with the undeniable fact that the boy is *yours*. And only yours. Anchor your puzzle on that fact Marcy! That's a start. Solve it from that perspective." Gwen paused again, and then her face and stance softened.

She continued. "Part of me wants to tell you to go speak to Ethan about that photo. That is what smart people do. It's your business, and his secret, not mine to tell. Go ask him. But another part of me knows that in this case, this stupid loveable boy will panic and mess this up. Not through guilt over the picture, because it's stupid and irrelevant. It's something deeper. So, I feel compelled to step in, and tell you in better words than he will, what you need to know to properly understand that photo, but even more so, the boy in it. But it's not my place, and I could lose my apartment — and even worse — a really good friend. Whatever I do is a risk. Perhaps it's better you do shoot me! Don't deny it; you were considering it." She broke the trance and drifted towards the small, oak bar nestled in the corner and reached for two wine glasses.

"If you plan to hear me out, we need to slow you down. And you need to ask me to tell you. I won't unless you ask me. Say the words, and then I will. And this will take a few hours and some wine. If I am going to betray a good man, I definitely need wine. A lot of good wine. Or you can turn around and walk back out the door and beat up Ethan [*no!*] or walk out of his life for good [*NO!*] or at least until he begs you to return [*OK, maybe that!*]. Or beat me until you feel better, and then feel worse." Gwen stood quietly now, her back to me, her shoulders tense, with the wine glasses in one hand, and the corkscrew in the other. Letting me think in silence.

As a daughter from an abusive family, and as a cop who did the domestic beat for years, I've seen almost all kinds of cons, manipulations and angles. Gwen was managing me — no question of that — but it didn't feel ill intended. And, damn it, it was working. She had successfully distracted me, and cooled me down a few degrees, and I must admit I wanted to hear more about what Ethan thought of me. *He talked about me? Us? My eyes?* I could still shoot her later, I thought, to quiet that nagging tough-cop voice in my head. I realized I had tears in my eyes and wet on my cheeks. *Shit, I never cry. This is deeper than I thought.* Not that I had let my brain think yet. I made a decision, lowered the Polaroid, and sighed. "This better be good! Where can I wash my face while you pour us some big glasses of wine?"

It was just past noon and the sun was hot on Gwen's balcony, but we had shade from an awning that extended at the touch of a button. Pretentious but very cool. Gwen sat at one end of a three-seater sun lounge, and I took my place at the other, separated from Gwen by several cushions. There were gardenias and petunias tastefully arranged on the low table in front of us, and Gwen had somehow conjured up some brie, cheddar, and crackers. No ice cream though; she was not perfect. Suddenly I was ravenously hungry.

I felt on guard, Unsettled. Desperate for peace of mind. My ego hurt. Suppressing the urge to stalk back and forth. Tired, and deflated, all at once. My face was sore from crying. God, I was *a mess*. I told myself to get my shit together. This is not me. I took a sip of wine and vowed not to sip again until something made sense.

Gwen began thoughtfully and carefully.

"A cop, with a cop brain and woman's intuition. Your face is pure conflict and suspicion. You know in your heart Ethan's a good man, but you've been deeply hurt before and you are not going to let that happen again. You are complicated, Marcy, and that's Ethan's big problem. Right there! You and your past."

I bristled. "Are you blaming this on me?" I asked incredulously, my bristles growing their own bristles.

"Easy, tigress," she said smoothly. "Our man believes he has a deep, dark secret. But really, it's not that deep or dark in today's world. However, Ethan doesn't really live in today's world: he is pure old-fashioned, macho John Wayne. He might tell a lesser partner, but only if he didn't care as much as he does for you. If he didn't worry about your troubled past. You do have a troubled past, don't you?" A separate and objective part of my brain – my cop brain — was impressed with the way she both seemed to know me, and at the same time was puzzling out the parts of me she didn't know and completing the jigsaw. She was fleshing out her professional view of me in real time.

"And don't worry, he has not been indiscrete; you know he wouldn't be. He's just unknowingly hinted enough for a woman like me to work it out. He has something that is deep within him, but not as deep as his love for you. For you, he could bury his 'thing' and even you may never see it surface. You might sense it at some level; you must be very perceptive. It might be a ghost you can never put your finger on. A niggle. But for him, I think it would fade away over time. He would forget it in the elation of you reuniting, and it may not ever reassert itself. He would unquestioningly do that for you. But then there's the Polaroid. That was my fault, and I am deeply sorry. It's given you the scent of something. If he brushes it away, it would eat at you. If he admits it, he will feel ashamed and worried you might leave him — or worse — stay and judge him."

"Is it something I should leave him for?" I asked, surprisingly earnestly.

"That depends, I guess," she considered. "If it were me, I wouldn't. I'd embrace it, to be honest. But we are all different people, aren't we?".

She let that hang in the air for a moment. "Let me tell you about me first," she continued. "I'm the fun, exotic, coffee-shop owner you met the other day, and Ethan's loveable and eccentric neighbour. I'm sex positive, a little kinky when the mood takes me, and not very shy about it. That's me for sure. But before all this," she gestured at herself dramatically, "I was a psychologist and teacher, specializing in relationships and sexual sciences. I have a PhD in both Yin and Yang but like to stay away from the 'woo woo' end of our spectrum and prefer to deal in the science and facts. I qualified as a shrink, and I am on the list of "kink-aware" practitioners. Yes, there is such a thing, and it's about time in our changing world. To borrow from Trudeau the younger, it's 2018. I know where Ethan's coming from with some, um, academic certainty. But my problem is, I don't know you at all. Ethan is crazy about you, and that means you are the real deal. As smart as you are cute. Tough as nails—that's clear. And a strong and vibrant soul. Nothing less would attract that boy. It's a shame you play for the wrong team!

"And you don't get to where you are in VPD by starting out as a Sunday School teacher, so I imagine you've seen it all. And maybe were driven to become a cop because you've been on the receiving end of violence, or abuse. Or maybe inflicting abuse, in some people's situations, which I doubt in your case. Is any of this true?"

Shit, she should interview perps with me—she's a savant.

"But I don't know where that's left you." She gazed at me trying to see through my Jedi shielding. No dice, I hoped, and I let the silence stretch out. She had me hooked, but I wasn't an easy reel in.

"Here is the nub of it, Marcy. Ethan has a minor, let's call it, kink. I discovered it in an unfortunate, but very funny accident. And because Ethan is a little bit ashamed of himself, he will think you will be ashamed of him, too. But will you be? If genuinely not, then there's no real issue between you, other than the pending awkward conversation you need to have with him. But Ethan knows you pretty well, doesn't he? He has thought much and deeply about you, and the boy is as smart as he is cute. He thinks you will have trouble with his foible, and if he thinks it, he may be right." Gwen stopped talking again, suddenly it seemed, and the silence grew louder, as it was clearly my turn to talk. But nothing was coming out. Oh, I've had a lot of erotic fantasies, both with me giving and receiving, but I've seen where they lead to in life, seen some awful outcomes, and that's not for me. Against my values. "If it's consenting adults and no one gets h—" I started. She cut me off.

"Oh, you're one of those are you?" her interruption reminding me of a slightly impatient mother, snorting and shaking her head.

Save me from lesbian Yoda, I thought.

Gwen laughed. "Those words are not far from the truth, but you and many people say them as a way to avoid a conversation about them because you avoid thinking about them." I opened my mouth to object vociferously, but she cut me off again. "Hear me out, Marcy. We are surrounded by a fire hose of data coming at us, and one of the brain's strengths is to create shortcuts so we can survive. We bundle things into groups and assign shortcuts. Literally. Politics south of the border? I skim highlights, dividing into real and fake news without questioning much. Anything mechanical or technical? Blah Blah. Cooking? I go deep, with no shortcut, because I am truly interested in the details. This wonderous technique both keeps us sane by letting us avoid overload, but it is also the source of bias and prejudice. We take a shortcut, when perhaps we should learn more and go a bit deeper. And there is nothing wrong in that. It is survival, as I said.

"Now, no one has to have sex, or kinky sex. Or think about the complexities surrounding the types of sex we are happy to block out. But all that just changed for you. Now you have a Polaroid, and it forces you to judge Ethan, and ultimately yourself. And you've never given kinky sex much objective thought or done the research to make a balanced judgement. You have a singular view. Ethan will mess this up because he will panic. You will mess it up out of ignorance!" Gwen punctuated the air with her finger as she toughened her tone. "Make a balanced and informed choice Marcy, not a knee jerker. And you will be much happier with whichever choice you make if you think it through."

I took some slow sips of wine. *Yoda makes a good point.* This is something I shy away from and know little about, outside of the crap I see through work. I lump it all into my 'abuse box'. But there be dragons in that box. My feelings towards Mom, Billy, and Dad, and why...*fuck' I'm getting upset just thinking about it. Focus.*

I offered, "I was raised old school, you know, sex can be fun as long as there is no 'funny business.' You are right, Mom and Dad were both abusive to all of us kids by today's standards, but back then it was just called 'strong parenting'. And as a cop, I've seen abuse, human trafficking, and forced prostitution. So, my old-school values tell me kinky is bad, and I know that much sex work is abusive and cloaked in fetish. I accept some people might enjoy some bondage and spanking, and if it is truly consensual, then fill your six-inch heeled boots; but I've seen where it leads, and it is not good, Gwen. I love Ethan, and if he has a mild kink, great, but it's a long stretch to accepting there is nothing abusive in those BDSM relationships. Let's say, for the sake of argument, he gets off on spanking and is totally fine with it. My whole career is based on enforcing that people should never hit people. Whatever he feels, why should I feel OK hitting him, even if he begs me to? What would that make me? My mom? My dad?"

"It would be going against your values, and you shouldn't. But that doesn't mean your values can't change. And not because the devil seduced you, Marcy. Values and laws change all the time, and the change agents are perspective and education. Here is a fact for you. Thomas Jefferson, US founding father and beloved person, once submitted a bill that men convicted of sodomy should be castrated. What do you think of that?"

"I don't believe it. He's supposed to have been one of the good guys."

"Actually, he was, in that he was attempting to reduce the penalty from the death sentence to just castration. Perspective and context make a difference. You say you are geared to defend the law. What's your stance on homosexuality? What about oral sex?"

Awkward. "Err...I'm very much in favour of same-sex marriage; I've even marched in the Pride Parade for it, Gwen. There is nothing wrong with it. And I'm definitely OK with oral sex. Why is that a legal issue and how does that relate to kinks?" *OK, that sounded defensive.*

"Well, it's not that long ago that most people used the 'consenting adults' line about gays, too. But we have learned a lot since then, and that knowledge changed our values. Let's forget gay marriage for a second. If two guys want to have anal sex, is that OK?"

"Sure, of course," I played along.

"Ever had a threesome?"

"No, not my thing. Maybe a college fantasy." I could feel myself blushing.

"But if three guys want a threesome that's OK?"

"Of course, yes!"

"Actually, no, it's illegal in Canada. Sodomy was partly decriminalized in the Criminal Law Amendment Act, 1968-69 (Bill C-150), which also decriminalized oral sex. Ironic that was in '69. The bill had been originally introduced in the House of Commons in 1967 by then minister of Justice Pierre Trudeau, who famously stated that, "there's no place for the state in the bedrooms of the nation." Despite a further progressive revision in 1987, the Criminal Code continues to criminalize anal sex, but with exceptions. So, it is basically a criminal act, unless the criteria for an exception are met, as opposed to a straightforward, legal act. The exceptions, which will mean it is not criminal, are for husbands and wives or two consenting parties above the age of eighteen, provided no more than two people are present. A threesome does not reach the threshold for the exception. It is criminal."

"But that's silly!!!" I blurted. *I'm a cop, I should know that.*

"My point is, you can't rely on the law to back up your values, as it gets very confused over sex. There is no law about kinky sex, by the way—nothing says BDSM itself is illegal — just laws about how BDSM activities might manifest as a crime. There are laws against harming people mentally and physically, for instance, but they are not explicitly about kink-related harm. There are laws against restraining people, but they get very confused by the consent language. Which is understandable. You know better than anyone how the abused can protect their abusers, so you have to be extremely careful about consent. Anal sex is pretty binary. You did or you didn't, however big the group. Yet they can't get a simple law to cover it. Consent is much more complex and non-binary.

"In the mid-nineties, the term BDSM was coined on a bulletin board. Us old folk used bulletin boards before we invented the internet. As I will explain, 130 years ago the lack of open communication stigmatized, pathologized, and for some acts, criminalized sex, but recently, online communications have been instrumental in providing a different understanding of the context. It's creating facts where there were none, and that is changing perspectives, which in turn can challenge our values. Our values may not change, but they will at least be based upon informed choice."

I went for another sip and found my glass empty. Gwen leaned forward and topped me up, — passed me more crackers which I gratefully accepted — and then continued.

"There are thirty-thousand-year-old cave drawings, parchments from ancient Greece, and many historical artifacts that make it clear that we have been having fun, kinky sex for thousands of years. We invented the dildo before the wheel. In ancient Greece, a warrior gave his girl an olisbos, a dildo made of leather or wood, to keep her happy while he was away. Olive oil, with its lubricating qualities, wasn't just a staple of the Greek diet back then. In Victorian London, despite the puritanism of the educated elite and growing middle class, kink was organized like no other time in England, even perhaps today. There were regular brothels, and brothels for gays, and houses for gay people to hang out openly which were not brothels, just hangouts. There were the houses of flagellation, both to give and receive as you like. Cross-dressing places. By today's standards we might call some of it barbaric, such as places that offered younger teens, both boys and girls. Women with 'the vapours' could go to a doctor who would manipulate her vagina to exorcize the bad energy. At a time when London had less than a million people, over 50,000 were involved in prostitution. Why? Because it paid well for fewer hours and was safer in more ways than the alternative workhouses. It was a time where you could access anything, but almost everything was frowned upon.

"But only recently has our culture evolved so that we can verbalize and share with the masses the difference between abuse and consensual BDSM. I'll give you some examples, but remember, it is not any single one of these; it is all of them together that capture the difference.

"BDSM includes activities to elicit pleasure for both parties, sometimes using pain, whereas abuse is the intention to cause physical, mental, or emotional harm, not pleasure – at least not for the recipient. BDSM is a consensual power exchange, with the submissive agreeing to give a defined portion of their power to a specific dominant for an agreed time. Even if they give away all of their power, so an experience seems non-consensual, it is 'consensual non-consent.' Abuse takes one person's power away without permission, or with permission but under duress. BDSM requires an equitable negotiation, reaching an explicit agreement before anything happens; but with abuse, the recipient doesn't know when it will happen and there is no consensual agreement as to scope, timing, or severity. Sometimes there is a feeling of tacit agreement; often this feeling is one sided, or the abuser is assuming a fear-driven lack of objection is meant as consent. BDSM creates excitement in your partner and is thrilling and rewarding, whereas abuse causes fear and makes you afraid and resentful of the abuser – and often resentful of yourself. BDSM creates and builds trust, whereas abuse can create a sense of dependency but destroy trust. BDSM is designed to help fulfil the desires of both partners, and abuse is cruel and often violent treatment of one by another. Both BDSM and abuse are similar in that they deviate from social norms, but different in that abusive activities are characterized by stress and dysfunction, where BDSM is not. Most importantly, BDSM requires open communication in a supportive environment, but with abuse there is little or no communication or emotional support."

As she talked, I weighed each statement against my personal upbringing and experiences as an adult. How she described abuse certainly resonated with my experiences, and how she described BDSM sounded different – and almost uplifting – but hard to fathom. I still couldn't imagine it being right to hurt someone when we know in our hearts it is wrong. And I said as much.

She considered my comment for a moment before continuing. "What our head thinks our heart tell us we think is wrong is based on what we learn since birth, and for generations we have been told both openly and subtly that it is wrong to inflict pain on others. Most forms of organized religion are against all forms of frivolous sex. The more progressive ones begrudgingly allow that sex within marriage can be fun, but never to excess. Most accept it in pursuit of procreation but would prefer it otherwise didn't happen. Much like the Victorian upper and middle classes. And actually, for historically valid reasons, since sex has many ways of undermining society and progress: Diseases, fights over partners, betrayals, and distractions happen so often that if you are trying to guide your flock in a predictable fashion, sex is not your friend. Despite nearly 1000 years of Christianity, where the Catholic church had come to an uneasy peace with sex, it was the syphilis outbreak around the year 1450 that eventually sparked a big societal change as five million people, or 18 percent of the European population, were wiped out by an STD. Hard to build civilization with that sort of uncontrolled result from casual sex.

"In the early 16th century, Henry the Eighth was married to his first wife, Catherine, and lusting after Anne Boleyn. He wanted divorce and the Pope said no. But Henry had bigger issues than that: He was at war with the French, and low on funds. The recently formed parliament was of little help; its primary function seemed to be to protect the lords and barons from monarchs overtaxing the populace to get money to fight wars, as had happened for centuries. To picture this time in history, think Robin Hood and Prince John, as Henry came right after Richard. Meanwhile, the Portuguese and Spanish were getting organized and creating trade routes that created more and more wealth for their countries. In particular, they had skilled sailors and navigators, whose rutters – or maps – were guarded closely, often codified for secrecy.

"Breaking from the Catholic church achieved a few key goals: It rerouted the funds that were leaving England for the Vatican into the royal purse, bringing in money and denying it to the Europeans; by selling twenty-nine monasteries, Henry created funds to build six warships the size and power of which had never been seen before, and a further 30 more ancillary craft to supply them and carry trade, as – up until then – there was no navy or organized fleet, just privateers hired on one-off contracts, so this was a game changer; and, he finally got to bonk Boleyn. In terms of sea power, Henry was poised to leap-frog the competition. Except sex undermined his master plan. As fast as he pressganged men to sail his ships, they bonked each other and died of syphilis.

"Up until that time, most sex-related acts were dealt with by ecclesiastical courts. Henry created the first English government-formed sex law, the *1533 Buggery Act*. It covered sodomy and zoophilia – or what we would call bestiality

– to protect the men and the farm stock the ships carried from the horny seamen. And so, the fleet began to become healthier, started to build and retain navigation, fighting, and sailing skills, and grew into a powerful navy.

"This concept of pushing away the distractions of sex grew steadily over the next 300 years, and although the 19th century Victorians were at it like rabbits – and often kinky rabbits – the educated elite and the leadership convinced themselves that sex, except for necessary procreation, was a bad thing. It was for the weak minded and a distraction if you want to build an empire. Do you smoke, Marcy?" The question surprised me.

"No, never. Why?"

"People are much less scared of distant, long-term physical threats than a mental threat. Smokers know their vice is killing them but still do it, even with the explicit packaging they look at twenty times a day. But a mental threat is a far more compelling deterrent. A threat to our sense of self, our soul.

"In the late 1800s, in that time of very puritanical beliefs – if not acts – the science of psychology really came into its own. It had been around for about 50 years as a notion, but the heavy lifting, much of which we use today, happened in England, the USA, Germany, and Austria between 1875 and 1900. They created the new science first by categorization, creating names for behaviours and acts; nymphomania, homosexuality, and many now-familiar terms were created and described in growing detail. And then those terms were classified as good or bad, and by degrees. Not surprisingly, when you 'know' in your heart for generations that anything except procreational sex is bad, then homosexual sex must, of course, be bad. Similarly, nymphomania must also be bad because you don't need excessive sex to procreate. A couple of days a month at most. In fact, almost all frivolous sex took on a bad image. But, as this was a science, these assumptions needed to be validated, even back then. Up to that point, it was great science and achievement given the times, but it was about to go seriously off the rails, largely because science lacked the experience we have built up since. Where do you find subjects to prove the theory of what is good and bad?

"No one would talk openly about sex, so Freud, Ebbing, and the other thought leaders of the time relied heavily on three sources: Firstly, literature. Some poets, fiction writers, and social documenters had published works that were studied meticulously. In nearly all cases, the creator was from a previous era and had died or was for other reasons not accessible, so was not directly interviewed. Two authors you would have heard of would be the Marquis de Sade and Leopold von Sacher-Masoch, from where we get the terms sadism and masochism. In today's world, de Sade would be deemed a serial sex offender and viewed as far removed from some fun 'slap and tickle' as you could imagine. Someone more akin to Ted Bundy. He was locked in jails or asylums for over 30 years of his life and was as abusive as they come. But he wrote about the joys he got from hurting others emotionally and physically, and his prose coloured the science.

"Masoch was a much more benign person, and one of his works even became a Roman Polanski movie earning 89% on *Rotten Tomatoes*. Masoch paid his mistress to treat him cruelly, wearing furs whenever possible. They signed a contract allowing that for six months she could do anything she liked to him and with him, and she so created a fictional manservant called Gustav, whom she took out in public, demeaned, and treated badly in front of other people. I think that would make an awesome movie today, but it's really until only very recently that society could accept it as anything other than a farce. Ebbing used these writings about 'Masochistic tendencies' in his work to define mental states, too. The Polanski movie was called *Venus in Furs,* by the way.

"So, hardly definitive input from the literati, but better than the other two available sources in many ways. In addition to literature, the budding scientists went to the only other place they could at the time: jails and asylums. There they proved beyond doubt – hah! – what they already knew in their hearts: the strong link between bad, evil, and broken people, and sexual perversion. Science back then was not rigorous enough to prevent the absence of balanced data to nullify the conclusions, so they stood as the truth for generations. 70 or 80 years went by before we even began to become more enlightened about same-sex attraction, and in perhaps 50 percent of the western world, attitudes to it have slowly changed from bad, to 'whatever consenting adults want,' to normality. There is still roughly half of the western world way behind Vancouver on that journey; there are still 14 states in the USA where anal sex is illegal — and several where even dildos are illegal.

"The growth of an organized BDSM community with stated conventions and definitions has helped separate fun from abuse; but more importantly, the internet is providing access to the data that Ebbing and Freud lacked. Our more rigorous science and the ability to survey both anonymously and openly, coupled with masses of data about people's lifestyles and online buying habits, are illuminating. Of course, there are abusive people who involve themselves in BDSM, but studies are showing that most people who enjoy and respect BDSM conventions, consciously or otherwise, are as sane and well balanced as the average person and disprove the other big misconception, that they must all come from broken homes and abusive backgrounds. But their social profiles are aligned with those of the control groups i.e. groups drawn from the general population.

"The two western bodies who regulate psychology are the *American Psychological Association* or APA, and the *World Health Organization,* or WHO. Five years ago, the APA reclassified most BDSM activity from a pathology, which is disease-like and potentially degenerative and dangerous, to a paraphilia. Paraphilia is, in laymen's terms, sexual activity that is abnormal in the sense it is atypical – not inherently harmful in itself, but it might embrace pain or higher-risk situations – and practised by a small minority. The WHO's recent advisory panel's findings suggest the WHO will follow suit in 2020, which is when their next publication will come out.

"The media are on the bandwagon, and kinky sex – and more and more female-dominant kinky sex – is reflected as positive on television. If you go to the magazines our older teens are reading today, next to advice on sex in general, and anal sex safety, the advice on kink is coming on quickly, openly, and with a positive light. With the most recent surveys of attitudes and buying habits now showing that between 25-30 percent of people have tried some form of BDSM, or are very interested in trying it, I think it won't stay a paraphilia for long as it won't be a minority. It will just be 'sex.' Remember, it's not that long ago that owning a vibrator was considered risqué. And not long before then, if your woman wanted to be on top you were shocked but quietly pleased, but if she asked for the light on, too, she was a slut."

"So, you're saying the science was wrong and based on that, our values are flawed? That's a big leap, Gwen."

"That's not quite what I'm saying, Marcy, but would it be so surprising if I were? Way back when, science proved the world was flat. More recently it proved homosexuality was bad and smoking was good. And women could not be soldiers, pilots, or cops, or much more than nurses, secretaries, and housewives, as far as our leaders and policy makers were concerned, at least. We recently legalized pot, and gay marriage has already been legal for some time. We are learning all the time and adapting our values. Kink is harder because it was painted much darker. Think of the many shows and movies where a key character turns evil. The first thing they seem to do is throw away their street clothes, dress in leather gear, and get kinky. OK, maybe I watched a lot of *Buffy* and *Lost Girl*, but you see what I mean. The media have used BDSM trappings as a subconscious signal for evil since the 1960s.

"In the 1800s, male and female masturbation was rampant but highly frowned upon, considered like a gateway drug. You know, if you play with yourself too much, before you know it you'll be having sex when you don't even want a baby and then we lose the empire. John Harvey Kellogg invented cornflakes in 1894 because he, and many others, believed masturbation and self-pollution could be avoided through better diet. Think about that over breakfast. Of course, that didn't work. They set back 'bopping the baloney' for a few decades by using psychological warfare in the form of if you play with *it* too much, you will go blind and get hairy hands. Some people still use that trick even today with their kids. There is nothing like fake news to sway and divide a people."

"But if that is not quite what you are saying, what are you saying?" I persisted.

"One: sex is not for everyone. We each get to choose freely. But if you like it, then be positive about it. Two: the definitions of abuse and BDSM are different; be conscious about it and unpack what you see so you can judge each part clearly. No shortcuts if you care for Ethan, and no need to judge him. Three: there are new data challenging our beliefs and so, as a society, we are reforming our values. We have different values from our parents, and our kids have already moved on from ours. Look at the data and see if it causes you to personally re-evaluate your values. It's a bit like the phrase, 'If you don't vote, you don't get to complain.' Educate yourself. Being ignorant could be stifling in this new world in general, and fatal to your relationship with Ethan."

Gwen stopped talking and took a long sip of her wine, and we sat quietly for a minute or two.

"I have so many questions," I began. "I still don't think I would like myself if I hurt someone, even if they wanted it. What would change that view? Why do people enjoy pain? And most importantly, why is Ethan naked with you in the Polaroid?" I was perplexed and confused, but I felt at some level that Gwen's words, if true, had power over me. Given my past, unravelling this stuff might be helpful. I looked up and Gwen was smiling warmly.

"Let's save the rest for another time, when you have had time to process all of this and have done your own thinking and research. You can use my computer if you like. I'm sure Ethan has his wired and tracked.

"So here is what this is all about, Marcy: I'm trusting you here as one good friend of Ethan's to another. Ethan has one declared kink, which may or may not go further if he lets himself explore it. When he was a teen, he got himself into a predicament where he was naked and at risk of being discovered while he witnessed a very intimate act. It left with him a strong sense of arousal in similar situations. This grew within him, and over the years he found occasions to take those risks and recreate the feeling. Only he didn't take really big risks, because he is too uptight and caring. He might actually enjoy getting caught but would be horrified if the unwitting person he exposed himself to was offended. So, he created situations where the risks were really low in reality, even if he thought otherwise. Trapped on a roof for an hour, in the middle of the night, in a secure building he owns. That sort of thing. But one day, in a bizarre set of circumstances, I caught him naked on the roof and forced him to tell me what was going on. You know our boy well enough to know no one can force him to do anything, so I believe at some level he wanted someone to know. He has a bit of a kink and wanted to tell someone about it, to make it real. Imagine having part of your identity that was important, but no one knows or ever sees it. Like having an MBA or PhD and never telling anyone." She grinned.

"I decided it would be helpful for him — and fun for me — to legitimize his kink to some degree, so I told him to make it right with me. For upsetting me, he had to let me get my revenge. He had to let me create awkward situations where

I was in control of his nudity and risk. That way, I thought, he could explore this in relative safety on the one hand, but I could help him take it further than his soft limits and see where it went. If he got caught again, it would be a stupid bet between neighbours and not something that could do much damage to his reputation. Our deal is that for the next ten cases he solves, he has to do everything I tell him without complaint, and I get to torment him by placing him in predicaments with nudity-risk scenarios. I love cat and mouse games. We don't have sex, and there's no whipping or anything extreme; I'm just the cat, and he is the mouse who sometimes gets naked. For two single friends, just some harmless fun. For him, this is wild kink and he worries about it and wonders if he is abnormal.

But that was then, and this is now. Clearly, he has moved from 'single neighbour' to 'neighbour in a relationship with you,' so this is where I bow out. Game over. Neither he nor I would want to continue this with you on the scene. And I believe he would prefer it fade away and never be mentioned, as he is head over heels with you."

We sat quietly, and she left me to my thoughts. *OK, I must admit that is a pretty tame kink.* If he were exposing himself around schools, flashing victims, or forcing himself on people, it would be unforgivable. But who hasn't had a naked-in-church type fantasy? I realized the tension had left me and had an immense sense of relief – which I didn't think was just the wine. I still had many questions, some for Gwen, some for Google — and especially some for Ethan — and I suddenly saw a way to do the latter.

"So how many times have you two played this game?" I asked, keeping my face deadpan.

"Five. And in addition to the first time I caught him, only once have I actually seen him naked. The other times I tormented him but let him escape unscathed."

I grinned. "And is there anything in your contract with Ethan that allows you to assign the last five sessions to a third party?"

"Oh, you wicked woman!" she chortled. "I definitely think there should be."

*

I stood naked in Ethan's large and tastefully appointed shower room drying off with a thick white towel that had his scent, and my eye fell on a small tattoo on my hip. It is of an upturned hand sharply signalling 'stop.' It was my constant reminder that I will never let myself succumb to abuse and would never stop fighting for it's victims. As intrigued as I am about this kink of Ethan's, and as crazy yet as sensible-sounding Gwen's words had been just an hour earlier, here on my own, the tattoo challenged me. Just as I had meant it to when Mary-Ann and I had designed it.

Mary-Ann — whom I had used for all of my inky artwork — does fantastic and exclusive work, normally charging a small fortune. We first met when she reported that her sister Alice was being beaten by her husband. As often happens with victims of abuse, Alice refused to admit — to herself and others — that her husband had serious issues. She made excuses for him: The pressure of his work, or that she was not always a perfect wife. Sadly, I saw this too often and even had similar thoughts myself as a child. I spent a long night talking to her sister and eventually convinced her that her life was heading in only one direction. I shared many true tales of other people who had not found the support to change their lives.

It took much persuading, but Alice eventually let me arrest her abuser. He spent a night in jail and then had a restraining order placed against him. It was hard to make a strong case, but at least we had stopped him in his tracks on this occasion. Mary-Ann wanted to thank me, which really wasn't necessary. I had no interest up to that point in tattoos, but she offered to do one for free, and I said I would think about it, not intending to take her up on the offer. But the idea needled at me – pun intended – and I was soon back there and we had a girl's night on the town talking about designs, locations, and where it hurt the least. A week later I had a small, swirly 'Mx' just below my left ankle, in memory of Max. I miss him so much, and this reminder is a comfort.

Mary-Ann's 'superpower' is incredibly elegant pictures made up of at most two or three unbroken lines, never more. The lines can be intricate and quite long, but they never overlap with each other. A year later I had chosen the design for the tattoo on my hip, which caught my attention now. It's a call to action, to stay strong; its challenge unrelenting, a reminder to ensure I don't get sucked onto that slippery slope. The fact that with Ethan I was potentially to play the part of the aggressor, not the victim, made little difference or if anything, made the imperative this symbol stands for even greater.

I finished drying, full of reflection, and found a long shirt in Ethan's closet to use as a nightshirt. I pulled back the Egyptian cotton covers on his king-sized bed and nestled into the fat pillows to think. I was transported back to when I was ten years old. Dad had taken Billy to a BC Lions Canadian football game. He'd already been drunk when he left and continued to knock back the beers throughout the game.

He got into it with some guy who was bigger than him on the Skytrain on the way home. He was in a fowl mood and Billy had fled to his room as soon as they came back in through the door. Mom had been working herself up all day, dreading his return. She had a beer ready for him, which he complained was too warm, and had dinner in the oven ready to serve, which he didn't want as he'd had a burger at the game. Dad yelled at Mom as she went to remove the casserole from the over, and she dropped it in panic. This was Dad's excuse, and he marched over and backhanded Mom across the face. He actually clipped her shoulder first, which took a lot of the weight out of the slap, but she fell to the floor anyway and cowered. Her leg landed on the casserole dish and she screamed as it burned her flesh and filled the room with a smell which haunts me to this day.

Dad swore at her clumsiness, turned, and walked out of the kitchen with his beer in hand. I went over to try to help Mom, but she waved me off. She was embarrassed. I went to Billy's door, but it was locked. He wasn't about to come out and investigate the noise. I went into Max's room and locked the door behind me. I played with him all afternoon, hiding. When I came out, Mrs. Graham, our neighbour, was sitting at the kitchen table, and the mess had gone. She told me that Mom was at the hospital having her burn seen to and would be home soon.

I knew the pattern. Mom wouldn't be hard on me today, but the situation would eat at her. Tomorrow, or the next day, one of us kids would say or do the wrong thing and we would get it from her. Much milder; perhaps a few slaps. It wasn't the pain from the beatings, it was the punishment to our souls that hurt the most. No one to tell. Or at least that is what we thought back then.

Back in the present, I wiped my eyes on the sheet, suddenly realizing I had been crying. My cheeks were soaked, too. Max was gone, and I had pushed the rest of my family away once I was old enough to realize what a broken bunch they all were. How does all that fit in with me being... a dominatrix? Is that who I am? I pictured Ethan lashed to a stool, butt in the air, me standing behind him, contemplating where to strike with a whip. Hard or soft? How would I feel? I imagined him really wanting it. Exquisitely nervous. Did it feel like he was a victim? I realized my pulse had quickened and my loins were stirring. Why? Ethan was nobody's victim. He was hardened and fearless. He was trained to fight and has a disciplined mind. It turned me on to think of doing something pretty taboo that made us both feel hotter than hell.

I wanted the control. Of the situation to be sure. Of him? Not in life, no, but to play? I loved the thought of playing cat and mouse with him. He is so powerful in reality that the idea of being able to play mind games that we both thought of as fun, suddenly seemed like a turn-on; the idea of taking something he really didn't want to give, a turn-off. The idea of being strong enough to help him find his limits? That's hot.

What about dominating him? Spanking, hair pulling, using him for my pleasure? I thought again about my childhood, and of cases I had attended. It began to feel clear to me, that if Ethan was excited about playing the submissive, and we acted with respect and not meanness, then that was very different from abuse. I suspect there are cases where those involved had less emotional strength and personal discipline, so that the line between abuse and consensual exchange of power for mutual fun would need much more careful consideration.

With that decision made, I set about planning a welcome for Ethan that he would not soon forget.

10: Removing Obstacles

[Ethan] — I drifted in and out with the drugs, but when I surfaced, I came up sharp. My limited-edition Manchester United *Tag Heuer* watch lay next to some apple juice on the bedside table and told me I had been out of it for about 12 hours. We had touched down at Vancouver General Hospital in the early hours, and it was now nearly 6 pm. The juice was staying down, so I decided it was time to get up. There were things to worry about: The Kingman was gone, but the threat from those who sent him so rapidly was not. These guys move quickly and lurking here in a hospital was just putting innocent people at risk. *The Bean* attack was too close; we had to be smarter.

I worried about who had overridden Dennis and thrown Marcy and me back into the fray. I was grateful but disturbed about the mystery player with the ground-to-air missile that saved our asses, then vanished without a trace. But mostly, I was worried about how they could sneak in and sneak out without detection. A carefully constructed, sensor-deflecting hide set up well before the action was one thing but moving around undetected with state-of-the-art drone technology scanning the environment was pretty much impossible. Or so I had thought.

Only two possibilities occurred to me. One was that the missile man had technology I didn't know about. This was possible. I'm briefed about most advanced technology through my business affiliations with the military, but there are always advances and leaps in the field it takes time to catch up on. The alternate explanation was that my scanning net was not as tight as I thought it was. Either Kelsie had dropped the ball, which was unfathomable, or something had interfered with our scan without being detected. Advanced jamming? I would need to talk to Darcy, although no doubt she was already thinking along the same track. To solve this puzzle, I needed to get home. And I wanted to catch up with Marcy. My chest ached a lot from the crash, but a little from not knowing where she was and if she was safe; I was too macho to say that out loud.

I pulled myself up and let my head clear from the resulting rush, then plucked the saline drip from my arm. I was hardly dressed for the street. My eyes took in the room: an exit door, a toilet, and a closet door. A tired stock picture of boats bobbing quietly in a west-coast bay at dawn. The serene scene in the frame was quite at odds with the ripe hospital smell that pervaded everything, part of which was probably coming from me. I visited the bathroom, stood in the shower until I could no longer smell myself, then searched the closet for clothes. The cupboard was barer than I was, so I shuffled painfully to the exit door and peaked outside. Heads swivelled my way, and if my team were surprised to see me up, they wisely kept it to themselves. I borrowed a long jacket from one of the guys and let them lead me to an elevator, through the underground parking area, and into our armoured Suburban. I didn't relax much, knowing there were folks out there with military hardware, even though they at least appeared to be friendlies. For now.

After checking we had the apartment block on lockdown, I let myself in, double locked the doors, and set the alarm systems behind me. Marcy's scent was in my space; I liked that and inhaled deeply. The primal hunter in me awoke. There was a soft light spilling from the main bedroom and I had taken four steps towards the bedroom when a sexy shadow cut through the beam of light and Marcy emerged.

"Hey dummy, you are supposed to be resting in hospital," she declared, smiling warmly, as if she had expected no less from me. She stepped close to me and our mouths met, and the world shrank to a small space for a second before expanding at the urgent insistence of several other parts of my body. We stood, hugged, and kissed, but mostly enjoyed the moment reflecting on our survival and that we had reconnected after all these years.

"I figured you nursing me would be better than the battle-axe at the hospital," I shot back.

"The nurse I saw stuffing your butt back together was a young, cute thing," Marcy teasingly snapped back. "I nearly arrested her. Seriously, how are you?" She looked into my eyes trying to work it out for herself, as if she wouldn't trust my answer.

"Bruised and a little sorry for myself." I grinned ruefully. "I couldn't rest as I am worried about some of the things that don't fit together and that I can't answer about the last 72 hours. But they can wait. First, I just want some time with you. This has all happened so quickly, and I want to stop and savour every second I can. I have to say this out loud and get it off my chest: For me, this last reconnection on the *Sea Star* was way more than casual. You know that, don't you? I know we joke about third time being the charm, but I'm serious. I want this to really work between us, and we can put everything else on hold while we sort it out. Whatever this is going to be, I'm all in!"

"Me, too," she whispered, without a hint of hesitation, and tucked her face into my shoulder. After a few shared heartbeats, she took a half step away, a troubling shadow flashed across her face. As she led me through to the bedroom, I let my hand slip down to her hip, and then her taut butt, and pulled her towards me suggestively.

"You seem to have enough energy in you to be a very troublesome patient," she said as she raised an eyebrow, tilted her head, and had a sexy challenge in her smile. I grinned back, and we kissed again. For a long time. When we eventually reached the bed, she stopped me, stood close in front of me, and then reached up and held my face with both hands. Slipping one hand behind my neck, she triggered bolts of tingles racing down my body. She looked deep into my eyes, her pupils devouring me. I melted and stiffened all at once.

"Ethan, listen," she breathed. "The last couple of days have made me kick myself for letting things coast for too long. I want to commit to finding out who we can be together as much as you do. And I really, really, want to get into that bed with you and take your mind off any pain and suffering. I'm all in, as I said, but we have secrets. I can't take this further until we clear the air and get on solid ground." I wasn't following it all but loved the 'bed' and 'who we can be together' parts. I nodded like a puppy. [*yeah yeah yeah...that thing! Woof!*]

"You shared some of your secrets on the boat. I had no idea of how you were using your financial resources and your technical capabilities. Impressive. Technically and morally. And your...let's not call it stalking," she grinned, "let's call it tracking me for my own safety. I'm sure there is more, and I need to hear it eventually so the air is clear. But I have secrets, too, Ethan and it's only fair that I reciprocate. It can't be a one-way flow. And, well...," she was blushing, "there's this one secret that concerns the bedroom, so before we climb into bed and get sweaty, I need to get this off my chest." I really couldn't imagine what her big secret was. And I was not sure I cared much, but whatever was on her mind, it was clearly important she say it. I liked the thought of nothing being on her chest, although the shirt she had borrowed from my closet was mostly unbuttoned, tight across her breasts, and looked rather awesome. I took an eighth of a step backwards, prepared to listen intensely.

"Sure, go ahead. I'm listening but relax. I can't think what you would have to worry about."

"Well, that's just it. I'm terrified that when you hear what I have to say, you might panic. Silly maybe, but I know if we can talk it all the way through without you or me losing it, we will be ok. So...," she paused and took a deep breath, "I have a big, big, big favour to ask."

"Anything. Whatever you need."

"This is going to sound crazy, especially as I want to talk about a little kinky stuff I'm worried you might freak out about, but..." She stalled again. Then very earnestly asked, "Can you trust me?"

"With everything Marcy! Name it." *Sounds serious.*

"Well, this is going to sound weird, so indulge me. I promise you won't be disappointed." Shy smile. "When I have bad guys I want to pin down when they don't want to talk to me I...well, I cuff them so they stay put. I want to know you won't—or rather can't—run away from me. I want to cuff you while we talk it through. That way, I know I can safely start this conversation without it ending before it's begun." She lowered one hand slowly down my side and across my hip and grazed the front of my pants. "I will make it fun, I promise," she winked.

What the hell? Total overkill. I couldn't think of a kink she would really have that would freak me out that much, but maybe the cuffs were part of it. I decided to play along. I kind of needed to play along. I nodded, and I nervously held out my wrists.

Marcy backed me up to the window where her gun, badge, and cuffs sat on the chaise lounge. She had me stand facing a chair she had placed in front of the window; and she picked up her cuffs, then slowly, one hand at a time, and one slow click at a time, cuffed my wrists behind my back. As each click locked me into place, my breathing and heart rate sped up a notch, too. And little Ethan got a little bigger. I felt her behind me, fiddling with each cuff to ensure I was comfortable.

"Ok, nearly ready. I don't want you running with your hands behind your back and falling, so hold still." Marcy pulled a housecoat belt from her pocket and, moving me slowly and reassuringly, tied each of my feet to a separate leg of the chaise lounge. I was stretched out and going nowhere. Then she stood up and gave me a long, deep, and passionate kiss, and pressed her tummy into my erection.

When we broke apart I whispered, "OK. Relax and spit it out. Let's hear what your kink is. I can't imagine it would upset me, unless you do weird things with puppies and kittens. I want to get back to that 'kissing me better' on the bed part."

"Oh, Ethan," she said, smiling playfully, "I said I wanted to talk about a kink, but I didn't say it was *my* kink, did I? I want to talk about your kink babe!" From her back pocket, she produced a Polaroid and held it for me to see. *Crap. Crap. More crap.* I looked back and forth between her and, well, the 'me' in the photo. I expected her to be angry, but she was smiling indulgently.

"Er...that's not what it looks like," I stammered, mind racing for what else it could be, if not what it looked like.

"Shush!" she said, kissing me quickly and putting one finger on my lips.

"Before you say something stupid, there's no need to explain. I've already talked to Gwen. I know about your game, and about your fun side. I want to know more. I want to know everything. Every detail. No secrets. This..." she waved the Polaroid, "I can deal with, and enjoy. Look, I'm having fun right now for instance." She gently cupped the front of my pants for a long second, then stepped back and continued.

"In the spirit of openness, I'll admit it threw me a curve ball, and I was upset. There was some arm-waving, and some threatening words, but Gwen and I had a long conversation about abuse and psychology and I ended up more intrigued than angry. She's a smart one. I'm adjusting to it, so if you are straight with me, you have nothing to worry about. Well, other than that now you are mine to toy with mercilessly. Gwen 'grand-mothered' the last five challenges you must complete to me. Woman-to-woman thing. Non-negotiable babe."

"Marcy, I don't know what to say. I'm not going to freak out, especially if you aren't. I worried that, with what you went through as a girl, this would drive a wedge between us. You can let me out of the cuffs and we can talk. I certainly need a big drink!" My mouth was dry, and I was sweating for Canada.

"Oh no, Ethan. I want to see what this game is like. Last night we killed The Kingman. We solved a case. You know what that means?" She was grinning from ear to ear as she rolled her plan fully into view. She reached forward very slowly and grabbed my cock and gently and very sensuously stroked it back and forth through my shorts. *Holy crap!*

"Let's get these clothes off and start the challenge, shall we? I figure you can afford to replace these rags." Without waiting for an answer, she reached under a cushion and pulled out a pair of kitchen scissors. She quickly cut away the remains of my clothing, and I was blushing, naked, and at half-mast. She had my full attention.

Marcy pulled the chair by the window to the back of the room and sat down in it, but I couldn't turn her way as my legs still straddled the chaise lounge. The way my legs were bound meant I was forced to face the window, and I had to look over my shoulder to where she sat to see her giggling back at me. She produced the remote control for the room and waved it. She touched a button, and all of the lights on my side of the space came on full. I was spotlighted, blinking and trussed up like a turkey; she remained in the shadows.

"I was playing with this clever device earlier. If I push this button here, all of the blinds go up." She touched it and, with a whir every blind in the bedroom slowly began to rise. *Holy crap.* I couldn't move or hide, tied as I was, with Yaletown and the west side of Vancouver about to see me in all my embarrassed glory. I was considering throwing myself facedown, despite my hands being behind me. Everything stopped, except my racing heart. And the sweat had leapt onto my body, trickling and tickling as it made its way over my clenched muscles. Marcy had pushed the button again and stopped the blinds, which had only opened a couple of inches.

"So here is my game Ethan. We are going to have a serious talk. I ask a question, then you can ask me one. Three questions each. If my cop spidey-senses tell me you are holding back — or God help you — are lying to me, then the blinds go up all the way and I walk out, and your maid can find you when she does the rounds. I'm not saying we would be over, but it would be a stumble and a reset. Instead, I want to give you what I believe you want. A high-risk encounter, and a chance for us to get closer to each other." She paused, and I waited. Little Ethan jumped about and twitched with excitement. He really is a treacherous little bastard.

"My question first. I know this is all a bit awkward, but I'm genuinely glad I discovered your kink. I would never have guessed, but had you never told me and hidden it, that would have been worse. So, question one: Can you be OK I found out?"

I didn't need to think about this at all. "Despite the fact I might die of embarrassment, yes. I think I'm relieved you know, if I'm honest. It's a secret I didn't want to have and had no idea how to resolve. Didn't think of this approach, but hey!"

She considered me. "Good. No show for Vancouver yet. Your turn. Ask me something!"

"Do you think my kink is an issue for us? It's not something I really need. It was just fun."

She pondered for a long moment. "I think you could live without it, Ethan, and you don't need it. But you want it. A lot. It's a part of you. I don't think you are lying to me, so you can keep your blinds down for a while longer, but don't lie to yourself either. To answer your question, I think it could be fun. I'd never considered it, and as you could guess I have to work out how it relates to my abusive mom and dad. Tonight is high stakes for us. We need to come out of this closer, and we seem to be headed that way." She had said that seriously but brightened suddenly. "After tonight, I get to play with you four more times and it will be more fun, and less risky. Well for me at least," she giggled. "OK my turn again. Any other kinks I should know about? And I have my finger on the button, Ethan, and I'll know if you are hiding anything. Don't try to cover anything up!"

I took my time. I was not sure I really knew that answer, but I wanted to, and I wanted her to as well. "To be honest, I'm not entirely sure where the line between a kink and fun sex lies, but I think this is the only obvious kink I've ever acted on. I have fantasies. I've had no one to explore them with. We can work that out together. Good enough? My question." I said, rushing out a joke to relieve the tension "Is Gwen still alive and out of jail?" That made her laugh out loud. If I weren't so vulnerable, I would have told her she actually snorted loudly.

"Yes, she's thriving. A hoot. We may have conspired a little. She's asked for a full report by the way. I haven't decided what to tell her yet! Maybe another photo? I'll think about it. That was your second question by the way."

"What?"

"Shush. I want to explore this side of myself. And I want to explore it with you. It's going to be hard for me sometimes — really hard — separating my emotions and memories from my abused early years and what I see on the job, from our fun and fantasy. I need you to ground me and support me. To trust that I can work through it, and not mollycoddle me. I would hate that. I'll get upset and confused, but I will deal with it. Just love me whatever. Accept me whether I like it or reject it. Question three: Can you do all of that Ethan? Can you be strong for me, and sometimes tough, but tender as needed? Support me as I work through it and not freak out when I freak out? And accept me wherever I end up? Promise me?"

"I can certainly promise to love you throughout this journey. That's easy. I want to promise I can support you exactly like you've asked, but this is new territory for both of us, and I am sure I won't get it right every time; so in such a vulnerable position as I am, I can't promise to be perfect. But I can promise to give it one 110 percent effort to always be what you need when you need it. Can that be enough?"

"Oh yes. And 'can that be enough?' was your last question." She laughed. "You are going to have to get better at watching what you say if you are going to make this harder for me." She walked over to me, wagging her finger, and slowly looked me up and down. My mouth was dry and cold. I realized I had been breathing hard. Marcy held the remote in front of me, where I could see her finger on the button for the blinds. *Click.*

Crap! She pushed it. She pushed it. I hadn't lied. I stood there in dread, getting more alarmed with each inch the blinds climbed. Marcy held my eyes locked in hers. When the blinds were up about three feet, the room plunged into darkness. She had killed all of the lights with the remote.

The city was revealed in its sparkling glory, and I stood bound and naked in its reflected glow, mostly but not completely hidden in the shadows. Marcy unbuttoned her makeshift nightshirt and let it drop and the night played across her smooth, creamy skin. She slowly knelt between my legs, reached up, and cupped me tenderly.

"That's good enough, Ethan. We are going to have some fun exploring together." And then, tentatively at first, she began to suck me.

*

From our magical reconnection on the Sea Star to the startling revelations of last night, I had been worried about money. Not mine — as I have more than God it seems — but Marcy's. She owns half a house, has some modest savings, and gets a cop's salary. If we were really going to be together, our financial disparity would become an issue. She is a proud woman who would shy away from taking from me. I had never thought that having too much money would be a problem, and it worried me. We lay naked, her head on my chest, her breath warm and salty on my shoulder. She slept easily, and I watched the dawn creep into the room and climb the bed as thought about money. I couldn't help it. I felt driven to remove all obstacles.

As it got steadily lighter outside, with pink hues turning white, I flipped a sheet over us both for modesty and Marcy stirred.

"Getting shy now?" she whispered, nuzzling my neck. God, she made me feel sexy. We came together and made the sheet jump around for a while, then lay back blissfully. Sweaty and satisfied.

"So, what's next?" she asked, with a more serious tone. I knew she meant with the traffickers, but I decided to risk poking the money bear instead.

"There's a big answer, and a small answer. The small answer is to go back to work, and wait for the authorities to do their thing, taking the precautions we can, and following up on the few loose ends that we can tug on."

"And the big answer?"

Here we go! "It's kind of the same, but if we are both 'all in' to being together, we don't stay in limbo, we can get on with setting up the life we want to build. In doing so, it would change the game plan. It could give us some strong advantages in fending off the traffickers. I have an idea to talk through with you, and I kind of want to cuff you to something to stop you running away or punching me. Oh and I think I owe you a taste of your own medicine."

She stretched like a tigress, arching and twisting, then relaxing to lie a foot or two away on her side, propped on her elbow where she could size me up dangerously. "I'm listening. No cuffing."

"Well, you're a great cop, which is not really a job so much as your life. Through it we have the advantage of being connected to the authorities, and that is helpful. But it also limits us, in two ways. Firstly, there are rules you must follow, both in terms of what you can legally investigate, you have to obey your chain of command, and secondly you only get a certain number of vacation days. Your job ties you down, both in our relationship, but also in our ability to remove the threat we face."

"Ethan, I couldn't give up my work, even if I wanted to. I have to eat."

"I know, but it's bigger than that. You are going to get mad if I offer you some of my money." She was beginning to look upset. I pressed on.

"But hold that thought. Let's jump ahead. Confirmed. Married or wherever. Our 'all in' has held fast. I'm not a prenup sort of guy, so just living with me for twelve months makes us common law, and legally we will be sharing finances more than you likely want to. If we are all in, we should be all in and jump ahead. I see you have three issues. The first is the biggest. You are, quite rightly, proudly independent. I love you for that. Secondly, you won't be financially dependent on me just in case down the road, we stop being together. You won't rely on me, just in case the worst happened. Third, you need to help people who need you, who can't help themselves. You need to protect people. You are a cop, a hero, and warrior. You can't change that, and I wouldn't want you to. It's part of why I love you. You are my warrior." That seemed to calm her a little.

"Also think about this: I help people too. I operate in ways you can't. I don't have your legal powers, but I don't have the limits you do. No boss or chain of command. No politics. Almost infinite resources. Maybe *Ethan and Marcy Crime Fighters Incorporated* could do more good as a team than we are doing separately. So, following that thread, if you worked for a private company, even if it didn't charge those who can't pay, you would expect a salary, right? But we are starting this fantastic adventure, and just in these few days I've almost pissed you off several times. [*Did she eye-roll?*] We can't say for certain today you should throw away your career for this new venture. If we broke up in a year, your future financing is disrupted.

"Now you know my net worth is ridiculous. On paper it's many billions. That's only Canadian dollars, but it's still ridiculous. If I had to liquidate and turn it into cash, really it is a mere three or four billion. Yet you would poke me in the eye if I offered you some. You don't love me because I have money, but it is a part of me. You love me partly because it doesn't mean everything to me. So don't hold it against me — against us — either. If we are going to be together, I want us to travel. Often. And live large. Are you really going to fly coach while I sit up front? If you were you, and I were a garbage collector—a cute garbage collector of course—and I said I couldn't be with you because of our financial differences, would you hesitate to offer me money to save my ego? Of course you would. Actually, Garbage Guy Ethan would be OK with being a toy boy, but let's imagine. But you would respectfully offer me say, five thousand dollars — perhaps as a loan — if it made a difference, yes?"

"Of course I would. That's not a lot of money for your happiness, sweetie," she purred with sweet sarcasm.

"Assuming you retire at 65 instead of tomorrow, I guess you would earn roughly two million or so. Two million out of my stupid pot of money, is way less as a ratio than if you gave your sexy, well-hung garbage guy five thousand. But ratio aside, it's too big to accept. I know that. But how about this: What if we put that much in a trust fund? If we ever spit up, it's yours without question. It's a guarantee that costs me nothing but lets you make this huge leap of faith with me. If you leave me, you can choose to give it all or any portion of it back." She was getting upset again.

"Park that thought for a minute. So, tomorrow you go in and resign, or maybe take a sabbatical if you like. We start our new venture. You can even start other business ventures. I use my pool of money as a resource; I don't really think of it as money. If we lived together you would borrow my car, right? You would swim in my pool, right? So use my money the same way. You won't even make a tiny dent, believe me. You are a force of nature. I know that whatever you do, given time, will bring in more money than you take out. I bet with a funding start, in a couple of years, you will have made that two million and paid back anything you borrowed. The yachts, the drones, the gadgets and bodyguards — just think of them as company resources. Put them to work, to help me. I'm trying to improve the lives of others. Help me. Think of it as spending for them, not for you. We will help way more people if you help me do it than we would separately. And have fun, too.

"I know it's crazy, but I want us to take on this adventure as partners on equal terms. It's not a case of swallowing your pride. You say you are all in, but is that just romantically, or is it to have a big life together too? If you want to continue being a cop, you have my full respect and support, of course. We can make anything work, if that's what you really want. Or perhaps, just perhaps, we can have more fun solving slightly different, but not less important, problems for way more people. I know fighting for people suffering from abuse is important to you. Do it with an army, not alone or with a stretched and jaded police force."

Marcy rolled onto her back and closed her eyes tight, and let out a long, long breath. It felt like she was blowing her old life slowly away, and I hoped her next breath would be a commitment to a new life. Suddenly, she threw the sheet off and jumped out of bed, and shamelessly wiggle-walked sexily towards the shower room. She called over her shoulder as she paraded in front of Vancouver's breakfast crowd, "You are truly nuts Ethan! But I'm on leave for a few days. Show me around this world of yours, and I'll see how it fits me. Let's start with your shower! Try to keep up, garbage toy boy— let's scrub you clean. Then a big breakfast." I found myself letting out a breath I hadn't realized I had been holding. I tried to maintain some decorum and dignity and not run after her too quickly.

*

The tour of the pool, spa, dojo, and business facilities took an hour, including fifteen minutes of Marcy talking to Gia and arranging her first training session for later in the day. There was electricity fizzling between them, and I knew not what it meant but was smart enough to stay out of it. We ended the tour at the operations centre, and Kelsie was a mother hen, showing off the capabilities and systems and fussing a little over her team to make sure they were at their best. It was cute.

Kelsie handed operations off to her assistant and we adjourned to a small war room adjacent to the control centre to go over what we knew. We had nothing new on who had overridden Preece, but Kelsie walked us through the logs of the drone traffic from the night at Stave Lake. She had taken the fact that the mystery missiler had gone undetected as a personal affront and had barely slept, as she analysed everything in an effort to explain it. I went through the data with her — more to make her feel better — as I knew that before we started she would have been more than thorough.

"What was found at the missile launch location?" asked Marcy the cop. All business.

"The evidence of a missile launch, such as heat damage to shrubs, chemical residue, and so on. Some size-ten partial boot prints, common brand in North America. Two pinpoints of disturbed lichen on a large rock consistent with the legs of a rifle's bi-pod. Someone had a long gun, possibly a Barrett 50 cal, pointed your way. Nothing else. The bank was muddy and the woods overhang the shoreline with a dense floor-covering under the trees. No footprints or other signs of disturbance, so the working theory is water-borne ingress and egress." Kelsie listed this all off professionally and concisely.

"A Barrett and a ground-to-air missile — or two — is not something you swim around with," observed Marcy, "so there would be a Zodiac or small boat involved."

"I think the same, but there is nothing on the drone footage. Look here," said Kelsie, her fingers alive on the keyboard, throwing images up onto the array of screens in front of her. "This is sped up, time-synchronized imaging from three different drones of that area for the period leading up to the shot." We watched it run through in silence, daylight quickly slipping into dusk, then into night. The image switched tones to a mostly black or green or blue screen depending on if we watched the natural, night-vision, or heat-vision footage. Nothing but water, trees, birds, deer, and seals.

On the third pass, it was Marcy, with her keen cop senses and analytical brain again who spotted the anomaly. I had been focused on the main body of water, and the launch site, but she drew our attention way off to the far side of the lake, which at that point was about a mile to the west.

Marcy asked, "What's that weird fuzzy distortion moving north up the bank?" Kelsey adjusted the natural light image back to normal speed and zoomed in as much as the footage would allow. We watched it for a few minutes.

"There's not really anything there; it's just the water on the beach moving," offered Kelsie.

But Marcy persisted. "Looking at this normal speed yes, but at the faster speed it couldn't be natural, could it? It's too methodical, moving along the beach. Go back earlier to when the boats left after setting up the cabin. What does their wake look like?" Kelsie did her magic and sped back to that segment and zoomed into the wake of the small boats as it rolled up onto the beach.

"On the shoreline it looks the same, except it has a wake attached between that effect and the boat generating it," I said, puzzled. "Does this mean there was a boat with no wake? If it is some sort of stealth craft that didn't leave a wake, then why the disturbance on the beach? This doesn't make sense." I looked at Kelsie, who was white as a sheet; shocked, and clearly upset, processing some horror I hadn't yet caught up to.

"Kelsie, what is it?"

"There's a boat, Ethan, with a wake. The footage has been tampered with. That's the only logical explanation."

"Then go back to the original stream, or the onboard buffer," I said. "We need to see that boat."

"But that's the point," she said painfully. "This is the onboard buffer footage. You can't alter that once it's written. There is no processor on the drone that can do it." She looked scared.

"Then what makes you think it was altered after the fact?" asked Marcy, before I could.

"It wasn't. I mean it must have been altered as it was being written—in real time. Live. An algorithm that duplicates the sea surrounding an object, laid over the object as camouflage. There are tools in use today that can do that on the fly. Some security forces do that when sending troops into an area that is covered by CCTV. It's analogous to the old movies where someone records footage, then plays it back so the bad guys don't realize it was interrupted — only better. We have high-speed processors and specialist microprocessors to render the new footage simultaneously. It has limitations if the background is too complex. It wouldn't work on a crowded street for example, too many moving things to create and recreate, but water or trees, or plain ground is possible."

"Are you saying our drones were hacked while they flew?" I asked, trying to catch up.

"I wish I were, no. Can't be done, as there is no link between the recording firmware and the flight telemetry or footage transmission system, and the camera buffer system."

"Do we need to get Darcy to come and look at this?" I asked. Kelsie was technically top notch, but her sister had crazy superpowers where this stuff was concerned. I reached for my cell.

"No. Don't do that." She stalled out, deflated and out of words. "That's the issue. You need physical access to the drone to do this, *before* the flight. And Darcy set these units up from scratch. Herself. She insisted on them being perfect as you were going into danger, and she essentially rebuilt each one and checked it personally. I can't believe someone would mess with her code, without her noticing. I'm afraid... I'm worried this was her doing but can't believe she ever would. Maybe she's being blackmailed?"

We sat in silence looking at each other. Marcy, who had never met Darcy and had no personal connection, broke the spell.

"Where is she? Let's just ask her. I want to speak to her if she knows something." As she said that, both of our phones chimed with a message. We both automatically checked our phones.

"LEAVE DARCY OUT OF IT. MEET ME AND I WILL EXPLAIN. THIS IS WAY OVERDUE ANYWAY. I FIRED THE MISSILE."

Marcy and I both stood at the same time and looked at each other. It was clear we had both received the same message — worryingly — someone was eavesdropping in our screened sanctum. I showed it to Kelsie. I raised an eyebrow. Kelsie nodded.

"WHERE? WHEN?" I messaged back.

"I'LL COME TO YOU. 15 MINS. TELL YOUR TEAM TO LET ME IN, ON FOOT, BACK ALLY DOOR, HOODIE AND JEANS."

I left and ran up to my suite while we waited and returned with a Glock 18. Marcy was already armed. When I came back into the room, it had chilled considerably, as Darcy had appeared. She and Kelsie were in tears, and Darcy kept apologizing. Her face awash with black streaks of makeup, eyes puffed and throat sore, she had obviously been crying for some time. Aside from confirming she had been eavesdropping on our conversation, and that she informed whoever was coming to visit us what we had discovered and begged them to let her come forward, she would not be drawn further. Eventually, she clammed up totally under Marcy's increasingly unsympathetic stare. Kelsie was beside herself, but loyally sat with her sister and offered comfort, glaring back at Marcy.

Under the supervision of my security team, the visitor was let in and patted down. We watched this on the monitor. He had a grey hoodie and blue cap so we couldn't see his face, but he seemed to be late twenties, very fit looking. As we watched him walk across the TV screen, something about his gait gave me a chill. Something was not right.

A minute passed before the door to the war room opened, and the visitor walked in, accompanied by two guards.

All of the air left the room; my neck hairs shot to the ceiling. I couldn't breathe. I looked at Marcy, but she was already on the move. She launched herself at the visitor, threw her arms around his neck and made an undignified gurgling noise. Max Bremmer, Marcy's little brother and my one-time best friend... back from the dead. Grinning like an idiot, teary-eyed, older, tanned but very much alive.

11: Rocks and Hard Places

As mad as I was that all of these years Max had let us think he was dead, once we heard his amazing tale, I was left hoping I would have had his courage and made the same sacrifices. I hugged him but wanted to slug him. My eyes stung, and I had a lump the size of a baseball in my throat.

Towards the end of his first tour, Max had agreed to go undercover for the MPs — the military police — in the Afghan theatre of operations. It was a very close-kept secret that some of the explosives and components in a recent spate of roadside attacks using IEDs had come from our own side. It is a relatively small force from Canada, so it shouldn't have been so hard to find who was selling us out to ISIL, but efforts to uncover who it was were stalled. Max had gotten closer to uncovering the source than anyone, and the traitors had panicked and evidently decided to set Max up for assassination. An IED took out the Hummer that Max and his partner were patrolling in, severely wounding Max's colleague, and it should have vaporized Max as well. However, through a bizarre twist of fate, Max was no longer in the Hummer when the explosive device went off. As the Hummer had pulled under a bridge, Max had stepped out to meet clandestinely with an informer, and his partner had continued on to circle the block, intending to pick Max up on the next circuit so that no observer would have known about the meeting.

When the vehicle didn't return, Max, suspecting the worst, contacted his handler and was devastated when he realized the blast he had heard from a distance had critically wounded his partner. In what transpired to be a masterly quick-witted decision, Max and his handler agreed on the cover story of Max being killed in the explosion, which would allow Max the freedom to continue the investigation totally under the radar. His informant had just confided that his cell was set to make their next trade for explosives that very night and revealed its location. Max went immediately to a small mosque that overlooked the location of the impending trade, and at dusk — at great personal risk — climbed the minaret to a high ledge from where he could observe the transaction and the identity of the traitor.

When Max later met with his commander, he explained that the amount he observed being exchanged was far bigger than the amount that was turning up in IEDs. The brass was worried that shipments were working their way up through Egypt and Libya and into Europe. There was a suspicion that this material was supporting some of the recent terror attacks in London and Paris. They left the traitor in place, but made it difficult to steal, or in a few cases let him steal defective explosives or weapons. No attempt was made to install a tracking device into the contraband for fear of letting on that they had been discovered.

Fluent in French, albeit Québécois rather than Parisian, dark-skinned, sunburnt, and with a contact already in a terror cell, Max volunteered to work to trace the route and expose it. It was highly dangerous, and Marcy grew seriously frightened as Max recalled the details, even though he had clearly survived.

Max spent time posing as a potential recruit and deepening his connections to the terror cell, posing as a disenfranchised French Tunisian, and eventually joined ISIL. The intelligence community had created a full backstory, including authentic documentation and references in Tunisia. The intelligence Max gathered proved to be some of the most important in the war effort in general and made possible only because we all thought he was dead. The operations lasted a year, and Max received two field promotions, and some medals he would not discuss as they didn't exist either.

When Max talked about how hard it was not to contact us, and even his parents, there wasn't a dry eye in the room.

Max explained that he was still actively in place, working out of St Tropez in France. His ISIL cell was working through a group of drug and human traffickers, who were smuggling their products out of ports from Marseille, St Tropez, and Nice, bound for the USA.

As part of his deal to stay undercover, he insisted on regular updates about his family back home and had followed Marcy's career closely, with incredible pride. He choked up again as he explained that, through his contacts in the military and CSIS — Canada's secret service — he learned about The Kingman's threat to Marcy, who it appeared coincidently was part of the group he had been working with in Europe.

Max also knew Jimmy Fullerton, Darcy's husband, who had flown out from time to time to brief Max on some of the newer surveillance technologies he was using, and when it came to light I was involved and we were both going to be used as bait, Max had dropped everything and flown directly here to provide an unofficial overwatch. Max's old commander had been transferred and now oversaw operations at Comox air base on Vancouver Island. He helped pull strings for Max to make the crossing from Europe, in the back seat of a CF18 training aircraft, and then by helicopter to the Stave Lake area.

Max had convinced Darcy and Jimmy to mask his involvement, and the combination of the threat of official secrets, laws, and his meritorious work against ISIL convinced them to play along, but it had not sat well with them, especially Darcy. Darcy had begged Max to come forward, and when it was clear Darcy's involvement was going to become a problem for her, he had agreed without hesitation. And here we all were.

"So how did you dodge surveillance before firing the missiles — thank you by the way — that saved our asses at the lake?"

"I picked the weapons up at Comox, courtesy of my old commander, who personally piloted me into the site in a Canadian Forces Zodiac. Darcy provided a thermally neutral tent, which I set up as a hide, and it was coated in light-absorbent material so as long as I didn't move, I was invisible. I was inserted while your site was still being set up, and my ride took off and left me there. Once I fired the missile, I placed all of the equipment in a weighted, waterproof sack and towed it fifty feet out into the lake, where it settled on the bottom and we picked it up this morning. I egressed using scuba gear and an electric underwater tug to the south shore, well out of surveillance range."

The conversation turned to less operational matters, and we all slowly withdrew to leave Marcy and Max to catch up with each other on family events. I wasn't sure I wanted to be there when Max learned I had been boffing his sister.

Darcy remained inconsolable, convinced she had shown disloyalty and would be fired. I did what I could to reassure her, reminding her that had she not acted as she had, I might not be here to fire her. Somewhat relieved, she left with Jimmy and Kelsie.

So now we had the answers to the two mysteries: Preece being overridden, and the missile. We had run out of leads so I looked forward to seeing if Max had any insights as to our status with the trafficking group, and advice on the next steps we had to take. In Vancouver, playing with small-time crime, I had many advantages but even with my wealth, I was totally over my head when it came to large-scale international crime such as this. Mostly, I was missing Marcy, and wanted to support her while she was reuniting with Max, and hopefully patch the huge hole in her heart his death had caused.

*

Alerted by the bang on the door, and after checking the security camera, I let Max into my apartment at 4:45 pm. He and Marcy had spent the afternoon catching up, and it was now our turn.

"Marcy had an appointment with someone called Gia, which she didn't want to break, so I've come to make my peace with you," Max offered. Part of me still wanted to slug him.

"You probably want to take a swing at me," he laughed.

"No of...well yes...and no.... Come here you stupid fucker!"

Man hug, back slap, man hug. All healed. *Not sure why women draw this stuff out so much.*

"Scotch?"

"Sure!"

"Since you left, we invented all this language for scotch: Peaty, smoky, a bunch of earthy adjectives. Any preference?"

"Smooth would do. I'm old school."

I poured us a couple of fingers each of Tamdhu 50. Well, it's not every day the man who is practically your brother is resurrected.

"So who's Gia?"

"She is my martial arts and fitness instructor. Mega hard-ass. Kicks my butt regularly, and according to my neighbour, a hottie."

"That explains why Marcy was all tits and attitude heading down there. By the way, you dickhead, she's mad for you. If you mess with her, I'll kick your ass in ways Gia hasn't heard of, brother!" He actually looked pretty scary.

I tipped my glass his way. "I love her too much, Max. There has only ever been her. And anyway, I mess with Marcy, and she will kick my ass. But if she's taking on Gia she is getting a surprise. Olympic banter-weight Taekwondo, Woman's MMA champ, and eats snakes for breakfast. It won't be pretty."

"Crap, should we go separate them?"

"You sure were banged around by that IED; you're nuts. Get between those two? I'm out. Let's wander down in thirty minutes on some pretext and pick up the pieces."

By unspoken agreement, we didn't talk about 'next steps' so we could include Marcy in the discussion, but in 30 minutes we covered almost all other aspects of our missing decade, at least at a high level. Max had lived on the ragged edge, on his wits and some unique but classified training, which he glossed over. I could gather he dropped out of his undercover life on occasion to take in the latest intel, fighting skills and techno updates and was some combination of Bruce Lee, MacGyver, and James Bond. But no details were forthcoming, despite D50 scotch.

After 45 minutes, I grabbed a couple of bottles of water and a couple of beers so we had both options covered, and we wandered down to the dojo. We entered to find Marcy and Gia talking amicably, both very sweaty, each with a towel around their neck. When they saw us, Marcy walked over to give me a hug but had a slight stoop and a limp that wasn't there before. As Gia turned, I could see she had the beginnings of a black eye. *That's my Marcy.* I held Marcy, and checked her out like her personal mother hen, as I heard Max say to Gia, "Do you have time to spar with me Gia?"

Oh-oh... protective bother.

"Max!" Marcy tried to call him off, but he was starting to circle Gia.

Gia squared fractionally, centring her 120 lbs over the balls of her feet, looking Max up and down.

"I don't mind putting two Bremmers on the mat in one day," Gia replied. *Is she flirting?* I must have sparred hundreds of times with Gia, and she was all business. Now she was a chemical reaction on legs, focused entirely on Max

This should be interesting. Marcy and I opened the two beers and took a seat on the weight bench.

I must admit, when Gia puts me down on the mat I don't see much: she's there in front of me, then I'm on the mat in some choke hold or other. So it was fascinating to watch her spar with Max. Max was fast. I could barely keep up with his moves from 20 feet away, in a ringside seat. But somehow from here Gia was like that speck in your bath, the one you try to catch but the bow wave of your hand pushes it away, so it continually eludes you. She appeared to be in slow motion, but always a step ahead of Max, who was striking like a mamba. He faked left and low, then swivelled, his leg whipping around at terrifying speed towards Gia's forehead. But she gracefully, and seemingly gently, leaned away and down, and like some fluid attracted by static electricity, seemed to spin with him and wrap around him. As her torso moved with his extended leg, her right leg swept the leg holding his weight, and they both went down hard. Gia's left elbow landed with precision and finality in Max's groin. I let out a long whoosh of air. *God that hurt. And she hadn't hit* me*!*

They both lay still, and to his credit, Max said, "Hit my sister again and I'll kick your ass again," and laughed.

"I want to tell you Marcy hits harder than you, but as you have yet to land a punch, I'll hold off on my assessment. At least Marcy landed a blow. A pretty good one at that."

Gia flowed like liquid up to a standing position and offered Max her hand. He took it. *Wow.* Hadn't seen him in years, but I could tell he was suddenly in love. And I'd be damned if Gia wasn't acting a little smitten, too.

"Ethan, I assume your mansion upstairs can furnish the four of us with cold beer," said Marcy, who walked over to Gia and put her arm around her inclusively. I went over and jokingly straighten his clothes and dusted him off, careful not to touch his left hand, which had been checking out the damage inflicted by Gia's elbow.

*

We ordered some pizza, and I called Kelsie to see if she could join us in a council of war. I asked about Darcy, who was still beating herself up but gradually coming around. When Kelsie joined us, and we had eaten, we discussed the traffickers and what we could do about them.

"Their principals are the Toussaint brothers, Landon and Seth," Max began. "Louisiana hillbillies with no scruples. Pure sociopaths, as is their mother Destiny, who is probably the brains. They operate out of southern Louisiana - though but no one knows exactly where — and have local and state law either in their pockets or too terrified to act against them. The FBI have had several runs, but don't have the resources to track them in the wilderness and swamps. Don't get me wrong, the FBI have committed manpower and aerial reconnaissance, but with the state and county radar operators on the Toussaint's payroll, they've been totally ineffective. What we know for sure is, multi-million-dollar yachts leave the south of France with both humans and pharmaceuticals on board, parade just outside the US territorial waters, and then pull into port without the product. They somehow transfer the girls and drugs across and into the Mississippi Basin, and they pop out in Montreal, Chicago, San Fran, or in your case Vancouver.

"The French police and Interpol are engaged in trying to interdict them across Europe and have had some success. When the yachts set sail, European law enforcement lose interest. To be honest, as bad as human trafficking is, it takes a second seat to terrorism, which consumes most of the resources these days.

"The US government doesn't really engage as it is outside the 12-mile limit. When the girls reappear, local law enforcement pick it up, but they are—no offence, Marcy—small potatoes, typically picking off maybe fifteen percent of the traffic."

"No offence taken. We know we are barely making a scratch, despite our full attention."

"Do you know which yachts carry their victims?" Kelsie asked.

"They never use the same ones. They rent from the thousands of luxury yachts for hire and pick a new one every time. But I have a contact in their organization. She can narrow it down for me to three to four candidates who set off together. No one knows which one actually has the girls onboard. We track them all on satellite and have intercepted one or two on a pretext, but no real progress is made. Even if we catch one—we save those women, which is definitely something—it doesn't stem the flow. We need to find the headquarters and take out the principals."

"What about interviewing the girls we free up here? They must know where they were taken."

"Not really. Blindfolded, drugged or in containers."

"I would have thought, with the resources you use to follow ISIL, Hawks, and Reapers and the like, you could follow them across the Atlantic." I offered.

"But that's just it, Ethan. Those resources are focused on tracking ISIL. They are not released on — and don't shoot me for someone else's words — minor trafficking duties."

Silence. After some glaring, Max put his hands up in surrender. Then came understanding; it was not his fault. We moved on.

"Ethan," said Kelsie, "remember when you solved the issue of the Asian whalers who were coming into local waters and poaching fish? Could we, you know...," she said hesitantly.

I smiled. I clinked beer bottles with Kelsie.

"Max, if you can line us up with a shipment, even if it is several vessels, we can track them and fill in the gaps between Europe and the Mississippi!"

*

Over several more beers, we fleshed out a plan. Marcy called Dennis Preece, filled him in and requested he use his contacts with CCIS and the FBI to be ready to swoop in if we located the Toussaint brothers and their HQ. We put a team together to go to St Tropez. Gia would not be left behind and threatened to quit if she couldn't accompany us as part of the personal protection team. I think Max was the 'us' she cared about most, but either way, she could not be put off. We seconded two men, Daniel and Barac from team Alpha, who both used to be French Foreign Legion. Although Max would help us get set up, he had to get back to his undercover role soon after we landed. We also seconded a crew from my Atlantic yacht, the Déjà Vu, which was currently being refitted in Copenhagen. They flew down and rented *Cassis*, a 130-foot 'boat' from Monaco, which was to be our Mediterranean forward-operating base. Kelsie and two of her team were packing up an impromptu, remote operations technical suite, gathering anything they could cannibalize or acquire hastily.

The oddest addition to our group was Gwen. I really didn't want her in the field with us, but I couldn't leave her here. Anyone close to me was a target for the traffickers, and *The Bean* was being renovated and 'de-bulleted.' In this first phase of the plan, the risks were low. We were an anonymous group of rich tourists. If our plan developed further, Gwen's extensive experience in psychology could be a valuable asset with victims of sex-trafficking we might be able to rescue. OK, busted: Marcy and I were also keen to pick Gwen's brain more about...you know...the kinky stuff.

Gwen was more than happy to join us for a Mediterranean cruise. She was aware that there was more to the trip, but we did not share all of the operational details. She was still shaken from the assassination attempt at *The Bean* and understood why it made sense to leave town until things cooled off. She was packing in a heartbeat, and I swear I heard her humming Ria Mae's *Clothes Off* as she vanished into her apartment.

12: Beware of Women Bearing Gifts

We worked into the night preparing, and at 11:20 pm a small convoy of SUVs rolled out of the car park and sprinted down First Street to Highway 1, then out to a smallholding we own just outside of Langley. We may have been being paranoid, but I figured it was possible that the major airports around Vancouver were being watched, and we couldn't rule out their being covered by snipers or worse. We were sneaking out via a circuitous route. We had two helicopters winding up as we arrived and transferred ourselves and twelve metal cases from the SUVs to the chopper's cargo holds; we were airborne within ten minutes of arrival. The choppers flew low, out to the north in a tight formation, and disappeared into the mountains. After ten miles weaving in a generally northern direction in the valleys, we wheeled left and climbed to 6000 feet, skimming the peaks until we could descend towards the Georgia Strait just east of Squamish, and drop down to 75 feet for the crossing to Comox. Comox has commercial air traffic but is primarily a Canadian Forces airport.

Max's ex-commander met us at the ramp and assured us record of our exit from Canada would be 'accidentally' delayed and our destination possibly even 'accidentally' mistyped. We boarded a rented Gulf Stream jet. All told, we were wheels up for Aruba 90 minutes after leaving Yaletown. Bruised or otherwise exhausted, most of us were asleep within 30 minutes of takeoff.

We landed in Aruba at dawn and rolled straight into a private hangar, where we showered and boarded a different rented plane and were lifting up and out over a shimmering turquoise sea by 8 am local time, heading farther east. The cabin staff served a light breakfast, complete with coffee and mimosas.

"I'm not pressing you on your future, Marcy," I quietly quipped just to her, "but as a cop you would be cooped up waiting for someone else to act, or at best, flying economy out of YVR. Just sayin', this is not only more fun, we are ten times more effective in this situation." Her reply was to dig her elbow into my injured side, reminding me I was not fighting fit and should behave myself. I was pretty sure the excited glint in her eye as she watched the golden Aruba beaches recede beneath us was a good sign.

We touched down at Toulon Hyères Airport near midnight local time, and again we were met by a contact of Max's. Toulon was far enough away from the operating area of the Toussaint gang and could accept international traffic on its nearly 7000 ft runway. Max's contact was a genuine French customs official, who inspected the plane briefly before recording its arrival, noting it was empty except for the crew. Purpose was listed as awaiting passengers headed for the USA. OK, that's a neat trick I can't use my money for, at least with my morals and scruples intact.

Feeling confident we had arrived unnoticed, we split into small groups and in rented cars, we travelled separately to a small villa owned by a friend in St Tropez. We arrived at just after 2 am and retired to our assigned rooms, exhausted. As I turned in, I got a text from Kelsie advising that the *Cassis* had departed Monaco and would arrive offshore St Tropez at 7 am.

*

The cases we had carried on the journey contained only equipment for the operations centre, some specialized drones, and some toiletries. So, after a light breakfast at 9 am — which had itself followed some leisurely, extended sex — Marcy and I set out on a shopping expedition. We didn't need much, our cover being rich tourists cruising the Med, and we didn't plan to host dinner parties.

The first two stores saw Marcy efficiently blow through, picking up several casual outfits, two bathing suits (a one piece and a rather fetching bikini), some workout clothes, some floppy hats, and some lingerie I was looking forward to seeing her in later. We gave everyone a small brick of cash to avoid leaving an electronic trail in Europe, and Marcy seemed to be getting comfortable with the idea of spending 'operational' funds. It was interesting to watch her shop: Quick and decisive—no grazing or browsing.

Our third stop was a menswear boutique, where we went through the racks and chose several outfits for me; I slipped into the changing room to try them on. After a few minutes, Marcy slipped quietly into the room with a pair of European-style speedo swim trunks. She leaned into me shyly and kissed me.

"Don't think I didn't notice we solved yet another mystery, Ethan," she whispered as she clipped me behind my earlobe with her pink tongue. *Oh-oh.* "The Caper of Max the Missile Man! Solved. Time to pay the piper, buddy; you are mine for the next few hours. Slip these on." I got hard so quickly I worried about squeezing into toy swim trunks. I obediently undressed and stretched out the speedo, trying to add inches to it, while she picked up the clothes I had been trying and said she was off to pay for them. Feeling very uncomfortable in the tight grip of the micro-trunks, I turned to put on my other clothes to cover them up. It was then I realized the crafty witch had scooped my street clothes, too. *Crap.* I was naked in a changing room, but for about 12 square inches of teal Lycra. I stood apprehensively, feeling silly but determined I wouldn't leave the store dressed like this, and was greatly relieved when Marcy popped back into the cubical with a pair of loose shorts, a Hawaii shirt, and some flip-flops. I hastily put these on before following her out.

She drove me out of town to the track of beaches to the west, and we passed several before she found the one she wanted. I worried a great deal that she appeared to have a plan, as that could not bode well for my modesty. We parked close to the dunes, locked the car, and stepped onto the sand. Marcy had purchased a small leather briefcase, which she opened and offered to me now.

"Shirt and shorts in here, slave." She laughed and threw her hair back with a dramatic flourish, which I actually found very sexy, and stepped away to watch me embarrass myself. I slowly stripped down to what was essentially a thong and flip-flops and reached to put my clothing into the briefcase. A bottle of sunblock peaked out of the case, and Marcy told me to lather some on. Apparently, I would be out in the sun for some time. She made some surprisingly lecherous faces as I slicked myself into an oily, nervous wreck.

"OK, slave. You are to play the role of my personal secretary. Look professional, confident, absurdly aloof, and follow me across the beach with as much dignity as you can muster in your fancy jock strap. Three steps behind me, carrying the case like a food tray." OMG, she was really getting into this.

As we topped the dune, we passed a sign that said "Clothing Optional" in English and French. I marched three really embarrassing paces behind Marcy as she strode confidently across the beach to the surf line, my eyes glued to the back of her head, not daring to look around. At the shore we turned right and paraded in full view of everyone on the beach. This section of the beach was about 300 feet wide, and a small fence marked the boundary to the next beach. A sign marked the next beach as "Topless", but not for the fully nude, and we quickly crossed that section to the far side, where another fence marked the next section as another clothing optional beach.

As we entered the next 'fully nude' section, I was slowly becoming more accustomed to my predicament and stole a few glances around. The beach was about 300 feet wide and 200 deep, some steep but short, wire-grass dunes at the top and a crisp and cool-looking ocean lapping across smooth, golden sand at the bottom. Marcy marched me to the middle of the beach by the water and stopped, took the case, opened it, and set it at my feet.

"The rest of your clothes in now, slave," she ordered with mock flare, eyebrows arching like an evil villain. I looked around. There were perhaps 50 people on the beach, most significantly older and in worse shape than me, and all looked totally comfortable naked. No one appeared to be paying us any attention at all. I took a big breath and peeled the Speedo down, scooped the flip-flops off as the scrap of material came over my ankles, and dropped the whole caboodle into the briefcase — along with my ego and dignity. Marcy picked up the case and snapped its combination lock shut with a click. *Crap.*

Marcy sat down gracefully on the beach and had me parade slowly left and right in front of her, and then even do a small work out; toe touching, dangling press-ups and all. The jumping jacks were spectacular. Little Ethan was obviously having as much fun as Marcy and managed to stay firm but pointed downward when not being swung in graceless arcs by my callisthenics. Thank God. Marcy reached into her purse and drew out a 20 Euro note and pointed to a woman selling ice cream at the top of the beach near the dunes.

"Go get us both a cone, ice cream boy!" she ordered. I found it incredibly erotic to be walking away from my clothes, which were locked out of reach in a case. I was having a problem keeping my erection under control. I thought about brick walls, cheeseburgers, Donald Trump, and anything to take my mind off being under Marcy's control.

If the ice cream seller thought there was anything unusual, I couldn't tell, but I knew I was glowing beet red as I stood holding two cones while she rooted around for change. The worst moment was when she offered me the change, but my hands were each holding a cone, emphasizing I clearly had no pockets. I relaxed slightly as I returned across the sand to Marcy, who was grinning like a loon.

"Oh my God! This is such fun," she sighed. "I can see you are straining against gravity, Ethan. Would it help if I told you what I feel like when I take you in my mouth? Or how great it feels when you slip your wet cock into me from behind when I'm on all fours?" *Oh my God.* I dropped my cone in the sand and ran into the sea to the sound of her squealing with laughter. I dove into the cool water, which had the immediate desired shrinking effect. I surfaced and stood waist deep, with gentle waves pushing my genitals rudely back and forth, to see Marcy standing up, briefcase in hand. With a wave, she took off at a brisk walk back towards the car and quickly disappeared into the topless-only section, leaving me stranded and naked.

After waiting for a few minutes for her to return, I realized she was not coming back. I waded a little deeper and swam parallel to the beach to follow her. There was no sign of her on the topless beach, so I kept going to the next clothing optional section, where we had started this little adventure, and saw she was waiting for me up by the dune. With a wave indicating I should follow, she vanished over the top, with the case containing my clothes swinging tantalizingly at her side. By the time I reached the top of the dune, she was already sitting in the passenger seat of our rental car, windows down, smiling back at me. I gingerly walked down into the parking lot and looked into the back seat for the case.

"Oh, that's locked in the trunk, Ethan. Here, this is to cover your blushes." She handed me the smallest hand towel in the history of hand towels. Barely a handkerchief. I used it to wipe off the excess moisture from the sea and slipped quickly into the driving seat.

"Home James!" she commanded.

"Really?" I looked at her nervously.

"Would you prefer to walk? Naked?"

I started the car and we pulled out of the lot, sinking as deeply into the seat as I could. So far with Marcy, I had been tied naked in a mostly dark bedroom and been nude on a nudist beach. It felt way more dangerous than it sounded, but technically it wasn't. But here, on the open road naked, we had changed gears dramatically.

There were not many cars around, and with my tiny scrap of cover spread strategically across my lap, we made good time back to St Tropez. As we came into town, Marcy reached over and gave me a few playful strokes and was rewarded by "little Ethan" the tent pole, who proudly lifted the hand towel completely off my lap.

Traffic was single file, and so other car occupants could see nothing but my head and shoulders, but I was worried about pedestrians when we stopped. No one seemed to pay any attention. We stopped at a set of traffic lights, and a moped carrying two girls in their twenties pulled up alongside us. I was glowing red like a traffic light. They were talking and had noticed anything amiss. Then with a sudden draft, Marcy whipped away the towel and cruelly threw it into the back behind my seat. To reach around to retrieve it would expose me to further risk of being spotted. I sat as still as a startled rabbit.

The lights changed and the moped took off, and we followed a little more slowly. Little Ethan was at full attention, even glistening a little with pre-cum in the late morning sun. Marcy directed me to a small, empty parking lot, and she jumped out and retrieved my clothes from the trunk. I gratefully put them on, then climbed out of the car. Marcy stepped up to me nervously.

"Am I doing this right, Ethan?" she asked honestly, looking up into my eyes to see if I was holding anything back. All I could do was reach down and slip my tongue into her mouth and kiss her eagerly. This level of crazy was more than I had ever done—or even dreamed about. I wasn't quite ready to admit what a kinky sod I was, even to myself. We kissed like wild teenagers, then broke apart embarrassed and got into the car.

"Marcy, that was mind blowing," I whispered hoarsely, as we sat catching our breath. "We need to make some time to talk about this...whatever it is. I love it, but shouldn't I feel ashamed? I don't, in case you are wondering. What can I do for you? It all seems a bit one sided!"

"Oh God no, Ethan. I'm wet and needy. I loved that, but I know what you mean. That was crazy and I'm not sure I'm a kinky person. But tormenting you like that? My God I loved it." We kissed again and then drove back to the villa, scurried like naughty teens into our room, and closed the door.

*

The *Cassis*'s tender picked us up in small groups and ferried us out to where the yacht was anchored, about 400 yards offshore. We selected the secondary reception room to be the main operations centre, primarily because it had a convenient window that looked out to a discrete sunbathing area where we erected various antenna, which we then covered with a tarpaulin, and doors out onto a large upper deck, which became our airport. The tarp would not impede our signals but would look to anyone overflying like some simple maintenance was underway. We tried to assist Kelsie and her team, but she quickly shooed us away, saying things would go more quickly without our help. Fair enough.

We had said a temporary goodbye to Max, which I could see was hard on Marcy, so soon after their reunion. Gia was nowhere to be seen. Kelsie had hacked Max's iPhone and given him a pair of *Bose Bluetooth* earphones, which were authentic but slightly modified. Her hack would secretly store any messages in encrypted form in the buffer of the headset and make a small crackle every few minutes if a message was waiting for Max to pick up. If he used a certain set of keystrokes on the phone, a hidden app would appear to facilitate voice or text communications with us but would otherwise always be hidden, even to most experts. There could be no chance that a message from us could ever appear when Max didn't want it to and give away the fact he was in contact with anyone outside of his covert persona.

The schedule of events was that Max would signal us when he knew the timing and yachts involved in the next trafficker shipments, and we had planned a test of our specialized drones for later that night. So all that was left was for the rest of us to pretend to be on vacation. On an amazing 130-foot luxury yacht.

Marcy, Gia, and Gwen seemed to become friends in no time, and as I had never socialized with Gia, I enjoyed learning her history and more of her personality outside of the dojo. With some subtle teasing from Marcy, and less subtle but genuine prodding from Gwen, Gia shyly admitted having an instant attraction to Max, which Marcy applauded enthusiastically. Whatever woman-to-woman shakedown the two of them had in the dojo that first day seemed to have erased their battle lines. Marcy had shared her initial impressions of Gia and admitted to some pangs of jealousy. Anyway, they had now switched from apparent prickly, tense eyeballing of each other to the beginning of what appeared to be a firm friendship. If I poked at either one for fun, I could feel them swivel together to defend each other at my expense. Good to know.

That night, Gia excused herself and left us alone with Gwen, who had not been at all shy to enjoy the trip so far. She told us about her tour of St Tropez, about a woman she had flirted outrageously with in the market square, and the breakfast she'd had al fresco at the wharf. She had been all over the *Cassis* and befriended the first officer, a cute little brunette her own age 'and leaning' Gwen assured us with a hammed up, lusty wink.

"How are you two lovebirds doing? Any questions for Dr Gwen yet?" She laughed. Both Marcy and I had fumbled through some pretty direct and embarrassing conversations with Gwen on our own but had never spoken to her together. Somehow it felt more awkward to discuss things within earshot of each other, but I thought that might be a great place to start.

"Gwen, we are clearly fascinated with this stuff, but I for one struggle to talk to Marcy about it. Ironically, it's easier to talk to you. Why?" I asked, more boldly than I felt. I sensed Marcy's gratitude next to me and it buoyed my confidence a little, so I continued. "I get that communication and negotiation what differentiates BDSM from pathological abusers, but it is hard to talk about."

"Well, think about it this way." She settled back on the couch into teacher mode. "The stakes are higher with someone you care so much about. That's why on edgier issues it can be easier to talk to your friend than your partner. It's counterintuitive, I know. You see each other naked, and have done all sorts of intimate acts, so why is it so hard to admit you like a specific kink? Because this uncharted territory is full of landmines, and if you tread on one, you could rock a fragile relationship. It's a charged topic, and any kink can polarize opinion and bring judgment, and you don't want to risk that with someone who matters to you. But me..., you like me, but it's not as risky."

I tried to confirm her idea with an example. "If I tell Marcy I like nudity risks, she says "OK, that's cool. Then I get confident and say that I like, I don't know -- spanking, say -- and she says 'great!' So, then I leap to wearing high heels -- which, for the record, does nothing for me -- and suddenly, I'm emasculated. Am I on track?"

"Exactly, but with me it doesn't matter if you rang a bell like that, which you can't then un-ring. It's just awkward. But emasculation is a weird bitch for several reasons. Firstly, I hate the word. There is an implication that for the woman to be on top in the bedroom, the man might be emasculated, but that in turn implies that for her to be powerful she must be more masculine. Times gone by, maybe. Want to be the CEO? Got to get your elbows up and act like a man. It's 2018 for God's sake. I am woman, hear me roar like a lioness, not hear me talk with a bull's voice. I say, a strong man can submit to a strong woman. That said, that is a common misuse of the word emasculate. Emasculate really means weakened, not less masculine. So again, are we saying if a man dresses as a woman he is weaker? So women should grow beards?

"Now don't get me wrong, I might hate the word, but never underestimate the negative force of emasculation. It can ruin a relationship in a heartbeat. It has two facets. Once your partner sees you emasculated, it is hard to, as I said, un-ring that bell. Not impossible, but it takes time to walk back from the impact of seeing your partner do something that really turns you off at a core level. The other issue, again often misunderstood, is that emasculation is in the eye of the beholder. You might wear high heels and worry about it because you see sissification as unmanning, but she might love it. Then you relax and scratch your arse then wipe your nose and—*boom*—she hates it and you are essentially emasculated. A minefield.

"BDSM, more than most things, is about trust. You are trusting her if you let her control your nudity or tie you up. Huge amount of trust there. But she must trust you to tell her what you like and don't. To say stop or slow down if she is hurting you too much. She gets you naked three ways you love but embarrasses you accidentally the fourth time. She must trust you are going to control your reaction to her mistake, and that it won't impact your relationship, or she can't take those risks.

"The more you talk about this stuff, the easier it gets, partly because you get used to hearing these crazy words coming out of your mouths, but more because you get used to seeing the other person hear you say something that isn't for them, and not overreacting or panicking. But you two have a way to go before you are completely comfortable with each other, and that is part of the fun." She laughed, with a hint of evil mixed with nostalgia, perhaps for her own more innocent times.

Marcy braved, "Well, we've blown through two of my challenges for Ethan, so I guess we are eager to find out what happens next, before we run out of excuses. What is reality going forward?" *Good question,* I thought. Wish I had been brave enough to ask and smart enough to think of it. Marcy reached over and took my hand, then swivelled in her seat and leaned back into me, pulling my arm over and around her in a defensive cuddle.

"That's both easy and hard. If you can get past the stigma, then the world is your oyster. You just have to decide if you like oysters, and if so, which variety. The hardest part is to get used to talking openly together about what you like, and harder still about what you don't. You need a mindset of going slowly and not getting worked up if you wander down a path that it turns out was not as fun as you thought, and have to retreat with or without upset or panic. Easy advice, hard in reality. But it's just practise and education."

"How will we know what we like?" I ventured.

"Well, there are probably things you've fantasized about. You could start there, by sharing them with each other. Wine helps. Or if you want to take a more structured approach, there are comprehensive lists online of almost every type of kink. Print them out and you can sit down together and rate each. You know, 'not interested,' 'curious,' 'not feeling it but will try if it appeals to you,' 'no way,' 'oh yeah, baby...' those sorts of ratings. That's an accelerator but can be quite off-putting to suddenly be discussing anal plugs and nipple clamps. There are even websites where you both separately put in your preferences, and then it tells you both your common areas and is silent about the conflicts. You can guess them, but it is a way to ease into it."

"I want to start slow. It feels accelerated enough as it is," said Marcy, looking up at me for support, which I gave with a squeeze of agreement.

I ventured, "I always imagined myself a big alpha male who liked to get naked occasionally? Am I a submissive?" That question had been plaguing me since Gwen and I first started our game.

"You have to work that out for yourself, but my radar would say no. Look, don't beat yourselves up; it is confusing. For some people their kink is existential; it is part of them and they live it every day. For others, probably most people, it's more akin to a hobby, like golf. They love to read about it, talk to other golfers, play a round often—pun intended—and they would miss it greatly if they couldn't do it, but it is just a hobby. Then, you can have submissives who like to lead, and others who like to be led. You can have dominants who enjoy pain and subs who enjoying being instructed to give it. Fifty Shades doesn't begin to cover the amount of variation and degrees. There is some science behind how we feel about and during a session, and BDSM has rules and conventions that people follow as a guide, but much of it is about being free from the society-imposed, largely heterosexual, rigid, and normalized rules, yet still safe. If it is consensual and healthy, fill your stiletto boots.

"Don't get me wrong, these are taboo waters for many, and still heavily stigmatized, so be careful around others. But if you are submissive, there are many types: Alpha subs, bratty subs, service subs, pain sluts. People who just feel safer, or more relaxed, if someone takes the stress of potentially embarrassing mistakes away. An endless list, which evolves and changes, and people blend the roles. The same for dominants: The teaser, who likes cat and mouse; the expert, who likes to demonstrate their expertise; the people who — not inappropriately — get a sense of awesome power bossing someone about, but the rules don't allow it in normal life; The sadist. Riggers who like tying, mommies and daddies, degraders, and so on."

"I like teasing Ethan with this little game. It's harmless fun, and I can see it turns him on a lot. And me too—it truly does—but I still don't understand the appeal of much of what I have heard about... that wasn't clear, let me try again. I think I could enjoy a light and playful spanking, even with my fears of abuse, but I don't understand *why* it appeals to me. I'm not talking real pain, but why would even a little pain appeal? Why do people like kinky sex?"

"I sometimes wonder the opposite. Why *don't* people like it kinky? What you will discover if you venture further down this path is that people who are open minded, good communicators, sex positive, and curious can be very open to sensation-seeking; and to trying BDSM. These competencies and values tend to make them successful in life generally, and so they typically have the resources, both personal and financial, to have a greater degree of choice about how and whom they have sex with, and they have more confidence to experiment.

"If you look at the statistics for sexually active 'normal' couples in North America, lovemaking on average takes nineteen minutes, which according to surveys is ten minutes of foreplay, in these enlightened times, and nine minutes of intercourse. Since women have learned in the last few decades more about their bodies, female orgasm rates have increased, especially where vibrators are involved in their lovemaking. But there is still an orgasm gap. Heterosexual non-kinky sex surveys say ninety-one percent of the time men have an orgasm, compared to just thirty-nine percent for women. Lesbians have a much higher hit rate. Women masturbating on their own survey in the seventy percent range. It's less awkward. You know what you like. You don't have to negotiate a special sex night or do it when the house is not tidy. My little vibe is always on duty but doesn't judge me if I am not in the mood.

"But largely 'vanilla sex' — as we kinky folk refer to it — tends to be limited to a small number of favoured positions that are repeated. And that is great. No issue with that at all. But compare it to the stats for those who practise kinky sex. BDSM typically, but not always of course, has a much higher degree of communication around it. Each session can be negotiated, but certainly the range of things are agreed in detail, in advance. We encourage research and education, partly because — like you two — it takes some working out, as it is more complex and potentially dangerous. Due to the way we approach it, it is normal for all parties to get what they want. Every time. If your schtick is to have an orgasm, you typically get at least one. On average, BDSM sessions are two to three times longer than the vanilla sessions, more focused on what people have agreed they like. The dominant is typically very focused on ensuring the sub gets whatever they asked for and more, even if that's denial or chastity, and of course, being in charge, the top gets as much of what they like, how they like it, too. So why isn't everyone doing it is more puzzling in some ways." *She makes a good point.*

"It sounds like fun, but it's not 'making love' is it?" Marcy asked.

"Making love is making love, however you do it, in my humble opinion. Society projects a mindset that lovemaking is a certain way, and absolutely it can be. But I would argue that making love is a state of mind, not a set of physical acts. It's being lost in each other, filled with passion and devotion. If you have that feeling, does it matter what you are doing at the time? I agree, it would be hard to sustain that lovemaking feeling if the scene were very ritualistic or staged, but what if Marcy had you strapped down and was riding you in total abandon and you were both lost in each other and that moment?" *Oh, I liked that visual.*

"What your mind is doing is one component, but chemically one of the key elements in creating loving bonds is oxytocin. It's released between parent and child — and in many other situations, like when a cat purrs — and it stimulates and binds relationships. In women it is released with rubbing and touching in the lead-up to orgasm. In men at time of orgasm. Post-coital cuddling is a pool of oxytocin. In BDSM, it's typical to have more and longer sex sessions, and we have something called 'aftercare'. Our sessions can be so intense, with large amounts of adrenaline and endorphins involved, that the cooldown period afterwards can be a problem. So aftercare is a planned and deliberate time of cuddling and support for each other, especially the sub, although more recently, 'top drop' is something we also try to manage. Anyway—too much detail— aftercare provides a further extension to the time we are swimming in oxytocin over that of a typical vanilla encounter. Ethan, how many times have you had intercourse, then just rolled over and fallen asleep? Don't answer that. BDSM practitioners typically present in surveys as having stronger relationships than vanillas. And it's not the whips and chains, it's the time they spend together, focused on giving each other what the other wants and need."

"Really?" I blurted.

"Yep. Surveys over the past two decades suggest that couples who regularly practise BDSM as part of their sex lives report more satisfactory sex, and stronger relationships, than the control group of 'general' society. There was also a study by Sargin, Cutler, and some others in 2009 on BDSM and stress. They measured the chemical cortisol, which is associated with stress, and applied some psychological tests before, during, and after BDSM sessions of fifty-eight individuals. During the scenes, cortisol increased in the submissive but not the dominant, as you might expect. Afterwards, for those who reported their session was a good experience, tests indicated a reduction in stress and an increase in relationship closeness. For those who reported a bad experience, it was mixed in these two respects.

"I need to keep stressing: No one should feel they have to want sex, or kinky sex, if they don't feel the urge. We all have a free choice, and the heart wants what it wants, but stigma aside, on paper kinky has a great deal going for it."

Marcy asked, "Why would anyone like pain? I realise BDSM is much more than just pain. Ethan and I haven't explored pain, and of course abuse often is mental, and emotional and not physical. And I guess my wonderment applies to all of the kinky 'seeming-counterparts' to abuse, but the enjoyment of pain seems the most baffling to me. If I could understand that better, it might help me get my head around why people like the other aspects of BDSM, which parallel the behaviours I associate with abuse and have battled for my whole life."

"Why do we like anything? Do you like hot curry or chili?"

"I do," I said. "As hot as I can stand it."

"Not so much," said Marcy.

"Hot baths?" Marcy put her hand up to that one.

"A masochist can enjoy being tied to a cross and whipped or spanked hard, have nipple clamps put on, or even get electric shocks and love it. But if they stub their toe as they dismount from the cross, they would probably hate it. They would hate the wrong person spanking but love the right person doing the exact same act. Spanking, chili, hot baths.... Many of us learn to enjoy different types of pain, some of it erotic and some not. Some of this is a mental state. Think of some of the biggest highs in your life. A big exam, a drug bust, learning to fly your helicopter. You probably had moments of fear and dread just before a key test, or even signing up and committing to learn. And the stronger that feeling of dread and the more you had to strive, for some, the more rewarding and thrilling the high of achievement. The more you make Ethan dread his next naked risk-taking, the bigger the high. Trust me. At least to a point. Knowing his limit is critical.

"And there is the chemical aspect. When we feel pain past a certain threshold, our bodies release endorphins. This is our naturally occurring opiate. The word itself is a contraction of *endogenous*, meaning internal origin, and *morphine*. We produce it and store it in a holding tank in case we stub our toe. When needed, the endorphin store dumps its complete load into our system and helps us tolerate pain. It doesn't numb the pain—we still feel it—but we are able to tolerate it more. You get in a bath that is too hot, you step out quickly, but moments later, you can stand to get back in—and add more hot water. A runner hits the pain barrier, then suddenly gets a second wind, leading to a runner's high. It takes roughly 10-15 minutes for the body to replenish the endorphin tank, and it won't release any more until the tank is full again. But once replenished, if you trigger it again, then let it refill and then trigger it a third and a fourth time, the opiates build into a wonderful high. Hard to control this repetitive cycle on a training run, or with a curry, but a skilled dominant in a sex scene? Absolutely! The effect of that high can be intense, and the resulting orgasms so memorable. It is literally, for a short time, mind altering. Again, it's not for everyone. But if it is for you, like chili or hot baths, or running long distances, and it doesn't damage you, and gives you mind blowing orgasms and a huge but natural high, remind me: Why wouldn't you?" *Again, she makes a good point.*

"Is it just the masochist who can get an altered state of mind?" I asked. I wasn't sure I wanted one, but it otherwise seemed inequitable and I was curious.

"It's been thought so forever, but only recently is data beginning to come forward. In 2016, in a preliminary study called *Psychology of Consciousness: Theory, Research, and Practice*, an altered state called 'Flow' was observed in both tops and bottoms. Flow has nine aspects, and the mix was different between the groups. Bottoms get there by giving up control and the chemicals relating to being dominated, but the tops get there by becoming hyper-focused on the task and taking care of their submissive in the right way.

"Look, it's important to take these things slowly. Going for the big payload up front is likely to lead to disappointment. You need to ease into it and understand yourselves as individuals, and as a unit. It is hard to get into the mood, especially in the early days." She continued. "Adrenaline helps, which is why roleplay and psychodrama are often an important part of a session, or scene as we call it. Start by talking about a few positions you might like — over the knee spanking, standing up, etc. — and try gently spanking each other, not just girl on boy. Make it part of a game, spanking-crib or stripping-chess. I've even played Kinky Catan. That's Settlers of Catan with dares thrown in. Roll a seven, the robber steals an item of clothing. Build a city, roll again and the number you throw selects a kinky thing you have to try. Rolling the dice takes some of the stress away from one person having to tell the other what they have to do next: The dice made me tell you to do it, it wasn't me!

"Try different spanking strengths, gentle at first building up to a little harder. Nothing too strong until you decide if it is for you or not and get a feel for how hot you like your 'curry.' Stick to the fleshy bits of your butt cheeks. Standing straight will be physically less intense than bending and touching your toes, as the skin is stretched tighter the more you bend. Being bent over an unmoving object is more intense than standing freely, as you can't flinch away. Tied up, or not. All things to experiment with. That's your homework. I'm off to bed, kiddos. Don't rock the boat!"

And with that, she left us. I could swear my butt was already tingling.

13: The Stakeout

Marcy and I decided to suspend our homework for a day or two at least, and instead spent the night cuddling and talking when awake, but mostly sleeping. The master cabin had a full king-sized bed, but we only occupied the space of a single. Being the stalker that I apparently was, I knew the bones of Marcy's career, and her time with her husband, but Marcy put flesh on those bones. Hearing which cases were her most important, some solved, and some not. Many not closed due to lack of resources. Many women, children, and, in a couple of rarer cases, men trapped in abusive situations. Marcy could do little about things except to threaten dire consequences, which did little to deflect those who had gotten away with it for years or couldn't help themselves anyway due to alcohol, drugs, or other issues.

We were up at dawn, grabbed some fruit and coffee from the galley, and went to the operations centre. Max had come through much faster than expected. On his return, he got drunk with an enforcer for the Toussaints and we had a message during the night via his secret app as a result. Four locations and four yachts. *Le Grand Rêve* in St Tropez. *Laurier* in Marseilles. *Missy's Mistake* in Monaco. *Astasha* in Nice. Kelsie had not slept, and she and one of her two operators had located each ship and all available information about each, including blueprints, ownership details, histories of travel, and current rental agreements. All four vessels were currently contracted by different individuals or corporations, which we tracked as we built up a picture of what we were dealing with and expanded our situational awareness. Our specialized drones had been distributed to these and other locations, along with base stations, which allowed us to control activity remotely.

Kelsie had personally supervised the drone in each city relocating itself to a discrete perch where it could land and keep watch on its respective target. To save power, each took a single, low-resolution picture every 30 seconds and compared it to the last. If there was any significant change in the picture, it alerted us and we turned on the main video camera. Each drone could maintain this low power, overwatch status indefinitely, thanks to solar film that covered its body and provided enough juice to keep the battery charged if it didn't fly too much. So far, all we had was routine and sporadic traffic that did not appear to be related to illegal activities. Now well into the morning, we assumed nothing of significance would happen until nightfall. We left one tech on duty — just in case — and all became vacationers for the day.

We elected to keep everyone on board unless there was a purpose to go ashore. Before it got too hot, I worked with Gia on some exercises to stretch out my side, which kept stiffening but was otherwise healing well. Marcy joined in, and when Gwen saw us, she did, too. Very soon we had a mini fitness class underway. To cool off afterwards, we lowered the rear pontoon platform and swam or paddleboarded for 30 minutes. I circumnavigated the 130-foot yacht, which was an effort heading towards the bow, due to the current and wind that had weathervaned *Cassis* around its anchor, but it was an easy drift back to the stern.

As I stepped onto the pontoon and grabbed the board before it drifted onwards, I noticed Gia and Marcy in quite an animated conversation. Whatever they were discussing didn't look likely to come to blows, so I left them to what appeared to be a private matter. I split my time diving and sitting chatting to Gwen for another 30 minutes, at which point the girls broke and we all agreed it was time for a leisurely lunch. Then, as we expected activities to increase overnight, Marcy and I retired to the cabin to rest. Which was a lot of fun.

At some point in our lazy afternoon on, between, and under the sheets, I inquired about the deep discussion with Gia that I had witnessed but stressed if it was none of my business, that would be ok.

"Not at all. Gia is pretty distraught about the victims of the human trafficking. She peppered me with questions about what I know from my work as a cop. You know, what happens to the girls? Do they all become prostitutes and house cleaners? That sort of thing. It was intense. We are all concerned for the victims, but she seemed over the top, and she eventually revealed she had a cousin who disappeared from a small village, and the rumours were that she had been taken by a gang for prostitution in Amsterdam's red light area. This was years ago, but Gia went there for four months looking for her and does a pilgrimage every couple of years. She doesn't ever expect to see her again, but talks to the working girls she seeks out, asking about her cousin and their own situation. I gather if someone needs help escaping from a pimp, Gia is more than happy to kick their ass; but mostly the girls elect to stay doing what they are doing. It's pretty sad — I see that all the time — and I can tell it weighs greatly on Gia."

"That's awful. Should I say anything?"

"No, I think she would be a little embarrassed. Anyway, enough about all that. I think you need some more kissing practise. This time with you lying on top of me!" I couldn't argue with that. I like to be at the top of my kissing game, after all.

*

At ten past four in the afternoon, the stateroom phone chimed, calling us down to operations. *Astasha* had weighed anchor, departed port, and headed east and out to sea. As the yacht transited down the coast, Kelsie relocated the drone to a point ahead of it, and we watched *Astasha* steam past. After another hour we exceeded the range of the portable base station's connection to the drone, but by then Kelsie had launched a different drone, a type we use for high altitude surveillance. A battery-powered, solar-refuelled glider that was super lightweight and small enough and shaped to be invisible to radar. It climbed high enough to be out of sight in a few minutes, and at altitude from which we could control it with a line-of-sight microwave unit directly from the *Cassis*. It picked up the *Astasha*, which was still following its earlier course, and we watched for another hour. Dalton, one of the protection detail who had accompanied us from Vancouver, took off in one of the *Cassis's* tenders with another base station with the intention of posing as a tourist cruising along the coast. He could stay a mile and a half from *Astasha* but allow us to bring back into play the drone that had been left behind due to range. Controlled via the new base station, the drone transitioned to the launch for a full recharge.

At 7:40 pm, *Astasha* dropped anchor in a small cove, and 30 minutes later our drone drifted onto a small ledge on a cliff 1000 yards away and we could retrieve the glider. All of this was exhausting [*eye roll*] so Marcy and I went and picked up food and beverages for everyone and then settled back to watch. No activity at the other locations. Soon the monotony took its toll and, except for the duty tech, we all took a break. I checked in with the captain and made sure Gwen was not making a nuisance of herself with the crew member she had taken a shine to. We slipped back to our rooms to relax and returned to operations at 2 am to witness the next — and to date highest risk — portion of the plan.

The drones we had brought were a unique design, with a couple of key characteristics. If moving at low speed, we could adjust the blades so they were almost silent. *Don't I wish I had that technology on the roof when Gwen caught me. Or do I?* The second characteristic was that once it settled down, it could reconfigure itself by deploying very thin plastic panels at various angles, to disguise itself by blending into its surroundings. We had painted them white that typically used on radar masts and fairings on luxury motor yachts most commonly use. *Missy's Mistake* had a dark blue mast, and Andrew, Dalton's partner, had sped out on a motorbike and spray painted the drone covering Missy appropriately. It wasn't perfect by any means but would work if it remained fifteen to twenty feet up a mast above an observer.

Kelsie's team had spent the day with high-resolution photos and blueprints for each boat and identified one or two locations on each boat that were not easy to get to — low-traffic, out-of-the-way parts of the boat structure — but with a decent angle for the drone's cameras to get helpful angles on the main deck areas. We had toyed with a plan that at each location, one of us would get close to a yacht on a noisy Sea-doo, drawing the crew's attention away from the sky and masking any noise the drone might make. We were worried that sounds on the water can be acoustically unpredictable and our stealthy approach may be detected. In the end we elected to go with the middle-of-the-night plan. It was highly unlikely a crew member would hear our modified drone approach, but if they did they wouldn't see it. Hopefully they would not spot it once it was in place. We hoped they would just suspect any noise was the wind, or if they identified the noise as a drone, believe it far away on the beach.

One by one Kelsie personally and skillfully piloted the small drones into place, starting with *Astasha*. Not an easy task, as she had to rely on the drones' own cameras, which lacked perspective of the surrounding 360 degrees, and it was doubly hard as the masts of the yachts swayed with the sea. The Laurier in particular took several attempts, and we nearly called it off. Once settled, and when we were happy with the coverage, Kelsie signalled each drone to deploy small arms, which had highly sticky adhesive that solidly bonded our camera into place. We could remotely jettison these anchors if we had to and leave them behind. With the excitement over, and diagnostics completed to ensure our view, stealth configuration, and solar charging cycle optimized, we stood down to watch. Well, Kelsie and team stood down; they did all of the hard work. But the rest of us let out the breath we had held for several hours and cheekily grabbed a beer. I sent the words "Bluetooth failure" to Max's modified headphones, which was our prearranged code word for this stage of the plan. Hopefully it would go undetected and allow him to maintain situational awareness.

I stood at the bow rail with Marcy as we watched for the first sign of dawn and wondered if we would be able to see the *Astasha*, whose relocation up the coast had brought it within 5 km of our current position. Kelsie popped out on deck.

"Game time," she whispered. Not that anyone would have heard if she spoke in her normal voice, but we tiptoed back into the operations centre quietly, just in case.

Astasha's drone's microphone had detected the approach of a launch, and we sped up the video feed's frame rate and increased the resolution. We flipped to image-intensifying mode and the screen flipped to a greenish glow, but the source of the noise was out of the shot. Eventually, not one but two launches — each at least twenty feet long, and both wide in the beam — eased up to the *Astasha's* fantail. Several large boxes were transferred from the first boat, followed by six women. As the first boat pulled away, the second slipped closer and a further sixteen dejected-looking females transferred onto the *Astasha*. All of the women were unkempt and bedraggled, but you could tell they were beauties. They wore jeans and t-shirts but no shoes or socks. The colours of the t-shirts were difficult to see with the green hue from the camera but looked like they varied and had a mix of logos and patterns. The women were led quietly and unresistingly down into the bowels of the yacht, seemingly accepting of their sad fate with barely a glance around—the luxury yacht just another station on their road to misery.

Within minutes of the second boat shoving off, the engines on the *Astasha* fired up. The crew stood over the anchor as its motor hauled it off the shallow bottom, and she pointed her nose seaward. She was soon making 22 knots west, presumably for the southern USA.

It was heartbreakingly hard not to chase down the *Astasha*. Intercepting it now would mean 22 souls would almost certainly be saved, but the Toussaint's would just continue and hundreds, if not thousands, would follow. Those of us in the operations room were silent and sick as the distance increased between us and *Astasha*. If it took me every last cent, we were getting those women back. Our frustration and heartbreak turned to disbelief and fear three hours later when we were urgently called back to the operations centre.

"We were going back over the footage to better calibrate the camera's night vision when we noticed this," said Kelsie, teeing up a scene. It was the fantail of the *Astasha*, rolling gently at anchor. Suddenly a thin, dark shape slipped out of the water and onto the deck, then slid quickly into a storage well on the port side. From the deck, the interloper would be invisible, especially in the dark, but from our perch high up on the radar mast we could see them pull what appeared to be a towel from a bag and quickly dry off before dressing swiftly in jeans and a t-shirt. They returned the towel to the bag and, with a quick scan to ensure they were still unobserved, threw it over the side. The shape crept stealthily down to the stairs and disappeared into the lower deck.

A few quick keystrokes and Kelsie rewound to the moment in time the swimmer pulled themselves onto the deck and their face was exposed to the camera, and then she adjusted the light and focus settings. Wet hair swept back by the tug of gravity, a dripping Gia was staring back at us.

14: No Return

[Gia] — At what point is there no return? As I slipped over *Astasha*'s fantail and hid in a puddle of my own making?

Or as I silently ascended to the fantail, holding my breath, fearing a single bubble might betray me, my world expanding and infusing with colour with every foot I climbed nearer to the silhouette of the yacht?

Or 50 yards earlier, as I slipped off the stolen paddle board? I had manoeuvred slightly east and up-current of my target, then let the board drift away parallel to but out of sight of my quarry. I breast-stroked diagonally across the current to intercept *Astasha*, and when I neared her sleek white hull, I sank without a ripple and dove deep under her keel.

Or earlier yet, when I slunk guiltily off *Cassis*'s deck? When I stole the paddle board, food, radio, and SPOT GPS tracker? Was that the point of no return?

Or in Vancouver, when I argued myself onto the plane on the pretense of joining Ethan's personal protection detail? Or when I all but interrogated Max, drawing out as much as I could about the traffickers, their operations, their tactics, their strengths, and their known weaknesses?

As I hunched breathless in the stowage well on the rear deck, I wondered these things. But the truth is, the point of no return was nine years ago. When I promised Jenjing, "Never again."

Nine years ago, I cried on her grave until my throat pained me and my tears ran out, their residue dried on my sore cheeks. Her coffin was six feet below me, topped with a plaque with her name and her dates. She would never blame me. No sane person in their right and objective mind would ever blame me. But I blamed myself, and I embraced the rage I harboured as my fuel. My reality and my comfort blanket, as much as my penance. My search for the last nine years was not for Jenjing; it was for atonement.

For the thirtieth time I considered the path I was committed to, my chest tight as I weighed my debt not only to her, but to all girls, and boys, and women I could not save—victims of monsters.

Taking responsibility for millions of souls I have never met and whose names I could never know is ridiculous, and in truth, that is not how I feel. I am driven. Driven to look for victimization, especially in the underbelly of the sex trade, and when I see it, honour my vow to Jenjing and her brothers and sisters. A vow that demands I act.

Nine years ago, I failed her. But my mission began three years before that. And a year before those three years I was 'normal'.

Born to a Japanese mother and Spanish father, I was a happy sixteen-year-old striving to conquer my four biggest problems: exams, boys, and our intertwined insecurities. And acne. Today, people describe me as sexy because of my unusual looks due to my mixed heritage. My almost pretty face, along with a sporty sinewy litheness that is attractive the way a leopard's movement captures you, combined with the undeniable self-confidence of a lioness. But thirteen years ago, I was Bambi with a naive face and an innocence that attracted monsters.

As a child, Alicante was mostly good to us, until it wasn't. A Spanish coastal town, straddling the old world and the new. A warm and genuine tourist destination with a typical mix of locals servicing that tourist demand. The town's rich, its middle class, the service industry imports and locals, and the quite poor. Concealed within each stratum of the pyramid, which has a much fatter base than peak, are its victims. Feeding its seedier needs are the brothels and pimps, gambling dens and drug dealers, all controlling the sex workers, the gamblers, and the addicts. At a local level, tragic enough. Those who struggle to stay above the surface avoid being sucked into a pool of desperation; they flail, making eddies that exist within a current of malevolent big business. Business that is part of a pan-European river of gluttony, which feeds a larger world avarice. I might have escaped if it were only the local pond, but the gravity of that world of avarice sucked me down.

For my first fifteen years I was one of the happy middle class. My parents had wholesome, respectable jobs servicing the better hotels. My mother ran a food service business, complemented by my father's laundry business. Their sweat bought me an innocent and happy life, and I was blissfully oblivious – as my parents had intended – to those I walked among who were less fortunate than I.

A week after my fifteenth birthday I was orphaned – in such a stupid way. I returned from a sleepover with a friend. My parents' cars were on the street outside our house, which was unusual for that time of day, and perhaps my subconscious registered that first hint of trouble as I opened the door. I stepped into the hallway, and in that instant knew for certain that there was something terribly wrong. The sound of the empty house has a low thrum of the air conditioner, a background road noise, and the drip of a tap. The echoes of all those sounds blended into an audible fabric you feel and wear as much as you hear. But somehow, that same house containing my dead loved ones has a distorted, quieter sound, and my lizard brain noticed. It stirred and commanded the hairs on my neck to stand and that I shorten my breath, ready for freeze, flight, or fight. I crept but did not understand why I crept; I only felt that something was terribly wrong. And like every female teen faced with an eerie woodshed, I moved towards it instead of fleeing for help and safety.

And as my head began to hurt, I smelled rotten eggs. That sulphurous smell added to natural gas to warn you of a leak. Assuming you are awake. Spanish building codes are not as modern as some more progressive countries, and in 2005 we had no gas alarms, so Mom and Dad slipped away quietly, spooning in their sleep, not knowing they had orphaned me.

My next three months felt to me like hell, but in reality, it was just the normal adjustment to tragic but not necessarily threatening circumstances. One of the hardest moments, outside of saying goodbye to Mom and Dad, was realizing I was no longer part of the same tribe I had been. Friends were not rude—quite the opposite—but they were awkward, now that I was tainted with tragedy. Awkward both when I joined a group walking to school through the mall and also awkward when I didn't. It very quickly became easier for us all to be neutral rather than exclusive or inclusive, but the emotional insulation this posture offered was subtly socially isolating.

I had no extended family to adopt me. There were family friends, but none who could accommodate a fifteen-year-old. So, I entered the foster system, where I met Jenjing, a thirteen-year-old, also recently orphaned. Her father's identity was never known, she had been raised an only child by a mother recently taken by cancer. In our grief, we bonded instantly, like sisters we needed but didn't have.

Our first foster family was kind, which with hindsight only made the subsequent twists of fate more bitter. Our new foster mother was diagnosed with ALS within two weeks of our arrival, and they understandably gave us back to the system. I don't blame them.

We were passed to the Gnomes family, who also were not bad people at heart. But they were weak people. To compensate morally and financially for their weaknesses—his gambling and her drugs—they took in orphans. And they provided what we needed. But stalking that provision was menace.

Mr. Gnomes had occasion to pay a large debt. Fifty percent of a week's paycheck was owed, and that would cause a fight with Mrs. Gnomes. Annoyed at his weakness, and not thinking, he took Jenjing with him to pay his bookie.

Perhaps that was my moment of no return.

If I was an almost-pretty-faced Bambi, Jenjing was Bambi with an innocent touch of Jessica Rabbit. She was not a tacky provocateur, but there was an undeniable base sexuality that, while good grown men would deny it touched them, the heads of monsters would swivel her way. Mr. Gnomes's bookie mentioned Jenjing to someone, who mentioned her to someone else, who was a talent scout for the sex trade outside of the local pool of misery, fulfilling the upstream pipeline to Amsterdam's street trade hundreds of miles to the north. This person stood smoking on the corner by our school and checked her out. He was not the scummiest of scumbags and, to his credit, he decided she was too young. *Perhaps in a year or two*, he probably thought. But then he noticed me. I was perhaps not as marketable as my younger orphan-sister, but at least I was of age in his world.

And so, as these manipulations often occur, Mr. Gnomes suddenly became luckier and we had a period of relative wealth. We had new clothes and ate out. We even had a long weekend in Barcelona. But soon, once the hook was in deep, his luck ran out again and he plunged into debt, and then into crisis. A crisis deeper due to the sudden but fragile accumulation of wealth. His bookie, ever 'his best friend', passed him to someone who could help. And in no time, and with almost no realization of what had occurred and to the guilty relief of his real family, he agreed to pass Jenjing and me to a different family in Amsterdam, no questions asked. They were desperate to offer children a good home and had the funds Gnomes would never possess. A win-win.

As we entered our third foster house, and as the front door slammed sharply behind us, our world collapsed in on us.

I will spare you the details of captivity, of beatings, of child rape. Of the machine that transformed us from innocent to obedient, subjugated sex workers in no time flat. Of meeting our new foster-father-cum-pimp, who we knew only as Anott, pronounced "Ai-noh." Instead, I will tell you of Señor Maffi.

Once a priest, he awoke one morning compelled to follow his personal vision of the Lord's work, as opposed to that of his church. For four years, he had been an independent aid-worker helping the trodden upon and abused. He could not provide shelter or sanctuary, only transparency, hope, and education.

He lived in the neighbourhoods we suffered in, among the victims and those who pimped out children. He would approach us on the street, and with little gestures gain our confidence, or at least mitigate our worst fears. Through that cracked window between our tortured world and his, he whispered of shelters and programs. Some lost souls like ours noticed and yearned. But he was careful to explain to those who chose to listen that although some escaped their misery through such channels, others eventually fell back into the trade and were worse for their 'disloyalty' to it.

The other education he offered was in martial arts.

As a prostitute, you have a duality of confidence. On the one hand, I had incredibly low self-esteem—zero confidence, especially when surrounded by my captors and abusers. They held my soul and squelched its fire. But after perhaps the first one hundred or so 'tricks', with mostly weak and flawed people, a different confidence is born. Learning from many bad situations allows you to become queen in many circumstances. I came to control the customers, placing myself in the path of those I could tell might want me and then ensuring they did, and leaving them satisfied in as short a time as possible.

The enticements of martial arts were to better prepare me for those rare times I could not control a customer. When your life is truly out of your control, and your comforting façade of being in control is torn away, that fear can be worse than a physical blow. Already in my short career, that had already happened on five separate occasions, and each time I had been terrified. One man gave me a broken rib; another a black eye. On the other three occasions, they just re-exposed my abject helplessness. For days after each occasion, the dread of subsequent customers was heightened, but then numbed again by repetition. Señor Maffi taught martial arts class so we could learn how to control and shape the course of such situations.

My first lesson was in the shower of a local hostel. When Maffi asked me to follow him into the shower stall, I was convinced he was just another monster, luring me in to fuck me in his kinky way. A sad joke, but not one I was unused to. I followed, as I had no fire left in me, hoping that perhaps afterwards he might pay me. In the oppressive space, with the door closing us into an echoing three-by-three-foot Perspex space, he told me the secret of Bruce Lee and Luke Skywalker.

"Which martial art do you want to learn, Gia?"

"I don't understand. Whichever you teach," I said, with some skepticism and impatience.

"Choose one. Kung Fu? Karate? I can't teach you all of them, of course, but I can teach you the secret they all share," he whispered. And smiled. It was the smile of conspirators.

"Can you teach me to street fight? I doubt artsy arm waving and the crane stance will be respected in the back alleys and doorways," I whispered, leaning in, anxious to get this done.

"Yes, I can. The secret is the same in street fighting, too," he assured me, pausing for dramatic effect.

"OK," I mimicked his tone — a trick to encourage our 'tricks' — not really knowing what else to say. He was a small man, with bad breath, but he had a kindly way about him. I wanted out of the shower stall. Or to drop to my knees and get paid. Whichever.

"You've watched Jackie Chan or MMA fighting, boxing, or any fighters at the top of their game. You've noticed that they move faster than their opponent. They counter an attack before it starts. They seem to see their opponent move in slow motion and dance around them."

"Yes, they seem superhuman. It is miraculous, but it's fiction," I said impatiently.

Señor Maffi reached behind his back and picked up a wet bar of soap from the rack. He held it out for me to take. I paused and looked at it, imagining the sick things my taking it would lead to. But it would not be the first, second, or third time. I reached to take the soap, but he let it go a fraction too soon, before I had it. It bounced off my palm, slipped away, and began to fall. Eight inches and a quarter second later, I caught it.

"What do I do with this?" I asked.

"Whatever you want. You've just discovered your superpower."

I stared at him, wondering if I should be worried about more than just being raped and thrown back onto the street. Maybe he was a total nutcase.

"How many times have you dropped the soap, and caught it so fast that you didn't even know you had even dropped it? How many times has someone thrown something to you and you grasped it out of the air without conscious thought? Swerved on your bicycle before you even saw the thing you were avoiding? Walked through a door and let it close behind you, then realized a child was following, and flicked out a hand and grabbed the door again without even looking?" I stared back. He continued.

"We all live in what I call the world of 'fast speed,' but our brains slow our world down to 'slow speed.' It's overwhelming to be at fast speed all of the time. If you've ever seen someone playing a first-person-shooter game on an Xbox or PlayStation, against another real-world player who is hundreds of miles away, you see their avatars move very quickly. Gunshots or spells are fired rapidly, as characters leap and roll from position to position on the screen. In the blink of an eye. But what you don't see is the reality. You see what some clever software, but mostly your brain, shows you. We play here in The Netherlands, and our opponent is perhaps in southern Italy. There is a minimum of a half second delay between you pressing the 'shoot' button and that gun firing on the screen of your opponent a thousand miles or so south of us. You should miss every time, or at least be consciously aiming where you think they will be in half a second. And yet we knock their soldier out of the air nonetheless, even though they leapt half a second before we saw them leap.

"Our brains," he continued, "are amazing at reshaping or hiding the world so we can make sense of it. Bruce Lee, or Neo, or Riddick look through that façade and fight in real time — *fast time* —, where most of us can't. They seem superhuman because they've practised seeing things as they happen, not when our brains think we should register them. They see a shift in weight to line up a punch before their opponent really knows they have even moved.

"When we drop the soap, our body is so practised at soap management, it knows what to do without engaging the slow but thoughtful part of our brain. But in fact, part of our brain slips into fast mode for a fraction of a second, tells our hand to grab the soap, computes intercept angles, instructs muscles, tracks progress — including how to counter its inherent slipperiness — retrieves the soap and then switches back to normal, returning to help you sing ABBA or whatever your conscious brain was up to. But soap wrangling is a thoughtless act or impulse. I can teach you to knowingly switch to *fast speed* for short periods when you need to, and make conscious decisions based on what your fast brain is seeing, rather than just practised reactions." He paused, letting me catch up. I was quiet for a while.

"So what? I'm weak and a woman and can't fight. Will fast speed get the sex over with faster, or will it make it seem longer?"

He laughed. "Hey, that's good, I don't normally get that joke from my students for several weeks." Then he straightened and said, "Of course. You need a fighting system as well as speed and strength and stamina. Without those qualities, you just watch clearly as the world comes at you and you see it beat you every time. But conversely, if you have just skill and strength but not 'fast speed,' with your stature, you are just a well-trained and angry gnat who might only beat people smaller than you are. You need both skill and fast speed, which I can teach you."

"When do I start? What will it cost me?" I inquired eagerly, and then, catching myself, suspiciously.

"There is no cost but your time and total devotion to task. And you can start as soon as you fully commit. But here is your second Jedi mind trick: You need to accept a critical emotional proxy."

"A what?"

"You need to do this for some purpose bigger than you. This training is practically impossible for someone not in the position you are. A 'normal' person. They control their life and destiny, whereas you don't. They have time at their disposal, which you don't. And most importantly, your emotional and spiritual backbone is broken. First your parents' death weakened it, and then before it could mend, Anott purposefully broke what was left."

"I can be strong!" I said, driven by the thought of self-protection.

"Yes, but for short periods. You were brave to trust me and come into this shower. But be honest, would you have dropped to your knees if I had asked you to?"

I said nothing. I felt angry that he was right, and I was defeated before I had even started, and that he was snatching back the hope he had offered.

"It is a hard, hard journey, and most people—even the strongest—can't do it for themselves. But oddly, sometimes they can do it for another — someone whom they treasure. You might not value your own life, but you would die for someone else. You might not be able to sustain the commitment for your own benefit, but you would do anything for Jenjing!" And as those words sank into me, something in my heart that was hard and brittle softened a little to become resolute, and something in my head that was overly pliable turned to granite. And there began my mission.

*

As a sex slave, my time was not my own from early evening until the early hours of the morning. Then I could sleep for two to three hours before the morning shift, or the 'husband shift,' as we called it in the trade. Wives are suspicious of husbands who come home late, smelling of sex and unable to perform; but few suspect men who leave for work early, return smelling of work, and possess a prowess formed from successful betrayal and from flattery of an illicit a lover about their performance. But between 9 am and 4 pm, I was mostly left to myself. I committed and maintained two to three hours per day, six days per week, to Maffi's lessons. For a total of fourteen months. Maffi and I both tried to convince Jing to join me in training. She at first said no, then tried, but she did not possess the discipline and drive — perhaps the belief that she could do it. She kept fit but was no fighter.

At first we worked on stamina and strength, interspersed with 'seeing' exercises. Señor Maffi preferred the term 'seeing training' to 'reaction training,' as he believed that our bodies know how to react fast, but they also need to learn how to see fast. Then think fast. Dropping the soap. Juggling, then juggling blindfolded. Touching surfaces that are unexpectedly hot and pulling away. Sometimes Maffi would take a stance, then attack as fast as a snake, stopping an inch short. I had to twist my body away from his attack, but stop just a fraction from where he stopped. A hundred other tricks.

The process reminded me of those Magic Eye pictures from the 90's, full of coloured dots which, if you stare at long enough and adjust your focal length, you can suddenly see a three-dimensional picture of a dragon. At first you stare for hours and don't see it, but with practise you can switch vision modes almost instantly. It is not a Jedi mind-trick; it's a knack. After a month, I could see with fast speed almost at will, but that was the easy bit; if it was something I had practised, like catching soap, my body just reacted and I watched. But learning to see fast, and make a choice of how to react, and then initiating a thoughtful action at that speed seemed impossible at first. But my granite mind, locked onto the certainty that one day I would free not just myself but Jenjing, too, drove onwards, over and over again. And in the fourth month it felt like I had a just a little more time, and I began to consciously direct my reactions in those precious fractions of seconds, rather than just allow my subconscious to run things autonomously.

In those four months, I was doing 90 minutes of structured exercise each day. Only then, when I was strong, supple, and could anticipate correctly, did we start on fighting systems. We began with systems built on speed, not strength. I could block and deflect a strike long before I learned to land one. Then we worked on systems of counter-striking. Deflect a blow and strike the gap created by the extended arm of your opponent. Arm comes up to punch me, knock it higher and strike under it, at the exposed liver if the target is turning with their punch, or the nerve centre under the armpit if not. Fast speed allowed me to deflect, and I increasingly found I had time to choose which target to strike in return.

Within six months, sparring with other students, I could get myself out of trouble against a far stronger opponent perhaps half of the time. I could hold my own against most men I was likely to encounter at ten months, provided they were not well trained in martial arts. Although this seemed slow to me, apparently I was learning to a quality and at a rate that put me in the top five percent of students Maffi had encountered.

By the time Jenjing and I had been in the trade for roughly eighteen months, we were known to most workers and pimps within a few miles of the red-light district. On my eighteenth birthday, I arrived to pick up Jenjing from Red Pearl's Spa, a massage parlour where she had arranged to meet a regular client, after which we planned to take a short break between customers for some cake, to celebrate my big occasion. I climbed the back stairs and heard through the door the raised voice of an angry man, followed by a slap, followed by a pained gasp let out in Jenjing's small voice. I don't recall entering the room. I was just between them; seeing his annoyance at my appearance; seeing him size me up and dismiss me as a threat; noticing his chest puffing up. Watching his eyes flick malevolently to my legs, breasts, then face; watching his weight shift to his front foot as he leant towards me; watching his arm snake out to mar my face. Watching my left hand encircle his right incoming wrist and force it sideways, while the heel of my righthand caved in his Adam's apple and crushed his larynx. He went down hard just from the shock, cracking his head on the table. A throat strike should have left him coughing, and possibly dying, but it was moot, as the head injury left him dead. Time froze, then quickly restarted with a jolt, and we ran. We hid. We hugged tightly, and we cried.

Anott, our pimp of eighteen months, knew who was with the regular found dead that day. After a brief inspection, he knew that he had not died of a simple slip and fall. The cracked head could have been explained, but not the crushed throat. There would be consequences.

I was for running. We had some loose change and a proven track record of being able to make a living off the street; with the open borders of Europe we could relocate to London, Paris, or a long list of places in which we could hide and survive. Jenjing, who had started on this path earlier in her formative years, and who had not gained the confidence I had in recent months from Señor Maffi, was desperately torn. In truth, had we wanted to, we could have run away any time over the past year, but the codependency between the pimps and us — their 'property' — left Jenjing with a bizarre sense of home for these sad few square miles that we had been living in.

I had been raised in Alicante, and had my life dismantled there. The brief foster stays a sham. Passed from post to pillar to post, and then eventually to bedpost. Circling the drain of poverty, it was pimps who offered us a sense of family. We knew that some pimps got their girls addicted on a heroine leash, but Anott said he wouldn't. He took all of our money and gave us back a weekly allowance. But 30 percent of what he took he put in trust for us. He had us open an account, to which we were the only signatories, and he paid our cut into that trust monthly. We had papers, in our own deposit boxes, which confirmed exclusive access to that account on our twenty-third birthdays. If we worked hard, we would be free, with around 50 thousand Euros, too old to work for the clientele Anott supplied. And in our time there, we had seen each girl that reached that milestone obtain their prize and freedom. A bizarre trust formed; a promise of a brighter future.

The pimp with the golden heart protected us and provided for us. Had he been in the Red Pearl's room that day, he would have intervened. Since our parents' death, he alone had offered stability of household, and trust. Not that he wasn't above the odd beating or forced abstinence from food, and in severe cases, fines to the offender's 'pension.' A girl once raked her nails down a John's face, drawing blood, and maybe leaving a scar. This was because her trick had beaten her during the act. Anott broke her arm and fined her five thousand Euros. What would the penalty be for killing a customer? And what would it mean to us to have this life, such as it was, dismantled? Would we survive without a pimp in London? If we had a pimp, would they treat us as kindly? I was for leaving, but she was torn.

We decided, after much soul-searching, to test the waters. I left Jenjing at a street-side café and went to the bar Anott used as his office. I found him on the patio, raging at his enforcers and anyone who was not a civilian that came too close. I approached and stood on the far side of the street where I could run if I had to and called across. When he saw me, he pulled himself together and straightened his grey silk jacket over his AC/DC t-shirt, and forced a calm on himself, which clearly did not fit. Uninstructed, his enforcers fanned out. Two at his side, one up the street, the other down the street, effectively boxing me in. They stepped across the road, but kept an even six feet from me, while Anott stepped right up to and into my face. Anott was a foot taller than I, and towered over me, using his height to intimidate. I was scared, but confident I could take him. The other four I would have to outrun. In broad daylight, I would have to make just enough of a public spectacle to ensure that help would come. Standing my ground and antagonizing him further in front of his men wouldn't be smart, so I adopted a frightened and conciliatory posture.

"Where's Jenjing?" Anott spat, without preamble.

"She's sorry, Anott. Really sorry. Scared shitless. The jerk was beating her. She panicked and flailed and caught his throat and he went down and hit his head. It was a fluke, not a rebellion. What can she do to make it up?"

"I asked, where is she? Not how is she feeling. She needs to be here right now. For her own good."

"She knows, but she's terrified. Of what you will do to her."

"It's not me she has to worry about, it's Buddy Taylor, the American shit. Were it just me, and she convinced me it was an accident, I would beat her senseless, but not to the point she couldn't work. That would be stupid. A lesson to others, but no impact to my business. If I thought it was deliberate...well let's not go there.

"But she did this at Buddy's massage parlour. He has had police there all afternoon, and they found drugs. It won't connect back to Buddy directly, but he has lost product, face, and money. And he says I owe him. He wants Jenjing, and thirty grand for the trouble a girl of mine caused him."

"Buddy never keeps his drugs on site there; that's bullshit. He would lose them in a raid, which he gets weekly. He's playing you, Anott."

"Doh! Why didn't I think of that? Idiot, of course he is. But Jenjing gave him the excuse to shit on me, and he is a bigger player who can now use her stupidity to muscle into my business."

"So, what then?"

"He wants Jenjing. He wants to make an example of her. He said I have to make it up by giving the both of you to him as payment. We negotiated, and he settled for Jing. I get to keep you; lucky me. You can work off the additional ten thou' he wanted from the negotiation. Jenjing? Very sad. He is not soft on his girls like I am."

My legs nearly gave way and my throat hurt. "Give me to Buddy. You keep Jenjing safe. She's still a kid."

"You know that won't satisfy him. Not when he has his foot on my neck like this."

"Well, I'm not giving her up. She will run."

"And go where? Anyway, you will give her up. That is not a variable. The variable is how much we have to hurt you before you tell us where she is."

He stared down at me, eyes red and angry. A fleck of spittle on his cheek.

"I'll go talk to her. See if I can get her to come, but why would she if she will just become a hollow-eyed addict sucking for Buddy for the rest of her life? She made a mistake and her life is over. Running has to be better than that."

"No, you will tell me where she is, and we will go and get her."

I made a decision.

"Well, you would be getting the wrong person, Anott. I was there. I heard her scream and went in, and I hit the guy. It wasn't Jenjing. Give me over to Buddy."

This made him take a long pause. He stepped back and considered. Somewhat deflated. Shaking his head.

"You stupid bitch. You should have known better. But that won't work. The big man made his statement, and if I tell him you were involved, he will just want you both and I lose out even more. There is no sense in that. Just give her over, Gia. There is no helping her. Just hurting yourself. Last chance; where is she?" I let him put his hand on my shoulder, buying time to think while surrounded by his oppressive stench.

A white *Ford* SUV pulled around the corner, and everyone tensed. Buddy Taylor eased up alongside us and dropped the window. He signalled with a casual wave and the rear window lowered, too. Jenjing's terrified face peered out, just over the beefy arm that encircled her neck. We made eye contact and I began to move to get her. I was not sure how that would happen with seven men between us. Anott tightened his grip on me.

"I've done you a fuckin' favour, Anott," Growled Taylor. "Figured you wouldn't be organized enough to give me what we agreed on, not today anyway, and time is fuckin' money. Know what I mean? This bitch needs to be popped up and on her knees, paying off her considerable debt to me, not sitting in some café having high tea and takin' the piss. I didn't want to have to add a late delivery fee on to our deal, so I went and picked her up for you. You can thank me and send the ten grand over tonight." He laughed and put the car in gear. The last time I saw Jenjing alive was in those few seconds as he pulled away, her eyes pleading.

"This isn't happening, Jenjing, I'll come for you. I will stop this, I promise," were the last words she might have heard from me, fading on the air through the roar of exhaust. My promise.

It wasn't just words, it was a solemn vow. I didn't say "I swear" or anything, but in that moment, my life was committed to a new course. As I stared through thickening tears after the *Ford*, one of Anott's goons came up in my blind spot and tasered me. Anott apparently caught me, walked me like a drunk over to his car, and we sped away. A roofie in my arm, and I was out of it for two days. I woke up groggy, with Anott standing over me telling me to "leave it alone" and take a few days, then get back to work.

"There is no helping it, and nothing you can do," he repeated. He had it on good authority that Jenjing had been shipped out of town to one of Buddy's other operations. And this proved true: She had.

She had not lasted long in Hamburg, riddled with drugs and in the hands of a harsh pimp who called himself Dragon Boy. I walked out of Anott's safehouse and never saw him again. I went instead to Maffi, who helped me search. We didn't find Jenjing, but I did find the brute who held her in the car. He and I met in a dark alley behind Buddy's club. I broke his arms and tied his ankles together, then pushed a piece of glass into his eye until he told me where I would find Jenjing.

I found Dragon Boy a week later and realized he was hard to get. He had presumably been warned I was coming and was not taking chances. It took me another week of stalking him and following his men. I found several locations where his girls operated and, one at a time, I staked them out. It was at 2:13 am that I noticed a familiar jacket around a girl propped up in the entrance to an alley. It looked like Jenjing, but at the same time, it didn't. It was her, but life had left her an empty and deflated husk of Jenjing. In her arm was a needle. With the crazy bitch sister from Amsterdam on the war path, Dragon Boy had decided to cut his losses, perhaps figuring I would back off once I had no sister to find. I later learned from one of his girls he thought she was useless anyway — broken from being abducted — and had not reacted well to the drugs he had forced into her veins.

I'm not proud of it, and I won't dwell on it here, but both Dragon Boy and Buddy died painful deaths over the following six months. I did back off, but only to let them emerge back from under their stones. Then it ended for them, and eventually, a long time later, began again for me.

Señor Maffi was the beginning, and from there I immersed myself in a different life. I travelled to other cities to train under notable martial artists in various disciplines, and while training, I helped street girls deal with their harsh lives in various ways.

In Montreal, I met a Tae Kwon Do sensei who took me to the 2012 London Games, where I placed fourth, then retired. It was a distraction I didn't want. I worked my way across Canada, from shelter to brothel to street corner, helping lost souls as I ran from my past. I eventually ran out of steam in Vancouver.

I took the job working for Ethan on a whim, to earn some money to get back on my feet and decide what to do next. I still had my vow, and it would always drive me, but it was perhaps time to be smarter about how I went about it.

I settled into the Vancouver martial arts community, sometimes travelling to Seattle, Portland — and occasionally as far as California — to train and spar, and occasionally compete. The more I learned about the work Ethan did for the community after I joined his family of misfits, the more it felt like it could be an emotional and effective base, and perhaps a home for me. I was planning to approach Ethan to see if he would sponsor me running a women's support shelter in my spare time, modelled on Maffi's methods.

When I heard of Marcy's takedown of the traffickers, I was torn in several directions. I marvelled at this woman who shared something of a similar mission to me. Despite her fears, she took on one of the biggest criminal gangs and slapped them in the face, knowing there would be retribution. But then, dragging Ethan into the middle of it, and nearly getting him killed, threw me for a loop. I was supposed to be keeping him safe. Fit and safe. That was my job. And if he died, so did my dream of helping girls on a bigger, more legitimate scale, and that would be another failure echoing that of Jenjing's fate. And, perhaps I was a little jealous.

When I first met Marcy, the night she came from the hospital, I was hostile. She had dragged Ethan into danger, then left him at the hospital. If she cared for him, why was she not at his bedside? I said nothing in the elevator, and was glad, as later that night, alone in my room, I cooled down and realized I was being stupid. She was a great warrior. I could sense that. And she was looking out for girls like me. And like Jenjing.

The next day she came after me with some purpose, and we went a few rounds on the mat. She was marking her territory and I let her come. On the first day I met Ethan, I had made my impression with a sucker punch, and Marcy did exactly that to me. Ironic. While I was distracted trying to decide how not to hurt her pride, she threw a roundhouse, and as I tracked it at fast speed and shifted to deflect it, she got in a good elbow and blackened my eye. A warrior.

I controlled the remainder of the session, and we fell into a competitive but less intense bout of sparing. We both worked up a sweat, which mingled as we fought, and perhaps that was the binding of the beginning of a friendship.

Max was the second surprise of the day. After years of being abused by men, it was rare to find one I could tolerate, let alone be attracted to. Over the years, when I needed comfort of that sort, I mostly slept with women, or on a rare occasion, a quick, passionate, but otherwise unemotional release with a male instructor. But only the ones I narrowly championed. Good enough to be worthy, but I had to own them completely.

As I cooled down with Marcy, Max and Ethan came in, and I realized how Max watched us both but only saw me. Something in me clicked. More like something long broken reconnected. Through that connection flowed so many emotions, spinning my head so fast that I did what I knew how to do best, which was to put him on the mat. But part of me wanted to keep him there a while longer.

Later, in Ethan's apartment, the tale of Max and Marcy, Max and the military, and the traffickers unfolded and reignited the mission within me. I all but insisted they included me and was warmed further when Max took my side in that debate. I peppered him with questions about what he knew about the girls, how they were transported, how they lived, and where they came from, and he told me. He trusted me as if he had known me forever. He told me how the girls dressed when they were taken to the boats. They knew where some of them ended up, but not how they got there.

*

So, when is the point of no return? For me, it was in Hamburg.

I admired Ethan's grand plan. Big picture. Track the yachts to the base and call in law enforcement on the Toussaints. Save perhaps thousands of girls, at least from that one gang. I knew vice abhors a vacuum, and a new gang would backfill faster than Ethan could fly home. But at least that new gang would not have a contract on Marcy. I got that. But I calculated that 15 to 30 women would be alone and defenceless on that yacht, and I could not do anything except move to protect them. In the best scenario, I would place the SPOT GPS tracker on the boat, to make it easy for Kelsie to track, and hide out until the cavalry arrived. In the worse scenario, I would be discovered and have to subdue everyone on the yacht. Or die trying. Or end up a drugged sex slave. There would be nowhere to run once we pulled up the anchor.

In all scenarios, I believed I would lose my job, my burgeoning new family, and Max. And this made me cry.

15: *Astasha*

I crouched in the storage well on the port side of the *Astasha*, deliberately waiting for the worst of the water I brought on board to trickle from my goose-bumped body. Once I was mostly drip dried, I opened the waterproof sack I had dragged with me and removed a towel. I dried the rest of the water off quickly, then slipped out of my bikini and into jeans and a t-shirt. I hoped it was close to what the women would be wearing and prayed that the intelligence I had from Max would hold up. I took a smaller bag out of the sack and replaced it with the wet towel and bikini, then lowered the sack over the side for the current to wash away. In the small bag was a radio, a SPOT device, eight days' rations of food and water, and a pistol.

Checking that the coast was clear, I slipped out of my hiding place and quietly climbed the mast, towards the well-disguised drone near the top. Several feet below it, I turned on the SPOT, and saw the green LED confirm it was sending our GPS position to a satellite service, which would forward our coordinates via email to Kelsie. I got the idea of taking a SPOT with me after hearing Darcy and Kelsie discussing why they had not designed this feature into each drone. They were focused on weight and power management at the time, but were ruing that decision in this situation. I climbed down several feet and stowed the bag in a cubby, hoping no one would discover it there and I could use it during my mission as needed. Then, unencumbered, I slipped down to the deck and down the stairs into the body of the yacht to find somewhere to hide.

I ghosted in bare feet across the main saloon. I could smell garlic from a recently cooked meal and hear music wafting up from the staterooms below. The *Astasha* was nearly 89 feet in length and, according to blueprints, had three levels. Bridge and saloons on top, with two large staterooms mid-deck, and another five small rooms for passengers and crew below. Max said these smuggling runs had between 15 and 30 women, and I tried to imagine how you would secure them for the crossing. You could either lock them in two large groups in the main staterooms, or you could split them into smaller groups and distribute them around the boat. We had been surprised such an expensive transport of superyachts was employed, when container ships were common for human trafficking. Max had explained that the yachts were being transshipped anyway, and for the higher-end women, the better conditions made a difference. Not one of the yachts had successfully been raided, and so it was a trusted method for their best product.

I peeked my head quickly into the bridge area, then ducked back. There were two men at the controls drinking what smelled like coffee — lounging in the captain's chairs — in front of an array of levers and buttons, lit by a green glow from four complicated-looking screens. I slipped down the main gangway into the bowels of the boat and checked each cabin. I found one man in a small aft cabin asleep in his bunk with the door ajar. I passed a door marked 'Shower' and heard activity inside. There was one more cabin with a closed door, which may or may not be have been occupied, but I didn't open it just in case. The other small rooms were unoccupied, so there appeared to be four or maybe five crew on board so far.

I climbed a small, steep ladder near the bow into another gangway on the mid-deck and snuck a quick glance into the two large staterooms. Up until this point, I had not been sure if this was the boat that would be carrying the women, but what I saw gave me relief that I was in the right place. Both had their queen beds removed and a series of bunks installed. The master room had eighteen, configured as nine upper and lower bunks, and the smaller had room for ten with four uppers and lowers, plus two singles near the bulkhead where it curved too tightly for a double bed. Twenty-eight bunks in total, so on a run with 30, two would have to sleep in a smaller cabin or perhaps on the floor. Both doors had bolts to lock from the outside, but both had an ensuite bathroom. Fifteen women to a bathroom would be difficult. I considered slipping under the bunks to mingle with the passengers as an option but decided to look for something better.

I slipped back down to the lower deck and edged aft along the lower companionway and found the engine room. Two large diesel engines stood side by side in a small, smelly space. At the back of the room was a series of small lockers, with tools, engine supplies, and various lubricants inside on neat shelves. Two of the lockers were empty and large enough for me to curl up inside. A quick trip back to the mast and I retrieved my food and water but left the radio and pistol, then nabbed a pillow from each of the two empty small rooms and made myself a small nest in a locker at the back of the engine room. I was concerned about fumes and thought I may have to relocate if it got too funky with the engines fired up.

I was already feeling hungry but didn't want to touch my supplies yet. I settled back into the darkness and listened to my heart slowly settle from its rapid rabbit thump to something more dignified. I had left my watch back on *Cassis*, as it tended to light up as I moved which could have given me away. After perhaps one to two hours, I heard activity above me for perhaps twenty minutes, and then — suddenly, and surprisingly loudly — first one and then the other engine sprang to life. The gentle rocking gave way to a more purposeful and stable sense of movement. At this point I knew I could slip back over the side and was confident I could swim to shore, but as the engines fell into a steady throbbing drone, I imagined that option fading as we presumably were heading farther from the beach.

At some point I wanted to do some reconnaissance but decided that should be much later, when hopefully the crew had fallen into a routine and were dulled by boredom. I decided to let myself drift off to sleep to the diesel lullaby.

*

I awoke in the darkness and felt stiff and groggy, unsure if it was just from sleeping an unknown amount of time or if the engine fumes were taking their toll. I slipped out of the locker and turned on the engine room lamp, and felt my head clearing quickly. There didn't appear to be much other than heat and noise coming from the engines, so I decided it was the effects of sleep; the space was adequately ventilated. I took a few small sips of water, ate a granola energy bar from my supply, and did some callisthenics to loosen up. Then I thought of a problem: Sooner or later I would need to pee, and sometime later something bigger. Recalling the layout, there were the two ensuites, presumably now behind locked doors, plus the head in the shower room I had passed which presumably the crew all shared. I had an image of dangling my ass over the side, with Ethan and company getting a bird's-eye view of my ablutions. As is always the case, as soon as I had limited options to pee, the urge increased.

I repacked my locker and turned off the engine-room light, then cracked the door seal and peeked out. The gangway stretched out towards the bow, and two of the smaller cabins had their doors open and were spilling light and — a bizarre choice for hardened traffickers — Andra Day's song *Rise Up* into the hallway. At least it masked the noisy engines that would sound louder when I opened the door. I closed the door, and turned on the light, and examined a small escape hatch I had noticed in the ceiling of the engine room. In my mind I pictured it emerging on the fantail. Not knowing if it was day or night, or who might be up there, I wasn't keen to open it. I examined it for anything that might be an alarm switch or wires. A light popping up on the bridge console and someone investigating wouldn't be great. I undid the latch in case I wanted to come in that way later but left it closed. Overall, I decided once I had scouted it out from above, the hatch would be a better choice than the door, as the engine noise escaping as I opened it was much less likely to be heard at the remote, stern area where the exhausts were already blasting away, than in a quiet, internal corridor. But for now, I went back to the door, doused the lights once more, and went silently into the corridor.

I crept slowly forward to the first open door and glanced in. It was empty. I stepped in and looked around. There was an alarm clock on the bedside that informed me it was just after noon. The room was clearly in use, various clothes were spread around, and a toiletry bag lay open. A pair of shorts, with a pair of underpants still snagged inside, sat on the floor at the end of the bunk; and on the bunk was a wallet, keys, and various artifacts. Looking at it all, I decided someone had just stripped and made their way down to the shower. On the bed also was a Taser. I quickly looked around and found no other weapons. That made sense. The girls were an expensive product worth all the cost of renting this boat and fuel for the trip and popping bullets into them was bad business. Keeping them drugged and stunning anyone who made trouble made more sense. I had very little concern about the men on the boat, provided they were unarmed. If it came to a hand-to-hand fight, in the small space on the boat, I was very confident I would win, even against all of them at once. I examined the Taser and saw it was one that shot fine wires into its target, over which the high voltage current travelled. Borrowing nail clippers from the toiletry bag, I carefully snipped the wires where they entered the unit. They would still fire, but hopefully not transfer the current. I poked the loose ends until they could not be seen, popped the Taser back into its holster and, keeping the clippers, slipped back out of the room. I made it a mission to locate and sabotage the remaining Tasers whenever the chance presented itself.

Since the head was occupied, I slunk back to the engine room and waited for what I guessed was 30 minutes. Retracing my steps, the door to the first room was now closed, so I slipped past and peered into the second. A tall man was asleep on the bunk with his back to me. I crept past his door, let myself into the head, and quickly took care of business. I grimaced as I flushed, but no one came banging on the door to see where the noise came from. I snuck back into the gangway and to the bow, passing several closed doors on the way, and climbed up to the mid-level. I carefully looked over the top of the staircase and saw a man sitting in the corridor on a deck chair, between the two large staterooms. The doors were bolted, but they appeared to need to be guarded, too. It crossed my mind it might be as much to protect the merchandise from the crew as it was to ensure no one escaped.

The ladder continued to the upper deck and emerged under the bridge, into a small cubby that led out into the main saloon. It was empty of people, but full of boxes. I examined them quickly. There were roughly 300 small ration packs, presumably two per girl per day, and about 30 cases of bottled water. Next to the water cases was a small table containing a jug, empty except for a turkey baster. Next to that sat three demi jars that looked like they came from a pharmacy. I didn't recognize the chemical names on the labels, but clearly the captors were drugging the water bottles before handing them out to the women.

I continued on through the saloon and looked up to the bridge, where three men stood talking and watching out of the front window. The yacht appeared to be on autopilot. I held my breath and tiptoed out onto the fantail, looking backwards to see if anyone could see me. I stepped quickly around a bulkhead, out of sight of the bridge, and let out my breath. I worked my way over to the port side of the fantail and located the hatch that led down into the engine room. It was discretely located, and I decided — all things considered — a safer egress point that the one I was using into the corridor. I popped it open and checked once more for alarm wires. Finding none, I lowered myself down and closed it behind me.

I dozed on and off for hours, and eventually nature decided I needed to make another trip topside. Still just for number one. When I inspected the top side of the hatch, I noticed a small hole in the ship's side where the ropes and cables ran to moor us to shore and decided I could try wedging my ass into it to pee. I carefully released the lock on the hatch, tipped it up an inch, then another, until I could see the coast was clear. I crept onto the deck, checked I was alone, and peed in the hole. I nearly cried out in surprise when a freak but saucy wave splashed up and found my bare bum, and I bit down quickly to keep silent. I decided some fresh air would do me good, so I climbed out on the fairing below the bridge, where I could only be seen by someone walking along the side of the boat, which was very unlikely. I was perched right under the bridge and could hear conversation from inside. I listened intently, but it was mostly soccer, girls, food, and where they would go once they were paid off. I sat out there for a few hours, and as the sky in the east began to grow pink, I slipped back down through the hatch and shut myself in. I ate an energy bar, drank some water, and dozed some more.

This became my routine for a couple of days. I made a point to maintain an exercise regime, designed to keep me sharp and limber. On the third day, I was woken by someone banging around in the engine room, right outside my cupboard. I held my breath and listened. From the noises, I decided it was a routine inspection, perhaps adding oil or checking other fluid levels. The noises went away after ten minutes and I dozed some more. Another day, then another. It was becoming hard to track.

It became routine for the crew. A man of North African extraction slept during the day and manned the bridge through the night. The others took the day shift. Roughly every two hours at night, the day shift took turns to rouse themselves and spend fifteen or twenty minutes with the North African. Whether this was for company, safety, or to ensure he was awake I couldn't tell, but it made it easy for me to slip around unnoticed once I discerned the pattern. Knowing where people were and when meant I had the opportunity to slip in and out of their cabins to reconnoitre and raid the water and food which had not been drugged. I was bored to death, but fit and fed. I had a fright one night using the head for number two, when someone tried the handle and slapped the door. I made a slight grunt and they left me to my business and racing pulse.

On what must have been night five, give or take a night, I slipped up through the hatch and found the weather cooler and a swell beginning to build. Perhaps bad weather was coming in. I climbed to my perch under the bridge window, but it was getting colder. After perhaps an hour, the first raindrop bounced off the fairing and hit my leg. I took one last look around and slid down the curve of the wall to the narrow walkway and edged my way silently back to the aft deck. As I bent to open the hatch, a shadow passed over me and I reacted. I dropped a little lower and spun to the right and came up into a loose Kokutsu-dachi stance, rear leg bent strongly at the knee, foot turned 90 degrees to the side; front leg straight, and my body turned 90 degrees my head square to the front. This is a basic karate stance — fantastic for counter attacks — and looks quite scary. This was a tactical error on my part because the wide-eyed North African standing six feet away panicked and reached for his Taser. Had I played the drugged, lost prisoner, he may have stepped in close and made it easy for me. I forced myself to relax and stand, a little stooped, and I held out my hand and croaked for a bottle of water. I knew I was in trouble as my fast-speed eyes saw his finger tighten on the trigger and his aim shift a fraction. I started to move. The North African aimed at my chest and got far enough to the left that the darts stuck into my right forearm. I was tensed for the painful, debilitating shock, but it never came. Some bitch with nail clippers was to blame.

The North African's eyes opened even wider and he stared at me and the Taser, confused, and he was beginning to register he had a problem. I continued moving to my left and leaped upwards towards a tall bulkhead, which I ran up in two small steps, parkour style, and bounced high to come down at him from above. Trying to fling himself away, he started forward, and my kick skimmed his ducking head. I followed through and landed partly on his back, my arm around his throat. Totally out of control, he kept running, beating at me over his shoulder, his head turned at me trying to decide what kind of demon I might be. By the time he realized he was about to sail over the side, it was too late for him. I flung myself off, but he grabbed my arm in an attempt to save himself. The only thing that saved me from following him into the dark-green, phosphorescent sea was the wires from the Taser snagged on the cleat where the mooring lines would fasten in harbour. He had dropped the Taser, and the wires ran up and cut into my hand, as the handle part smashed into a knuckle. I grabbed it and held on tight. The lines tensed, but it was enough of a jerk to tear his sweaty hands off my rain-smeared shoulder, down my arm, and away over the side with a terrified cry.

I was half over the side, one arm and one leg dangling perilously, and feeling that any second I could slip off of the wet deck. I gingerly edged back onto all fours and caught my breath. Unwrapping the Taser wires, I kissed them, and flung them off after the sorry North African who was already lost in the darkness. I stood quickly and took shelter to the side, in case anyone had heard the commotion. After a few minutes, no one had appeared. My heart rate had dropped a little, and my hand had bled a small pool by my feet. I sucked on the cut and ventured up to the now-empty bridge and raided the first aid kit for disinfectant cream and a Band-Aid. I considered attempting a radio call but was put off by the daunting array of technology.

The ship would remain pilotless until someone came to check, and then a search would ensue. After they checked the North African was not using the head, they would scour the boat inside and out. This was a problem. My first thought was to slip into a stateroom and mingle with the women. Hide in plain sight, so to speak. The padlocks on the doors defeated that plan. In the end, I felt I had two choices: Either climb the mast and hide there in the dark as best I could—I had heard somewhere that searchers rarely look up—or I could retreat to my locker and hope they didn't look there. The increasing rain, and fear of still being there frozen as it got light, made me come down in favour of the retreat plan. I grabbed a towel from the saloon bar, cleaned away any trace of blood, and disposed of the towel into the sea. The bar gave me an idea. I left a glass and a bottle of Bourbon on the gunnel on the aft deck, hoping it would look like the missing crew member had taken a break and slipped over the side. I dropped back through the hatch, fastened it tight, and used my stolen cushion to mop up the small amount of rain that had followed me down. I spent a long time tensed for action in the locker before I eventually fell asleep without hearing a sound from the remainder of the crew. The next night I crept out, and a new guy was manning the bridge, as if nothing was untoward.

*

Perhaps six or eight days passed in total with little more variation to the routine. A measure of time was spent watching the cut on my hand slowly heal. One night, as I sat under the bridge in the dark and listened to the men talk, a radio call came in. The conversation was in English, rather than the French I had been listening to for days, and the speaker had a deep voice and Cajun accent. I gleaned that we would rendezvous with, of all things, a submarine at 10 pm the following night. The sub would carry half the girls and take them to a transfer point where they would be met by a *Zodiac*, then come back and repeat the process for the remaining women. The second rendezvous would be at 3 am. This was information I needed to relay to my allies on the *Cassis*.

I waited an hour until all seemed quiet inside and peeked into the bridge. The new night man was monitoring the controls, and the others seemed to have retired. I clambered carefully up the mast, pulled the radio I had stored in the cubby earlier, and tried to contact *Cassis*. The radio remained quiet, and I decided *Cassis* must be outside of the four- or five-mile maximum range of the unit, or the battery had drained to the point the range was much shorter. I made my way back down to the saloon, found some paper and a pen, and climbed back up to the drone. I made several notes in crisp print and held them in front of the camera for a minute each. Hopefully my message about the rendezvous, and that I would attempt to transfer the SPOT tracker to the submarine somehow, would make it through. I picked up the tracker and radio and returned to my closet for the duration of the next day.

The SPOT battery was two-thirds drained, so I turned it off to save it. Rough math said when I turned it on, it would go for perhaps 48 hours more. I had not thought to bring a charging cable. I spent a lot of time thinking about how I could attach it to the sub, so Kelsie could keep up with the women. Perhaps I could slip into the water and find something above water level on the sub to attach it to. Perhaps break into the stateroom and give it to one of the women to carry. Nothing I came up with seemed very viable, so I decided to pretty much do what I had done to date: Wing it.

The next evening, I emerged early and slipped up to my hideout on the fairing. I reasoned everyone would be focused on the fantail and not looking up at me. There was a cold breeze and I shivered. Or perhaps that was fear. I heard noises below and peeked over the fairing, looked down onto the back of the yacht. The prisoners were being brought out and made to sit on the floor in two lines. I counted eleven women. The engine slowed and all was relatively quiet, *Astasha* rocking in a light swell, the distant sound of seagulls providing an eerie backdrop. After ten minutes or so, a light came on perhaps 50 feet to our stern and started travelling towards us. Out of the darkness came a small fishing boat; it approached the fantail at a slight angle and drifted slowly past to our starboard side. Then, following the fishing boat came the weirdest sight: A man seemed to be standing on the water, travelling our way holding a flashlight. As he got closer, I could see he was standing on a platform that was so low in the water it was almost invisible. Using a headset, he helped the sub's pilot to steer the sub right up to the rear of the yacht's fantail, where he caught a line and secured it to a cleat on the platform by his feet.

One at a time, the women were helped across a plank onto the platform, then they disappeared down into the submarine. There was no way I could get close to the sub, and if I had been able to, almost none of the sub showed above the waterline, and I doubted the SPOT would work underwater. I would have to come up with a better plan by the time the sub returned. Half of the women had crossed over, and the transfer was proving hard due to the drugs the men had given their prisoners, which made the women unsteady and sluggish.

As the next woman stood, a large wave rolled in and lifted, then dropped the stern and she lost her balance. One of the crew had been steadying her, but she fell away from him and plunged towards the water, falling onto her face at the edge of the deck. The man dived to her and grabbed her before she slipped over the side, and the only other man on the deck also moved to help. Without thinking, I dropped quickly down onto the fantail, sat next to the last woman in line, and lowered my head, looking as drugged as I could. I quickly stuffed the SPOT into the front of my jeans and tensed and ready for battle. If I was discovered, I would take out these men and jump into the sub after the girls.

The woman who had slipped was helped up and onto the sub, and then the routine recommenced. No one appeared to be keeping count, and eventually I was helped to my feet. I leaned heavily onto the man helping me, and in no time at all, disappeared into the hatch into the darkness below.

THE NUDE DETECTIVE

16: Worship

[Ethan] — We stood there silently, looking at Gia's ghostly image staring back at us. I felt sick and my guts twisted in horror. My concern for the twenty-two women in peril paled in comparison to the concern I felt for Gia; I felt a flush of shame for thinking that way. I shook myself and noticed the room was looking at me.

"Do we go after her?" Kelsie verbalized the question we all had on our minds.

"We need to buy time while we think this through." I reached for the intercom phone, called the bridge, and had them prepare to leave immediately. It would normally take almost an hour for such a complex ship to secure all watertight spaces, set up navigation, and get underway, but the crew did it in less than thirty minutes. Kelsie provided the bridge with the course and direction to parallel and overtake *Astasha*. It was helpful knowing all traffic leaving the Mediterranean passes through the narrow strait south of Gibraltar, so we made an arc which took us three miles to the south and poured on 32 knots — our top speed.

Using our secret method, I sent Max our agreed emergency code but did not know when we would hear from him. I knew I could rapidly call on a lot of capabilities but storming a moving superyacht at sea was not one I felt I could attempt without putting the women on that ship at risk. We needed professionals. Assuming *Astasha* was heading for the southern USA, a distance of roughly six thousand nautical miles, and if they could maintain 25 to 30 knots, the transit time would be eight to ten days. Plenty of time for Gia to be discovered. If she was, there were several possible outcomes: She could be killed and tossed over the side; she could be captured and complete the transit as a prisoner; or she could take down the few guards we had seen and need our help. An alternative scenario, as we didn't know Gia's motives, was that she had no intention of allowing the yacht to get far and was attempting a rescue, from which she might need help sooner rather than later. Marcy and I were discussing these and other scenarios when Kelsie broke into our conversation.

"I've just received a message from Gia on my personal email. Or rather, it is GPS data from a SPOT tracker, complete with a message."

"Please explain what that means," Marcy replied.

"Satellite communication takes a lot of power, and bandwidth is expensive. The way SPOT devices work is to send one of three very short codes to the satellite, which relays that code to a ground station. The codes include the GPS location of the SPOT. In mode One, it just repeatedly sends the position data on a pre-set schedule. You can vary the frequency from once every five minutes, to hourly. More frequently gives a more detailed position but uses more power. These positions are posted to a private website that has a map and posts the locations like a trail of breadcrumbs. People with the web address can follow the progress of the SPOT as it moves. On first transmitting, it sends an email to a pre-set list with the link to the map. I was on that list, and it looks like Ethan is, too.

"Mode two is triggered by pressing a button on the device and it sends a different code but does not repeat it. When the service gets the mode two code, it sends a pre-recorded email to a different email list, but in our case, it is a duplicate of the first list. The message would typically be something like 'I am OK.' In this case, Gia sent a longer message. It looks like she triggered mode one and mode two together. I have a link to the map, which tracks to our radar data of the *Astasha*, confirming the SPOT is somewhere on board. The mode two message reads, 'Accept you are tracking *Astasha* with intent to follow to locate base. I am riding shotgun to protect captives. Intention to hide, and only intervene if anyone is threatened.' End message." There is a mode three, a cry for help mode. Once triggered, it routes the GPS location to emergency services, who would assume someone is injured or lost and respond with a rescue."

"Well that explains what the hell she is doing, but not why she has taken off on a solo mission," growled Marcy. Marcy the cop was not happy with civilian interference. It didn't seem like the right moment to mention she and Gia had exactly the same authority—none—outside of her jurisdiction. That was Marcy the cop; but Marcy the woman looked stricken with worry for Gia. I suspect had she thought of it, she might now be there at Gia's side.

Thirty minutes passed, then my cell rang. It was Max, the cell signal relayed via the ship's satellite service. I briefed Max on events and asked him if he could connect us to regional law enforcement, who would be interested in human trafficking and had the capabilities to intercept a ship at sea in a hostage situation. After some thought, he explained that it would be a jurisdictional nightmare, given they were already in international waters, but left the call to make enquiries. He called back 40 minutes later, and I put him on speaker so Marcy could contribute.

"This would be a gong show," he said. "My Interpol contacts seemed more interested in why you are running a clandestine operation in French waters than they were interested in helping. I've got them to put that aside, but the reality is, *Astasha* is now running along the edge of Spanish international waters. If she sees us approaching and cuts towards the coast, she will enter their jurisdiction, so it would have to be a joint French/Spanish endeavour. We could wait until Gibraltar and ask the Brits, or we could wait until they are out in the Atlantic and try for a US response. The most likely response would be something like a Coast Guard cutter interception, and they would flank the target with helicopter and Zodiac-borne officers. Nothing stealthy. If the crew don't surrender, it becomes a nasty hostage situation. And the crew will be more scared of the Toussaints than of law-abiding law-enforcement personnel."

"Any good news or suggestions?"

"Sure. I have two buddies who are ex-SEALs. The three of us go in at night by Zodiac and storm the ship. They've practised this often, and I've done some similar hostage-rescue shit. There will only be half a dozen crew. We can launch from Gibraltar and lie in front of them, and as they come past, slip in behind."

"Hang on," interrupted Marcy. "Your plan sounds better than the Coast Guard plan, but it is high risk to the women, and — not to mention — you. I just got you back, Max! On the other hand, if we do nothing, the yacht steams to its destination. If Gia stays undetected, we could intercept them at the far end. Which might be better or might be worse. And if Gia is detected, the crew better be good or she's going to kick their asses anyway. What if we wait until they make landfall? I'm mad at Gia for going in half-cocked, and without a plan. But if that were me, and you charged in like the cavalry and got me shot, I would skin you alive. If that was you, you would hate the idea we were even thinking of second-guessing you. We are treating her like a *helpless woman*. We could try trusting her and see this as an improvement in the half-assed plan we had anyway. We are overreacting because it is someone we know. We didn't plan to do this for the other twenty-two victims."

Max and I were quiet. We both wanted to tell her she was wrong. But she wasn't. It was worth considering. Then Gwen added her thoughts.

"The other consideration is the prisoners' state of mind. Obviously, getting them back in any condition is the priority, but getting them the best medical and emotional support as quickly as possible once we have them will make a significant difference to their chances of recovery. They are no doubt drugged and being kept relatively safe during the crossing. Intercepting them in a port, where we can provide the right help quickly, would be preferable to trying to manage them afloat with very limited options, and for possibly a protracted period. If we do have to go on board in an emergency, we should be ready with a plan to keep them sedated until we can get them off and to a better facility."

"How about this," I ventured. "Max and his guys transfer to *Cassis*, then we close the gap on *Astasha*. The Straight of Gibraltar is a natural funnel, so us moving in is not unexpected and should not cause them any concern. If we think the shit will hit the fan, we can launch the *Zodiac*, and we can bring in a helicopter, too. *Cassis* has a pad. I assume one of your buddies could bring and fire a sniper rifle and we could remove the chopper's doors and provide limited air support. We could monitor the situation and make a final decision at the narrows. If all is quiet, *Cassis* could parallel *Astasha*, and when we get an indication of their destination, we could set up something for that end. If things remain quiet, we can let it run and follow the SPOT all the way to the Toussaints' operation and have US federal enforcement take them down."

"I hate to ask though, Max," Marcy interjected softly. "Don't you have a job to do? Can you get time away again?" Max didn't answer immediately, and a heavy silence hung on the airwaves.

"I've um…kind of resigned already." He seemed embarrassed. "Seeing you guys really bought home how much I miss family. It would one thing when you didn't know I was alive, but now…and err, I know this will sound almost infantile, but I want to pursue Gia. She's…different. I can't get her out of my head."

"Can you just walk away from being undercover, Max? Will they let you?"

"To be honest, they don't have much choice. In the early days, my position was unique. We had this one-time opportunity to insert ourselves into their operation covertly. But once we mapped out the ISIL operation, I really just became another operative. I can resign my commission at any time. Sure, they would love a better transition, but when my sister is putting herself in harm's way seemingly on a routine basis, I don't really give a shit. I'm coming home. Anyway, I already resigned, as I said. It will just come a little sooner than planned, is all."

I pulled Marcy to me. Max couldn't see the impact his words had, and I guessed Marcy didn't want me to tell him she had tears streaming down her cheeks. I was choked up. All she said was, "Well don't think you are coming to live with me and cramping my style, little brother!" He laughed. I think he was overcome, too. The rest of the call was about logistics, timing, and planning and went on until morning.

*

Within twelve hours, we were slightly ahead of *Astasha*, just off the Spanish coast, and slowed to allow a Bell Long Ranger rental to settle onto the large and hydraulically extendable fantail, which doubled as our chopper pad. Typically, when carrying a chopper, *Cassis* limits her speed, but some impromptu welding and chains ensured the chopper was going nowhere, no matter our speed. Max introduced his buddies as Jim and Terry as they stepped out of the helicopter, and I wondered if those were truly their names. Both insisted on unloading their own equipment and locking it in their assigned stateroom before going to check out the Zodiac we had earmarked for operations. Max, Marcy, and I hugged and slapped backs, then went down to the operations centre.

Over the next 24 hours, nothing material happened and *Astasha* appeared to have fallen into a routine. At night we occasionally caught glimpses of Gia, who was clearly finding ways to stay unobserved and out of trouble. As we neared Gibraltar, we met in the operations centre to make some decisions. We had talked about many options, and now it was time to pick one.

The decision came fairly quickly: Kelsie and Max and his buddies would stay with *Cassis* and trail *Astasha*; Marcy and I would helicopter off to Gibraltar and fly back from there to the southern US via a circuitous route. We would take Gwen, as she would likely be safer there than on the crossing. We would assume landfall would be somewhere near New Orleans, and we would set up a base there and be ready to intercept. Via Dennis, I would connect with FBI agents and we would work out some sort of plan to roll up the Toussaint operation once we identified the location of their base.

Max's contact in Comox arranged for us to arrive secretly at Uplands Airforce base in Ottawa, from where we crossed the US border by car using our own passports. There was a fair chance organized crime might have contacts that could alert the Toussaint's, if they were still looking for us, but Max's contacts could not get us into the US the same way we had slipped into Europe. We figured crossing the border near Ottawa would give the Toussaint's no indication we were focused on them, and hoped they just believed we had been holed up in hiding.

At 43,000 ft over Greenland, in the cabin of the rented Gulfstream, we began to relax a few degrees. Making the decision that Gia knew what she was doing, and activating a plan to support this brave woman, mitigated some of the horror and helplessness we had been feeling. Somewhat shamelessly, as Jake, our cabin host, retired to wherever they hide during the flight to give their customers privacy, Marcy and I struck up a conversation with Gwen over a gin and tonic about our new favourite subject. This time Marcy kicked it off.

"Ethan and I were talking. Are you up to answering a few more questions?"

"My favourite subject I presume? Of course." Gwen laughed.

"We were relaxing on *Cassis* and lover boy here offered to give me a foot massage. He had even dug up some cream from somewhere and had it ready. Not being an idiot, I flung myself on the bed and raised a foot in the air for him to get busy rubbing. It was just a nice gesture rather than a preamble to anything kinky, but of course — with all this on our minds — we started joking about him being my foot slave."

"Nothing wrong with that," Gwen giggled. "If you want to rent him out... Just kidding!"

"Anyway, the joking got us thinking, and I asked him if he liked it. You know, rubbing my feet."

I interrupted and took over. "It's funny. Before she made the crack, I hadn't thought about it. I've seen fetish images about PVC-clad men licking and worshiping women's high heels. I love women in heels, but a fetish? I don't think so. A bit far-fetched for us we think, but when I reflected on how I felt massaging Marcy's feet, there was something more than just being kind and making her feet feel better. I know you were joking, but if I rubbed your feet it would be like a friend doing it for a friend, but doing it for Marcy—there was a slight feeling of, well," I stumbled, embarrassed, "well, worship. It was a very mild version of worship, but it was there nonetheless." Marcy jumped in and took back her story.

"So to return the favour, I then massaged his feet and felt something similar."

Gwen smiled. "There's worship-worship and then there is *worship*. Different flavours and degrees. The hardest part to get your head around is worship as part of sex, as that instantly feels wrong, but check that thought for a second. As humans we are riddled with worship genes, and examples are all around us. Gods and deities of course, for some. But for others, sports stars. Movie celebrities, parents, valedictorians, war heroes, the person who found your lost cat and even bosses on occasion. We are wired with the urge to be liked, and our society has a desire to put people on pedestals. We do the same to a lesser extent to things. Crosses, exotic cars, mansions, and so on. So worship is all around us. If you think about it that way, it would be odd not to do it in the bedroom too, wouldn't it?

"Try this," she continued, now on a roll. "Assume for the sake of argument, when you settle in together, you split the cooking evenly, assuming billionaires ever cook, of course. Say you like cooking. It's not a chore. This goes on for months. Then, one of you cooks dinner for the other's birthday. You make an extra effort. Part of that effort might be to spend a little more time, light a candle, set the table differently, put extra effort into making it come out well. My point is this: cooking a birthday meal feels different from cooking daily. It is a meal cooked from love, rather than the need to eat. Worship is a form of showing love and devotion. Service slaves are a type of submissive who like lists of chores to perform for their dominant. Sometimes it's people who enjoy the feeling of being humiliated. Sometimes it's people who like to be made to do things as a punishment. But for people who are not full-fledged service slaves, and their dominant tells them to do some household chores as a fun forfeit, perhaps naked, there is a similar feeling to worship. You pay a little more attention and take a little more care than a regular chore. Your master or mistress might inspect your work overtly, which they don't in regular situations. The thought of this raises your feeling of psychodrama, and the juices of arousal in our brains start to flow.

"A fetish is defined as arousal or gratification to an abnormal degree from an object or body part. Most of us find women in high-heel shoes mildly arousing, so a shoe fetishist does so a little or a lot more than most. If a dominant knows their sub is aroused by shoes, they can increase the psychodrama of a scene by having their sub hold, or kiss, or otherwise focus on the shoe. Like cooking or doing other work because your goddess asked, kissing her foot can induce that worship feeling for some. If worshiping, or being worshipped, makes you feel special in any way, and in a loving or sexual situation, tell me why that is worse than worshiping Ovechkin or Trudeau?

"There are other reasons for making your slave kiss your feet, of course. If you are into D/s, — dominance and submission — by definition there is a consensual imbalance of power. In some scenarios it is fun to dramatically emphasize that imbalance by the top making the bottom do acts of extreme servitude, such as grovelling or foot worship. I use the word 'dramatically' in both senses: to 'accentuate' and to raise the sense of drama in the scene. Think of psychodrama as a catalyst in most sexual situations. Some like a lot of ritual in their BDSM: costumes, protocols, and so on, as that is high psychodrama. Some find that too much and like it much more casual, but the drama is still present and it helps to be conscious of how you play with it."

We lapsed into silence as we each let our mind process this information. I got up, refilled the G&Ts, and settled back into my chair.

"Why is psychodrama so important?" I asked.

"I think there is a chemical reaction to it in the brain, but that is still being proven. Remember, this is a field that has had very little research funding to date. But chemicals aside, there is a psychological mechanism in play for both dommes and subs. BDSM currently exists outside of societal norms, and for some that 'taboo-ness' is the attraction. They like to be different. But for most, we have an internal conflict to deal with. Society enforces rules, and for good reason, of course. You have to be fair. Things must be equal. You can't tell people what to do or embarrass them. You can't inflict physical or psychological pain on another. But in some scenarios, we actually want to, or want someone to do it to us, but we feel that is 'wrong.'

"Here is an analogy: If I wanted to sing and perform in public, I would feel too afraid. I'm not good enough to be hired in a bar. I could busk, I suppose. But effectively the rules don't allow me to feel comfortable. Except for karaoke. Karaoke is a permissive scenario. In a karaoke bar, the rules change. I can get up there, and I am still judged, but with different rules and consequences. I can even allow myself to be reluctantly dragged up. BDSM is a bit like that. Ethan, I think you like the risk of being exposed nude as opposed to actually being naked in front of others, but for some they actually want to be naked and have others see them. But they can't. The rules of society don't let them. But losing at strip poker, or accepting a dare—change those scenarios and it becomes within the rules. So does BDSM. If your dominant demands you strip in front of their friends, then it is not your fault. They changed the rules and forced you. Or permitted you, where you could not before. They would also be demonstrating in front of others the consensual power discrepancy you two have created and are exploiting for fun. That others are witnessing that is also permissive and gives feedback to that part of yourself that otherwise is never witnessed and lacks its own feedback."

"Creating a stage that these parts of your psyche can be permitted to act on freely reduces or resolves the conflict. It is suddenly OK to tease or torment someone. Or strip for them. You have temporarily suspended your belief in the normal societal rules. This is now guilt-free activity for some, but not everyone can fully disassociate. And that is the power of psychodrama. For some, it helps if it is very overt. Uniforms, overt domme or sub roles, and stances; For others it is equally permissive with small gestures that substantiate the new stage you want to act on.

"Ahead of a session, we communicate what we want and what we don't. Some call it the negotiation, but I don't like that term, as it implies one side is attempting to win things from the other that they don't want to give up. Anyway, both sides should share, as transparently as they can, their likes, dislikes, and hard and soft limits. They should talk about things they are open to trying, and if they are personally drawn to or curious about it or just happy to support the other's exploration. What is vital to build trust is to be very clear about what you don't want to do. If your limits are not clear and the other goes there, it can dissolve trust rapidly. And, you agree this as your general set of rules, but then when you get to an actual session, double-check once more that the rules stand. You might be generally OK with anal, but on a specific day not feel like it."

"But I thought the idea was to take control away and make a sub do things they don't want to," said Marcy. "That's why I associate it so closely with abuse."

"Yes and no. We are learning to separate abusive or psychopathic acts from BDSM paraphilia by highlighting 'true' consent and honest and open, two-way communication. Consenting to something just to keep your partner happy, especially when you are significantly worried and stressed about the consequences of doing so, is not freely consenting, or being honest in your communications about your feelings. We have a principle that it should be safe, sane, and consensual—or SSC. I think everyone agrees they want it to be sane, although interestingly, some activities can actually be temporarily mind-altering. Some, however — like Ethan — like some risk rather than it being completely safe. Some like a lot of risk. Some love it when they give control to another and it feels non-consensual. But there is a clear difference between giving someone that power versus them taking it against your will. So what we try to create is 'consensual non-consent. We give power for an agreed period and within guidelines, and we should have a way to take the power back if we need to, such as a safe word. So BDSM folks have also coined the phrase RACK, or 'risk-aware consensual kink'. You are aware of the risk, perhaps like a skydiver or boxer. You give consent to take control. It can be a little control or almost all control, but I would never be happy seeing anyone give up total control.

"Ethan's little game is to consensually put himself into a position where fate, or you, chooses if he is going to be caught naked, or not. Ideally, he would say if he just wants to feel it might happen; sail so close to the wind that it might happen by accident but really prefers the risk never actually materializes; or say if he is truly OK if he gets caught. If the former, and accidentally he is exposed, it is OK for him to be a little upset, but he has to accept that was the risk he took and not be mad at you. He chose to put it all on the line, which for him is a big high."

"I'm right here guys," I reminded them, with a blush, and continued bashfully, "I like the skydiving analogy. I would never want the parachute to fail, but the feeling of anxiousness — even dread — leading up to the moment of truth is exhilarating, and as it is sexual in nature, arousing. It's thrilling to test myself with emotional and physical challenges which stretch my limits, but it is important that it is unpredictable too. Marcy tests me the same way, and I like it."

"That's quite a common attitude," said Gwen, "but one of many. Some hate the dread. They want to know exactly what will happen, and that it shouldn't vary. Everyone is different, which is great."

Marcy said, "I want to go back to the motivation for the dominant. You've talked about several drivers, but I worry about being mean."

"Being mean, or being seen to be mean? That's a more interesting question than it sounds. Let's assume meanness is like temperature: I might be comfortable between sixteen and twenty-two degrees, and you might be comfortable between nineteen and twenty-four. We are both OK where we overlap, but am I a bad person for liking it a little cooler than you, or you for liking it warmer? Of course not. If society came along and declared us *normal* if we like it between eighteen and twenty-two, we both have part of our comfort zone slightly out of the norm.

"I recently read some work involving nearly 100 participants tasked with choosing one of four very challenging jobs. Then they had to do the job several times over and then report back. The jobs were a) enduring the pain from standing in icy water to clean the university fish pond, b) cleaning sewers, c) killing locusts which were used in the lab, or d) assisting the people killing the locusts. Now I'll say up front, that no bugs were really hurt, but the test was designed to convince the subjects that hundreds of insects were killed by loading them into a cremation-like device that made a horrible burning smell when they activated it. The containers the bugs came in were even labelled with cutsie names."

"My God, and people chose that?"

"Actually, eighteen percent chose the icy water, and twenty-nine percent the sewer cleaning. So just over fifty percent signed up for locust killing duties, half assisting and half actually pushing the button. The bug brigade also reported slightly higher satisfaction rates, or at least were less dissatisfied. So a lot of people have parts of themselves that are at the lower and higher end of that temperature scale and are even prepared to crank the dial to feel comfortable, if the other option is experiencing personal discomfort."

"So what does that tell us?"

"Nothing really conclusive, but then think about this: For some, they might enjoy being a little mean. Not horribly so, but they like getting another person worked up and off balance. Don't confuse that with people who are pathological or narcissistic. I'm talking about people around the edges of what we've apparently deemed as the norm, as opposed to those way off the chart. You see latent meanness in youngsters more than in adults because as we grow we normalize to society's rules and suppress or even let go of that aspect of ourselves. But it's there as part of them, and it might get a kick from coming out to play if no one, especially themselves, would judge them for it. If everyone in the room likes seventeen degrees, or a degree below the socially accepted norm, why not turn down the dial? Remember what I said about BDSM temporarily changing the rules, and making things more permissive? If someone genuinely likes to be tormented and teased, or spanked or spat on, and they truly invite that activity, and if you've been suppressing a part of yourself which gets a satisfying response from doing that activity – and here is the important part- *and* there is no lasting emotional or physical harm to either of you, then it is OK, and maybe even therapeutic, to let that part of yourself out to play. But do it to someone who doesn't like it, and you *are* mean.

"The other thing the study reminds me of is that some people genuinely want to participate in BDSM activity but choose a role because they don't like the other roles for some reason. You may be a true dom. Or, you might not want to be a sub, and default towards dominant to avoid taking the submissive role. Someone might be uncomfortable with being tied up or directed, so they become a top. Some might not want the stress of making all the choices, and so choose the bottom. It's not always the desire to do something, it is the desire to play the game, but at the same time, to avoid a stressor.

"I know people who could drive down the same two-lane road and four miles ahead they have to be in the right lane to turn. Some get in the turn lane four miles early because it is a stressor if they are not ready for the turn, and they hate changing lanes. Others are stressed if they are stuck behind someone for four miles and are more relaxed changing lanes and at least feeling they are progress faster. And both are valid, but zigzagging dangerously at high speed is not, and neither is driving in one lane at thirty in a fifty zone and holding people up. It's OK to choose a less stressful path, to a point."

I wondered how prevalent these feelings are in the world, so I asked "But in all groups, this is just a very small number of people, right? Most love room temperature, don't they?"

"Remember, we don't have much data on this, but as people are feeling the stigma around BDSM decreasing, they are trending to be curious and accepting. Here are a couple of recent studies. Sticking to Canada, at the University of Quebec, Joyal and Carpentier published findings in 2016 from just north of a thousand respondents. They only looked at a small number of paraphilia, but over half of the respondents expressed interest in at least one, and a third said they had tried one at least once. Interestingly, there was very little difference between men and women around sadism and masochism.

"A recent study in Belgium polled a thousand and twenty-four people about fifty-four BDSM activities and fourteen fetishes, so a lot more detailed break out than the Quebec study. Seven-point-six percent of respondents self-identified as full on BDSM practitioners, but the survey was from the general population. Nearly forty-seven percent of respondents had performed at least one activity, and an additional twenty-two percent had fantasized about them. Twelve and a half percent said they do one or more activity on a regular basis, and twenty-six percent said they were interested in BDSM.

"They are the more scientific studies, and decent but not perfect data and methods. For example, one weakness in the study is the practitioners are all from Belgium. Does that mean Americans, Russians, and Pakistanis are the same? On a much larger if less academic scale, a large online dating agency called *OK Cupid* published a survey of its members in 2017. Of the approximately four hundred thousand respondents, half or more said they sometimes enjoyed kinky sex or fantasized about it and wanted to try it.

"Now, the trap some fall into is when they hear unfamiliar and perhaps scary terms like BDSM, their thoughts leap straight to dungeons, sex clubs, PVC outfits, and forced enemas; but the bulk of people like something much more moderate. Remember, the stigma originated from society turning against all sex that was not aimed at reproduction. That's like saying the temperature must always be eighteen point five degrees. I believe what we are seeing is the realization that actually a broader range is OK. We are much better educated and protected from sexual diseases, and so many of the causal reasons for the stigma have diminished. There are still limits to be respected, but it is OK to relax a bit and let some of our natural wiring come out to play, especially if we believe a fair percentage of the population are doing it too."

We sat quietly again, and Gwen deliberately slurped the end of her G&T, so I obligingly refreshed the glasses. I think we were all consciously but quietly giving Marcy time to place her next question as she untangled her complex feelings about abuse. She broke the silence again.

"I like the idea of all this, but still it gives me heartache. Ethan and I need to talk about what we both like a lot more and map this out."

"Yes, but you don't need to map out everything all at once. Take it a section at a time. You have your whole lives ahead of you."

"Maybe one day I would like to try the submissive role, but I'm not ready to go there. In fact, even though I thoroughly and genuinely enjoy teasing Ethan, to a surprising degree, I don't associate that activity with who I think I am."

"And you might never do so—many don't. Especially if you don't have that hidden mean streak to begin with, it is hard to create it. Here is a trick that helps some people: Create a persona or a character, or several. Build that person up in your mind. What sort of domme do you want to be? Give that character a personality and attributes. Maybe have a few characters for different occasions. When they have some substance, you can assume their identity, then step away from them when you are done. Then treat it like a game of sorts. If your character is supposed to have skills, you will need to build them, too. She might need to be an ace with ropes, or skilled with a whip, or know how to keep her man on the edge of exploding and tease him until his balls turn blue. But you don't know how to do those things. So like any avatar, you have to level up. Take your avatar out for a spin and work on simple knots first, and as she learns, so do you. Give her a name if you like, and when it is used, everyone knows it's her, and her rules and your conservative rules remain intact. Another permissive proxy 'trick'."

"That's interesting, but not me. I want to be me and find out who I am. Or could be."

"That's very common, too. These are difficult aspects of yourself to accept if you want to use them, and you want to own that responsibility and be authentic."

"Yes, that sounds more like me."

"Then to be equitable, you have to accept Ethan as being equally authentic and trust what he says. Let's imagine you decide to dabble with physical domination. He is tied up in front of you, and you get the urge to grab his hair, pull his head back sharply, and kiss him hard. Then you force him roughly to pleasure you with his tongue. Later you feel embarrassed and guilty, and you ask him what it was like for him."

I was thinking *bloody hot*, but I let her continue.

"If he says he loved it, trust him. Your instinct might be to think he was just saying that because he felt he had to, because sometimes it is harder to trust when someone admits they are turned on by something you feel guilty for enjoying. When you both come to terms with the fact you both enjoy a certain thing, and that no one was harmed, and you really are two consenting adults, it gets easier with repetition. Trust me."

*

Once in the USA, we drove to a small civilian airport where one of my companies operated a shipping business, and I commandeered a Cirrus SR22 aircraft. Small, fast, and very common in the US. I did not file a flight plan, which in theory limits how far you can travel, but I piloted the three of us 600 nautical miles to the west to another small airport, where we hopped onto a chartered jet that took us to Baton Rouge, Louisiana.

Again, to stay off the grid, one of my team in Ottawa booked a room through *Airbnb* in their own name just outside New Orleans. We arrived tired from travel, but hopefully without drawing attention to ourselves. After a brief shower, a check-in with Kelsie, who confirmed *Astasha* was steaming west as expected, we left Gwen and drove to a bar called The Toadstool. The bar was busy and noisy, with people shouting over a local band that had the stage. We had been told our contact was African American, five feet ten, would be wearing a white golf shirt with a red collar, and had a bald, shiny head. We went up and introduced ourselves. FBI Special Agent Robert Douglas Chave showed us into a booth he had reserved at the back, where it was a little quieter, and asked us to call him Bob. He explained he had been partly briefed by Dennis Preece, and we filled in the missing details. Once we were all on the same page, he leaned forward and spoke.

"First off, I want to make sure we all know the ground rules," said Bob, in a not unfriendly way. "As a civilian, Ethan, you have no authority at all, and Marcy, you are acting in the official capacity of Liaison for a Canadian law enforcement agency and as such can carry a concealed weapon for self-defence purposes; but effectively you are a silent observer, should this situation evolve into an active status. I'm obliged to say that shit and have done so. Off the record, nothing I have said changes, but I want you to know that anything you can offer us within those limits is as welcome as a keg of beer to a man in the desert. We've been circling the Toussaint's organization for three years and have made no inroads to speak of yet lost several good agents. We know this group operates somewhere out of the swamps and wetlands of the south Mississippi Delta but have had zero success locating their base. We have intercepted what we are told were drug and human trafficking ships in conjunction with the DEA at the twelve-mile limit, and there was nothing but a ferry crew each time. We have track nothing unusual on our radars, so we deduced the cargo must be offloaded in the Caribbean; but despite arranging both aerial and shore-based monitoring as they come into range we have seen nothing that explains where their 'cargo' is offloaded.

"We know the local state police are either in the pocket of the gangs or terrified of them, and who can blame them? In two years, four officers and their families who got close were executed by gang enforcers. Even the governor has been extremely cautious in this matter due to the vicious nature of the Toussaint family."

"We've seen firsthand how aggressive they are," said Marcy. "A sniper attack on me personally in Vancouver, followed closely by a helicopter assault with missiles and machine guns, which took the lives of two RCMP officers — and nearly ours too."

"I heard that from Dennis, and you were very lucky. I've never known these guys to miss their targets, and you dodged them twice."

"I imagine you have attempted to get a handle on their financial transactions? Follow the money and all that?" I asked.

"Sure, we have located four separate shell companies that they move some of their money through. We think it's just the tip of the iceberg, and we've left these companies in place so we can monitor and hopefully expand our understanding of their network. They are very well organized. Getting warrants for each step has proved very difficult, and we believe — but can't prove — that certain judges were suborned. In fact, I get pressure from my own chain of command to move on to other cases where we might have more return on investment, so to speak, and I wonder sometimes if someone above me is being influenced."

"We were penetrated in Vancouver," Marcy reminded us.

"On that note," I interrupted, "Dennis vouched for you personally. Apparently, you two have history. But who else down here knows, and how do we know who we can trust?"

"To be honest, I don't really know. We are pretty leaky. At this point I've told no one. At some point, I need to widen the net and get warrants and such; but when we do the danger increases exponentially. I appreciate this is an imposition, Ethan, but the more you and your group can handle this, the safer from exposure we all are."

I chimed in, "So we have twenty-three women, one of which works for me, headed this way, and we have GPS tracking that will let us know if the yacht stops to transfer them to another vessel; We have the potential for video surveillance if we can get within a few miles and capture the signal. I have a team working out how to do that now. Our ship, the *Cassis*, is paralleling *Astasha* but staying at least five miles south so as not to raise suspicion. We've filed papers to dock at Galveston, which implies our yacht is being moved to the US under a potential long-term contract for a wealthy family based in Texas. If anyone is checking, they will hopefully at least not see anything unusual there. As we get nearer to the coast, and the seas calm some, we can launch small boats from the *Cassis* with equipment that can access the cameras we planted on board. The boats are small enough the radar on the *Astasha* won't pick them up.

"Let's talk about the likely scenarios, and what the FBI can do," I continued. "Firstly, if it makes sense to just rescue the women, do you have a seagoing hostage rescue capability? Secondly, if the women are transferred to a different vessel, can you track it to their base? Lastly, if we find their base, can you take it out?"

Chave didn't hesitate and confidently, if exasperatedly, replied, "We could certainly mount a water rescue, although I think we all know that is a crap shoot. The bad guys wouldn't get away, but if they see us coming, they could kill the women before we could board and secure them. We've attempted to track suspected Toussaint movements on the Mississippi and so far have either lost them in the clutter, or they detect us and just moor somewhere to wait us out. They certainly seem to be able to detect any water and air surveillance we put up. We suspect they are somehow plugged into the DEA search radar and sonar facilities used to interdict drug runners and are using our own system against us. As to shutting down their base if we find it, we can bring in resources from out of state — like FBI SWAT and other tactical teams; but until we know the situation on the ground, we would be going in blind and that would have two implications: The safety of innocent civilians would be at risk, and we would have no way to confirm the Toussaint's are actually on site. When we show our hand, we certainly want to take them off the board. In fact, the latter has a secondary issue, especially for you. Just because they are in custody doesn't mean that through their lawyers they can't hit back at us with assassinations."

We discussed several other scenarios and agreed to meet daily here at the bar as *Astasha* made her passage westward.

17: Gopher Hunt [Landon]

I turned and spat over the rail into the swamp, but I didn't give ground on my stare with Kemper. We called Kemper 'Knickerless' partly as his given name was Nicolas and we swamp hillbillies like to seem juvenile and naive, but also to remind him of the hold we had on his genitals. Kemper is head of the US Drug Enforcement Agency, or DEA, in Mississippi, and as we always do, once a month, we had him and his perty wife Addison come to the ranch for a nice lunch. At these here meetings, Kemper would divulge anything we asked because his wife would be in a cage hanging over the swamp and her panties would be sitting on the table between us. We insisted she always arrived wearing some, and they always must be pink. Had her buy a pack from Walmart just for these occasions.

He had seen, with his own eyes, us drown his predecessor in the cage, then feed his remains to the gators. He has no doubt in his little ole mind that first his wife, then himself, could easily go that way if we chose to end our productive relationship. And if that was not enough, his two girls were left behind in child care within easy reach, and he knew we had no compunction in adding them as assets in a future batch of girls we sell around the USA if he didn't toe the line.

My brother Seth reached over and stroked Kemper's wife's knickers with his middle finger to re-enforce our hold on him and repeated my question.

"Did y'all not hear my brother Landon ask where the billionaire and his slut cop girlfriend are hidin' out?" He banged the table to punctuate the sentence good, which made Kemper jump some. Seth is as skinny as I am fat, and when he get mad his eyes bug and spittle flies about.

"Do y'all really want us to dangle lil' Addy there a bit lower so her feet are in the water for them snakes, gators and p'rannas to nibble?"

Seth was truly terrifying to behold, an' we agreed he would do the bullying in these situations. I think I'm meaner, but I tend to look a bit like a teddy-bear gone crazy. Frightening in itself, but it leaves room for doubt. Seth's form of crazy is an absolute promise of bad things to come.

"W...w...we might have just had a break today. As I've said, they dropped off the grid and I took a lot of risk to find them, pulling in favours and all. We just got a hit as they crossed into the states in New Hampshire. Figured they were holed up out in Montreal until now. He has a lot of business interests in the US. He was seen in a rental car and we have the plates. It's just a matter of time now."

"When y'all find him, have them both taken into custody and put somewhere we can get at them. I don't like the notion that others might get from him giving us a black eye. Makes us seem weak!"

"Yes sir," sweated Kemper.

We toyed with Kemper a little more and made sure he knew where his resources should not be for the next few days, then sent him and his wife on their way. We always give him many fake locations his teams should avoid, to mask the real shipments we plan. In the next few days we have a full load coming through. We have two large shipments of 'H' heading up through Mexico, which is freighted across to our base here at La Hatch, just south of New Orleans. Three dozen women from Colombia and Mexico on a freight barge inbound to Galveston. They come in containers and then truck across to here. Our submarine will pick up four cases of drugs and a couple of dozen girls coming in from France, and ferry all of them up into the Mississippi and transfer them to *Zodiacs*, which will bring them here.

We cut and repackage the drugs, then truck them up to Baton Rouge to the Danstead shipping facility. The wonders of online shopping have helped us amazingly. Danstead is an aggregator of shipments for small to medium-sized businesses who can't compete with Amazon directly, that ship their products around the world. Danstead has a network of massive, robotized warehouses, and we have a guy who programs the robots and the tracking system. We take our product into a loading bay at the Baton Rouge facility, and robots mix it into the millions of packages being shipped around North America, essentially invisibly. No trace of our shipment appears in the system, but a robot at another location delivers it onto an untracked truck some days later. Been doing this for three years without a single issue. Magical. We would have it made if we could just ship whores that way too.

The girls we give medicals and fix them up with clothes and a hairdo, then photograph and video them for their auction. On the dark web, our customers across North America select what they need and we deliver in the most expedient way.

At the Louisiana and Mississippi state level, including feds who focus here full time, we have enough government and law enforcement people in our pockets to avoid any issues. The only area that is harder to control is the sea border with the Coast Guard and law from out of state. Their long-range and airborne radar means they know pretty much where every vessel is, and they can board them at will once they reach American waters — or before if they get agreement or have sufficient reason. From South America we can rely pretty much on land travel with our contacts looking the other way, but anything from Europe, which really means Russia or the Arab nations, we used to have many losses. It was Destiny that solved that problem years ago.

Our mother, Destiny Toussaint, took her aunt Patti's kids to Disney World in Florida and they went on an undersea adventure. There was a network of underwater tunnels with transparent, see-through walls. Tourists would walk through and gaze at the fish. There was also a miniature submarine that took them a few feet down for a quick ten-minute tour. As she sat there with her nephew on her knee, she reasoned — correctly as it turned out — that a similar network of tunnels here in the swamps would be undetectable and that a submarine that could ferry our contraband from international waters to the swamp might make that part of our operation invisible.

It took nearly four years to build both our under-swamp base and our submarine. Submarine might be a little grand a word for our vessel, but that's how we think of it. We've named it The Crawfish. The Crawfish doesn't dive far or have an engine. It is a long tube with canvas seats and a bottled air supply that can take twelve small people, including the pilot. The pilot has a little control over buoyancy using air and water tanks and some fins if the Crawfish is in motion. Propulsion comes from the tug, which tows it through the water.

The tug is a real fishing vessel, which actually makes some nice money when not in our employ, but as required will tow the Crawfish back and forth on a two-hundred-foot tow line. It's been inspected a dozen times, but as the coast guard comes close, she just drops the tow cable. Once the coast is clear the sub pops up and they grab the tow cable and continue.

The girls are so out of it, most don't remember the journey. We've had a small number that did. Well, they are the cost of doing business I guess, and won't be telling no one now the gators had their fun.

From the back of the ranch here, we have an under-swamp tunnel that runs a few hundred yards beneath the river to the far bank, then on a little farther to a slightly raised bluff a few hundred yards wide. Under the buff, the tunnels fan out into a series of rooms we use as the main base of operations. Here at the ranch, the tunnel entrance is well hidden. In the back wall of our garage, a three-feet-thick concrete wall on a hydraulic hinge opens the way to a staircase that leads down to the swamp base. If we were searched and they x-rayed the wall, they wouldn't see much as it's too thick for them to penetrate. We've hosted many law-abiding cops here, on various pretenses, and watched on our hidden cameras as they all snoop when given the chance, and they clearly dismiss the ranch as an active part of the business.

On the far side of the river, the swamp base is invisible from the air, and we have installed our own air and water microbeam radar, which will spot anything as big as a frogman. Our biggest issue is false alarms from gators. Although we scare Kemper and many others with the threat of feeding them to the gators, the reality is we use machines to cause tiny tremors in the water at a frequency that annoys them, and they mostly keep a few hundred yards away.

Above the underground swamp base, we've built a legitimate operation: An ecology centre and a service giving tours on airboats, *Zodiacs*, and on foot to tourists who come in by bus daily. Between all of the buses and trucks we use supplying that operation, there is plenty of ways we move product invisibly out of the swamp base. We have some great ex-navy types who run the 'ins and outs' for us as tightly as a possum's ass.

This undetectable pipeline positioned us to become one of the major pipelines into North America for both our own product and others', on which we collect a hefty import fee. This money gave us leverage to hire mercenaries and assassins at an international grade, which we use mercilessly as enforcers. Again, it was Destiny, our Ma, who argued we should be the biggest bully on the block to protect our pipeline asset. But the weakness of a bully is that if a smaller guy blacks your eye, other bullies take note, smell blood and start circling. It was bad enough The Kingman missed the cop in Vancouver the first time, but having given him a huge firepower advantage, a dirty cop on the inside, and a second chance, it was devastating that he missed the second time. The wrong people now see we are vulnerable, and pressure has mounted fast.

We know the cop took up with some millionaire flyboy private eye and they are now on the run. The clock is ticking for us to make an example out of them, and we are not going to miss a third time. We had feelers out through Kemper and our contacts north of the border. We were pretty sure our pesky gophers were holed up somewhere in Canada, as we would hear if she used her passport but running her to ground was proving difficult. We had looked to pick up anyone close to her and persuade them to tell us her whereabouts, but no one promising had presented themselves to our men on the ground. Both of their parents and her remaining brother had dropped off the radar, too. Our VPD contact was also out of the loop and was pretty confident his boss Preece was also ignorant. So it was with some relief to us when Kemper relayed that the gophers had popped their heads up at the border, heading into the US, where we have more reach. Even if they had popped back off the radar for now.

Cho cleared the table of all dishes, glasses, the tablecloth, and other accoutrements, then bought a small silver tray with a small glass of premium Kentucky Bourbon each for Seth and I. It was unusual for Cho to serve table, but the regular woman was sick, and we deliberately kept the staff to a minimum when we had product coming through the facility. Cho was Seth's favourite helper in the 'training pens,' as we liked to call them. Seth typically tested or worked with the girls where we had question marks about their talents or if they had to be trained for a special client. He enjoyed the work more than me. I tended to work our network and the money side. He said Cho seemed to have a mean streak and enjoyed helping him when he needed an extra pair of hands. She had been with us for nearly five years and was as close to being part of the family as we let anyone. Due to her involvement in the work, she was as culpable as any of us, so we knew we could trust her in most situations.

Cho withdrew, and Seth and I discussed the situation; we were not agreed on what should be done. I thought the best approach was to let the law arrest Ethan and we would take him once he was in custody. Our network of contacts in jails could do it, or we could simply bomb a precinct or FBI office if they were held in such a place. Seth wanted to get more personal. He felt the insult to our reputation warranted a more overt strategy. He wanted them somewhere feeling safe, and then we go in and gut them. It was getting heated when Ma came out onto the porch and settled it for now. She was right, as she often is: Just wait and see where we find them and go from there.

18: The Very Friendly Phoenix

[Marcy] — In four days we had accomplished a great deal. I wasn't quite ready to admit to Ethan that perhaps he was right, and I could accomplish things professionally as his partner that I never could in the VPD.

Ashanta entered the Caribbean, steaming towards the Gulf of Mexico. There is a natural path all such traffic follows, so it is common for boats to almost be in convoy. This gave *Cassis* some cover, and she now ran slightly ahead of *Ashanta* and to the south, typically staying within four to six miles. She was deliberately running a few knots slower, so she would be overtaken; the gap closing without suspicion. For a person at sea level, *Cassis's* mast would be over the horizon and out of sight with the distance we now had between the yachts. For someone sitting on top of the *Ashanta* mast with binoculars, the 30 or so extra feet of altitude meant they might be able to see us if they tried. We knew they were not observing us that way, however, because we now had one of the three launches always motoring between the boats so we could pick up radio and access the telemetry from the drone. The drone and the SPOT concurred in every respect, so we had no doubt as to the ship's location, and as we got occasional glimpses of Gia, we knew she was at large and safe and sound. It felt as routine as one could ever imagine such a precarious position could be.

Kelsie, Max, and Darcy met every four or five hours as we hatched out various plans and contingencies. Max was working his network for ground support. The situation in the US regarding access to millions of guns is a massive social problem for the country, but incredibly convenient if one is trying to quietly acquire weapons. Max's contacts were plugged in to gun clubs up and down the country, and Ethan's money did the rest. Max called upon Steve, Dray, Sarah, and Cazz — short for Casandra — who were all ex-forces specialists recently retired but still in shape. They had all agreed to join us in Baton Rouge, and after checking out all of the firepower that was rolling in, they had relaxed and were enjoying an all-expenses-paid vacation by the pool. They looked like any group of friends partying it up, except they were all ripped beyond belief and none of them touched a drop of alcohol. At the drop of a hat, they would be in motion to the airport, where Kelsie had air transport of different types on standby to get us all anywhere along the south coast toot de suite.

Kelsie and Darcy had also been busy with our electronic weapons needs on two fronts. Firstly, they had relocated Darcy and every toy she possessed to Louisiana. She had rented space in a small hangar at Stennis International, where all of her toys were unloaded and set up, ready for deployment. She and three trusted technicians were working on some adaptations that would allow them to work in the swamps. They sprayed them a colour closer to the environment we expected to operate in, modified them to operate in a warmer and moister climate, and adjusted the software to help them operate in a swamp with minimum human assistance. They had already completed several field trips into areas to the west of New Orleans to practise deployment and test the new configurations.

The second front they had opened up was cyber warfare. Darcy had approached a friend she used on occasion to help ensure her laboratory and computer systems were impenetrable, who connected her to a trusted contact who was prepared to work around the rules and without legal warrants. SkyLox, as she called herself, was based somewhere near Portland and was deeply moved when she understood the mission our team was attempting to pull off. She made no promises but agreed to start researching options for intervention. Within eight hours, she had a feel for which dark websites were linked to the Toussaint business and was well acquainted—read: had already hacked in to — the four shell companies Bob Chave had identified. I asked SkyLox how she had got in so quickly and she admitted she had followed the trail she picked up where the FBI's cyber team had also penetrated and could tell me where they did well and what they missed. After 36 hours, SkyLox called us with the good and the bad news.

"I've mapped out the main financial routes, including banks, Bitcoin funding, gold and diamond deposits, investments in rare earth metals, and who the major downstream customers are, and I can estimate their net worth is roughly $187 million. They would have trouble liquidating much of that, but no doubt they are well funded."

"Perhaps I should just buy them out," whispered Ethan.

"Although I have a high-level map," SkyLox continued, "I have very little detail. It's clear to me the real data is not kept anywhere online. I can see evidence they have a computer system that tracks their empire — a sort of bad-guy-ERP system — which is kept physically separate from any internet or wide area network system. I suspect they are comfortable bringing extracts of data out on thumb drives or similar, but any data they want to bring into their closed system is probably manually typed, every time. It slows them down, but without physical or network access they are safe from cyberattack. We need to find that and bridge into it to do real damage to their operations."

We had constructed the bones of a plan to attack the Toussaint assets electronically. SkyLox was prepared to either scramble data and make it useless, including backups that she could reach, or in many cases actually transfer the money out of the Toussaint's accounting system to accounts of our choosing. This created a dilemma as it was all the result of criminal activity. On the one hand, we should turn it all over to Chave, but if we did that, it could get caught up in red tape and get back to the Toussaint's one day; on the other hand, we didn't want the money, or to be linked to a criminal act ourselves. SkyLox was confident she could firewall us from the latter and could park the money in a cleansed and untraceable bitcoin fund and give us the key to it.

Ethan had been researching Gia a lot more deeply than the original background check, and we were aghast when we uncovered her earlier years and the pain she had suffered at the hands of the likes of Toussaint. Ethan had come up with an idea for what to do with the stolen money, a plan we agreed to keep quiet about, and it did have a certain satisfying irony. It also pretty much meant I would be leaving the VPD.

*

Almost as a separate life, as we worked up our various options to take on those who would want to kill us, we explored our sex life. The first few days in Baton Rouge were hectic, but we found time to be together and have — you know — normal sex. Which was pretty mind blowing, I must say. I know you should never compare, but I had been happily married to Terry, with a good sex life, and somehow this was a different gear again.

On the fourth day around noon, we grabbed a couple of light salads, that oddly, were shaped like cheeseburgers and fries. OK they were cheeseburgers, who cares; don't judge me. They had lettuce and tomato. And fries. We sat out on the patio, just the two of us, and it was fantastic to be alone and not exhausted.

I have really been wrestling to reconcile my feelings around abuse — reinforced by years of pursuing and punishing abusers — with the strange tingly feeling I get tormenting Ethan. If you had asked me a year ago if I could respect someone who liked to give up control in such an odd way I would have laughed at you. But I have such strong feelings for Ethan and his thing is so innocent, or he is—I'm not quite sure which — that it doesn't seem wrong in this case. It seems right. And interestingly, when I thought about it, neither he nor I were thinking of taking his thing any further until Gwen suggested it. Again, I would have thought I would rebel against the idea. The thought of me liking being dominant isn't so odd in the sense I am always assertive — some might say aggressive when out of earshot — but I want to be with someone who stands up to me. And he does. Ethan will kick my ass if I'm a jerk.

Gwen's explanations have helped. She says we have different layers, when I only saw a single layer. It's a bit like having only eaten wedding cakes with sweet, sweet icing on the top, and that awful fruitcake on the inside. I thought I hated all such cakes. Then someone introduces an iced cake with chocolate torte inside. Now it's an adventure.

But so far, playing this game that Ethan and I have agreed to play is like a dare. Raising a hand and hitting him is a whole different cake. As would be dominating him in other ways. I spoke to Gwen, and she gave me a few thoughts on how to dabble a toe in the water, but I really didn't want to follow her script—that would be creepy—so I spent some time in the bath alone last night and recrafted them into something Marcy, rather than Gwen, could do. I was feeling very apprehensive even bringing the subject up, let alone following through.

I remembered what Gwen had said about some people finding it easier to create a persona they can step into. That still didn't feel like me, but I played with it for interest sake. I was finding this journey is partly about trying on ideas for a while and seeing how they fit. Some you keep in the wardrobe, and either you wear them often, save them for occasions, or save them with the tag on and never take them out—but you are not ready to part with them. Some, after a while, you jettison. To be honest, I couldn't get into the build-a-character mode, although I saw the appeal. There was one aspect I liked after some thought: having a naughty name.

A name kind of naturally occurred as I floated in the tub, which captured my life's journey to date. I had started off in life a bright, happy, well-adjusted child, then the successive issues with my parents drove me down to rock bottom. But I broke out and forged a good thing for myself. As I climbed up, Max's fake death, and then my husband's real death, really brought me again to a very low point. I was lost, but ignited by a spark from Ethan, I focused on work and rose out of the ashes, and now with Ethan I am flying again. Like a Phoenix. Equally, and this sounds immodest, but I love it when Ethan sees me walk into a room; his eyes light up, like I'm some magical creature. I thought that perhaps my naughty name might be Lady Phoenix. Nope. Not me. Just Phoenix. That felt like it added something and opened a door to somewhere I could go. I might like it if he called me that while we experimented. Then I could cast it away later if needed. In the bath, Phoenix modified the script even further, and now she wanted to try it out.

*

As we picked at the last of the fries, I could tell neither of us wanted to hurry back to the room we had commandeered as our base. I gulped down some courage and ventured into the discussion I had been dreading.

"Can we talk about our kinky adventures for a few minutes? I know we have to get back, but I have something on my mind." Damn, that sounded ominous. Great start Phoenix.

"Sure."

Deer in headlights. But he thinks I am going to say something bad. I hope I am not. Plunge ahead. "I really like what we have been doing, but at some point, I want to take another step. Are you up to that tonight?"

"Yes, sure! Mistress?"

Looks relieved and interested. He's leaning in, and his pupils just dilated. OK. Keep going. "There seem to be so many ways we could go. So many subjects to pick from it's hard to know where to start. I have a suggestion, but first, do you have any thoughts?" *Try and 'sure' that buddy.* I didn't want to do *all* the work.

"I haven't had time to order *Kink for Dummies* or my new wardrobe yet," he smiled a little shyly, trying to keep it light.

"How are you feeling about pain? A little light spanking maybe?"

"That's been on my mind, in a good way." He glanced guiltily down at his lap, and I could tell it was a happy thought, "but is that where you want to start?" A slight cloud crossed his face. *He is worried about me. Sweet.*

"I do. You know me, I'm kind of a face-things-head-on girl. Striking you when you can't fight back would be a hot button, in a negative sense, and I want to test if it could be hot in other ways."

"OK but let's go slowly. Not for me — I'm sure my butt will recover — but let's do something small, then slowly work up to where we are comfortable, rather than blowing it in a rush." The double entendre flashed across his face, but he was smart enough to let it slide away.

"I agree. Are you OK if we don't overplan this? I'm getting embarrassed, and feel a little silly even talking about this, although I must admit I find it a bit hot thinking about it. Gwen says we are supposed to negotiate everything up front."

"Well how about we agree to wing it but stay in the realm of what we have already tried, plus some light to medium spanking, pinching, and so on. If you feel like venturing further, trust me that I will say yellow or red if I need to slow down or stop. You do have to trust me, more than I have to trust you in a way."

We hugged it out. I was about to walk back to our makeshift operations room, but he held me a little longer and gave me a deep, slow kiss.

"OK, I'm hot and horny! Perfect for going back to the office. It's going to be a long afternoon," he laughed.

"Wait until tomorrow, Ethan, your ass will be tingling all day."

*

The afternoon both raced and dragged. It couldn't go fast enough, but at the same time I was nervous about how things would unfold. Would I make a fool of myself? Would I panic and have to step away? Ethan was putting no pressure on me, but I put it on myself. It was with relief more than trepidation when at 8 pm we closed down the planning meeting and headed up to our suite.

Ethan, thoughtful and overprepared as ever, had ordered ahead from guest services, and we were greeted by a *chardonnay*, a *sauvignon blanc*, a *chablis*, and a dry *riesling* all on ice but unopened, some reds; chocolates and strawberries, and a large tub of peanut butter. Funny guy. I thought we should get into the mood, so I walked over and grabbed him roughly by the hair at the back of his head, pulled him down to me and kissed him. His mouth was cool, like he had been breathing quickly, and his taste was on the front part of my tongue where sweet and salty register.

"Go shower and come back in just a towel. I'll pour us a drink!" I command-whispered when we came up for air from the kiss.

As he walked to the bathroom I could sense in his stride the conflict between the alpha male ego, the man who wanted to be tested, the cheeky party guy, and the nervous newbie. Realizing how tuned into him I felt made me feel more confident. I poured us both a tall glass of Chablis, then went to the dresser drawer and took out a long silk scarf and a pair of my clean cotton panties. I brushed my hair and dabbed on some scent. I already had killer underwear on under my jeans and tee, and I kept my heels on so they might echo on the hardwood floor. Ethan was eager and emerged minutes later, a little red from the hot water, a short white towel around his waist, but wearing nothing else other than a nervous smile. As he opened the bathroom door, the trapped heat rolled out and pushed Ethan's scent across the room. I could tell he smelled of high-end astringent soap and musky Ethan. *Yum!*

"Come over here!" I said, pointing to a spot in front of me. He stood close to him — an inch away — and let him feel my breath on his shoulder.

"Stand still. Face the wall, eyes front, and look only at the back of the woman's head in the painting!" The picture was of a woman in a red, off-the-shoulder gown sitting alone at a bar with her back to us, the viewers, and her hair was the same colour as mine.

I walked slowly around him a couple of times, dialling in a bit of sass and swagger with each circuit, treading hard so my heels sounded clearly. He was relaxed, confident, and manly on the surface, but I could sense him tracking to the millimetre where I was in relation to him, and I could sense the adrenaline coursing through his veins.

"Hands on top of your head!" I stood behind him quietly for a few seconds, then ran a nail across his shoulder blade, and a tremble shivered down his back to his right leg.

"That's right, you can feel gravity tugging on that towel, but you can't touch it now. If you didn't tie it tight enough, you'll be naked once more. I might call room service while you stand there. Ask for a knife for the peanut butter." I had a wild thought about smearing it on his taught buns. *Concentrate, Marcy!!*

I shushed him when he opened his mouth to talk.

"You can talk when I tell you to, and not before!" I raised my voice a few degrees with the order. Part of what I had understood from Gwen was to create the mood by getting Ethan off balance. He was so accomplished in many ways, so this wouldn't be easy. I fully committed to working on it, ratcheting up my focus level another notch. His breathing was already elevated, but I told him to breathe a little faster. I had heard of breath control, and always assumed it was about belts around the neck and plastic bags over the head. Dr Gwen had again said that was asphyxiation, and breath control could be subtler. Have him breathe faster to elevate his senses or hold his breath for twenty seconds. From looking at the towel around his waist, I could tell he was aroused. I could see it in his eyes, and how his throat moved. *Keep the initiative, keep a step ahead of him, and get him even more disoriented,* I told myself.

"When I'm ready, I'm going to slip this towel off you and spank your ass. Gently, then harder, and then even harder. We will try it like Gwen suggested. Standing there with your hands on your head. Then, when it's as hard as you can bear, I'll tell you to bend at the waist and hold your ankles. Then we will start again, and you can tell me how the two felt different."

As I explained my plan, a shadow crossed his face.

"Is that OK? You can speak!" I added quickly.

"I like the idea of just standing there while you spank me; it's more erotic in some ways being bound by your order than by a rope. But I'm not sure of myself yet, and how I might react. I had imagined you would tie me up again, then I wouldn't have to worry about it. It would just happen to me."

"I thought tying you up might freak you out more, but I'm definitely game. What did you have in mind? I don't have my police cuffs."

"We have the belts from the dressing gowns," he said, nervously. I was glad he'd said that, as it confirmed that he had been planning, too. Gwen had prepared me for a moment like this. Most people are not good at knot tying. It's surprisingly hard to tie someone with a rope, tightly enough that they can't escape, but not so tight as to cause nerve damage or stop blood flow. It takes practise that we haven't had. It can also be a bit of a mood spoiler him standing there while I work it out. I put to work what she taught me.

"This might be hot work, and I need to take off my clothes, Ethan, but you haven't earned the right to look at my body today, so I'm going to blindfold you." He drew himself up a few degrees taller and the towel got a little tighter. I pulled his face to mine again and kissed him, letting my tongue swirl around his lips some, then I pulled away and stood behind him again. He obeyed well, and kept his head faced forward. I folded the scarf lengthwise and slipped it around his head, tying it off behind with a deliberate jerk. The blindfold had two purposes: One to get him off balance, and two, so he couldn't watch me fumbling. It would also distort his sense of time a little, and if it took me a few attempts at the knots, his not knowing what I was up to would add anticipation, not impatience. I kept in contact with his shoulders for a few seconds so he could feel me as he adjusted to the darkness.

I walked to the closet and pulled out the belts, and then collected the clean panties from the bed. I reached round to his chest, and I let my hands slide slowly down his pecs and over his flat stomach. *I'm glad Gia kept him in such great shape. Oh, that thought will get him an extra hard spanking!* I eased my fingers under the top of his towel and slowly undid it, letting it slide down to the floor. I kept my hands on his tummy, just above his perky manhood. *Oh, I think I have his full attention.* His balls were already tightening with lusty fullness.

"Kneel down," I commanded, "and hold your wrists together and in front of you." He did so slowly. I walked around and used my foot to push his knees a good eight inches apart, exposing him.

I didn't worry too much about making unescapable knots; I just wanted to give him the sense of restraint. I folded a housecoat belt in half, put the midpoint on top of his wrists, then looped the loose ends under and around and through the 'U' of the midpoint I had created, then cinched it back the other way. The belt tightened, pulling his arms closer together. I kept a finger-width-worth of air gap to protect his circulation, then wrapped the belt under and back once more. Then, once I had the ends back at the top, I tied them off with a shoelace bow. He would just have to pull the ends to undo it, but the ends were tucked under his wrists and hard to reach, and he couldn't see them—and he was unlikely to be trying anyway. I would have to 'level up' my rope skills.

I pushed his hands back onto his head, then stepped in and put my tummy to his face, and let him smell me. I hoped my standing over him, with my hands in his hair, would emphasize my dominance over him. I pulled up my tee so my belly was exposed and pulled his head to me. His cheek stubble grazed me softly, his tongue shot out and circled then slipped into my belly button, and my breasts lit up like Christmas trees. I just wanted to rip my clothes off, drop and straddle him, and abandon my plan, but I held it together.

"Stand up!" He did and I led him over to a light fixture on the wall. It was pretty robust looking, and I checked it with a solid tug. I quickly tied one end of the second belt to the one around his hands, looped the opposite end over the light, and pulled slowly, pushing his arms up encouragingly. He got the hint and stretched higher.

"I know you can afford to pay for the light fixture, but I order you not to put too much weight on it, you hear?"

I stepped back and checked out my handywork as I quickly shed my own clothes. His legs and ass looked great, and stretched slightly taller than he would normally stand, the muscles on his back and arms were rigid. Gwen said some subs go into themselves during a scene, while others can be very outward-focused. I got the sense that Ethan was tunneling in somewhere, lost in his imaginings. I could not take my eyes off his bod right now, and I was also noticing every need and twitch from his bones to his aura, as if I suddenly had a direct line into his nervous system. Just like most good dommes apparently, I was totally focused on my submissive. But I had to be patient. Keep him waiting.

I stepped quietly up behind him and let my nipples trail across his back. We both shuddered at that, and I felt that tremor across the top of my chest, in my tummy, and further south too. *Fuck!* My left leg just flicked back at the knee like I was a teenager having my first kiss at my Prom. I strutted to the bed, picked up my clean panties, and returned to Ethan, letting my high heels click sensuously on the hardwood flooring.

"I don't want you talking and spoiling my concentration, or yelling and bringing security down on us, so I'm going to push a pair of my panties into your mouth as a gag. I'll confide they are clean, but who knows next time. That will depend whether you've been good or bad. I'm not going to tie them in, so you can easily push them out if you need me to stop or slow down. I trust you to stop me if it is too hard. No manly, manly shit, OK? But we don't have to try gagging if you are not ready for that. What do you think?"

He answered by slowly turning his head towards my voice and parting his lips. I lifted onto my tiptoes and kissed him. His mouth was really hungry. I made sure the panties were tightly rolled into a sausage and pushed them into his mouth sideways, so he looked like a happy dog with a bone. As a 'well done,' I reached down and slid a hand around his other bone, which was horizontal and heading north with each second. I felt him swell in my hand, and I let my fingers curl around him, holding him lightly.

"OK, first step back a quarter step. That's it. And I want your feet a little more than shoulder-width apart. Good. And I want your ass out where I can get at it." He complied, and I made sure my hand followed with him. As he steadied, I made my hand slowly pull his cock back and forth continuously, just a fraction of an inch. He gasped. I did a little too, as I felt a little excitement trickle out onto my fingers.

I straddled his thigh sideways, so I could hold his cock and balls, and rubbed his ass cheeks a few times with my other hand. I let my warmth graze his quads. We used each other's bodies for a few seconds. Things were building intensely.

"I've decided I need a name when I do this to you," I whispered in his ear, hoping my nervousness didn't betray me. I wanted this to work.

"It's both the name I'll use when I do this to you, as well as a secret code word between us. If I say or show you this name, you know you must obey my commands. It might be in private, or around others when I want your obedience." I dropped my hand down around his balls and held them softly, but with purpose. "A reminder that I own these!" I let go, then grasped the base of his shaft and his balls together. It was a sexy handful.

"I put some thought into this name, and also what my first try at spanking should be like." I played with him more and more, working him up quickly.

"Should I start really light, and work my way up? Then I thought no, we want this moment to be one you remember, not some wimpy attempt at it. I am a strong and powerful woman. I've kicked criminals in the ass. I've taken down assassins with my awesome ATV skills. And right now, I am your domme, and this occasion is going to make a lasting impression. The name I have chosen is Phoenix!" With each hard SLAP, I spelt a letter of my name, and he jerked sharply in my hand. SLAP. SLAP. SLAP. SLAP. SLAP. SLAP. SLAP. I rubbed his butt a few times and looked at the hand mark I'd made. A little pink blush. My warm and personal brand on his skin. I slipped my hand up his ridged erection and started stroking him harder and faster. His legs stiffened, and he went up on his toes, his head to the ceiling. I reached up and tugged the gag from his mouth. He sucked in air.

"OK, you have to repeat the spelling of my name as I spank you. We will repeat it over and over, and I will spank harder each time until either you ask me to stop, or you cum in my hand. Say 'Yes Phoenix,' if you understand and want this as much as I do."

"I want this!" He said it. Firmly and passionately.

He came hard in my hand halfway through the forth iteration of Phoenix. And riding his thigh as it clenched and twerked with each stroke, I nearly did, too.

*

Ethan had gone slack in my arms, and I quickly fumbled all of the bindings away and he turned and all but carried me to the bed. He had taken his time and been very generous and skillful, and as his ardor got harder we made love intensely. I was now propped back on a pillow, and Ethan lay across me sleeping the soft sleep of the content. I stroked his hair gently and glanced a little guiltily down his back at the two red moons glowing below. I could see a couple of lightly broken blood vessels, and I bit my lip. *My God.* My heart sank and my stomach contracted and for a second, I thought I might want to puke. I was back at home, aged ten crying in my room, standing in front of the mirror with my dress pulled up around my waist, twisting to look at very similar marks on my sad tush. Only the hand prints and marks were from a bigger hand on my tiny frame. A series of women's and children's faces with black eyes and hopeless looks flashed at me from cases I had worked, and worked hard, until the bullies and addicts who make such marks were down and done.

I felt tears on my cheeks, and my throat hurt. Ethan was instantly above me — my sobbing had woken him- caressing me protectively. He just held me softly and didn't try to talk, 'shhh', or coddle. He gently mopped my tears with the corner of a sheet and rolled over and lifted me onto his chest, his arms around me. A safe place for me to fight my demons.

I had known I would get to this place at some point, and I was determined I would pull my big girl panties up and objectively evaluate where it left me, putting the guilt aside. It was actually easy to separate everything philosophically. What Ethan and I had just done was one hundred percent consensual, the planned and desired act of two adults in their right and curious minds. Ethan was clearly very happy with it and had no second thoughts. His ass would heal by Friday. My memories, in contrast, were the work of bent minds filled with anger, lack of control, rage, drugs, hopelessness; power taken not given; broken communication — all resulting in physical and mental injuries which both victim and abuser might never recover from. I could rationalize the difference mentally, but emotionally it was a messy, illogical soup. I stewed in my soup a while, then put it back in its box for later and opened a different box. Did beating Ethan's ass make me think less of him?

The answer "no" was clear and strong in my mind. In fact, I thought more of him, not less. But that in itself raised the question: Why would I think more of someone who is OK with, and even turned on by, a spanking? What does that say about me? A little casual voice in me said, *Who cares, he is wholesome and this is hot. Don't over analyse it.* But the bigger 'analyst' voice in me strangled that crazy bitch. I needed to unpack this to get comfortable with it, or see through it.

I thought about all the reasons I had heard that men like a spanking. The British institutions of eroticizing their strict childhood nanny? Nope. The CEO who wants release from decision making? Nope. Well he is a CEO of sorts, but carries the weight of his friends and society perhaps more than the companies he owns. Still that does not feel right at all. He is confident, curious, adventurous, sex positive, and does whatever he wants. No indication he wants to be 'in service' to a greater power. Nothing wrong with it if he did, but that wouldn't attract me personally. I bet he is as puzzled as I am as to why he would get a kick out of it. Gwen said people get a big rush, and I guess he did. He is still my big alpha, and I am drawn to him because he takes risks, trusts me, is open minded, and listens to his bod. And mine.

As I lay in his arms, I realized I had shifted a little to thinking about other ways I could toy with him — and which might excite him the most — and away from the boxes containing things past. Those boxes seemed less important somehow when I thought about the two of us exploring the interesting and alternative ways to drive each other wild sexually. I felt suddenly closer to Ethan and recalled Gwen's lesson on oxytocin. *I like it. Perhaps we should create a little more and see if that helps.* I snuggled in tighter and let my hand drop to his thigh and felt the muscles there at rest suddenly perk up a little. I turned my head to initiate a sexy kiss. The mood was snatched away as suddenly, both of our phones pinged. Something was up.

We broke apart and each checked our messages, simultaneously seeing the same thing from Kelsie. Contact from Gia and a submarine rendezvous tomorrow night. Kelsie was calling everyone to a virtual meeting to discuss the implications. Part of me wanted to ignore her and hide here, but I followed Ethan out of bed towards the shower. As his sexy, bare ass disappeared through the door, I glanced a final time at the marks I had made, which spread out from the middle almost like wings. I shook my head. *I'll be damned if it didn't resemble a Phoenix branded on his tush.*

19: Eyes On

[Ethan] — I eased tentatively into the chair at the head of the table, a tingling on both my upper and lower cheeks. The latter from Marcy's administrations and the former from the absurd concern that everyone might guess what we just did. I was doing my best to park that experience and focus on the perilous situation Gia and 22 other women were in but concentrating was not as easy as it should have been. I really wanted to talk with Marcy about her tears. She was having such a hard time with it all and I needed to ensure she was truly OK, but my gut told me just to give her space to process it.

Kelsie was running the meeting from *Cassis* via a big screen we had hastily installed here, on which she had maps projecting options for where the rendezvous would happen if *Astasha* maintained her current course and speed. Our working assumption was that the submarine was not ex-navy surplus or anything with a long range, which aligned to Chave's suspicions about the base of operations being in the Mississippi River, and not further afield. The river delta, when extended out to international waters, and the likely rendezvous point, were a close match.

Our primary scenario was that the transfer would take place and Gia would remain hidden on board. *Cassis* was too big to make much distance up the river, so she would track *Astasha* to where it anchored, and Max would find a way to lift Gia off. We could then download any intelligence she could share. We had chartered two small fishing boats that would be strategically placed to assist as needed, and we had the drone and SPOT reports. Darcy had developed a series of sonar pods that our drones and other craft could drop into the river periodically to try to pick up traces of the sub after we lost contact. We were not optimistic and hoped Gia's information would help pin down the location of the base.

Our secondary plan assumed something went wrong during the transfer, most likely Gia being discovered or her taking some action. We now had consistent footage from the drone, from which we would hopefully monitor developments, but we needed a backup observation point and a capability to react well to various scenarios. We decided to risk a small, high-level drone glider, which we would launch ten kilometres upwind from the rendezvous and that would be on station with both optics and the ability to relay short-range radio signals. The latter was important because our response capability included Max and Jim in a borrowed SEAL stealth version of a *Zodiac*, cruising as close as we dare, which was roughly eight hundred yards out based on moonlight forecasts. They would drop Terry in scuba gear to get in closer, perhaps right up to the *Astasha*. At sea level in those conditions, radio range would be very limited, and so the drone's relay would make the difference. Since we were roughly estimating the rendezvous location, this plan would be less rigorous than we would have preferred, but we would have to make do.

On a different front, Kelsie relayed SkyLox's latest report. SkyLox had been busy tracing assassins who might be in the employ of the Toussaint's, starting with The Kingman. The dark web is truly a scary shopping mall, where you can find anything from stolen network credentials, bank records, pedophile resources, drug access, and weapons of almost any type, to the people willing to use them. SkyLox was the first to say her information was speculative, but her research into financial transactions suggested the Toussaint's worked almost exclusively with a shadowy group called Chiyome, thought to be primary employer of Kingman.

As legend has it, Mochizuki Chiyome was the wife of samurai Mochizuki Nobumasa, who died in the Battle of Nagashino in 1575. Following his death, Chiyome stayed with Takeda Shingen, her husband's uncle and daimyo, or king of the Shinano domain. Takeda asked Chiyome to create a band of kunoichi, or female ninja operatives, who could act as spies, messengers, and even assassins. Chiyome herself was from the Koga clan, so she had ninja roots. Chiyome recruited girls who were orphans, refugees, or had been sold into prostitution, and trained them in the secrets of the ninja trade. These kunoichis would then disguise themselves as wandering Shinto shamans to move from town to town. Then they might dress up as actresses, prostitutes, or geisha to infiltrate a castle or temple and find their targets. At its peak, Chiyome's ninja band numbered between 200 and 300 women and gave the Takeda clan a decisive advantage in dealing with neighbouring domains.

It was believed the modern-day group of assassins borrowed the name, as they specialized in supplying female and young assets for espionage or assassination and had a quid pro quo arrangement with Seth and Landon for new talent.

SkyLox had also reported three days ago that Destiny Toussaint had a small ranch on the Mississippi River, and Kelsie and Darcy had deployed assets nearby to observe it—and had already hit pay dirt. Two nights ago, several waterborne drones had been released up river from the ranch. These drones were disguised as small drifting branches and washed downriver, but each had very small propulsion units that could steer their course. Two had washed past the ranch in the strong current, but two had made it to the shore across from the ranch. Using very subtle steering, so as not to look like anything but drifting debris, each unit had wedged itself into the foliage that lines the riverbank and dropped their small anchors. The ingenious part was that each had state-of-the-art electrical generation capability, essentially from mini turbines that are turned by the passing current, that produce enough charge to keep their batteries topped up. The drones then operate in one of two modes. In static mode, their cameras can swivel and zoom to a target, which they transmit via cell service if available, as in this case. In mobile mode, the top half of the drone detaches and can fly quietly for short ranges and perch somewhere convenient to offer a different view of the target, returning to the tiny base to recharge as required.

The two units in place had been active for nearly two days in static mode, monitoring the outside of the ranch. On the first day they had already identified both brothers to be in residence, entertaining a man and a woman who agent Chave later identified as DEA agent Kemper and his wife. The drone had seen them arrive and leave but had not been positioned to capture the meeting. Darcy was actively working to position additional drone units into the area to gain audio and better video, but at least we had 'eyes on.'

Cazz and Drey, posing as tourists, had reconnoitred the area, including the conservation centre, and seen nothing amiss. On the way out of the area, they had posted a few dozen static devices — like the ones deployed in Vancouver that had located Marion's Mom — programed to search for Seth, Landon, Destiny, their cars, and anything else we could come up with.

At 10:15 am we called a halt and retired to sleep as best we could but were fed and back together at 7:30 that evening to watch the 10 pm rendezvous take place. *Cassis*, Max, and the *Zodiac* team were busy as they launched their mission, and with the help of frequent updates on the track of *Astasha*, by 9:40 pm were riding quietly about half a mile to her southwest. A light cloud-cover was dimming the moon and starlight, and we had plotted an angle of approach which we thought to be the best to avoid detection. Here in Baton Rouge we were tense, fidgety onlookers, with little to do but pace like expectant parents.

It was about this time that we became interested in a small craft, which our overhead drone showed us was a fishing vessel. It had stopped meandering ahead of the *Astasha*'s track and slowly swung onto an intercept course. *Astasha* began to slow as the two vessels approached each other, and so it was time to trigger then next phase.

Kelsie, who was running the operation, signalled Max to make his approach and they slowly closed to seven hundred yards, which was as close as they dared come without detection, then stopped dead in the water. From our onboard camera we saw Terry check his gear a last time, then lower his electric DPV over the side and follow it into the water. Kelsie reminded us a DPV was a diver propulsion vehicle and looks like an air tank with a propeller. It would drag Terry across to the *Astasha* quite quickly. Max lined up his sniper rifle, which was mounted on a gimble that compensated for much of the boat's motion in the water, but realistically we knew his accuracy would be very low if he risked a shot. Perhaps it would be more of a distraction than a killing weapon. Terry would take time to come close to the *Astasha* and when he got there, he would lurk under the surface and observe any activities through another Darcy invention, which was a camera disguised as a discarded float, tethered by fibre to a display in Terry's facemask. A small control unit on his wrist allowed him to orient the camera, which was stabilized with some image management software.

It was through that camera that we saw Gia vanish into the hold of the submarine and learned that all of our plans were for shit. Max reminded me later on that it's in moments like these you must recognize the professionalism of hard action teams like Rangers and SEALs, who do this work successfully day in and day out, whereas playboy private eyes play crapshoot. Fair point. It was Max who broke the silence at this point when we heard his crackly and slightly delayed voice come through the speaker.

"Mother One, I recommend holding. Going active now is maximum risk, over." Squelch. Silence as us amateurs really didn't have a clue. But I keyed the mic and ventured, "The sub is supposed to make two runs. Let's back off and see if we can take advantage of the next run at 3 am."

"Roger, Little Duck One, recover to Big Duck."

"Double click of acknowledgement."

We spent the next three and a half hours reworking contingency plans and monitoring to see if the Mississippi sensors gave us any indication. The fishing boat moved off with the sub and we had to make a decision if the drone or Max should try to follow. Neither really had range, and we surmised the fishing boat was a spotter for the sub, and might have enhanced radar or similar, so we let it go. We could follow it next time when we were organized. It tracked towards the swamps to the north. The Mississippi dumps into the gulf, with the main dredged waterway flowing through a channel, ending at the appropriately named Pilottown. The fishing boat bypassed that to the east and picked its way through the myriad of tiny isles paralleling the main channel, which also nullified our makeshift sonar net. Projecting its track from where we lost it, it appeared to be heading towards Little Lake, from where it could pick its way up towards Lafitte, where the Toussaint Ranch was located. The only issue with that idea was that the fishing boat's speed was too slow to make that journey and return by 3 am. We speculated that either the base we were searching for was miles south of the ranch, which would make sense, or that the sub transferred the girls to another vessel or vehicle, then turned around for its second run. Or they went to the moon: We knew we were guessing. Our best plan to date was to load Terry up with air tanks and send him back in and have him attach himself somehow to the sub and ride it in. We were MacGyvering a way to do that when the problem solved itself. Or rather, Gia solved it.

Kelsie had added a forwarding rule to her email to relay SPOT messages to a system that alerted on her screen and popped up the SPOT map each time a new update arrived. She had overlaid that screen onto the virtual meeting we were using, so we all saw it. At 2.04 am, the screen dinged, and a new breadcrumb appeared. It was a green "I'm OK" message, a few hundred metres from the Toussaint Ranch. Bingo.

20: Beware the One-Eyed Frog

[Gia] — What saved me is that bad guys can't count. My dumb, panicky stunt landed me as the thirteenth person in a twelve-person sub. As I dropped into the hatch and saw there was no seat for me, I instantly realized my stupid mistake. I was operating at 'fast speed,' where everyone else was either drugged — or in the case of the pilot — focused on rebalancing the little craft's buoyancy as we all came aboard. The seating was configured two by two, with a seat each side of a small aisle, in six tight rows. The pilot sat to the left at the front, and one of the women to his right. I had a moment to react, and I saw the space behind the rear bench and dove into it. My other option was to bounce back up the ladder ready for battle. I held my breath until I heard the hatch clang shut overhead. No one spoke, and soon the movement of the boat changed, and I guessed we were underway. There was no engine noise to speak of, but the sound of water rushing past had increased and there were hydraulic sounds from the ship's controls and a slow hiss from the oxygen system.

Condensation and stuffiness built quickly, and in no time, all the girls were asleep. I risked a glance down the cabin and saw that the pilot had a mirror mounted where he could keep an eye on things, but he was very focused on keeping our depth steady. In the reflection, I could see he had a personal oxygen mask.

I made myself relax but stay awake, despite the stuffiness, and occupied the time with plans on how to fight my way out as we reached the other end. I stealthily observed the pilot and soon decided I couldn't take him out and pilot the sub myself. If I were discovered en route we would have a standoff, and I would try to take out his communications to keep the element of surprise on my side against anyone topside. I decided I couldn't hang back and let the others off, as they would all walk past me and climb out. If they were still as drowsy as they were now, someone might have to come down and carry them off, or at least shake them awake. My plan must be to try to be the first off, and once above the surface, slip away and try to stay hidden.

At regular intervals, a radio crackled, and the pilot swapped status information with someone. After an age, he was notified that we had arrived at our destination and to get ready to surface. The noise of water outside rapidly diminished, and with much hissing and pumping, we rose to the surface and the rocking of our vessel increased. I felt lightheaded. Some of the hissing must have been related to oxygen being pumped into the space, and I noticed the other women were waking up and becoming more animated. A woman two rows from the front started to sob and hold her ears. The pressure had changed rapidly which — along with the sudden increase in oxygen — had her upset. As the hatch overhead banged open, water dripped in and my ears popped aggressively. I didn't wait; I just surged upwards, tensed, but trying to look sloppy and drugged. I aimed at appearing a little panicked by the situation, which apparently was common, as the greasy thug at the top of the ladder mumbled something that ended with "honey" and directed me over to a large rubber boat, not unlike the ones we ride in when whale watching in Vancouver; but this one had a large airplane propeller mounted on the tail ahead of two large fins. Then, bizarrely, another man handed us all bottles of insect repellant and had us spray each other down. *Protecting their product, I suppose.*

It only took four or five minutes to get us all out of the sub and strapped onto the airboat's bench seats before the large Chevy engine roared to life and we started to move. In seconds, we were flying down the narrow channels of the swamps, gliding over lily pads and under low-hanging willows. Conscious that the driver was sitting behind us and could see us clearly, I didn't want to bring out the SPOT, which was still wedged in my pants, but I did reach in and turn it on. It wouldn't find a satellite hidden in there, but I wanted it ready to deploy rapidly if a chance appeared.

After perhaps an hour of what in other circumstances would have been a wonderful experience, we slowed and nosed up to a small, softly lit platform that had a path leading away. Three men stood on the platform and briskly helped us climb over the side of the rubber boat. Once we were all on firm ground — for the first time in many days — they led us through some closely packed shrubs towards a modern-looking building. As we got closer to the building, I could see it was a tourist ecological centre. I was near the back of the group, trailing head-down up the path, watching for an opening. As we passed a white propane tank mounted on a large concrete bunker, I shamefully tripped the women in front of me, who squealed and went sprawling face-first into the shrubs to the side of the path. The rear guard stepped past me saying, "Hey, easy with the merchandise," and I pushed the 'OK' button on the SPOT and flung it onto the roof of the bunker—and prayed quietly that I hadn't just tossed away salvation just before we mounted the next form of transport to hundreds of miles distant. I felt relief as we were hustled into the facility ahead of us, through a gaping hole in the wall and down several winding flights of stairs to what looked and felt like the holding area of an abattoir. It wasn't the fear of being slaughtered that raised the hackles on my neck, it was the dreaded recognition that I had seen a room exactly like this before through much younger and more innocent eyes, in Arnot's basement.

The door above us hissed and clanked loudly closed with a finality we all felt in our guts. I stood near the middle of the pack, copying the body language of those around me, smothering the growing rage within. The lights flickered higher, and onto a small stage near the back of the room stepped an elderly but spritely lady, perhaps in her early seventies. She scanned the room, showing us her leathery, freckled, dour face peering out between straggly grey braids as she took us all in. Despite her millions in illicit and cruelly obtained dollars, her trailer-trash pedigree shone through. Her eyes paused longer on me, I felt, than the others, but then they moved on. There was something ominous in her expression that drew us to her, and the steady murmur died away as silence filled the space.

"I knows y'all speak some English, but perhaps not the good accents God gave us here in the South, so ah'll talk slow for all y'all. Let me start with a heartfelt welcome to America." She paused for us to get her joke. Instead I thought of Darth Vadar hissing, *the sarcasm is strong with this one!*

"Ah's not gunna lie to y'all; we are all women here, and you has some tough days ahead of you that'll make that lil cruise we just gave you seem like a vacation. But y'all can trust me that today, and tomorrow, will be easier. Y'all take some advice from an old woman. Use the time to gather your spirit. You'll need it later, true enough." She stopped and looked across us again, seeing if her words were having whatever effect she thought they should.

"We'll let you sleep soon, after we've fed y'all. But first we has to clean you up and give you a check out. Now there is an easy way and a hard way, this can go. We'll start with all of the men folk out of the room, and us girls can just get this done quietly between us. Any fussin' and the men come back in. Each nook around the room has a shower and some soap, and a black bag. When I tell you so, y'all will pick one, place your clothes and anything you have in the bag, and give yourself a very thorough shower. Wash the travel stink from you. Then, one at a time, y'all come to the table over there and I will give you a medical. I have my nursing training. I'll look you over, but y'all should tell me if there is anything you need fixin'. This is your one chance most likely. Then we give you replacement clothes, send you next door to eat, then to the dorms to sleep." I reminded myself that the food or drink would be drugged with sedatives — or worse heroine — and to pretend to consume.

"And last of all, we won't take no sassy backtalk from you, but no one is to mess with you either. You are *my* product, and you represent my brandt, and you *will* arrive in damn good shape at my customers or there'll be hell to pay. So, if any of the men folk get fresh with you, let me know. My name is Destiny Toussaint, and I will have the pecker off any man who messes with my girls without my saying so."

She stood up, scanned the room quickly, and snapped, "Now get to it!" with such venom that we all stumbled towards the showers.

With 23 naked women mingling around, no one was paying me much attention, which I realized was a good thing. Max had said the women on these yacht shipments were — to use a terrible phrase — 'high-end product,' aimed at the more lucrative end of the trafficking business. There was a variety of attractive body shapes, but none like mine. My musculature and build were very different. Warrior verses Victoria Secret babe. It would show in the lineup for the medical, and if it didn't, I expected Destiny would notice quickly during the examination. The other thing I noticed was that Destiny had an assistant, who was logging into a computer next to the medical bay. I began to strongly suspect she would have an inventory that I wouldn't be on. I racked my brains, but there was not much I could do to hide. I would have to brazen it out and be ready to fight if things went south. Deep South, I guess it would be here, in both respects.

I took my time and made sure I was near the back of the line. I didn't want to be last, but I wanted time to watch the process and prepare the best story I could.

Destiny was efficient and processed each person medically in a few minutes, taking blood, checking pressures, teeth, eyes, skin, and all of the holes you imagine she would. Asking probing questions about marks or scars, that hid previous broken bones or injuries. She asked each their name and age, and the assistant correlated our answers against her records, and copied down any comments Destiny made into their database. *Merde!* Destiny cross-checked which location and pimp each woman had come through, and maybe here was my only glimmer of hope. As the line dwindled and my turn approached, seven of the nine ahead of me came from Amal Jaz, a pimp in Sarajevo whom Max had mentioned in his briefings as running a major piece of the pipeline. I recalled Max had also mentioned Jaz was fighting a turf war with Bobbi Three Face, who operated to the west of him, out of a city called Mostar. The name had stuck, as Max had explained that Bobbi was famous for having a pleasing face for his customers, a business face for his associates, and a harsh face for his stable of girls — hence his moniker.

As my turn came, I noted the tray of needles and tools, pencils, the rubber tube from the blood pressure machine, and the cables from the computer as potential weapons. I wouldn't need them for the assistant or old lady, although that one looked like a mean bitch. She had something odd about her I couldn't place but that looked familiar. The potential weapons might come in handy for the guards. As I stepped forward, Destiny sat up and stopped me.

"Well ain' you different," she started. "Turn around and let me see you." I did, trying to look as unthreatening and meek as I could.

"Name?"

"Jing!" I said quietly. I meant to say 'Sylvia.' Destiny looked at her assistant, who worked some buttons, puzzled, then shook her head.

"Where you from, Jing?"

"Sarajevo." I said. She frowned.

"А ко је био твој макро, а?" *Damn.* I could guess she was asking me who my pimp was, but it could equally be one of a hundred other questions.

"I'm Spanish. From Alicante," I said truthfully, but then launched into my fabricated story. "A girlfriend and I visited Mostar last month and she got sick. The hostel we were staying at said they called a doctor, but two men picked us up and took us to a pimp called Bobbi. Bobbi Three Face, although we didn't dare say that when he was around. Bobbi put us out on the street, and a couple of weeks later an SUV pulled up to haggle. I got in and was whisked off to Sarajevo. I don't speak Serbian but picked up enough to understand that Amal could make more selling me on to someone and let Three Face think I had just run away."

"So why didn't he put you on his list?" she asked, suspiciously. I just stared back, trying to appear at a loss. It wasn't hard to appear frightened. Destiny's face took on a frustrated but calculating expression.

"Well, you're here now and if you are not on his list, he won't be sending me an invoice, will he." A statement, not a question. "Was that your first time out on the street?" At least I could answer this one truthfully, sadly.

"No. When my parents died, I ended up on the street for a while, but mostly I pulled myself straight and got cleaned up. When things got hard I still 'privateered' some, but I wasn't working at all for the last two years. I had no intention of falling back into this, but I understand these are not choices for me to make right now. I don't like it, but I can hack it."

"We'll see," was all she said, and waved me off to the dressing area without the examination. Ominous?

*

They fed us surprisingly well. Salads, vegetables, light fish, and other high protein, low-salt and low-fat food. It was healthy and natural, designed to improve their 'product.' I didn't touch the water and was careful what I ate; I needed to remember these were not dumb hillbillies. They put us in a dorm and we slept, and a few hours later were disturbed briefly by the rest of the *Astasha* group's arrival. It was clearly a relief for some women, who had struck up relationships and then been split up, to be reunited. *Peu de pitié*, I thought. It meant 'little mercies,' but it translates ironically to 'small pities,' which struck more of a chord.

The dorm had no windows, but there was a spiral staircase in one corner, which lead up to an exit that opened onto a small garden. The small garden had a dense canopy overhead and a wire fence between us and a river flowing past the property. We were presumably allowed to get some air if we wanted to but could not get far. A low bench was by the fence, and in front a sign said 'beware snakes and gators.' It was well into the morning and we had not been disturbed, so I sat on the bench and thought about my situation and my next move. I was beginning to believe I would have no choice but to fight my way out. I could always go Rambo or Trinity on their asses, and perhaps I need to initiate that on my terms, rather than be on the defensive.

I was distracted by a small blue light flashing furiously from inside a clump of dead or dying shrubs that had been floating in the river but had snagged on the fence at my feet. I peered closer, and suddenly six of the leaves spun up like mini helicopter blades and a small drone lifted up two inches and hovered for a second or two, before dropping back and reverted to being flotsam. *Kelsie Kobe, I love you.*

I glanced around and I was alone. I looked closer at the mystery bush, registering that the drone and the blue flashing light were separate units. I reached through the fence into the bush and pulled out the object with the light.

It looked like a frog — a clever disguise — and the blue light was its one eye. It was the length of my hand and made of plastic. It clicked and cracked open. I quickly pulled it apart, and two objects dropped onto the grass by my feet. One was a USB memory stick, with the USB connector at one end and ethernet network port at the other; the other object was a small device like an old-fashioned radio pager, with a tiny keyboard and screen.

The message on the screen flashed, "WE ARE CLOSE BY. PLAN INFILTRATION TONIGHT. IF ABLE, PLUG USB DEVICE INTO ANY NETWORK OR COMPUTER TO AID HACKING ATTACK. THANK F YOU OK. E WET HIS PANTS. HANG TIGHT. MAX."

I replied "WALK IN THE PARK HERE, BE WAITING FOR YOU ARMY BOY. CAN'T BE CAUGHT WITH THIS TOY. WILL LEAVE WITH DRONE" and I gave said drone a wink and thumbs up. I heard people coming up the stairs, so made an exaggerated motion behind me and pushed the one-eyed frog and the pager back into the shrub and palmed the USB stick.

More women came into the garden as the morning wore on, and I moved and sat by myself in the corner. I quietly removed one of the sneakers they had provided. It was a little oversized, as they had not expected me, and I pressed the USB stick in between my toes and crammed my foot back in, hoping I was not damaging the device. I casually got up and wandered down the spiral stairs, back into the dorm, and surreptitiously tried the doors leading out. The door to the feeding area was open, so I went through. There was no one in that room, so I quietly tiptoed on to the shower room Destiny had addressed us in on arrival. The assistant's computer was turned off, and the keyboard was missing. I looked at the back of the computer, and all of the ports were sealed off by a metal plate to prevent tampering, but the network cable snaked out through a small hole and made its way to the wall, where it was plugged in. I unplugged it. Using my t-shirt, I wiped any trace of my sweat and finger prints from the USB stick and inserted it into the socket, praying it was in fact ethernet. I noticed another network port in the USB plug, so I plugged the network cable from the computer into it, to at least make it appear it was connected to the casual observer. I backed away, not knowing if I had done well. And not seeing the huge, catlike smile spreading on SkyLox's face thousands of kilometres to the northwest.

21: Collar of Control

Things went horribly sideways at just after seven that evening. We had been taken to eat at noon and again at five — I had pretended to eat both times — and we were now in our bunks. The garden door had been closed as we ate dinner. It was padlocked, and I'd had no way to open it, so I'd retired to my bed, trusting the rescue team would come ready for such obstructions.

Just after seven, by the clock on the wall, we were roused by the door clanging open and a bear of a man pushing himself through it. He stood swaying, wedging his thumbs into the tight gap between his paunch and his belt. He surveyed the room, looking for someone. His eyes met mine and I looked away, but it was not to be that easy. He walked over and towered over me.

"Y'all mus be Jing. No mistaking that. Stand up. I have a job for you." I nodded demurely and obeyed his command.

He continued on around the room, looking at each woman, and each cowered as his eyes touched them. He eventually stopped by the bunk of a petite woman with mousey hair. She was very pretty and youthful, and I could tell from my experience that she was not a pro. She had cried pretty much all the time she wasn't drugged, had made no alliances for protection, and curled into a ball at night. The man grabbed her wrist, hauled her to her feet, and marched off with her towards the door, indicating that I should follow. He marched us down a corridor and through some doorways to a smaller room, which had a single bed, a basin unit, and a chair in the corner.

He introduced himself simply as "Landon," but his tone suggested we should already know who he was, as if he was royalty. On the basin unit sat two collars, and he handed us one each, indicating we should put them on. The mouse just stared at him. I hesitated. This didn't look good, and I wasn't going to let this asshole hurt the mouse. I felt my control slipping as I flashed back to Amsterdam, the mouse becoming Jing, and nobody was going to hurt her. But I also had the presence of mind to know I had to let this play out a little more before turning into the yellow hulk. This might just be a fashion show, trying a look he thought he might sell to the customer.

I examined the collar, which was a mix of leather and metal, quite typical of some I had worn in fetish scenes. These versions had a plastic box attached to the side, and the buckles I was used to were replaced by metal snaps here. What the hell — we should play this out and wait for the cavalry. I wrapped the collar around my neck and snapped the snaps, then partly to put this dick off his guard, I gently helped the mouse to put on hers.

"Good girl," the mountain growled at me, "I hardly have to explain your role. Here in the south, we like to do things easy. If we have a mare we want to set to stud, but she's too flighty or feisty, we bring a more experienced lady hoss that's past her foal-bearing days into the stall and the filly settles down. Eva here was snatched off the street for a purpose. I has a client who likes this type but wants them more experienced and less snively. So we have to break her in and toughen her up. Normally Seth would enjoy this, but he's away taking care of business and we need to get started." He paused, admiring what he thought was his own cleverness. The mouse quivered and backed away into me, terrified.

"Destiny said you men are not to touch the merchandise or she'll take your pecker!" I shot back. He roared with laughter.

"She's done that, true enough. Ma's inclined to keeping discipline. But that's for lasciviousness in the troops. This here is planned training for y'all, of which she approves. She assigned it to me in Seth's absence. Seth's my brother and is normally put to ensurin' you girls are trained and y'll represent the Toussaint brand properly., I'm the smarter, older, and handsomer brother. I'm the business development brother, so to speak. But not today. Today I'm the whore trainer!" he grumbled the last resentfully.

"Well, we are not going to do this today" I asserted. "Your ma said we get a couple of days of peace."

"True, she likely did say that. But lil' Eva here has a great deal catchin' up to do." He squared up assertively, a shade less than menacing, annoyed I was standing up to him.

"Here's is how this is gonna work. If Seth were here, he would be scaring the living shit outta y'all. There would be yellin' and spittin', an' he would have you backed up against the wall until he has you cowed. Maybe he'd get his pet maid to hold you down or rope you up. He has ways of hurtin' that leave no marks. But that's Seth for you. Passionate in his dealin's. I consider myself a whole lot more civil, and more modern. I have this technology!" He reached into his pocket and brandished a small black device. My heart caught in my chest as I thought it was the device Max had passed to me via the drone. But looking closer it was bigger, and just had one button on the top, which he pressed with his tree trunk of a finger and my world lit up. Icy pain shot through my body from the collar down to my toes. I'd been tasered before, and I'd accidently touched a utility socket or two, so I knew what an electric shock felt like. And this wasn't it. A Taser is painful but quickly overpowers your muscle control and you are on the floor twitching. The socket makes you jump and can burn you at the contact point. This was shear agony, like nothing I had ever imagined. It was over for a few seconds before I realized it had ceased. Eva and I stood there panting, dribbling, and our noses and eyes were watering and red.

"Microwaves and ultrasonics. It stimulates the nerves in your spine in a whole new way, 'til recently not known to science. I do hear the CIA are considerin' this here toy as opposed to waterboardin'.

"Now to bizniz. Our client — y'alls new owner — likes just two things. He likes good old-fashin' blowjobs, and he likes that anilingus stuff. That's when you lick his ass. Not my thing, but the customer is always right. And believe me, this ain't so bad. Some folks are into a lot worse. Many of the girls out there would swap beds with you in a fleetin' heartbeat, let me assure y'all of that fact." Sadly, he was right. *But this still is not happening.* I readied.

"Jing, what am gonna ask you to do is to coach young Eva here. With your experience an' all, you must know the tricks of the trade. Eva's gonna practise with me until Seth gets back. Now, we are all this in this together—well, more properly you two are anyway—and I have this one here button to make y'all diligent in your trainin'. Oh, and that was just level six out of one hundred, that just made you flap some. I'm now turnin' it up to thirty. No one has refused me a thing at thirty. Seth tried it at fifty on one poor woman, more to see what happens then for obedience sake. Sad waste of product that was." He stopped talking and let it sink in. Eva had started crying again but looked oddly resigned. No one would last long with that level of pain. I hung my head, but *fast speed* was ready.

The second-to-last mistake Landon made in his life was placing the remote control down on the basin while he fumbled under his belly for his belt buckle. My right hand shot out, first and second fingers extended together, the rest curled back. The strike started from my left foot, powering my body to swivel rapidly, whipping all of my energy into the twisting motion as I uncoiled and sprang low to high driving my full bodies inertia behind the impact. My aim was dead on, and the sharp, straight fingers went into his right eye, knuckle deep. A smaller man would have died. Dead before he dropped from the shock to his brain. A bigger than average man would have gone down and suffered and likely died in minutes or survived with severe brain damage. This mountain shuddered and stepped backwards, stunned and marred., Then he roared and ran forward at me blindly, his arms outstretched to mash me. That was the last mistake of his life. To me, he was moving in slow motion, and I ducked under his arm and then leapt, landing a roundhouse kick at full power at the base of his neck, forcing his head into the wall, cranked to one side. The angle of impact cracked his spine, and he slipped quickly down the wall, dead.

I landed knees bent astride his tangled legs, then steadied myself and reached to steady Eva. Rather than looking at me or Landon, she was staring open-mouthed towards the doorway. I turned and saw Destiny just inside the doorway looking horrified, her lip trembling, her left hand to her mouth, and her eyes buggy and wide. In her right hand was a thin knife with a nine-inch blade. It resembled a fish filleting knife. She looked from Landon to me, eyes filling with unholy rage.

"Amal never sent you!" She spat slowly. "Ah's was coming to skin you alive, but...you took my Landon, like a fighter would take him. I wanna skin you, but you'd just take me, too, and then who would look out for Seth?" She looked sad and regretful that she couldn't gut me with her bare hands. Reaching behind her back, she pulled a small pistol out of her belt and pointed it at me. Hand steady. I stepped between her and Eva instinctively, and the gun tracked me exactly. *They say it takes one to know one.* The gun didn't just follow me, it was mirroring my every reaction and nuance, and I felt in my heart that Destiny knew *fast speed* too. My training and youth would beat her in a fist fight, but she could track any dodge or feint I threw with her gun. Which was irrelevant in the next second when Max blew her head off with his silenced Glock 23 pistol.

I recognized Max in his tactical gear and ski mask instantly, not by his shape or voice, but by his body language, which embraced me on sight. I felt that if we were in a crowded party, I would feel him wherever he was in the room, through some invisible link. I felt... connected. My body responded at the lizard-brain level.

Eva fainted and dropped beside me. I reacted and got my hands under her and broke her fall and lowered her to the ground. Then I ran to Max. Like a little girl. At least he ran towards me too, sparing me a little dignity.

"You look OK. Are you?" he said, holding my shoulders and peering deep into my eyes, as if he could check my body and soul for damage that way.

"Relieved, and whole," I whispered back.

"The FBI SWAT team is about twenty minutes out, and they can't find me or the team here. They know you are here. Are you up to hanging in a little longer? Seth is unaccounted for, but the rest of the gang is dead. We are locking the cooks and cleaners in with the... um'... other women. If you are up for it, we will lock you in, too, then we fade away before the cavalry show up and start asking questions. You can tell them you have no idea who we were, just grateful to be rescued by soldiers with hot manly bodies and awesome skills." He was surely grinning under the mask. "They know you work for Ethan and stole aboard the yacht with a SPOT, but nothing else."

I nodded. He stared into my eyes meaningfully.

"I would kiss you hard right now, Gia, but we don't know what surveillance there is, and that would look...well...weird. But I'm coming back for a kiss. Shining knight, and all that!"

"I'll count on it!" My breath was a little gaspy. *Get a grip Gia, for God's sake.*

22: No Coins for a Dead Man's Eyes

[Ethan] — Although we had been monitoring for nearly twenty hours, it was only 90 minutes since we told Agent Chave we had a location for Gia and were moving drone assets into place to get a visual for his team. He was revving up his SWAT squad in anticipation of a 'go' order, eight kilometres away in a staging area at a school field. As prearranged, Max and his team put two of the Toussaint's men in areas visible from the tree tops, then faded into the swamp back to their boats. Once clear, Kelsie withdrew our existing stealth drones, letting them drift off downstream where they would be recovered tomorrow or the day after. She then brought up a live stream to Chave from other, more commercially available drones that were inbound to the area, where they 'discovered' that something seemingly lethal was in progress on the ground. Chave triggered the assault.

There was one paved road in and out of the environmental centre, and Chave's HRT team entered in a disguised vehicle. It looked like a large, empty flatbed truck., totally unthreatening, which could easily be a lost shipment on the road. Concealed within the space below the truck's bed, hung between the wheels and running the full length — including into the cab — was a boxed container where eighteen men, their weapons, and assault gear could crouch and from which they could deploy rapidly. Clever paintwork and mirrors gave the illusion it was an empty space and axels. It would not pass close physical inspection, but for driving swiftly past security cameras and guards it was perfect. As the truck pulled up outside, a false set of rear wheels fell away and the SWAT team poured out swiftly and silently, then fanned out. Fifteen seconds later, the air was split by the thunder of Blackhawk and Eurocopter helicopters barreling into the clearing at treetop level. The Blackhawk went straight to the far side of the facility and, from a hover, more SWAT members disgorged on four abseiling ropes. The Eurocopter had no doors attached on the rear compartment, and instead had a platform where two black-clad snipers lay strapped down. Hovering two hundred feet overhead gave them total air domination; of course, provided there were no more missiles as there had been in Vancouver.

While this was happening, three large *Zodiac* attack boats zoomed up to the ranch at the far side of the river, and another HRT entered and swept the property. Within seven minutes, the reports came in that all was secure, and all targets were down, without a shot being fired.

Marcy, Kelsie, and I watched all of this unfold firsthand on the helmet cameras Max and his team wore, and then on the feed relayed from the HRT teams via Chave's command post. We were relieved when the lead SWAT agent popped open the door to the dorm where Max had locked Gia and the captives and thanked God that the HRT team held their fire, cleared the room, and set up a protective perimeter. Within minutes of the 'all clear,' the captives and staff were led up to the front of the compound, and paramedics arrived in a small convoy of ambulances.

Marcy was still miffed that she could not go in with Max. All of her VPD hostage-rescue training and her new kinship with Gia demanded it of her, but we had agreed she and I would be visible on the video link to Chave and that would be our alibi. Max and his team were unknown to Chave, and therefore off his grid. Chave would no doubt suspect we were involved in the takedown but had no proof, and we didn't think he was overly motivated to find any.

Marcy, Max, and I had a long debate on the ethics of our plans, which in the final analysis boiled down simply to our survival. If the Toussaint's lived, even in jail, their reputation and deep pockets meant they would come for us, likely sooner than later. We could hold it off, but we would slip, and with the expertise and resources they could employ, we were dead. And other innocents probably along with us. The FBI HRT team might kill them for us, but their priorities would be first to save any captives, second make arrests, and third defend themselves with deadly force only if necessary. So, when the news came that Seth was unaccounted for, it was deeply troubling. While the HRT action unfolded, we were quietly but furiously going over all of the footage from the cameras and roadside trackers we had stored. Many vehicles and boats had come and gone as we had surveilled, but none had triggered our face-recognition or human-operator checks. Once the body count was complete, Chave put out an all-points bulletin for Seth.

[Seth] — When we met with Chiyome, it was never casual. The bitch-whore liked drama and left me always wanting to get her alone in some position where she was helpless and where I was the boss. She never bullied or threatened, but she didn't have to, and that's what made me so mad. The bitch-whore had an air about her, complete and utter confidence that she was deadly as a mamba. She scares me, and so I hate her. I've been scared of no one else in the world since Pop died. Well, maybe Ma a little bit, when she gets her dander up.

The drama — or maybe's ritual is a better word for it — was always Jap-flavoured. Like she's Kill Bill or sum'it. This morning I got the text on the burner phone we keep. A single letter as always. The letter 'A' means check your messages, 'B' means we are done, never contact us again. Even her texts are designed to subtly show us who is the boss. *Filthy bitch-whore.* This morning we got an 'A.' I opened the laptop she gave us, which had this one function: Checking messages. There was only one icon. I clicked it and it connected to that there dark web and downloaded a new installation of a TOR browser, then connected to a freshly created mailbox, which had the tricky bitch-whore's message in it. We could chat back and forth, but as we finished, the software deleted itself and reformatted the drive and ended up back as we started, with no trace of what occurred. When I used the laptop, the blue camera light told me she was watching us. I had to sit there and let her. *Bitch-whore. God help me, her time will come.*

Today's message simply said, "Marcy Stone located. Meet me at Parsons Hotel, Baton Rouge, 8 pm tonight to negotiate terms." I didn't answer, even to acknowledge. Wouldn't give her the privilege. I just hit the power down button and the machine ignored my command, instead starting its self-cleansing routine.

When we meet Chiyome, I take incredible precautions. But somehow, she tracks me. I've tried a variety of routes and subterfuges, arriving at the rendezvous believing I've shaken her watchers, only to have her evil greeter step out to meet me as I arrive. The greeter is a piece of work, too. Kimono, make up, bowing and polite, but never speaks. Wears so much white paste makeup on her face you can barely see the slut underneath it.

Leads me into the meeting, kneels and serves us that crappy green tea, sits there motionless until it's time for me to be shown out like a puppy, then she leads me out again. She's another bitch-whore I'd like to spend time with. I'm not scared of this one, so maybe I'd take it out on her for both of them, if I ever got the chance.

But this time I was too juiced to try to sneak up on them. They knew where the slut cop was hiding out, and I wanted that information. I wanted to go play with the cop for a while and get some of the dignity back she stole from us. After she'd told me how she'd rubbed my nose in the shitter in Vancouver, I'd fuck her in front of her boyfriend and kill them both. I'd laid down in the back of a delivery van so no one saw me leave the ecology centre, but changed into my Red Corvette once we were up the interstate a ways. Sure enough, when I pulled up at the Parsons Hotel valet, out stepped the bitch greeter. No matter.

With her little pigeon slow step, she led me to the elevator and up to the seventh floor. In room 709, we did the usual security check. They never patted me down for weapons, expecting me to be too scared to try anything. Which shamefully was true, and another bitch-whore trick to show her foot was on my throat. But they did check me for bugs. The evil greeter passed several electronic wands over me from head to toe and then led me back out to the elevator to another floor. Chiyome was in room 411. As always, the room had been redecorated just for the occasion. Gone were the beds and pictures and curtains. The room was gutted, but for a tiny, low table. We had to sit on the floor to use it — mats for Chiyome and the greeter, but not me — and on a carpet, which was not in the room when they'd rented it. At every meeting, they always had a carpet which created an optical illusion. It's one of their trademarks. This one gave the appearance the table and mats were suspended on the surface of a clear pool, with koi carp swimming beneath. *Who travels with their own carpet, for fucks sake.*

Chiyome was standing on her mat, waiting for me. As is her way, she gave me a little bow. I dutifully bowed back, then we both sat, and the greeter poured the tea. We took a sip, then business could start. I was impatient.

"So you know where the slut cop and her rich boyfriend are?" I opened.

"Yes, and I am watching them," she replied, in her always measured voice. That was another part of her scary routine. Never used the word 'we' or 'my outfit.' Just 'I,' like she was omni-fricking present.

"How much for you to tell me where she is then? I want to kill her myself, not pay one of your assassins." She regarded me silently for a long time.

"Today, I will tell you this information for free, I think," she said.

"Well that's a first!" I blurted, and instantly regretted it. Not for being insolent, but for losing control.

"They are right here, in this hotel," she continued, as if I'd said nothing. "This same room, one floor above us."

"I don't understand," I said cautiously. "I get they are here, upstairs. I don't get why you are just telling me this. You must know I woulda paid a fortune for that little snippet. Is this 'be nice to Seth' day?" As a reply, she reached into her kimono and set on the table in front of us two Jap coins of some sort. Odd fella on them waving a fan around.

"In a way, it is be nice to Seth day. And these coins are a gift, from me to you."

"Still don't get it."

"No, you wouldn't, but I will explain for you. In order for you to hire me, you need money. By our count, your organization keeps your funds in seventeen separate accounts, which we monitor, in different countries and currencies around the world. Today, just after five pm, they were all emptied. At the same time. In effect, you and your family are now penniless. Except for these pennies, which I gift you, as I said."

"That can't be; that's stupid." *What game is she playing? She's working an angle on me, I'm sure of it.*

"And it's your lack of money, Seth, that gives me a problem. I live by many laws and rules you would never understand. But one of them my grandfather taught me, due to his profound respect for those poor who have nothing at all in life, was that if a man does not even have two pennies to cover his dead eyes with, then you should never kill him."

What does that even mean? The greeter came to life slowly and moved purposefully with grace. I'd forgotten she was there. She sat up and put her hands on either side of her face and pulled. The face came away, and I realized it wasn't make-up; it was a cunningly constructed mask. She put it carefully onto the table in front of herself. She had Cho's face. The face of the woman I use to help me train our girls. What could Cho be doing here? That was the second-to-last thought that went through my head. In Cho's dainty left hand, a nine-inch needle with a tee handle — like a wicked, straight, giant corkscrew — appeared. My very last thought was one of understanding why someone would go to the trouble of carrying their own carpet from place to place. There wasn't time to have another thought before I died.

THE NUDE DETECTIVE

22: Gia Gets Her Dream

[Ethan] — Marcy, Gwen, Kelsie, and I flew directly back to Vancouver by private jet the next morning. Darcy stayed to collect all the toys she had spread around Louisiana and Mississippi, and Max stayed to wait for Gia, who was still answering the questions of an increasingly frustrated Bob Chave. I had called Chave and asked pointedly if Gia needed me to get her a lawyer, and he promised she would be released within 24 hours. They had no intention of prosecuting her; they were just trying to tidy up a mess everyone wanted swept under the carpet.

We were feeling safe enough to travel in the open since receiving the package. The package, as we called it — a little freaked out — had been left anonymously at reception. An ornate Japanese red maple box, tied with a voluminous, deep-blue silk ribbon. We opened it cautiously, as no one knew we were here, or so we had thought. Inside the box were several photos and a card. The photos were of us moving around the hotel for the last few days, candidly taken, and the final photo was the dead body of Seth Toussaint, a white corpse with a silver penny holding down each eyelid and a red dot between his left cheek and eye socket. The card said cryptically, "Our customer cannot pay, and so our shadow moves on. Well played, Ethan. Chiyome." SkyLox had told us who, or what, Chiyome was, and I guess we were lucky that the assassins were business people first and foremost. She could have killed us at any time in the last couple of days.

We reached home tired in many ways and agreed we would meet at 6 pm at *The Crazy Bean* to inspect the renovations we had left in progress when we'd fled the country. We woke up an hour before, to a message that Max and Gia were already en route and would just make it to *The Bean* to join us at 6:15. *The Bean* was whole again and bustling with locals, as if nothing had happened just two weeks ago. The only change was that a picture of local First Nations Art had been replaced by an impressionist painting of a white man, naked at a window, with the frame just covering his blush. Funny, Gwen. Funny.

As seems to be the way at *The Bean*, there was only one table open, enough room for us, and Max and Gia when they arrived. Otherwise it was full of locals and their dogs, including Frank the Cap and Elvis. The latter wandered over, licked Marcy's hand excitedly, and curled up to sleep at her feet. By the time we had inspected the place, talked to the locals and staff, and sat down, the door opened, and Max and Gia entered. Gia almost ran to Marcy, and they embraced like old friends. *Women.* She hugged Gwen, Kelsie and me, and I man-hugged Max.

We sat, and I realized Gia had been crying, and not just in the moment of reunion. Her tears were older—hours, not seconds.

"Hey what's up? Are you ok?" I asked. Gia just hung her head, in a very un-Gia-like fashion.

"She is upset because she thinks her crazy-assed stunt means you are firing her today," said Max. "You're not, are you? She loves her job here, and she...well, she told me about her past, and...." he faded out. Gia kept her head down, dejected.

"God no," I laughed. "Our plan was no better than hers. We would never have resolved this without her stunt. I think a little warning might have been nice, I'll admit, but we owe her everything. Chiyome was on our trail and would have killed us. We owe you our lives, Gia, not our anger. You took on personal protection and, wow! You are committed!"

She looked up and around the table at us all looking back. I'm not sure who had the oddest expression. We had no idea she'd be carrying that burden.

"As for her job? Well it's hers if she wants it, but...well, Marcy should say this, not me." I passed the torch to Marcy.

"Gia, I resigned from the VPD today when we landed. With time owing, I'm effectively out of there already. I've probably done more for helpless women in the last two weeks than all my time in the force. Not that I regret that—it is a noble job, and I stand by it one hundred and ten percent. I have a chance to do things others can't, and I'm hoping you will help me. Or, more the other way around actually. I want to help you."

"I'm not following you Marcy, slow down," said Gia.

"Max will have told you about SkyLox, no doubt. When you let her into the Toussaint network with the box we slipped you, she downloaded details on all the girls, boys, and others who the bastards had trafficked in the last several years. There are literally hundreds of poor souls. And we know which customers they all went to. We've already passed that on to law enforcement, who will sweep up the criminals. But no one speaks for or looks out for the victims. If we do nothing, they will be picked up by new pimps and madams, or be slaves to others, at any rate."

"SklyLox placed all of the stolen money into a charity she created called 'Silent Souls.' It needs a leader, and, well, we hoped that would be you, Gia. And I want to help. It would be your baby, for as long as you need it to be. With millions of dollars, and what you know about that life, you can do good work." Marcy stopped to let her absorb it.

Max quipped, "Marcy and I can be your military wing, not that you need us to kick ass for you." He finished quickly, realizing the implicit insult to a martial arts guru.

Gia gripped Max's wrist tightly, her tears flowing full force again, looked up at the sky, and said cryptically, "I promised you once, Jing; I renew my promise."

Epilogue

[Marcy] — It had been two, very busy weeks. A whole floor of our apartment building was cleared and had become Gia's first base of operations. On the same floor, she and Max shared a simple corner apartment. She still took time in the dojo with Ethan and me, but that would change soon. She insisted on selecting her replacement personally, and we consented. A staff had been drafted who were doing their best to keep up with law enforcement's activities across the globe, as well as making direct contact with the women named on the Toussaint list. Ethan and I had helped to get Gia started, but it was time for her and Max to make *Silent Souls* their own, and for Ethan and me to step away and let them. I would circle back to help later, as I genuinely wanted a part of this once she had put her stamp on it.

Ethan and I decided we wanted that break in the sun we had talked about, and there will be a plane waiting for us at the airport tomorrow, fuelled for Aruba. *Fabulous*. Yesterday I went shopping with my new unlimited credit card. Part of me hates it, but what's a girl gonna do to keep up with a billionaire? New clothes, including bikinis, lingerie, and a luggage set that had one extra small locking bag for whenever Phoenix wants to separate Ethan from his clothing. And speaking of Phoenix—*she* had a couple of surprises for Ethan before we flew.

This morning we took the Seabus over from Vancouver's Waterfront Station to Lower Lonsdale, an area on the North Shore that was coming alive with new condos and restaurants. We took a cab up to the foot of Grouse Mountain and ran the Grouse Grind together. The Grind is a 1.8-mile trail, climbing rapidly 2800 feet. Normal people climb it in about 90 minutes, fit people smile if they beat 60, and we ran up in 40. Sweaty and out of breath, we had a beer at the top before riding the gondola back down. I asked Ethan if we could pop out for a drive for a couple of hours in the afternoon, just the two of us, and he readily agreed.

After a light lunch, we went down to the garage, and I jumped ahead of him, pulling him over to the Aston Martin. I hopped into the driver's seat and indicated with my thumb that he was riding shotgun today. He squared off jokingly, then grinned and slipped into the leather seat beside me.

"Where are we going?" he asked pleasantly for the fifth time today as I revved the throaty engine, giving it a second to warm up. I loved the sound.

"I told you, it's a surprise!" I said, in mock exasperation. We motored down Davie, turned left onto Burrard, and headed south over the bridge, then turned west, which pointed us out towards Kitsilano and the University of BC. As we passed Kitsilano and Jericho beaches, the destination options narrowed to UBC and the endowment lands. We stopped at traffic lights, and I leaned forward and pulled my t-shirt off my right shoulder to show him my latest acquisition; my new small tattoo. I had visited Mary-Ann last night, when Ethan thought I was out for a walk, so it still had a sterile dressing over it and was raised and raw.

Mary-Ann and I had emailed some design ideas back and forth and had eventually settled on a design using just two lines. The first, in ochre, swept and looped and spiked to make a flaming pyre. The second, in an electric Cadbury purple, was much shorter and was a proud, regal Phoenix, winking cheekily. Even in its new state, it was stunningly beautiful, and I could tell that Ethan was dazzled.

"You do remember what it means, Ethan, when I show you a Phoenix?"

"That you turn from princess to goddess?" he quipped. "I wondered why we are heading this way. Wreck Beach I suppose." He pretended to sigh patiently, but I could almost hear his heart thudding in his chest. *Wait until he sees the real plan*, I thought. Public nudity is technically illegal in Canada, but like in many jurisdictions, the law turns her blind eye to certain events and locations, and Wreck Beach is a world-renowned nudist area that can be reached via a long set of steps from the rear of the university campus. I let him think that was our destination and smiled, pulling away with a 'zoom' as the light changed to green.

After a few blocks I added, "Don't think I forgot that the Booker Detective Agency solved another case down in Mississippi. I was thinking while we are in Aruba, we could design a *Fifty Shades*-style 'little room of fun' for the apartment."

"That could be a fun project," he agreed, squirming as much as the bucket seat would allow.

I surprised Ethan again as we drove through the campus, by pulling off into the art faculty building parking lot, shutting down the engine with a throttle-blip-roar, and hopping out gaily. I grabbed a small bag from behind the seat, which I had hidden there the night before.

"Keep up, slow coach, I don't think you want to make me wait for this," I giggled. He hopped to it and we left the Aston with a beep as the doors locked. I led Ethan through several doors and into a small room, which I locked behind us.

"Gwen told me about this place. I think you will love it. Totally up your little kink's alley. Here, put these on." I gave him the bag I'd brought from the car. He tentatively reached in and pulled out a small white towel, a bottle of baby lotion, and a pair of men's black *Micro Modal bikini* briefs.

"You have one minute to strip and slick yourself up all over with the oil, except your feet. Don't want you slipping. Then you can put on your Saxx. Leave everything else in here. Wait for me to come back. Don't keep The Phoenix waiting!" I didn't wait to see the expression I imagined on his face. I stepped out before my 'domina' face dissolved into giggles of anticipation. I quickly popped into the next room and double checked that everything was as expected, returning pleased that it was perfect. I waited a few moments, then stepped back in to find Ethan had followed the instructions and was just folding his discarded clothes. *Neat, glistening boy.*

"Leave them. Put the towel around your waist and show some modesty man!" I teased. "Follow me then!" His face was a picture of concern, but his personal enjoyment indicator was revved up and bulging nicely.

He tentatively stepped out into the hallway, and I opened the next door and ushered him in. In a small semicircle sat five women and two men, easels and charcoals at the ready for their art class; Gwen had arranged for Ethan to be the subject. He froze, looking at the scene, from the people chatting quietly and ignoring him, so far, to the small, spot-lit dais with a simple wooden chair waiting for him, and then he looked back to me.

I leaned into him and whispered softly and sexily into his ear, "Don't worry, you can keep your towel on. At least for now. Darren, the professor, agreed I could bring a model and choose three to four poses over the next hour when I made a modest donation to the club. These are all fourth-year students, so they've seen everything before, so no need to be shy, honey. Our game today is that you can start with what you have on, which is not much I grant you. Just before I choose your next pose for you, I will ask you a question. Get it right, you keep your clothes on. Get it wrong...."

I pushed him towards the dais and took my seat at the one empty easel, picked up my charcoal, and smiled brightly at my funny, loving, incredibly sexy, if crazy, man.

End.

What's Next?

I sincerely hope you enjoyed meeting Ethan, Marcy and the gang as they tackled their first adventures – thank you so much for reading this far. As a new author, your reviews of my work on www.Goodreads.com could make a big difference to me, so I would appreciate any support.

Book Two of the series, **The Nuder Detective** is already available, and contains the same characters and themes, and adds some new ones. Ethan and Marcy must race around the world to rescue an assassin's daughter from some seemingly supernatural 'bad guys.'

At time of publishing Book One, Book Three is underway and already taking shape. Keep up with developments at www.melissajaneparker.com

Thank You,

Melissa-Jane

Acknowledgements

My fantastic partner and fun collaborator, who believed in my writing ability — perhaps before I did – and who helped me maintain my drive and discipline (no pun intended). The only personal fan club I could ever need.

Anita Kuehnel, whose unrivalled editing skills (and matching tact), combined with some invaluable story suggestions, helped me make a better book.

Cappy, a thoughtful test reader who provided many perceptive and valuable insights.

The women, men, and recently acknowledged variations — in our new non-binary world — who have battled for equity and recognition for their gender, race, age, orientation, and/or kink.

The many brave people who have researched – often at significant professional and personal risk – the psychology, physiology, culture, history, and evolution of BDSM and similar topics. Fascinating stuff. Thanks to their efforts, and freely shared findings, I was able to reach a more educated viewpoint than would have been possible in previous decades.

I encourage anyone with an interest in BDSM to do their own research and form their own opinion. Whether you end up with a conservative or liberal viewpoint at the end of that journey, at least it will be based on the new data, which didn't exist before this century, instead of the dogma from the 1900s and before.

The inventors of the internet. A fascinating part of my journey was realizing how the internet allows us to amass data to *combat stigma,* and provides the ability to connect and find out that *we are not alone.* A dramatic acceleration to social change. If we are ever to reach fairness and equity in our lifetime, the internet is invaluable to our quest.

About the Author

If you read the *Acknowledgements*, you will find that the author was inspired by the courage of many people, over many generations, who risked the backlash of stigma associated with some of the topics contained in this book. But, this author is not that brave. Well, I'm not! Melissa Jane, or MJ as I've become to know her, is my beloved pen-name. That admission dispensed with, I affirm that the following is all me.

At school, I was a lover of math, the sciences, geography, and sports, with little use for the likes of foreign languages, history, and written English. The latter is now, of course, a handicap (see *Acknowledgements* below – thanks Anita).

In my pre- and early teens, I read encyclopedias galore; quiz books, locations of countries, their cities, populations, and their flags. At the time I felt incredibly knowledgeable, compared with my peers, but looking back, I'm sure I was more of a Cliff Clavin. If you feel that some of my novels have a few too many sex or technology factoids, this is why. Let me know what you think about any aspect of my work via my website: www.melissajaneparker.com

Some of my early literary influences were: — E.E. Doc Smith's *Lensman* series, anything by Asimov, Piers Anthony's *Xanth* and *Adept* worlds, James Clavell's *Shogun*, and Eric Van Lustbader's *Linnear* series. Later in life, Rothfuss, Rowling, and Mr. Martin's *Game of Thrones* (if he would just finish the damn series) fuelled my love for Sci-Fan, while Ken Follet, Dan Brown and P.T. Deutermann built on my interest in historical fiction. Lee Child, Chandler, Grafton, Baldacci, Larsson, and James (P.D.) are some 'go to' authors for detective novels; and in case you are wondering, I prefer Joey Hill, Tiffany Reisz, and Jacqueline Carey to E.L. James. The best book I have read in a long time is Esi Edugyan's *Washington Black*, for which she justifiably earned *another* Giller Prize. Ms. Edugyan has strong affiliations with Victoria, BC – Vancouver's near neighbour. There is something about this part of the world which is good for authors, and I hope some will rub off on me. A close second to Esi, in my admittedly biased opinion, is my daughter's latest effort. Good luck, my girl.

Interview with the Author

What gave you the idea for *The Nude Detective*?

I drafted a story 12 years ago about a rich private detective in Vancouver. This was when personal-use drones were just showing potential to be commercially viable, and I thought they would be a cool slant to differentiate my story. Back then, there was a girlfriend who was a VPD officer. The PI also had the same 'nudity' urge resulting from those same events on the island in his youth, that you see in the book today. In that early draft, neither of the characters had an overtly kinky side, and there was no story about BDSM. That came ten years later, when I decided to get serious about finishing the book. Drones, while not yet passé, are common, and I wanted to add in something else as a differentiator.

Is your new differentiator BDSM sex?

Yes and no. I wanted the story to stand on its own merits, and although there are a handful of short 'kinky' sex scenes, *The Nude Detective* is far from a hot and steamy erotica novel. I had recently completed some research that didn't start out to be about BDSM, but it led to a history of sexuality – and how sex influenced history — going back over 1000 years. I found it fascinating and thought it could be a compelling sub-theme (no pun intended). In particular, the emergence of the internet in the last 20 years has, in a very short time, provided data that suggest what we have thought about sex for the last 200 years could be quite wrong.

This new information led me to look at the psychology of traditionally highly stigmatized topics, our physiology, sex laws, and even how the media has operated in the last few decades. I considered writing a novel where the main character was someone like Gwen, who gets caught up in this new sexual revolution. It challenges everything she has believed and taught for the past three decades. In the end, I chose to take my original detective story, and weave this new information in as a sub-theme. One differentiator is the numerous sexual factoids that pepper this story [as distinct from writing a sexy book].

The second, subtler differentiator, is the relationship between Ethan and Marcy. BDSM erotica, in my limited experience, has primary characters who are already experts in BDSM. If there is a novice, they are cast against, and led by, an expert within the relationship. The dominant is most often a man, or if a woman, one who has already amassed experience as a dominatrix or similar. I took two very strong and independent people who were ignorant about kink. I cast Marcy in the more sexual, dominant role as a dominant female is statistically atypical. But most importantly, both protagonists are very much novices, and their awakening is unsure, fretful, and full of the many questions I think most people could have. Am I normal? Why do we like pain? Receiving and, *especially,* inflicting pain. Isn't it against everything we are taught? Where is the line where kink becomes abuse? With Gwen as a guide, they explore together.

What was your initial research about, that led you to BDSM?

It was a strange mix of two unrelated, rapid, societal shifts. The first was watching the early days of the last US Election, as Donald Trump made his run for office. I'm not political and didn't know much about any of the parties or candidates, but based purely on what I saw in the media here in Vancouver, I couldn't conceive why a person, let alone a party, could consider him a rational candidate. I wasn't thinking about his politics; it was the way he was portrayed as a flawed, angry person with a total lack of respect for the office. I initially concluded, and am probably partly right, that his supporters must be seeing very different media than we see here in Vancouver.

The second change was how much nudity and more explicit sex we began to see on TV. I remember one *Game of Thrones* episode that began with a full-screen close-up of a half-erect penis, and the same happened in *Shameless*, too. In other shows, erections were 'popping up,' more frequently on screen alongside mainstream Hollywood mega-star actresses. Sex toys such as 'strap-ons' in Marco Polo and Deadpool. Shows with meaningful characters into BDSM, acted by stars such as Maggie Sith and Paul Giamatti. A light came on for me that, to a person with strong, socially conservative values, this might seem like society was on the verge of breaking down.

Then it hit me: Vancouver is very, very progressive. It is openly supportive of liberalisation: Gay marriage; cannabis; pro-choice; racial and gender equality. Everything that in my youth in England I was taught – in the home, the church, school and at work – was wrong, and a sure path to trouble. Back then, my values were conservative by my current standards. But that was 30-40 years ago, so why the big values gap today? Well, I concluded, the population — spread over an extensive western world – of over one billion people, simply doesn't all change at the same pace, and the internet has factored in as an extreme accelerator in some senses, and a polarizing agent in others. Change at a steady pace is one thing, but a country where at one end we change the laws to admit homosexuality, and at the other we can't own a sex toy, is a lot of pressure on collective values.

I don't want to suggest that the GOP and their supporters are old-fashioned; that is not my intent, so please don't assume that it is. What I do know is that, to someone like me back in the 1970s, Obama might have seemed like *the devil*. Today, I'm positively drawn to the Obamas because they are so respectful, eloquent, educated, progressively minded, anti-violence and confrontation, and representative of equity – people of colour in the White House – and so calm and rational. They are so compelling when they speak. Now, the Obamas promote what some people with strong conservative values genuinely fear. Imagine having the Obamas fighting to dismantle what you strongly believe in, backed by Oprah, Ellen, and other 'reasonable' and successful influencers. That could be truly frightening. I could see people voting for a very strong alternative, even if that person has some 'issues.'

How did this get you to the research into sexuality?

While considering this gap in liberal vs conservative values, spearheaded by increased sex on TV, I wondered how liberalization actually worked. In my own experience, it's been a one-way journey towards increasing liberalization. So, I wondered, were we super uptight 2000 years ago and have we been slowly 'relaxing' ever since? Or is it more like a pendulum, swinging back and forth? I could have chosen other points of reference, but I chose sexuality to study as it seemed to be on a liberalizing tear on TV, and I looked back in history in search of patterns.

What did you discover?

Well, much of it is reflected and discussed in the novel, so I won't repeat it here. I would encourage everyone to do their own research; to look at the emerging information with an open mind. Fact-based education typically reduces stigma, and the minimum I would hope for is that if people retain conservative social values after looking at the new data, at least they might be more understanding and tolerant of the other points of view.

I discovered that there is – or at least was – some sound rationale against sex that is non-procreational (i.e., not in pursuit of children), in the sense that historically, sex has been very disruptive to progress. Some examples: Sex might cause fights and disrupt business or political alliances due to infidelity; nearly 30 percent of Europe's population was wiped out from syphilis in the 1400s; and, in the 1500s, England could barely operate a navel flotilla due to the impact of sexual practises, and were it not for Henry VIII, we may never have had an empire. (Some would say that would have been a good thing, of course.)

As fun and compelling as sex can be, it can be a trouble maker. I can see why religions and empire builders alike have tried to temper and even ban it. But at the end of the day, it is fundamental to how we are wired, and it comes in many flavours. We are roughly 2000 years into trying sexual suppression tactics, and rarely, if ever, have they worked.

Our science and connectedness today are enabling us to collect meaningful data on what makes humans really tick, and better define what is natural, normal, and healthy for our species. Freud, Ebbing, and the others whose wisdom we embraced in the late 1800s didn't have the ability to gather enough information to round out their conclusions, and those dead geniuses still strongly influence us today. But then again, just because something is physiologically acceptable doesn't mean we need that to be our societal norm, of course. Men are typically physically stronger and more aggressive than women, but they should not, just because of that, be in charge.

I think we are getting many of the distractions out of the way: *Don't have sex because it spreads disease, or you get pregnant; if you vary from a very narrow, heterosexual, vanilla sex, you have a mental illness; BDSM leads to abuse, and all people who are not 'normal' come from abusive or broken homes.* None of these statements are, or at least need to be, true today. In fact, it looks like it may, to a degree, be the opposite. So, there is a chance to define a new norm in a safe way, more in line with the way we are actually wired. If we survive 'fake news,' I think we will see this in our lifetime, and I thought it would make an interesting sub-theme in the story, for people eager to get more information in this increasingly sexually positive and tolerant age.

Some very recent studies suggest that over 50 percent of the population have incorporated something traditionally considered as kinky into their relationship. I think this says we are redefining 'normal' behind closed doors: let's legitimize this shift.

THE NUDE DETECTIVE

28078445R00120

Printed in Great Britain
by Amazon